PAST
AND FUTURE
SINS

Other books by the author include:

A Wing And A Prayer (1st Book of Gabriel)

Belladonna (2nd Book Of Gabriel)

Dealing With The Devil (3rd Book of Gabriel)

A Long Way To Die (4th Book Of Gabriel)

PAST
AND FUTURE
SINS

THE FIFTH BOOK OF
GABRIEL

ERNEST OGLESBY

iUniverse, Inc.
Bloomington

Past and Future Sins
The Fifth Book of Gabriel

iUniverse books may be ordered through booksellers or by contacting:

iUniverse
1663 Liberty Drive
Bloomington, IN 47403
www.iuniverse.com
1-800-Authors (1-800-288-4677)

ISBN: 978-1-4759-3600-1 (sc)
ISBN: 978-1-4759-3601-8 (hc)
ISBN: 978-1-4759-3602-5 (ebk)

Library of Congress Control Number: 2011901153

Printed in the United States of America

iUniverse rev. date: 08/02/2012

This book is dedicated to my children, Luke and Emma, for their love, and their lives, for which I feel truly blessed. I hope one day they'll both read my books, but I won't hold my breath.

Prologue

he village settled down for the night, as it did every night, once the sun went down. Villagers settled in their homes, the wives preparing the evening meal, helped by some of the children. The old men sat and talked, some smoking their pipes or cigarettes, others drinking some of the home-made fermented brew they cultivated amongst themselves. Occasionally, one of the village dogs would bark. Around them the odd bird-call would sound, and the jungle came alive in the darkness.

Up in the temple, on the fringes of the surrounding jungle, one of the priests rang the bell which marked off the hours, and then returned to evening prayers.

The temple was old, it's origins lost in time, and the village had grown up around it, as people came to seek spiritual aid. The red mud walls had faded over the centuries to a more dirty brown, but the architecture still stood pronounced, depicting its Khmer origins. It's only deference to modern times, was the generator which provided limited electricity to the temple and village below. The fuel to run it was paid for by trade with the cities and various companies interested in marketing their craftwork, and artifacts.

In ages past, the Khmer had been a mighty people, until history had denigrated them to a bunch of illiterate thugs, in the Khmer Rouge. Only fading outposts such as this temple remained to remind people of a once proud heritage.

In one of the private dormitory rooms, Radna attended his blind charge, bringing him fresh food and water to drink. The food and water were accepted graciously and consumed, and then Radna set about his daily grooming, combing the angel's hair, and applying oils to his wings and feathers. He was molting quite badly these days.

Nathaniel endured, as he had done for centuries now. The confinement was nothing more than he could expect with his blindness, and his wings now all but useless. Without sight, he could not fly, and without flight and exercise, the muscle wastage had a detrimental effect on his wings.

The first sign of alarm was the increased barking of one of the dogs, followed by a single gun-shot, and then ominous silence, as the Khmer began their infiltration into the outskirts of the village.

Then came shouting and screams, more barking from the dogs, and more gunshots. Automatic fire carried all the way up to the temple, and some of the priests looked down at the carnage unleashed in the village, as some of the dwellings were set on fire, and the growing flames revealed the black clad men overrunning the village, like a swarm of ants.

Radna was alerted, and ran to the wall to see for himself what was going on. He and his fellow priests were horrified. The Khmer Rouge were on the rampage once more. They had never truly disbanded since the fall of Pol Pot. This was not good.

Besides the damage they were inflicting below, Radna knew the temple itself was not safe. They were averse to anything which reminded them of how far they had fallen. Once they saw Nathaniel, they would likely kill him on sight. The Khmer hated anything they didn't understand.

Radna rushed back to the dormitory area, and grabbed blankets, and got Nathaniel to his feet. "What is it, my friend? What are those noises I hear?" the angel asked.

"Come with me, Nathaniel. Bad men are in the village. We must hide you where you will not be found. You must stay there till after they are gone." He tried to explain. Not really understanding, but trusting his friend, Nathaniel allowed Radna to lead him from his room, down many steps, along many corridors, until there was earth below his feet, not stone, and then Radna hurried him along the jungle path, to where there was the sound of running, then roaring, water, and Nathaniel gathered he was close to the river's waterfall.

There was some sort of tunnel or cave, as Nathaniel felt stone under his feet once more, and a closed in sensation encompassed him, as Radna led him deeper inside. Behind the waterfall was a cave, known only to a few. It was the best refuge he could offer his friend for now.

"I am frightened." The strange figure cowered, finally, on the rough bed that Radna had made up for him in the cave. "All those loud noises assail my ears. Why must I stay down here?" The feathers from his withered wings were molting again. The priest simply picked them up and added them to the bedding.

"Bad men have come to the village, Nathaniel. The Khmer are still active, and they overrun the temple, seeking to enslave my fellow priests and the villagers. You would not be safe wandering around. They would not know what to make of you, my friend. They kill what they cannot understand." Odd gunshots could still be heard, all the more noticeable by the blind, and Radna put his hand on the angel's shoulder, to try and comfort him.

Radna remembered his childhood. The angel had always been there in the temple, and cared for by the priests. Blind, he had to be helped about, and as a child himself, he had been regaled by the angel's tales of time gone by, for Nathaniel had lived through countless ages, and many priests had come and gone since his first arrival in their temple.

The tale of his coming was written in their scriptures, but still hard to believe. Failing eyesight had caused him to come to earth, and the priests of the temple had offered him what succor they could, eventually giving him a home here amongst his people.

Radna blamed himself for the misery now being inflicted in the village. The priests were always looking to help finance the village to repay their kindness for the food and clothing left by the villagers, and it had seemed harmless enough in itself, offering the molted feathers of the angel to the trader, a representative of the Blue Elephant trading company. As trade with the company increased, more strangers began to appear.

Now the Khmer came in force, and there was no resisting them. His people must endure, as they had done through the centuries. But he pitied the angel, as the two of them now cowered in this hidden cave. While they were above, he must remain below, and out of sight. Death waited at the hands of the Khmer.

Dawn's light revealed the full horror of the Khmer occupation. Three of the dwellings were now just burnt out husks, the timbers still smoldering. The entire population of the village, those that were still alive, were now huddled together in a small clearing, surrounded by the black pajama clad men of the Khmer.

They were not all men, truly, for some of them were mere children, boys and girls, who had no option but to join the Khmer or die, and some of them relished their savage new lives, treating others with the same cruelty they had experienced themselves in years past.

Alongside the villagers, were the remnants of the priests, for many had been shot during the night. Anyone showing the slightest resistance had been killed out of hand. Radna hung his head in shame, as he cowered in submission to these men with guns. But there was nothing they could do against so many weapons. He listened as the Khmer leader spoke of occupying the village, and turning it into a refuge for his men. Villagers would be relocated and expected to give up some of their homes to house his men. The temple itself was not to be spared, but would house himself and some of his senior men, and radio operators. He spoke of other men arriving in a few days, doubtless to increase his personal army.

The villagers were expected to comply, or die. Assist and support his men, and they had a reason to live. Otherwise, they were surplus to requirements.

Over the coming weeks, more men arrived at the village, and tented accommodation was set up just outside the village, though before the onset of the jungle. These new men were foreigners, and dressed strangely, some in robes and turbans. Most wore full face beards. Radna did not understand their language, and he surmised only a few of the Khmer understood them, but they seemed to take orders, and a makeshift training camp was set up. Some of the larger rooms in the temple were given over to be used as a sort of classroom, and various maps and documentation were stored there. Other documents were being forged, and the priests were expected to help in this. The Khmer generally had no use for such, and so one of the newcomers was organizing this exercise. He still took his orders from the Khmer leader, and the radio room they installed was constantly kept busy relaying orders back and forth from someone far away.

As weeks turned into months, some of the newcomers would leave, and be replaced by others. Radna assumed this was some sort of staging post for these people. Brought here for familiarization, and then let loose into the wider environs of the world.

Sometimes the complement of Khmer would reduce for a few days, though those remaining behind had enough weapons to keep control of the villagers. Then the Khmer would return, sometimes minus one or two faces. Radna guessed some sort of action had taken place away from the village, by the fresh bandages on some of the returning Khmer.

In all this time, Nathaniel was confined to his cave. Radna could only steal away at night to smuggle him food, and to escort him out of the cave, to wash in the river under the stars. His lonely existence had gotten a lot lonelier since the coming of the Khmer.

Chapter One

It was about one o'clock in the morning when the man came out of one of the waterfront bars. It was quiet at this time of the evening, with only the lapping of the waves against the jetty and the odd squawk from one of the seagulls.

Jakarta had attempted to modernize its tourist face after the student riots of the nineties, and many such establishments now littered the waterfronts as the vast docks were extended and renovated.

The taxis weren't allowed too close to the waterfront, mostly a pedestrian zone these days; and so it was a short walk south, which usually allowed the prostitutes to ply their trade along the route. Strangely tonight, there didn't seem to be a living soul about, but even as drunk as he was, he couldn't help but notice the lithe lovely in the black cheongsam who was smoking a cigarette against a wall, half-lit by the nearby streetlight.

The red dragon across her bodice stood out, accentuating her chest where it bulged nicely, and her long legs were nicely revealed by the slit in the side of her cheongsam. She blew cigarette smoke into the air, and he watched it spiral, highlighted by the artificial light from the streetlamp.

He wasn't too drunk as yet. The alcohol hadn't fully kicked in, and the fresh salty air had a slightly sobering effect. This gorgeous looker with her long black hair looked interested enough, and he was certainly interested in her. He still had money in his wallet, and he glanced around as he considered his options.

Muggings weren't uncommon, but the area looked safe enough. As long as he didn't stray too far with the girl, he should be okay. He didn't want to take her back to his hotel in case someone blabbed to his bosses. He was staying at the Hilton till the conference was over. He also didn't want to take a chance on taking her somewhere she knew, but he didn't. That meant doing her somewhere close by. The docks were quiet and deserted at this time of night, and activity wouldn't resume until about 3am, when the boat-crews would start readying their vessels for the early morning tide.

"Hey baby, you look lonely. Want some company?" he smiled as he approached her. Her eyes slowly ran over him, as she took another drag on her cigarette, making him wait for her answer. As he got closer, he could see she was no Asian, though she looked and dressed like a Thai. Her skin was white, not just made so by the streetlight. A Caucasian hooker out here? Well, it wasn't unheard of. He had heard stories of some bored housewives of businessmen who turned tricks at night, and there were rumors of girls being made available at the right price to the right people. Mail-order, so to speak.

"I'm expensive," the woman warned, with a faint smile on those blood-red lips of hers, and he caught a glimpse of her white teeth, as she slowly and sensuously licked her lips. He felt his blood rising just where he wanted it to rise.

"Are you worth it?" he asked, amusedly.

"Oh, yes," she smiled, revealing brilliant white teeth.

"How much?" he asked. She chuckled.

"My price is high, but you'll pay it after we're done. Every man has willingly paid my price," she boasted. Now it was his turn to chuckle.

"That good, eh?" She turned her head sideways, and shrugged. She dropped the cigarette, and ground it out under her foot.

"Let's go somewhere quieter, and you can find out," she suggested, and linked arms with him. He was all set to protest, but she led him out along one of the piers, where there was no suggestion of anyone lying in wait for him. At this hour of the night, it would be private and secluded enough for what he had in mind. The click clack of her stilettos and the gentle lapping of the waves against the wooden pier was the only sound he heard. Even the seagulls were mostly quiet at this time of night. He felt her hip brush against him as they slowly walked, and he found himself getting even harder in anticipation.

The end of the pier finally came, and they could walk no more. In the moonlight, she was even more beautiful, and she melted into his arms as he embraced her and their lips locked together in a slow passionate kiss. She pressed against him, moaning into his mouth, as his hands began to move over her body, pressing the silk of her cheongsam against her flesh. She slid her own hand in between their bodies, rubbing his stiff length, and making him groan.

He slowly sank to his knees before her, hands lifting the slit of her cheongsam to one side, rucking it high on her hips as he pressed his lips against her pale belly, eyes widening at the colourful snake tattoo that wriggled and undulated in time with her belly, vanishing down into her black silk panties. With one hand, he pulled them aside, and his eyes widened even more at what was revealed. He opened his mouth to speak, but a firm hand on the back of his head forced his face into her crotch.

"Suck it!" she ordered, enjoying the feel of his hot mouth on her sex, and he dutifully obeyed, pleasuring her with his lips and with his tongue, sucking on her sex, and making her gasp and hunch her loins into his face. They remained locked like this for almost two minutes, before she cried out, and achieved orgasm, shuddering against him, fingers locked in his hair.

When she let him go, he gasped for air, and then started laughing drunkenly. "My God! No one would fucking believe I just did that," he laughed. "I always wondered what it would be like. I heard there were people like you out here, but I never thought I'd run in to one. But now it's my turn, baby. Now you get to suck me, too. Fair's fair." He fumbled with the bulging zip of his pants.

She smiled broadly, exposing those white teeth again, as she watched him hurriedly unzip. "Don't worry darling, I'm going to suck on you real good," she promised, and leaned forward to lightly kiss his exposed neck. He chuckled, enjoying the feel of her lips, and succeeded in exposing a stiff erection, which she reached for and began to manipulate lightly in her cool fingers.

She leaned closer, wanking him off against her thigh, as she took another playful nip at his neck, and this time he felt her teeth, though the sensations from his cock were paramount in his brain at that moment. Then those red lips fastened on his neck, and he gasped in undreamed of pleasure, as she drew blood, mouth fastening on like a leech, and drawing hungrily.

The distended fangs bit deep, injecting a paralysing venom, which also acted as a powerful stimulant. The sensation was all-powerful, and he was helpless to resist the sheer pleasure of it. His legs went weak at one point, but powerful hands held him up, and she sucked voraciously, with the hollow fangs draining him of his blood.

It took her nearly five minutes to drain him unto death. There was hardly any blood left in him, and he would die soon enough. She raised her head finally, lips and chin red with his blood, and then leaned forward and bit once more, ripping a huge chunk out of his neck, to disguise the wound. She spat the flesh out into the lapping waters, and then, after rifling his jacket and pocketing his wallet, threw his almost dead body into them as well. He would drown, too weak to swim, and the outgoing tide would take his body out beyond the docks and into the open sea. Fish and crabs would feast on the body, and if it did resurface at all, it would leave very little for the police to go on. She would dispose of the wallet later, and popped it into her handbag for now.

She tidied her appearance, and smoothed down her dress. Damn! He had come against her thigh, the semen soiling her cheongsam. She would have to get it cleaned. Even in the pale moonlight, she no longer looked pale. Her skin had a nice healthy pink glow about it. In fact, she looked almost human.

The click-clack of her heels rang out along the deserted pier, as she made her way back towards land. The night's fun and games were over for now.

Chapter Two

ONDAY: The two women joked and chattered away merrily as they walked through the souk. Both women were dressed lightly for the hot sun. Laura wore a thin loose white dress, while Belle dressed in slacks and a loose blouse. Both wore dark sunglasses against the glare from all the white painted walls and the hot sun.

They had only arrived in Cairo a few days ago, and were still acclimatising, before seeing the Valley of the Kings, the Pyramids etcetera in typical tourist fashion. In the meantime, a bit of retail therapy never went amiss, and they spent some time touring the back-alleys of the souk in search of bargains.

The background noise of chatter and Arabic music blaring out from the various establishments deafened them at times, and the exotic strange smells of heavily-spiced foods and strong coffee, tantalized their taste-buds. They say only mad dogs and Englishmen go out in the midday sun, but the heat of the day, at least, kept the flies down, otherwise they could be quite a nuisance. There were other nuisances to consider, of course.

"Basta!" Belle complained to her mother. "That's three times I've had my culo grabbed in the last half-hour. They sneak up on you through the crowd, and get their hand away before you even see them, they're so small. It feels like they're following us around and targeting us, though I'm sure they get up to the same antics with the other tourists."

"Yes," Laura grinned, amusedly. "It's hard not to react, but it only gives them more enjoyment. We're two hot looking ladies, and I'm sure they'd rather target us than some old fat broad. Even the old shopkeepers find it funny. All part of the tourist package in this part of the world."

"Back home in Italy, and even in Greece, it's something women come to expect, even appreciate, when a man pinches your derriere. It's a macho thing, and no woman wants to consider her ass too ugly to be pinched." Belle revealed. "Here, the men leave you alone, and it's these little urchins that play grabass. Just not the same," Belle sounded disappointed.

"They're just young boys, having a little fun, that's all. Probably the closest most of them will ever get to a western woman. Ahhhhh!" Laura stiffened, crying out suddenly as a tiny hand went up between her own legs, and she whirled as the grinning youngster disappeared back into the relative safety of the crowd, after giving her crotch a friendly squeeze. Much muffled laughter went on around her, including Belle's, who had watched the boy's approach and deliberately said nothing. Laura glared at her daughter for a second. "Liitle Bastards!" Laura cursed, trying to regain her dignity. "That fucker nearly shoved his thumb up my ass!"

"Yes, mother," Belle replied, smugly. "Welcome to Cairo."

"Damn it, Belle! It's not as if we're asking to be molested. We are dressed quite conservatively, even considering this is a Muslim country. They all look the same once they blend into the crowd, so the only way I could catch them would be to get my crotch dusted for fingerprints."

"It's a difference in cultures, as you say. They're Eastern males and we're Western females. Eastern males have a low opinion of women, and their own women aren't usually allowed out in public by themselves, certainly not showing their faces. Such women are looked upon with a lack of respect, and that's how they see us, I guess," Belle shrugged her shoulders. "Foreigners are always an easy target, I suppose."

"Thank God not all of the Middle East is like this. At least at the hotel we can behave more normally. In a crowded market like this, it just makes it too easy for them."

Belle joked, "The only reason I can sunbathe topless by the pool is because some of those young waiters like to gawp at my tits," she giggled. "Not likely to snitch on me if they can't get a free flash," she added.

"Yes, this part of the world is a nice place to visit, but I certainly wouldn't want to live here, or anywhere else in the Middle East. Too restricting, and full of hypocrites and double-standards," Laura agreed, and then drew her daughter's attention to yet another shop display.

*   *   *

The old Arab shopkeepers were either very polite or very pushy, sometimes inviting them in for coffee and haggling, others just kept tugging in a very bad mannered way on their arms, to try and get them into their shops. It was hard to say "No" and get them to accept the refusal. The old Curiosity Shoppe caught their eye with the strange exotic display in the window, and the two women soon found themselves in an Aladdin's Cave inside, pouring over old tomes and strange objet d'art, as the proprietor, who introduced himself as Abdullah, ushered them inside and showed them around. Some of the books were covered with what looked like skin or flaking leather, and some of them had a damp musty smell to them.

Abdullah showed the two women around his establishment, drawing their attention to all manner of strange and exotic items he had gathered 'from the far corners of the Earth' if he could be believed, though they had both heard similar spiels before, in other establishments. His English was cultured and polite, and he was fluent in both German and French, too, as he was quick to demonstrate. Of indeterminate middle age, he wore simple western clothes, albeit with a small, tassled fez on his head. The short goatee beard and moustache were kept well-trimmed.

Many years of dealing with all manner of tourists had made him quite glib in his manner, well used to people of different cultures.

It was Belle who found the feather, larger than normal, and she assumed it was from some Eagle or other bird of prey. It had been made into a quill-pen, and the two women both laughed. "I bet Gabriel would just love it," Laura enthused. "I have to buy it for him," she insisted. "I'll see if the hotel will send it off by special courier for me."

Laura bought the quill pen, and Belle fussed over a small statuette, though eventually refrained from purchasing it. She hummed and hahhed over one or two other items, but couldn't make her mind up. They still had a few days here, before moving on, so plenty of time to see what else was available in other shops before paying a return visit if necessary.

*   *   *

The special delivery arrived at Gabriel's villa on the outskirts of Buenos Aires five days later. The villa was west of the city itself, away from the tightly packed barrios of the second largest metropolitan area in South America. Only Sao Paulo was more congested, and Gabriel spent as little time as possible in the concrete jungle. Located on the western shore of the Rio de la Plata, Buenos Aires had a massive population, and one name among many was very hard to trace. It might not be the most aesthetic of places to live, but it served its purpose in the anonymity it gave him.

Gabriel was taking a breather from his workout in the mini-gym in the basement. His hollow bones, and strong musculature helped make it easy to keep his body in trim. He took a sip of water, from the dispenser, and used a towel to dab at his sweaty upper torso.

The package was delivered to Gabriel by his aged manservant Manuel, who left his master to open it in private. The card dropped out first, and it said simply 'Thought you'd enjoy this, Love, Laura.' Then Gabriel upended the package a bit further. It was so light, he wondered if there could be anything in it at all, and then out dropped the quill-pen, and the absolutely unmistakeable feather.

He gasped, taken aback. The last time he had seen a feather like this had been in a laboratory complex in Madrid. After scientists working for the Sword of Solomon had taken Matthias to pieces in their efforts to find out the secrets of the angels' longevity.

It could be a fake or it could be genuine. The only way to tell would be to have it analysed, and the research facility in Cordoba would be able to do that quickly enough. They could also carbon-date it to tell how recently it had been grown. But unless Gabriel was wrong, this feather came from one of his kinsmen, another angel.

Gabriel quickly made a phone call to the medical research facility he funded, and spoke to Luis Montalban, one of the few men alive who knew of Gabriel's unique physiology, and origins. Some of his staff might guess, but all of them depended on Gabriel's sponsorship, and so they could all be trusted. Luis was now Gabriel's personal physician, and was in possession of all the data Gabriel had retrieved from Madrid regarding the physiology of his race.

*　　*　　*

Cordoba was about 700km northwest of Buenos Aires, in the foothills of the Sierra Chicas, but in the same time zone. Luis looked up from his desk, and enjoyed the view out over the Suquia River for a moment, as he interrupted his work to pick up the receiver. "Yes?"

"Luis, I have something urgent for you." Luis recognised Gabriel's voice. "I'll be sending it by courier tonight. You'll know what it is when you see it. Run whatever tests you can, and give me a report no later than tomorrow morning."

"This is all a bit sudden, Gabriel, but of course I'll get onto it straight away. I know you wouldn't ask the impossible, so if you think I can get whatever tests you want doing by tomorrow, then of course I will do so. The last plane arrives here around eight pm. I'll mobilize the staff in the lab, and we'll work through the night."

"Thanks Luis. If this is what I think it is, I need to act on it fast, while I still have contacts in place. Call me at any time. I'll be by the phone, or Manuel will answer. Thanks again, old friend."

"The man with the chequebook always calls the tune," Luis joked. "Tomorrow then," he promised, and Gabriel severed the connection, to ring the courier service he normally used, to get this package on the last flight to Cordoba.

*　　*　　*

Belle spent the early part of Saturday evening on her own, as Laura complained of too much sun, after touring the Ezbekiyeh Gardens, and decided to have an early nap, promising to be refreshed in time for the midnight jaunt they had planned, so after eating alone in the restaurant, Belle tried her luck in the Casino, though not going mad. She won enough to keep her playing, but made a small loss on the evening.

As she was otherwise occupied, she didn't notice Laura leaving the hotel just before sundown, and taking a taxi to a nearby restaurant, where a handsome figure waited for her.

Laura's late arrival back at the hotel did not go unnoticed by Belle, however, who had called earlier to check on her, and found her room empty, and her key left at the desk. She had hung around the lobby, and finally saw Laura getting out of the taxi, before rushing to collect her key, and get back up to her room. Curious, Belle went out to quiz the taxi driver before he pulled away.

Half an hour later, Belle heard a knock on her door, and there was Laura, now all dressed and ready for their little jaunt. "Ready when you are," she smiled. Belle said nothing, as she grabbed a dark sweater, and small knapsack, and left the hotel with her mother.

The taxi driver had been booked with the aid of Reception, and he was well used to such late night journeys by some of the tourists. They crossed the Nile, and then headed south, towards Giza. They could see the Great Pyramids lit up in the distance, illuminated by floodlight. The main viewing areas were closer to the Sphinx, which was in the East. The western sides of the pyramids were in darkness, with a great cemetery behind them.

The taxi stopped near the cemetery, behind the Pyramid of Cheops. The Pyramid of Khephren was just south, and from here they couldn't see the smaller Pyramid of Mycerinus, even though it was set on higher ground than its larger brothers.

The driver was prepared to wait half an hour, no more, and so Belle and Laura moved quickly, using wire-cutters to cut a small flap in the chain link fence, while the driver opened the boot, and took out the spare wheel to pretend to be fixing a flat tyre.

The towering rear face of the Pyramid stood out against the night sky, 450 feet high, and built by Cheops or Khufu (people still argued). Khephren, the builder of the second pyramid, was also held responsible for the re-carving of the face of the Sphinx in his own image, for reasons unknown, but there remain dark tales of the Sphinx before Kephren's time, more than 2000 years ago. Some say that face wasn't human, but belonged to some dark Elder-God. In the shadows, and under the pale moon, the two women shivered, even though the night was warm. Egypt was old, and they could sense it still held it's mysteries after all these centuries.

Undaunted, they set out for the foot of the pyramid, staring up at the crumbling stone blocks that built this monolith. In years gone by, when access was freer, seven minutes used to be the record amongst some of the Arab children, whom tourists would pay to race up and down the Great Pyramid, but weathering and a few accidents had caused concern over damage to the ancient monument, and now access was more restricted, but some tourists still vied to make their own climbs. It would take a bit more than seven minutes at night, and in the dark, but Laura and Belle were fit and agile.

It took them just over ten minutes to reach the worn plateau on the top of the pyramid, and both women looked out over the large expanse of ruins, against the glare of the floodlights. It was hard to see, and both women hesitated to linger too long near the edge, in case the light of the floodlights made them visible to the guards below.

Belle took out the bottle of champagne, and two wrapped glasses. Laura uncorked the bottle with a small POPPP, and poured some into each glass. Laughing, the two women toasted their success, and then re-corked the bottle, and put bottle and glasses back into the knapsack for the climb back down. The taxi driver would wait if he wanted paying.

Belle and Laura were exhausted and sweating by the time they got back to the hotel. Night didn't greatly reduce the heat, but did increase the humidity.

It was nearly dawn, yet both of them were still enervated by their clandestine climb to the top of the Great Pyramid by moonlight. No one was allowed on the actual pyramids these days, but one or two people did their best to sneak past the security guards and make their own personal ascents, which the two women had done that night, and had laughed and joked at the peak in the light of the moon.

They had to be just as careful coming down the pyramid in the darkness, away from the spotlights, to avoid security once more, before making their way back to their hotel. "That was fun," chuckled Belle, as they rode the lift up to their floor.

"A hot shower to get the dust and sweat off me, and I'll sleep till lunchtime," Laura stretched.

"Think I'll do the same. Then maybe another run round the Kan El Khalili Market. But we really need to start packing if we're moving on tomorrow."

"Yes, you're right," agreed Laura. "Whatever we buy, needs to be small and light, unless they can freight it home for us."

"Either that or we buy more luggage," Belle giggled.

"Who's going to carry it all? Not me, daughter. I'm getting too old for all that shit!" Laura laughed. "Good night, then," she smiled, pulling her key-card out of her pocket and opening her room door. Belle gave a small wave, and opened her own door. The comfy mattress called, but once she was curled up in bed, she found sleep hard to come by.

Her brain was too active, trying to think of a reason why her mother had held a clandestine meeting with Marco Falcone, her former lover, for, from the taxi-driver's description of her escort, it could be no other. What was he doing here in Cairo? Too much of a coincidence.

*   *   *

Gabriel got the news he wanted before 8am the next morning. "Yes Luis, what's the verdict?" he asked impatiently.

"DNA isn't an exact match, but damn close. Dried blood dates to within the last year," he confirmed. He heard Gabriel breathe a deep sigh at the other end of the phone. "Where did you get this feather from?"

"I didn't, Luis. It was a gift, and one I've now got to track back. Within the last year means it didn't come from Michael, or Matthias. It means that somewhere out there, is another one of my people. No guarantee he is still alive, but I have to look for him."

"I wish you luck, and I stand ready to assist if I can, you know that," he assured Gabriel. "I'll keep a medical team on standby for the next couple of weeks. Keep me updated."

Gabriel disconnected, and rang for the International Operator, as he mentally checked the time. Lunchtime in Cairo, and the girls had less than a day before they were due to catch their plane to continue their Middle East excursion. "Yes, operator. Connect me to the Golden Tulip Hotel in Cairo, please."

*   *   *

SUNDAY:The Golden Tulip was set on the southern banks of the Nile River, in the diplomatic district, in the Heart Of Zamalek island. It was within five minutes walk of the bustling city centre, and a popular hotel with foreign visitors. Belle and Laura were having a late lunch, after sleeping away most of the morning, when the call came through from Reception and one of the waiters alerted her. She left Belle at the breakfast table while she went to Reception to take the call. "Hi, darling. Checking up on me? No, I haven't run off with a handsome oil sheik just yet," she giggled. "Most of them are fat and ugly anyway," she added.

"No, I trust you (about as far as I can throw you, anyway)" Gabriel joked. "I'm really calling about that feather you sent me. It's for real!" he added, pointedly.

"What? You're joking, surely? It's just some silly toy made up for the tourists." She found it hard to believe what she was hearing. "I just bought it as a joke," she explained.

"Fraid not, sweetheart. It's genuine. Luis ran some tests and found the DNA too close to be any sort of coincidence. There's another angel out there somewhere. Alive within the last year, that's all Luis could say. But I need you to try and track this thing down for me, till I can get out there. I don't want to spoil your holiday, so just do what you can in the time you have left, and I'll take over once I can arrange a flight and get to Cairo myself. I'd join you on your holiday, but I'm probably going to be a little preoccupied on this," he warned her. Laura knew what he could be like when he fixated on something, and this was going to be one of those times.

"Well, okay, I guess. Me and Belle will go back to the shop and do what we can. We'll leave word for you here at the hotel, and as you are going to be in this part of the world, if you can finish off your investigations, it would be nice if you could join us, oil sheiks or no oil sheiks," she chuckled, and then blew him a kiss down the phone line. "Love ya."

"I'll do my damndest," Gabriel promised. "I love you, too."

Belle was obviously lost in thought, sipping on her coffee, as Laura rejoined her to finish off her breakfast. "You'll never guess . . ?" she started. Belle looked around.

"Who you met last night?" asked Belle, smiling sweetly, though her eyes sparkled, now that she had decided to broach the subject.

"Oh," Laura gasped, taken aback for a second, and looking guilty, then she reached for her coffee. "How did you find out?" she asked, hiding her embarrassment behind her coffee-cup. Belle shrugged her shoulders.

"You weren't in your room when I called to check on you. Your key was left at the desk, so I hung around the lobby in the background. I saw you come in, and had a quick word with your taxi driver while you got changed. What was Falcone doing here, Mother, and why was he meeting you?"

"He didn't explain what he was doing here, just asked me to meet him. The call came as a surprise. I had no idea he was here, or how he knew we were here. When I met him, he said he still loved me, and wanted me to admit my renewed relationship with your father isn't going as smoothly as I'd hoped. That's about it. There, is that being honest enough?" Belle took a few seconds to answer her.

"I know things can get a little strained in relationships, but more importantly, what did you say to him? Who do you love, Laura? Be honest. I won't tell on you. It's a decision you need to make for yourself, but if you don't make it, I won't let you hurt him."

"I love your father, Belle. I never did love Marco. Liked him, and he was fun for a while. I needed him at a bad time in my life, and I used him to fill a void. After the Church had told me you had been stillborn, my mind snapped, and they put me on some serious drugs. Didn't know where I was or what I was doing for a while. My gift of prescience ended up with me being farmed out to a remote monastery in France after the war, as the Church utilised my skills as a modern Oracle. That wasn't fun either, but at least it weaned me off the drugs. That's when they sent me to the training camp, and I met Marco there. I needed someone in my life at the time, after thinking your father had abandoned me so cruelly. He's good to talk to, and a good sounding-board," she insisted. "Gabriel and I are trying hard to make this work, but having spent so long apart, we're two different people than when we first met. He thought I was dead, and I thought he had abandoned me. That's led to quite a few emotional problems we've both had to overcome. Reality doesn't always live up to memory. Gabriel's always been a loner, and he doesn't confide easily. He finds it hard to let me in. I need him to confide in me, to need me, as much as I need him." She was lost for words for a moment. Belle reached out and took her hand.

"Do you want me to talk to him?"

"What? A little emotional blackmail? No I don't think so, though I appreciate the offer. But this is something your father and I need to resolve for ourselves," she insisted. "Happy Endings are usually reserved for romance novels, Belle. They're a little harder to organise in real life. You need luck as well as hard work to find one."

"Alright, I'll leave it for now, though I'd better tell you, some friends of mine are making enquiries back in Italy. I was talking to Donatello about the various bombings in Italy, and he was there at the fashion show when I got injured. He remembers a suspicious person sitting at the back of the show. The brief description could fit Falcone." Laura gasped at the revelation. "As you know, that bomb wasn't designed to kill, like most of the other bombs Al Qaeda set off. Dad didn't agree to help Solomon until after I got injured. If it's not a coincidence, I'm going to want my pound of flesh," she warned. "If it turns out to be Falcone, I suggest you don't get in my way." Her look chilled Laura. Belle had been raised as an Italian and she knew all about Vendetta.

"Let's not talk about Marco just now. Leave him for the future. Your father gave me some unexpected news." Belle leaned closer, waiting for her to explain. "That feather we bought in the souk turned out to be the real thing, at least as far as the laboratory in Cordoba could verify. Your father is on his way here, but he wants us to make what enquiries we can to locate its source. We've still got a day before we're due to leave, and we can leave word at the hotel desk for him to follow it up. You still remember which street that shop was on, don't you?"

"Yes, I think so," Belle replied.

"We'll see if we can get the old man to reveal his supplier, and then Gabriel can track it down once he gets here. With luck, it won't take him long, and then once his enquiries are over, he might join us later in the holiday."

"That would be nice. A family holiday for a change." Belle smiled at the thought.

*   *   *

As Gabriel got Manuel to make reservations for him, he once again studied the lab report on the feather, trying to take his mind off that conversation with Laura. The product of genetic experiments by an alien survivor of a crashed star-ship, he had lived for over two thousand years as far as he could remember, and in that time he had had dalliances, relationships with many women. Such relationships grew more awkward with the advancing years, with 'civilisation' effecting changes in the natural relationships between men and women.

He had known Laura, for sixty years and more, though that relationship had been interrupted for a fifty year period. She was not like any of the former women he had known, more self-assured, more obstinate, more 'pig-headed'. He smiled, and mentally stopped himself before he went too far.

She was her own woman, as well as his. Strong-willed, and forthright. Her judgement didn't always follow along the same lines as his own, and she often chose her own path. He hoped, for once, she'd heed his advice, and let him continue with these investigations on his own.

Chapter Three

Abdullah Bey was not surprised to see the two western women reappear in his shop, as many tourists often came back time and again, haggling for this and that. It was a way of life in Arab shops, and had been thus for centuries. "Ladies, so nice of you to visit my humble shop once again. Please, would you like some coffee?" he asked, snapping his fingers for the young boy he employed as a helper, and the child scampered off into the rear of the establishment to bring two cups of the strong sweet coffee that was always brewing for his customers.

Laura and Belle returned the greeting, and as they waited for the coffee, they began examining the varied curiosities the old man had displayed in his shop. Laura really laid her American accent on thick. "Gee, Mr Abdullah, you sure do have some neat stuff in your shop. I've never seen such a variety of things. Not like your usual run of the mill stuff that's readily available for the tourists in the other shops," she complimented him.

Abdullah Bey bowed, graciously. "Madame is too kind. I merely do what I can to make my own shop a little more unique, and hope that visitors, such as yourselves, appreciate what I offer." The young boy came out from the rear with two small cups, on a tray, and both Laura and Belle accepted them, thankfully.

"Where do you get them all from? I've never seen anything like this before." Belle was examining a small bronze statuette, holding it up to the light to examine an inscription on the base. The old man laughed.

"My sources make my shop unique, as you say, ladies. They must remain my secret, else my shop will be just one among many," he explained.

"Can you at least tell us where you got that neat quill-pen I bought here last week? My husband thought it was real cute, but it got damaged in transit, and he'd really like a replacement," Laura used the story she'd dreamed up on the way here. It sounded quite plausible.

"I have many different sources for many different things. Some are more easily obtainable than others. What you ask is rare, and I do not know if my sources may be able to replace it," he held his hands out, in apology.

"Could you at least try?" Laura asked. "My husband is a writer, and he really loves neat things like that," she smiled, sweetly, turning on the charm.

"Such as you ask is not readily available," Abdullah Bey explained. "It may be many months before I can arrange a replacement, assuming one is possible."

"Could you put us in touch with your source? Perhaps if I contacted them myself, I could persuade them to make a special allowance to help me out. My husband is quite wealthy. Money is no object," Laura explained. Abdullah Bey appeared to consider for a moment.

"Ladies, my sources are not the sort of people who like their identities publicized. They are certainly not the sort of people you would like an introduction to," he warned, politely.

"We'll make it worth your while," promised Belle. "Let us worry about that."

"We just want a name. I appreciate your concern, but my husband really does want another one of those quill-pens." It sounded real lame now, Laura thought, but they had to pursue it. They had less than a day before their plane left, so no time to break into the place and rifle the old man's files. Abdullah appeared to consider their request.

"How could you make it worth my while?" he asked. "I am wealthy enough for my needs. I live only for my shop, and the uniqueness of what I can offer my customers," he explained. The way he looked at them, both women knew he didn't really believe their story, but he was considering obliging them in their request. It was just a question of what he wanted in payment.

Belle thought she knew, and made a show out of leaning forward to put the statuette down on one of the lower shelves, right in front of the old man, her neckline and cleavage drawing his eyes. Abdullah Bey smiled.

"I'm sure we can come to some arrangement, Mr Abdullah," Belle smiled, as she took her time about standing erect again. Laura caught her eye. Surely she wasn't thinking what Laura thought she was thinking?

"Do both you ladies have your passports with you?" Abdullah Bey asked, strangely. Both the women looked at each other, and then nodded. "As you know, I deal in rarities," he reminded them. "You both have something I can get a good price for," he smiled, knowingly. "Perhaps if you came into the rear of the store?" He went over to the door, and locked it, drawing the blind. Looking slightly puzzled, the two women followed the old man into the rear of the store.

He led them into the rear of the store, and at a signal from him, the young boy let himself out of the rear door. Abdullah Bey locked that door, too. He pointed up to a small security video camera near the ceiling. "Would you two ladies please take out your passports, open them, and hold them up so that the camera can record your identities? This will help in the authentication," he smiled. Puzzled, the two women did as he suggested. First Laura, and then Belle let the camera scan their passports.

"Is that it?" asked Laura, still puzzled.

"No, not quite," Abdullah Bey chuckled. "Now I want you to take off your underwear," he smiled, as both women's jaws suddenly dropped in surprise. "I intend selling your briefs," he grinned. "You, my dear, will remove her panties, and then she will remove yours," he chuckled, enjoying being in the driving seat, as the two women looked at each other in surprise. "I want this on video, to verify you as owners of the garments," he explained.

"Is that all?" Belle asked, for she had thought the old man had wanted one or both of them to have sex with him.

"In your own time, ladies," he chuckled, sitting back on an ornately padded sofa. Laura looked at Belle, and Belle looked at Laura, who shrugged her shoulders. Belle hesitantly began to ruck up her dress in front of Abdullah Bey, but turning her back on the cctv camera.

The old Arab grinned as Belle's grey silk panties came into view, and she raised her hemline up to her waist. Laura knelt in front of her daughter, looking up. Belle's eyes met hers, and nodded approvingly as Laura reached for those briefs, and slowly pulled them down.

Belle's debriefing was duly recorded on video, as the old man grinned, admiring Belle's black pubes as she stepped out of the briefs.

She noticed the lump in the front of his trousers, as he was getting turned on by her display.

Laura dropped the briefs on the small coffee table, and then, as Belle smoothed down her own skirt, Laura raised hers. Abdullah Bey smiled at the white silk briefs that Laura displayed, and then Belle knelt in front of her, hands reaching for, and pulling down the panties. A natural blonde, as Abdullah suspected. Laura put a hand on Belle's shoulder, as she stepped out of her briefs, and they too joined Belle's underwear on the coffee table. She smoothed down her own dress, now that they had complied with the old Arab's request.

*   *   *

Some time later, Abdullah Bey escorted the two women from his premises, smiling knowingly, as the two women hurried to get away. The old goat had gotten his money's worth, and all they had in return was a business card with the name of Al Raschid Trading llc. Exporter of Exotic Goods, Salalah, Oman. Belle realized the significance of the address. Muscat, in northern Oman, was their next port of call. Salalah was in the south, and a short flight from Seeb International Airport was all it would take to get there. She knew the way Laura's mind worked. They had a head-start on Gabriel, and if they could help track this thing down before he got here, it would give them more time to spend together as a family.

*   *   *

Abdullah Bey smiled knowingly as he watched the two women walked back out into the souk, the blonde hanging onto her skirt as a mischievous breeze lifted it. The two pairs of panties would now need to be hermetically sealed in plastic bags, ready for sale to some of his more discreet clientele, some of which were rather unsavoury, for he had many underworld dealings. That was how he got some of the stranger and more exotic items in his shop. The Al Raschid Trading company was one such outlet, and he had honestly warned the two women about contacting them.

They liked their privacy, for their own reasons, and to cover his own back, he would have to contact them, and let them know of the women's interest. He would blame their knowledge on his young helper being indiscreet, rather than admit his own role. An easy matter to send those details on to his contacts.

*   *   *

Sunday evening, after the two women packed, they sat down to dinner in the hotel restaurant, and discussed the day's events. Laura was hesitant to raise the subject. "Belle, in that shop, we . . ."

"We put on a show for the old man. It got us the information we wanted, didn't it? We didn't even have to give him a hand-job." The wine helped, and the two women ordered a second bottle. It would help them settle for the night, and then a sound sleep before catching the morning plane to Oman.

"You know he's got us on that cctv video?"

Belle scoffed. "We made sure it never saw too much, and you know what poor quality those things are. Beside, who's he going to show it to out here? It's not as if anyone is going to know us," she reassured her mother. "We've got a lead to track down. Al-Raschid is the Arab end of this conduit, and an outfit called Blue Elephant in Asia. We'll start with Al Raschid in the morning."

MONDAY: The international phones were down the next morning, when Laura tried to contact Gabriel to advise him of their change of plans. Always a problem abroad, and that meant e-mail as well, so she had no choice but to leave a letter for him at the desk, as she knew he would be calling here. She laid out the name of the Al Raschid company, and it's address in Oman. Gabriel knew it was on their itinerary, and so would not be too surprised to learn they were already following up this lead on his behalf. He would be no more than two days behind them, depending on connections. There were numerous baggage handlers' strikes going on across some of the major airlines at the moment, causing numerous disruptions. The Arab airlines weren't too concerned with unions, and certainly not with possible terrorist atrocities, and so were usually the most reliable way of flying in this modern world.

*   *   *

The Al Raschid Trading Company was a front for a smuggling operation which covered the whole of the Middle and Far East, one of many, no doubt. The news from Abdullah Bey of these two western women taking an interest in their activities caused concern. It would not be the first time that western agencies had tried to infiltrate their organization, concerned about the drug pipelines into the EEC from the East, which they helped supply and maintain, quite profitably. Abdullah Bey had e-mailed jpeg's of their passports within minutes of the two women leaving his establishment. Mohammed forwarded those details up the line, to his superiors. Bird and the Dragon-Lady would want to know such things, to ratify a course of action should the women indeed turn up here in Oman. Dead westerners always meant the authorities would poke around a lot more closely than normal, and bribes, however lucrative, weren't always guaranteed to work.

Mohammed had been working for Bird's organisation for nearly ten years now, working his way up to his present position of seniority, head of operations in Oman. In his late fifties, his light coloured skin could make him pass for European. He kept his face clean shaven, and his hair short, which had the unfortunate side effect of revealing his bald patch. Only his hook nose gave away his Arab descent.

He had already contacted his people at the airports, and they had checked and advised him of the women's flight details, arriving at Seeb on the Sunday afternoon flight, and reservations at the Ruwi Hotel. By the time they arrived, he would have his instructions.

*   *   *

The Dragon-Lady was bored. The position she now held in Bird's organization was important, as was the job she was being asked to do, organizing and running the Indonesian end of his smuggling racket, which helped pay the mercenaries he was recruiting in Cambodia, in preparation for his long awaited rise to power among the Thai elite.

Jakarta had its attractions, and a lot of those were ready to hand in the Jelan Kendal, where her operation was based, nominally known as the Jade Gate Brothel, just one of numerous establishments in Jakarta. It was here that many of the western women caught up in the Middle

East's still flourishing slave trade, ended up. They were broken in, or just simply broken, and the ones that ended up accepting their new lives were sold on to brothels all over the Far East.

This was also the clearing house for the antiques and rarities that the Al Raschid organization distributed throughout the Middle East, including jade and ivory products, the export of which was still banned. They were helped in this regard by the many corrupt government officials in this part of the world, which was still dealing with the aftermath of the big tsunami strike across the Indian Ocean in 2004.

Disasters were there to be exploited, and not just by the News Organisations. Charity groups and distribution houses could rake off what they liked in such harrowing times. There was never enough proper organization to keep track of all the donations, and less than 10% ever got to the people who actually needed the aid. Grain and other supplies were often diverted onto the Black Market, and Bird and the Dragon-Lady made sure the funds generated from those illegal activities all got redirected back to Bird's coffers.

The e-mail from Cairo was just one of many, and it took her a while to get to it, as she worked at her computer. Thank God for the air-conditioning, for without it, the use of such equipment in these sultry climes was haphazard at best. She wore little under the green cheongsam, with the black climbing vine motif down the side. A small fan under her desk was allowed to give a slight breeze to keep her legs cool. Long black hair hung down past her shoulders, and was cut straight in typical Thai style, yet she was no Thai. Her pale skin and the eye makeup merely gave that impression from a distance.

Occasionally, there were hiccups with security, requiring different solutions. Where westerners were involved, one simply couldn't kill the people concerned. They had to be disappeared first, to avoid diplomatic hassles from a variety of embassies.

Where western women were concerned, they were always popular in harems or brothels, once they were taught their new roles in life. Now there was this little matter of two nosey women arriving in Oman, after making too many enquiries in Cairo. But then her eyes caught the names, and she quickly pulled up the jpeg attachments of their passport details, comparing the photographs of their faces. "Oh my!" she gave a little chuckle. "Such a small world after all." Coincidence? Or were they tracking her down, somehow? It made life a little more interesting, that's for sure. Where those two women went, could Gabriel be far behind?

Two e-mails were called for, one to Oman, and another one, forwarding details to Bird, and advising him of Gabriel's possible involvement. Was the Church involved, too? Her contacts there had reported no indication of any urgent enquiries directed her way since her abrupt departure.

Borgia had taught her a lot about spinning webs, and snaring prey. Action against the two women would undoubtedly attract Gabriel's attention, and she didn't necessarily want that, but she did want the two women. She really couldn't let such an opportunity pass her by. She studied Belle's photo on the screen, and felt herself getting aroused. "We wants it, Precious. Oh yes, we wants it," and she slid her hand in under the slit of the cheongsam, to slowly stimulate herself.

*　　*　　*

Bird checked the e-mail from his partner in crime, and was momentarily puzzled. He had heard the name of Gabriel over the years, and had also heard, on the grapevine, of his supposed death in Italy. Was he still alive? If so, why was this man suddenly interested in events in the Far East? He knew a fair bit about Gabriel's reputation, fancied himself as good with a knife. Bird was good with a knife, too. He had never met his equal, or anyone that even came close.

Agile and still limber, despite his eighty-plus years, he pushed back the chair and stood up from his desk. He stood six foot eight inches tall, slim and emaciated as looked most Asian men, but more so. His hands reached down almost to his knees, and together with his long legs, gave him an almost unbelievable reach. He had the appearance of a crane or heron, though a bald-headed one.

He had won well over a hundred knife fights, as he had clawed his way to the top of this criminal organisation, and now he was finding himself fighting against the government as they attempted to crack down on the swiftly growing criminal organization, before it got too powerful.

Perhaps it had been a mistake to start up the supposed charity group to distribute 'aid' to the tsunami victims, and making sure he got more than his fair percentage for all his distribution work. It cut into the governments' own scam organizations for receiving foreign aid. Hence his involvement in funding the recruitment of his own private army from the remnants of the scattered Khmer Rouge in Cambodia. Combined with a little corruption in all the right places, he was well satisfied with the expansion of his powerbase, even considering a possible coup if events could be turned to his own advantage.

The current government was a corrupt as all the ones before it, and there was certainly money to be made in "politics". He looked upon his political aspirations as a natural progression, enabling him to consolidate everything he had done so far, and help cement his empire.

He walked over to the wall, and pulled out the stiletto that was stuck there, the impaled fly falling to the ground, as he flipped the knife from side to side. He folded the blade, slipping it into his pocket, as he deliberated. Events in Jakarta would bear watching.

*   *   *

When Laura and Belle collected their luggage at Seeb, they were ushered into an enclosed area by local Customs officials, who insisted on searching their luggage for contraband, drugs or whatever. Eventually, they fought their way through the throngs of people in the terminal, wheeling their released luggage in front of them, and they checked on availability of flights to Salalah. All fully booked. Nothing available for three days.

"We could always hire a car and drive down I suppose. But if we make reservations now, it gives your father chance to join up with us, and we can all go down together," Laura suggested, so that's what she did, producing passports and booking herself and Belle on the flight. Gabriel would have to make his own booking once he got here. But he needed to realize the two women didn't need to be protected all the time, and she knew that was one of the reasons Gabriel preferred to do things on his own, if there was an element of danger. "Let's grab a taxi to the hotel. I daresay Muscat has changed a bit since Gabriel was last here, though he told me a lot about the place." The two women eventually wheeled their luggage out to the front of the airport, where a sea of taxis waited, with drivers all trying to attract their attention. Westerners were always found to be bigger tippers, hence the fight for their custom.

The two women allowed one driver to load their luggage into the boot of his vehicle, and then sat back enjoying the air conditioning, as the taxi drove along the dual carriageway, heading into Muscat, some thirty kilometres away. The view was bleak to say the least.

Oman was not one of those Middle Eastern countries with rolling sand-dunes. Apart from the odd raised jebel, it was more flat, and gravel and shale. The only real sand-dunes of note in the north of the country were near the border with Saudi Arabia, where the oil-deposits of Lekhwair were still disputed, as the Saudis accused the Omanis of directional drilling under their border to steal Saudi oil.

The heat haze restricted their view to a few kilometres in front of them. Nothing to see but a few camels idly grazing by the side of the road, until they got closer to the city, and they could see the Jebel Mardar mountains in the distance. It took less than half an hour before the city came into view, and the traffic started increasing in volume, once they got past the Oryx Sanctuary, Oman's most famous wildlife, which was a breed of long-horned gazelle.

The dual-carriageway took them into the heart of the city, undulating up and down strangely, as Belle looked out of the window and noticed the roundabouts underneath, that the dual-carriageway had been raised frequently to avoid, as though built over an existing road system, which it indeed had been, in the early eighties.

The taxi turned off onto one of the ramps, down onto one such roundabout, and then pulled up to the Ruwi Hotel on the right, only a few hundred yards from the dual carriageway. Belle hoped the windows were double-glazed, to keep out the traffic noise.

The porter rushed out to open the taxi door for them, and other staff hurried to collect their luggage and escort them into the cooler reception, out of the hot afternoon sun. All the staff were Indian or Asian, which was typical in the Middle East. Arabs thought such work beneath them, and with their wealth, it was an easy matter to import labour. If truth be told, most of the Middle East was run by India, at the most basic level anyway. In one way or another, India had been taking over the world for the last thirty years.

Belle and Laura checked in, Belle reviewing the usual tourist brochures on the lobby desk, while Laura signed the register. A bit of sightseeing and a trip round the old Port of Muscat in the morning, and then lounge by the pool in the afternoon sounded a good plan. A trip to the old oasis town of Nizwa in the interior could wait till they got their bearings, and would depend on when Gabriel got here.

As the maitre-de allocated rooms, he noted the names of his new guests, and recognized them from the fax he had received earlier that morning. A simple phone call would alert the people concerned of the arrival of the two women, and he and some of his staff, who were already on the payroll of Al-Raschid, would follow whatever instructions they received regarding the two of them. Al-Raschid was well organized and integrated throughout the main cities in Oman. There were only really the two of them, Muscat in the north and Salalah in the south. It was an easy matter to install paid informants in the main hotels.

Laura noticed his interest, as he checked them in, but assumed it was a typical 'Don't touch the white woman' sort of thing. Eastern men were always attracted to white-skinned women, she found, and thought nothing more of it, as one of the bell-boys wheeled their luggage into the lift, and took them up to their floor.

The two women were allocated two double-rooms close to each other on the fourth floor. There was another room between them, but they found all the rooms were identical in layout, though opposite hand.

A nice large mirror opposite the bed was illuminated for vanity purposes, and there was a hair-dryer plugged into the wall beside it, as well as other utility sockets. Complimentary bathrobes were hung up in the en-suite bathrooms, and the balconies afforded a nice view over the walled pool area, and the city beyond.

Laura and Belle set about unpacking in their rooms, and took a quick shower. When the two women went down to the restaurant for a meal, the maitre-de used his pass-key to enter their rooms, and he searched their luggage for anything out of the ordinary, any reason they might be of interest to Al Raschid. He found nothing unusual, though enjoyed going through the women's lingerie, particularly the discarded panties in the laundry baskets, which he enjoyed sniffing. Both had the most delightful perfumed musk.

*   *   *

Mohammed had by now received word back from the Dragon-Lady. Slavery still existed in parts of the Arab and Asian world. Salalah was one of the age-old capitals of slavery, and it still went on to this day, though it was kept hidden from the civilized world. The two women were to be taken alive, and shipped to Indonesia, where they would spend the rest of their days. No bodies for the authorities to find and investigate. So much cleaner that way. It had been done before, and would be done again, he had no doubt. Quite a few of the pretty stewardesses earned their money on their backs these days in the Far East. He picked up the phone. Time to make some calls and some arrangements.

*　　*　　*

The next day, the two women took a taxi into the old Port of Muscat, and following the street-maps, they soon found the Embassy district, where Laura checked in with the American Embassy and Belle did likewise with the Italian Embassy. Both sets of passports were fake, but good fakes, and they liked to keep up appearances. From there it was only a short walk to view the palace of Sultan Qaboos, at least from the outside. They got as far as the row of black cannons before the military guards lined up to bar any closer access, and so they were left to admire the place from afar, before turning their attentions to the souk and more retail therapy.

After a small lunch in one of the few restaurants, both women walked out along the concourse, amazed at all the concrete obelisk sea-defences, which seemed to go off into the distance for as far as they can see, and then they continued down to watch all the dhows unloading their cargoes of fish and spices. The spices were aromatic. The fish stunk in the heat. As the sun got hotter, they took a taxi back to the hotel. Time to relax around the pool.

*　　*　　*

Gabriel finally arrived at the Golden Tulip hotel in Cairo, and checked in at the front desk, when the concierge passed him the letter that Laura had left for him. He opened it once he got to his room, and inwardly groaned as he read it. Just his luck that the supplier was based in Oman, Laura's next port of call.

He knew the two women too well to think they would not get themselves involved in this. He phoned down to the desk, and asked the concierge to book him on the next available flight to Muscat, and then asked to be put through to the Ruwi Hotel, and then waited as Laura was paged.

"Gabriel, darling, how nice of you to call," she chuckled, when she finally got to the phone.

"Laura, do we have to do this all the time? I know you mean to help, but I'd feel a lot better if I did this on my own," he explained.

"Belle and I are already here, and we're not going to go off on our own, don't worry," she reassured him. "Happenstance and Coincidence all at the same time. We'll be good, and we don't plan on making any inquiries ourselves. We'll just wait till you get here. But we do want to help. If you'll let us?" she pleaded. Damn the woman, but she knew which buttons to press. "We won't get in the way, but three heads are better than one, surely?"

"All right. We'll work on this together, but no running off half-cocked and doing things without my approval, okay?" he emphasized. "I know Oman and its people. I've spent time there before. You haven't," he pointed out. "Once the trail moves on, then I move with it, and you two just get on with your holiday. Okay?"

"Anything you say, darling," Laura purred down the phone. "When will you get here?"

"I think I've missed the flight tonight, so I'll rest up and catch a flight tomorrow. Assuming there's no complications, I should get there tomorrow evening."

"Good, I'll look forward to it. There's a real nice double bed just waiting for you," she promised.

"Hot and cold running chambermaids, too?" Gabriel joked.

"You wouldn't like the chambermaids, darling. Definitely not your type, and if I catch you even looking . . ." She didn't have to finish the sentence. Gabriel laughed.

Chapter Four

Angelo Zoro worked the streets, his face was now getting known in the area, and people came up to him, discreetly and not so discreetly, to buy the drugs he was offering. He sold soft and he sold hard, nothing big, and all in small enough packets to be ditched easily if the police happened by unexpectedly. Angelo was in his mid twenties, and in far better shape than his street appearance belied. Hair unkempt, and tall for an Indonesian, he wandered the streets in almost-anonymity, talking to the beggars and the street-vendors. He was getting a feel for the area, becoming familiar with the regulars, and learning to notice the strangers, the people who did not fit in.

Angelo had joined the Army fresh from University, and had risen rapidly through the ranks. His youth, fitness and intelligence had all served to get him noticed among his superiors, and his eventual transfer into the Kopassus, Special Forces, and he had volunteered for this current assignment after the J.I. bombings had started.

Muslim fundamentalism was a growing force in this part of the world, as it was across the Middle East. Ordinary Muslims were no longer allowed to follow their religions in peace. Always, the agitators were there in the background, stirring up unrest. The backlash from the Christian communities was only a matter of time, and Indonesia prided itself on its diversity. It could not be seen to be allowing a civil war to develop within its own borders. Hence Angelo's current assignment, to rout out any Muslim insurgent groups who were trying to operate in the area.

Jakarta was a crowded and noisy city, even after the riots of the nineties, teaming with people from all walks of life, and from many areas of the country. Sukarno had modernised and westernised the city during his regime, despite his many other faults. The wide avenues and dual carriageways gave a false veneer to visitors, and it didn't take long to wander away from these thoroughfares, and find the backstreets and shanties of the main populace.

Over 200 different dialects could be heard on the streets, and you were more likely to make yourself understood with a smattering of Portuguese, English or Dutch, than you were trying to speak your own tongue. In such a diverse metropolis, it was an easy thing to lose yourself on the streets and move about away from the eyes and ears of the authorities.

*   *   *

His mother was both pleased and worried about his current chosen profession. Retired now, though still on the board of 3M Industries, a supplier of stationery to the Engineering Industry, Denny Zoro lived a life of luxury on the outskirts of Jakarta, in a small but sumptuous villa. Once just a rep for the company, she had used a little windfall to invest and buy shares, and eventually rose to a position of power within its ranks. Truth to tell, she enjoyed the luxuries of life these days, which were a far cry from her youth, but life itself grew boring. She had never really been accepted by the elite of Jakarta society, which was still dominated by foreigners, 'orang-putihs' as they were called by the indigenous population. Sometimes she longed for the excitement of her youth, which was far behind her now. Still attractive and sprightly enough at 53, she had had lovers, though no husband. She didn't need more complications in her life, which revolved around her son. So like his father, he could never be satisfied with the quiet life, and his obvious skills had left him little choice of a worthwhile career in Indonesia, though she had tried and failed to persuade him to channel his efforts into Engineering, for which he had the aptitude, and had easily obtained the relevant qualifications. He had wanted more excitement in his life, and she couldn't blame him for that, for it was her own curse, if it could ever be called that.

*   *   *

Although Angelo had his own flat, he still had his room at his mother's villa, and was due there this evening for a small birthday meal with his mother, with whom he kept in touch, as often as he could. The present he had bought her was on his mind, as he continued his charade on the streets of Jakarta, taking notice of the faces. So many faces.

One or two had caught his eye, acting slightly suspiciously, and he filed the faces away in the back of his mind, to check out at Police Headquarters that evening, where he was allocated an office, before leaving for his mother's villa. He preferred the undercover assignments to the more boring and mundane work that the rest of the police in the city were generally used to. Used like this, his face did not become known to the criminal elements, which was how he preferred it.

He was following a man, though at a distance. The man kept looking back over his shoulder, trying to spot a tail, and this action had first drawn Angelo's attention to him. He kept back just on the periphery of the man's vision, trying hard not to attract attention. The man met up with a second man, and Angelo kept the corner of his eye on them, as he spoke to one of the other men on the street, as if touting his wares. This looked promising, but one of the disadvantages of not carrying a wire, meant he needed a phone to call in to Headquarters. There was a limit to what one man could do on his own.

The two men turned back, and started to walk back in his direction, and Angelo casually turned and began walking in front of them, though crossing over to the other side of the street. This type of surveillance was both difficult and dangerous. As he allowed them to pass by on the other side of the street, he took a long hard look at their faces, and decided he needed backup. No sense getting killed. He would check known mug-shots tonight at Headquarters, and arrange for the area to be staked-out in the hope of picking one or the other up again, if he couldn't identify the faces readily.

Angelo spent over an hour going through the mug-shots and filing a report on today's activities. He failed to put any names to the faces, though worked with a sketch-artist to produce reasonable likenesses. They would be circulated through the computer links with other agencies around the world. Two more men were assigned to help him on the streets in the same area again tomorrow.

Parts of this job were tedious, but he was glad of the change in assignments. He had been getting nowhere on the first case they had given him, chasing up the bloodless bodies that the tide kept bringing in from the open sea. Three bodies in the last six months, but too eaten up by fish and crabs, and only one of them identifiable from dental records.

Post-mortems had turned up little apart from the total drainage of blood from each body. It was a no-win scenario, and driving him nuts, so he was quick to volunteer for the undercover work on a new case.

*　　*　　*

It was nearly nine when he turned up at his mother's villa, and her female maidservant opened the gate to let him in. He nodded to her silently, and made his way up the path and into the house. "Ahhh, my son, my wonderful son."

"Mother, I bid you Happy Birthday," he smiled, bowed, and held out his offering, a small parcel wrapped in pretty blue paper, with a yellow silk bow around it. Denny smiled as she accepted the gift, which she would open later, in private, as was her custom. Mother and son embraced, and she accepted a kiss on her cheek, as he leaned down, and a tender hug.

"Dinner has already been prepared. Let us enjoy the meal, and talk of your latest successes," she suggested. Angelo nodded, and followed her into the dining room. His eyes were drawn by the framed photos on the wall, still there after all these years. One showed his mother, as she was twenty plus years ago, frolicking almost naked in the dawn surf at Cerita Beach. She looked happy then. She was happy enough today, but the smiles, however frequently he saw them, paled before the smile she wore in that single photograph. It obviously meant a lot to her, yet she had never explained it, save to confirm where it was taken. The other photo was never spoken of at all. It showed a western man, in his early thirties, Angelo guessed. He was sat with his mother at some restaurant table. She now beckoned him into the dining room, so he put the photo from his mind,

A nice Thai green chicken curry awaited him, flavoured with lemon grass, one of his mother's specialities, and Angelo sat down to enjoy his meal. His mother was always curious about his work for the police, and Angelo was always reluctant to speak of it, knowing it was a breach of security, however mild. There was a lot about his work that he didn't dare discuss, for there was widespread corruption throughout the force, and you never knew who you could trust, outside of a few close confidantes, and even they could be bought for a price. Indonesia was not a wealthy country, and the companies and the criminal elements (not much to choose between them really) had the money, whilst the honest men did not. His mother was still involved in corporate business, if only as a consultant these days. Best not alarm her with how much he knew about what some of the company boards got up to with their tax and pension scams.

After the meal, they sat out on the veranda, drinking coffee, and enjoying the night air, listening to the many sounds that drifted across the city, car horns and traffic, the noise of children still playing in the dark, faint bits of numerous conversations as people came and went beyond the protective walls of his mother's villa. Years ago, people living in such villas were often targeted by petty thieves, and they relied upon magic spells and charms to keep them safe. Angelo had insisted his mother invest in a more modern security system, and motion detectors lay at the foot of those walls, ready to signal an alarm should anyone venture within the grounds. His mother kept a gun by her bed. Illegal, and obtained for her by himself. It was untraceable, should she have occasion to use it. He had shown her how to use it, and told her what to do, if the occasion arose, particularly with reporting the incident to the police afterwards.

"You know I can't talk about details, mother," Angelo continued their conversation. "These incursions by Al Qaeda and their splinter groups are becoming more frequent, and we need to be alert to movements of any suspicious individuals. These terrorists seem to be everywhere these days. We think there is some sort of conduit into the country from the mainland, somewhere on the Malay Peninsula. The fake documentation some of them have had on them, seems indicative of some of the previous forgeries we've seen. There's a lot of movement of people without formal papers, since the big tsunami. We're trying to track them down. We have a good team working on this. Don't worry, I'm not trying to be a hero. I call in backup when I need it. I don't put myself at risk if I can help it."

"Good, my son. You have a lot of life ahead of you, and I wish you to live well beyond my own years." She smiled, and put her hand on his arm. Angelo smiled, and patted the frail hand. "This world is becoming a troublesome place in which to live," Denny smiled, wryly.

"There are fanatics and criminals the world over, mother. We already have our fair share, and we don't need any outsiders coming into our country to make the situation worse." He patted the back of her hand, again, reassuringly.

"When I was your age, the world didn't seem as wild. Oh there were criminals, and greedy politicians, but now the religious fanatics are out in force with the coming of the new Millennium, and everywhere I look, there is violence on a scale I've never seen before."

"That's why people like me will always have a job," Angelo joked, to lighten the mood, and his mother playfully punched him on his arm. Denny Zoro felt herself drifting back through the years as she sat here, enjoying the evening, with her son. The wild days of her youth were far behind her, now, but she still had her memories. Some of them were painful, and some very pleasant. She brooded momentarily, as she ruminated on the decisions and choices that had shaped her life. Could it have ended differently, she thought to herself? But then she looked at her son, and knew she would not have changed events if they had shaped such joy in her life, to replace the joy she'd lost all those years ago.

She had known his father for only a few months, and those months had been blissful, if hectic. He had worked as an Engineer at the power station on the Muara Karang peninsula, in Pluit, and all had seemed fine when he had left for Singapore to renew his visa. He didn't return. No phone call to explain, but in the weeks that followed, as she found herself pregnant with his child, she received a letter, simply explaining that his visa had been revoked, and he would not be allowed to return to Indonesia. There was no return address. He did not know of her pregnancy. Indeed, she had laughingly told him she could not conceive on that mad evening at Cerita Beach, when he had no condoms, and the heat of passion had quickly overcame the both of them.

The letter went on to explain that his salary had been paid into the ABN Bank in Jakarta, and it had scarcely been drawn upon. Another letter had been sent to the bank, instructing the manager to turn over the contents of his account to one Denny Zoro, upon production of suitable identification. There had been nearly fifty thousand dollars in that account, a fortune which she had wisely invested to secure herself a seat on the board of the company she worked for, and maintain herself and her child, a child who would never know his father. It was hard bringing up a child without a father, but Denny thought she had done a reasonable job, looking at the handsome man sitting next to her. So like his father in many ways.

*   *   *

Night in Bangkok was a splendid sight, the colours of the neon lights and advertising reminded him of Tokyo at times. Bird looked out of his office window onto the Mae Nam Chao Phraya river. The traffic flowed in an endless neon procession across the Phra Pokklao Bridge.

His office was on the north side of the river, just south of the Sampeng Market, and Chinatown, but his apartment building lay south of the river, in the quieter suburbs, though only a short drive away. The incense he kept burning in his office acted to disguise the smells from the market, on the occasions he kept the window open.

The hubbub rising up from street-level was unique, and Bird never tired of listening to it. He had come a long way from his days as a tour-guide for the many foreigners, and it was that past experience, and knowledge of the geography, travel routes, and contacts with people from all walks of life, that had helped re-build his life in a direction he had always dreamed of going. He was in his eighties now, yet almost as fit and agile as he had been in his prime, certainly more powerful now than he had ever been.

He had fleeced some of the paedophiles through blackmail over their activities, which he had helped set-up, in places where he could obtain the necessary video and photographic evidence to carry out the blackmail. The money had been used to grease palms, and climb the social ladders in Thai society. When the people from Al Qaeda had contacted him, he was quick to see the opportunities that were opening up for him. Arab money was readily available, for the right sort of assistance, and again his experience was invaluable.

Bird had now found the ideal location for their training camp, not in Thailand itself, but in the remote highlands of Cambodia, East of Angkor. Remnants of the Khmer Rouge still roamed around Cambodia, often foraying across the border into Thailand, and they had agreed to assist in the training of these Muslim fanatics, in exchange for a profitable sum of money to purchase their opium crop. Their occasional forays across the border, stirring up trouble for the current Thai administration, allowed him to take advantage of their embarrassment and put himself forward in the public eye.

The Royal Thai Army, or RTA as they were known, were often harried in border skirmishes in the north east, to keep them occupied when moving some of the Muslim insurgents across the border further south. Sound diversionary tactics Bird had learnt in his own compulsory military service when he was younger.

Travel was less closely monitored over the border, and the Khmer's activities were less likely to be associated, should they by some chance be discovered. The present world climate was there to be exploited, and the Arab money was used to finance a few "charity" organizations which his contacts in the Thai government helped secure control of world aid, flooding into the country after the tsunami.

His organizations helped that money along, minus a few "operational expenses". There was more money coming in than could possibly be needed, after all, and his need was far greater. His operational expenses were high.

In the aftermath of the tsunami, with all the displaced people, travel was less controlled than before, and it was easy for him to set up a conduit for the Muslim extremists of Al Qaeda into the south. From their training camp near Kampong Thom, through Aranya Prathet, and into Bangkok, where they exchanged travel documents and identities, then South through Hat Yui, and Perlis or Khota Baru, eventually ending up in Singapore, where ships sailed daily to the islands of Sumatra and Java. Passage was easy to arrange. The Indonesian government was more unstable, and security forces corrupt and untrustworthy.

Bird thought of the future for a moment, and wondered what would happen if Al Qaeda targeted the likes of Bangkok, once he had taken his place in the Thai government? His contact with them had been discreet, and he had operated through a number of cut-outs for the last few years. Few people had seen his face, or knew his real identity. It would be a relatively simple matter to eliminate the few that had, once his aspirations for public office bore fruit.

With what he knew about the Al Qaeda operations, once he made that information known discreetly to the right authorities, he could ensure that the Al Qaeda threat to the region was all but eliminated altogether, if not causing them severe setbacks in this region. No, he felt secure from that threat in his own lifetime.

He had his finger in so many pies these days, both legal and illegal, whilst maintaining the front of being an upright citizen and businessman, involved in various charitable works, he was also involved in smuggling, prostitution, and gambling, as well as the opium trade. Strangely he did not deal in the stronger narcotics, but opium was more of a heritage in this part of the world.

The trick was to keep his head below the parapet, and avoid getting it shot off. He diversified his money, making sure his face and name were readily associated with the more legitimate parts of his financial empire, and avoiding any known association with the others.

Because of his physical attributes, he was a man not easily forgotten, and so he tried to control public exposure, and only released head and shoulders photos to the media and press. He tried to keep as low a profile as he could, whilst climbing the ladders of power, but already he could see the top of the ladder. Once he achieved the public office he sought, then he could step out of the shadows, in the knowledge that no one alive knew of his past dealings.

Chapter Five

Mohammed sent an urgent e-mail to the Dragon-Lady, reporting Laura's phone call, and advising her that another player was expected to join them. The reply came quickly. "Take the women tonight. I want them alive, and in more or less good condition. Take no action against Gabriel, for now, if he turns up. Tell him the two women checked out, and left the hotel. Let him chase shadows looking for the two of them."

Mohammed had arranged similar disappearances before. The route south and across the seas was tried and trusted. By truck to Salalah, offshore by dhow, and then transferred to a larger freighter to cross the sea to Indonesia. Destinations sometimes varied, but the Dragon-Lady was adamant she wanted to play with these two pretty little things herself. White women fetched a tidy price in Asia, as well as Arabia.

* * *

Laura and Belle dined in the hotel restaurant, which was set back from the foyer. Across the other side of the foyer, was the entrance to the hotel bar, where they ended up for a few nightcaps before retiring for the evening.

Gabriel's plane would arrive tomorrow afternoon, and they planned on at least one more night here at the Ruwi before making arrangements to travel south to Salalah. The bar was full, with a mixture of ex-pats and Arabs, and more than a few female airline stewardesses.

*　　*　　*

The drugs had been administered in the food, which had been heavily spiced, as was the custom with food in the Middle East, disguising any lingering under-taste, and Belle had suspected nothing. It acted in concert with the alcohol the two women imbibed, and caused tiredness, which neither woman found unusual. They retired back to their rooms before ten pm. By ten thirty, both women were in a drug-induced sleep.

Mohammed had organized the truck for four am, the next morning, and the women, and all of their luggage, needed to be on it and heading south out of the city before the majority of its inhabitants were up and about.

He opened Laura's door himself, and switched on the room light. She laid asleep on the bed, the sheets partially down to expose her breasts, as she slept almost nude in the heat. Her chest rose and fell, rhythmically, indicative of a sound sleep. The windows to the balcony were open, and the balmy evening air wafted in, carrying faint sounds of the traffic. Mohammed took the syringe out of his pocket, and took the cork off the end of the needle, lightly depressing the plunger to ensure there was no air-bubble in the hollow needle. Sitting down on the edge of the bed, he pulled the sheets down further, letting his eyes roam over her body, and then with one hand he rolled her slightly to one side, exposing her pantied bottom. Pale yellow briefs with embroidered roses on the crotch.

He pulled the skimpy briefs to one side, and the needle went into the soft flesh easily, as he injected her with a more powerful drug, to keep her under. Mohammed put a second syringe on the dresser unit. His subordinates would need to inject her with the contents of that syringe before they put her into the truck. He had another set of needles in his other pocket for the brunette. Both would remain unconscious for their journey south to Salalah. Satisfied, he rolled Laura back onto her back, and re-corked the needle before replacing it in his pocket. She was indeed a beautiful woman, he thought, looking at her. He took her arm, and shook her lightly, and Laura moaned as the second drug coursed through her system.

"Have a nice night," he chuckled, as he got up from the bed, and went to the door to let two of his subordinates into the room. "No bruises, and see she is dressed for the journey," Mohammed warned the two men. "All her luggage as well. It will be disposed of in Salalah. Leave nothing behind," he instructed.

The two men set about their tasks as Mohammed left the room, walked down the corridor, and used his passkey to open the door to Belle's room.

Mohammed rolled Belle over onto her side. He pulled up the teeshirt, and pulled the black panties to one side, sticking the needle into soft buttockflesh, as he pressed the plunger. She too was given the same drug. Mohammed placed the second syringe on the bedside table, and went to the door to let the second pair of men into her room. He gave them the same instructions regarding Belle as he had Laura. Mohammed left them to it. His subordinates could be trusted to do a thorough job of removing all traces of the women's presence.

All Mohammed was concerned about was that the two women disappeared by morning so he left his men to it, and left the hotel itself, to go home, and report that the Bitch-Queen's instructions had been carried out. If all went to plan, the women would never be heard from again.

*   *   *

As Mohammed left them to it, the four waiters had their own plans for the two women. They didn't often have such an opportunity as this, as they intended on making the most of it.

Belle was carried into her mother's room. What nightclothes the women had on were eagerly removed, and then the waiters began removing their own clothing.

The men pushed the two single beds together to create enough space for all six of them to occupy, and the four waiters then began to enjoy themselves. The women were intended for the brothels of Jakarta, so the might as well get used to their new lives.

Unconscious or not, the two women had marvelous bodies, and the four men intended to make full use of them while they had the opportunity.

The four waiters cleaned up Belle and Laura in the early hours of the morning, and pushed and pulled them into a couple of old abeyyas for the journey. They were given renewed injections to keep them unconscious. Manacles were used to fasten their hands behind their backs, and then they were carried out through the service entrance to a waiting truck, where their luggage had already been moved.

The men had ransacked their luggage for any useful items, such as cameras etcetera, and had also helped themselves to a few personal souvenirs. One of them grinned as he reviewed the avi footage on his mobile phone. The truck pulled out, and the waiters, content with the night's work, drifted off.

*   *   *

Belle awoke gradually, being tossed about by the rough driving as the truck changed direction on the outskirts of Salalah. The interior of the rear of the truck was getting unbearably hot, having suffered the fierce sun all day on its journey south, and the small vents for air did not do much for ventilation. She recognized the horrible taste in the back of her throat as proof she had been drugged, and probably so had her mother, who was still unconscious on the floor of the truck.

She found the two of them dressed in long black grubby abeyyas, which was rucked around her knees at the moment. It felt like she was naked beneath. Rolling over, she tested the broad iron manacles that held her wrists behind her back. Very much olde-world in design, they were nonetheless effective when you didn't have a key. The hinge-pins could be worked upon, but not by herself and not when they were behind her back. She would need Laura awake to help her.

They were being transported somewhere, by someone, for some purpose, and she didn't know what that was. Coincidence? Or the result of their enquiries into the Al Raschid organization? They hadn't even had time to begin to make enquiries here in Oman.

She nudged Laura gently with her foot, and when that elicited no response, she nudged her less gently, raising a moan. "Wake up, mother." She kicked Laura's ass hard, and Laura rolled over, groaning.

"My head." Laura's eyes flickered open, and then she turned away, dry-retching, as the after-effects of the drugs began to make themselves known. She raised her head, taking in her surroundings. "What do you remember about last night?" she asked.

"More than I want to remember," Belle replied.

"Drugged and kidnapped," Laura stated, shaking her head to clear it. "What a mess! Any idea where we are, or where we're heading?" she asked.

Belle shook her head. "What you see is what you get. South, by the angle of the sun. We won't know more till the truck stops. Turn around and give me a good look at those manacles." Laura did as Belle asked, letting her daughter study the things. A thin knife blade would be enough to open the crude lock, but they didn't have one. Then she noticed the suitcases. "Let's get them open. If all our stuff is inside, I might be able to use my nail-clippers to jimmy the locks on these things," she suggested.

The suitcases weren't locked, but it was difficult opening them with their hands bound behind their backs in this fashion. Clothes had just been stuffed inside, but many personal effects were missing, obviously having a marketable value in Muscat. Belle's vanity-set wasn't there. Neither was Laura's. "Basta!" she swore.

*   *   *

Gabriel arrived on the late afternoon plane into Seeb, and he was pleased to notice the place had improved greatly since his last trip here. It was still as crowded as ever, but the concept of queues had been introduced, and it was a lot easier to get through customs, collect his luggage, pay for his visa, and make his way out to the taxi-ranks. He sat back to enjoy the air-conditioning during the taxi ride into Muscat, letting the sights and feel of Oman wash back over him.

It had been more than twenty years since he was last here. The desert never changed, but the few outposts of civilization that were scattered about showed signs that the oil money was being well invested by Sultan Qaboos. He was a benevolent ruler, compared to many such in the Middle East.

The highway, new in Gabriel's day, was showing its age in places, now, and his stomach didn't enjoy the constant up and downs as the city neared and the highway raised up to cross the many existing roundabouts, and then down again.

The Ruwi had been given a facelift, sandblasted and freshly painted. There were newer hotels here now, but the Ruwi had a certain charm about it. Small, cultured, and in a nice downtown location.

The rooms were nice and comfortable, and the air-conditioning was first rate. Gabriel was accustomed to the heat and humidity of places like Muscat, but no need to suffer it if there was no need. He liked the comfort of modern technology.

The taxi pulled up outside the foyer, and Gabriel paid him with some of the riyals he had exchanged at the airport. He went to check in at the reception desk, and a smiling face, possibly Indian, welcomed him. "Good afternoon, sir. How may I help you?" he asked, courteously.

"Angell. My wife is staying here. What room is she in?" The man consulted his register, running his finger down the list of entries.

"There must be some mistake, sir. Your wife was checked in here yesterday, but she checked out again early this morning." Gabriel was dumbfounded for a moment.

"Can I see that?" he indicated the register. The clerk turned it around and laid it on the desk for Gabriel to study by himself. There were indeed Laura and Belle's signatures, with an indication that their stay had only lasted the single night. "I phoned my wife yesterday, and she was expecting me to join her here. Why would she suddenly check out like this? Did she leave any sort of message for me?" he asked.

The clerk checked behind the desk. "I'm sorry, sir, but there's nothing here for you." He opened a cash box and started riffling through a number of receipts. He pulled out a visa slip and the original booking form. "Here, sir. You can see for yourself. She has only been charged for the single night." Gabriel studied the paperwork. It was customary to let the desk swipe your credit card on arrival, and the signature was indeed Laura's, but it didn't explain her sudden disappearance. His mind was working furiously, trying to think of explanations, and not wanting to think the two women had gone off on their own again, despite their promises to him.

"Is the room my wife used still vacant?" he asked. The clerk checked, and nodded. "Very well, I'll take the same room. Book me in, and I'll need to make an overseas phone call as soon as possible." He handed over his passport, which the clerk scanned in, and handed back to him. Then his credit card was swiped, and Gabriel authorized the debit. The balance would be input on his departure. The clerk handed him a pass-key.

"Room 249, sir. The lift is over there, and it's the 2nd floor, on the right as you come out of the lift." He rang a bell on the desk, and one of the porters came and insisted on carrying Gabriel's cases.

"Thank you. I remember the way." Gabriel took the key-card, and went to call the lift. The reception was technically on the 1st floor, with the ground floor beneath them, as the hotel was built on a slope. The porter got into the lift with him.

He used the key-card to open the door, and walked into the room, eyes everywhere. It had been valeted during the day, but he was trying to imagine it with Laura in it. Surely she wouldn't go off by herself, even with Belle, after agreeing to wait for him? What could have prompted her to do such a thing, having been in the country less than twenty four hours? He tipped the porter with a few low denomination notes, and closed the door.

Picking up the phone, he first made a call to the Hotel Tulip in Cairo, in case she had tried to contact him there while he had been in transit. No luck there, so he made a second call back to Argentina to check with Manuel, his manservant. Again, he drew a blank. Preoccupied, he looked about the room. Something about it didn't feel right, but he couldn't put his finger on it. Oman was a big country, and he had no current contacts here.

The SAS still maintained an operational base in the south, but after his last encounter with them, he realized that Whitehall preferred him dead. Contact with them was out of the question. How then was he to find the two women? He couldn't even call on Solomon, as this was a Muslim country, and the Catholic clergy could not maintain any sort of high profile here. Churches were few and far between across the Middle East, and it was hardly a sphere of influence to expect Solomon to maintain any agents here.

He picked up the phone and called the front desk again. "Yes sir, can I help you?"

"How do I call a taxi?" he asked.

"If you look at the welcome pack on your bureau, sir, you'll find the numbers of a few different taxi companies. They will pick you up at the front reception. All rates are fixed by the Ministry, so they will all charge you the same amount. You can call them direct from your room phone. Most speak English."

"Thank you," said Gabriel, hanging up and leafing through the welcome pack. No scribbles to indicate Laura had thought of using one. He started ringing the companies one by one, asking each one in turn if they had picked up two western women from the Ruwi hotel, sometime earlier today. Each answer was in the negative. Gabriel thought it unlikely that they had walked across the road to the Ruwi high-street in the hot sun, with their luggage, and manually hailed a cab. That meant transport of another kind, maybe an organized lift, or someone's car. But how had all this been arranged in so short a space of time?

The welcome pack also gave the addresses of hire-car companies, and Gabriel called them each in turn, but none of them could confirm renting any vehicle to a western woman either yesterday or today.

Gabriel next called the airport, and verified that neither of the two women had been booked on any of the outgoing flights that day or the next. Which meant the two women were somewhere in Oman, but it would be like searching for two grains of sand in a desert. Western women wandering about were not uncommon, with the ex-pat workforce working for Shell and PDO, but due to the fierce heat, not many people wandered anywhere. People drove from place to place, and who took much notice of passengers in cars? Many of the vehicles today also had tinted windows to keep out the bright sun, also. It was not going to be easy. He decided to make one last phone call.

"Jim?" there was a silence on the other end of the line for a few moments, and then a click, and Gabriel knew the call was now being scrambled.

"Will you fucking well stay dead?" an angry voice deafened him.

"If you're going to shout that loud, there's not much point in using the scrambler, now is there?" he reminded his friend, amusedly.

"Gabe, you almost got your head handed to you in Italy. I was the one ordered to do it. Have you got a death wish? Whitehall thinks you're dead. Let them keep thinking that. For fuck's sake, man, stop phoning me here." Gabriel could visualize Jim Maddox pulling his hair out.

"Jim, I'm in a bit of a fix, and I need help. I can't think of anyone else I can call under the circumstances. I wouldn't on my own account, but Laura and Belle have gone missing, and I'm out on a limb. I'm back in Muscat," he explained. "I flew into Seeb today, and was supposed to meet them here at the hotel, only to find they've checked out, and I can't find any trace of them. I can't contact anyone in the Regiment, and you're the only one I trust who has the resources to help me." Maddox was mumbling something indecipherable to himself on the other end of the phone.

"Europol doesn't have any official ties to the Omani government, Gabe, and if I use my old connections with the Regiment down near Salalah, sooner or later your name is going to crop up," he explained.

"I know that. That's not what I want. Laura was tracking down a company called Al Raschid, who deal in antiquities and curios. That's the only lead I have. There has to be a connection. One night in Oman, and they go missing. It's too much of a coincidence. I need all you can find out about that company."

"Where are you?"

"Ruwi Hotel. Room 249." Gabriel replied. He heard a chuckle on the other end of the line.

"Memories, memories. Give me a few hours," Maddox advised. "Go and get some of that good Cous-Cous, see if they still have some of that Pusser's Rum in the bar, and see if the Air France girls are still as friendly."

"I'll do my best," Gabriel confirmed. "Give my love to Rebel." He hung up, and hoped his friend would prove fruitful with his enquiries. Gabriel unpacked, showered and shaved. Nothing else for it but to take his friend's advice, and so he went down to the restaurant to order a meal.

After dining, he called into the bar, for a drink. The place had been revamped, but the clientele was more or less the same, mixed with affluent Omanis and ex-pats, all vying for the attentions of the stewardesses that did stopovers here in Muscat, usually the only single and available women. He didn't stay long, and went back to his room.

More relaxed now, as the alcohol worked on his system, he realized what had caught his eye the first time he had walked into the room. A couple of light spots on the wall. Gabriel went over to it, and examined it in more detail. He touched a finger to one of those spots, and felt it give slightly under pressure. He had worked surveillance with the SAS, and realized what it was he had just found.

Someone had drilled the wall partially through from the next room, though not enough to break through the wallpaper, to insert surveillance devices, a microphone and maybe a fibre-optic. This was not the work of amateurs. Someone had had Laura under surveillance, probably Belle as well.

Gabriel sat back down on the bed, not looking at the wall directly, but out of the corner of his eye. The room behind that wall would tell its own story. Someone could be observing him even now, but why? He lay down on the bed, fully-clothed, turned out the light and pretended to take a nap. He was debating how to handle this new information when the phone rang by his bed. He sat up, switched on the bedside light, and answered the phone. "Yes?" It was Maddox.

"The company you asked about does indeed deal in antiques and such. They are technically classed as importers and exporters, though what they export from a place like Oman is anyone's guess. Do you have a pen?" Gabriel grabbed one from the welcome pack, as Maddox reeled off the address of their offices, and phone numbers. "One worrying little thing . . ." Maddox hesitated to speak further. "Remember how we tried to close down the slave trade during our stint down South? Well it's still going on from what I can gather. Westerners are rare, maybe one or two a year, but women are disappearing out there as much as they ever did. If this company's export side is handling that, and your good lady was sticking her nose in, so to speak, she may have bitten off more than she could chew." Gabriel nodded to himself. "If you need assets on the ground, I can make introductions with some of the Regiment down South, but you know the risk you'd be running." Maddox offered.

"No thanks, Jim. Sounds like something I need to do on my own. One man is less noticeable. I'll let you know what I find out." Gabriel put the phone down.

*   *   *

Back in Brussels, Jim Maddox shook his head. Gabriel and he went way back, and Maddox had met Laura in Italy, when they had helped rescue his former girlfriend Rebekah from the Al Qaeda terrorists who had tried to explode a dirty bomb and irradiate the Vatican City.

A man alone in the Middle East stuck out like a sore thumb, and he could do with some help. His options were limited, as Whitehall had ordered Maddox to carry out Gabriel's death sentence. He had fooled them into thinking it had been carried out, and it was best if they kept on being fooled.

Chapter Six

The truck arrived in Salalah in the early hours of the evening. The sun was just going down and left a unique brown and yellow glow in the sky, as night approached.

Heading west along A'Robat Street, to the south of the airport, the truck continued along to the westernmost outskirts of the city and the Raysut Industrial Area, close to the docks. The two women could hear the sounds of seagulls, and they could smell the sea, even above the fumes from the exhaust, as the truck finally came to a halt. Manacled the way they were, there was little the two women could do for now, other than await what their captors had in store for them.

The rear of the truck swung open, and three grinning Arab faces stared in at the two women, who were huddled back against the far side of the container. The men were dressed western fashion, workers, not your average citizens. One of the men began to climb into the back with them, swinging a knotted length of what looked like ship's rope.

"Hey, Missy, good to see you awake. Hope you enjoyed the ride, yes?" he chuckled, in his broken English. "We got nice ocean cruise planned for you two ladies. Very nice, the sea air," he added, and reached for Belle to pull her to her feet. Belle didn't resist, and when she was standing, he helped Laura to her feet also. Both women made eye-contact. No use trying anything in the confines of the truck. Best wait till they were out in the open, and they could assess their chances of escape better.

Neither of them thought their abduction was any coincidence. You just didn't hear of tourists going missing these days. It had to be connected to the Al Raschid organization, though why they would go to such lengths to kidnap two foreign nationals she couldn't fathom. What could they be up to, more than small-time smuggling and customs fraud?

The two men reached to help Belle down from the back of the truck, as she looked about. The truck was stopped outside of a warehouse, where crates were stored. Another smaller vehicle was loaded up with a couple of the crates, and one such stood open and empty. Neon lights from the roof of the warehouse illuminated the immediate environs, and in their glare Belle couldn't see much else, though by the sounds and impressions she got, there were more warehouses in the immediate vicinity.

Belle struggled down from the high step, onto tarmac which burned her bare feet, still hot after baking in the hot sun all day. One of the men held her arm, while the other reached to help Laura down. They weren't rough, just firm. They had their orders.

"Now, little ladies. I must ask you to get into that crate." He pointed at the open crate on top of the smaller truck. "It will be necessary till we leave the harbour. It would be better if no one saw you. If all goes well, the crate will be opened once we get out of the harbour. We wouldn't want to accidentally drop the crate over the side," he grinned, showing a broken front tooth. "If you make a noise, that might actually happen," he warned.

"Where are we, and what do you plan to do with us?" asked Laura, wanting to know where they stood, and how much these men, obviously underlings, knew. Broken Tooth answered her.

"Where you are is not as important as where you are going," he laughed. "To us, you are just another cargo. Behave, and we will treat you as such. Misbehave and you will be punished," he warned her. "Now get in the crate," he ordered.

Belle was lead up onto the tailboard of the smaller truck, and one man held her as she swung a leg to climb into the crate. His eyes enjoyed the length of bare white flesh that was revealed, and Belle settled herself in a squatting position inside the crate, as Laura was helped up onto the tailboard. She, too, was made to climb inside, and as she squatted down beside her daughter, the lid was put in place, and their ears hurt as nails were driven down to fasten it in place.

"What now?" asked Laura, in the darkness.

"Nothing we can do till they let us out of this crate. Sounds like some sort of boat trip. Apart from Muscat, the only other big port is Salalah, and I'd guess that's where we are by the length of the journey.

We've pissed somebody off, that's for sure," she joked, trying to keep her spirits up.

"Where are they shipping us to, then? If they'd wanted us dead, we wouldn't be talking right now."

"I thought all those tales about white slavers were just urban legends. Looks like I was wrong. I heard Tokyo was quite a popular place for this sort of thing," Belle speculated.

"Can't be any of the other Arab states this side of the Gulf, but the Arabian Sea isn't that wide. Iran is too extreme, unless they're looking to take out some of their frustrations on a couple of western women for all the shit Bush and the rest have thrown their way over the last few years. India is too westernized."

"Either way, I don't plan on finishing this little cruise. Once they let us out of this crate, I think we'd better make a move at the first opportunity. One of them likes my legs. Should be easy enough to distract."

"We need to get out of these shackles, first. Won't swim very far with them on, and these waters are shark-infested," Laura pointed out. They were jolted suddenly as the second truck started up and pulled away, driving slowly on the relatively short journey to the docks. The two women heard men moving around and shouting to each other, and then shackles were fastened to the crate they were in, and they felt it leave the ground. Both women hoped the shackles held.

The crate was hoisted through the air, and lowered into the small hold in the centre of the dhow. The shackles were removed, and nothing happened for over an hour. The two women were getting cramps before they felt the change of direction which indicated the dhow was now leaving the quayside, and the swell of the tide could be felt beneath the deep keel.

After about an hour, two women heard the renewed activity on deck, and the fresh application of shackles once more, and then the crate was lifted a second time, high above the sea, as the crane relocated their resting-place from one hold to another. There was a sudden jolt, as the crate came to rest on steel deck-plating.

There was more activity around them, and crowbars were applied to the top of the crate, loosening it. Harsh light from the floodlights in the hold blinded the two women as the top of the crate came off, after their long confinement in the blackness of the crate, and they struggled to focus.

Rough hands pulled them to their feet, and Belle cried out as her abeyya caught on a projecting nail, ripping it and almost piercing her thigh. Her captors paid her no heed, and pushed her out of the way, as Laura was dragged out of the crate in similar fashion. Both women made the most of the opportunity to get their bearings, making eye contact.

The sailors herded them out of the hold through one of the bulkhead doors, and shoved them along a narrow corridor, and then up a narrow and steep staircase. Laura felt the Arab behind her lifting her abeyya to peer up underneath as he made her climb before him. She heard his chuckles, but there was nothing she could do about it. With her hands manacled behind her back, climbing wasn't easy, and he used the excuse to put his hands on her ass, squeezing and chuckling, as he pushed her upward.

A small cabin had been set aside for the two women, and they were pushed inside. The single porthole was too narrow for either of the two women to climb out of, and the only egress was the door by which they entered. There were two bunk-beds against the wall, with a small dresser unit in between. A shower/bathroom unit was behind the door, obviously crew's quarters.

"Can we lose these things now?" Laura said, gesturing with her manacled hands as best she could. "We need water, and food," she pointed out. Two of the Arabs remained just outside the doorway, whilst a third came closer to unlock the manacles. Both women were relieved to be released from the rough metal manacles. Belle rubbed her wrists as the man collected the manacles, and stepped back towards the door.

"We will bring food and water," one of them informed them, and then the door swung shut and they heard the key being turned in the lock. Belle instantly checked out the portal, opening it and sticking her head out. About fifteen feet above the water, and twenty or so below the main deck. Laura checked out the bathroom. The place was bare of anything they could use as a weapon.

"What do we do now?" Laura wondered.

"We wait. Sooner or later, we'll get an opportunity. We just have to take it when it comes. If we can lower a lifeboat, we stand a chance of getting back ashore, and making our way to the Embassy. I'm sure the ordinary Omanis would help us." Belle and Laura made themselves as comfortable as they could, laying down on the bottom bunks. Rest would be important.

After half an hour or so, the key turned in the lock again, and two of the men had returned with a tray of food and a plastic bottle of water. There were no glasses or cutlery offered, and one of them entered the cabin to hand the tray to Belle. She took it as he backed away out of the cabin, and the door closed and locked behind him. Laura watched as Belle broke the seal and unfastened the top of the bottle, taking a few swigs before handing it to her. As Laura drank, Belle sampled the food. Now she knew how they had drugged them before, it was easier for her to detect the under-taste of the drugs behind the spiced food. "More drugs in the food," she announced. "They obviously want to keep us quiet for the trip." She took the plate into the bathroom and swilled the food down the toilet, flushing it. She put the empty plate back on the tray. "Let them think we're nice and docile, and maybe they'll drop their guard," she suggested. Laura nodded. Water was more important than food, and they swallowed what they needed, but no more. The half full bottle might be needed at a later date.

Unsure of the time, the two women trusted their body-clocks, and lay down to try and sleep. Rest while they can. It felt late evening or early morning, and no telling how long they would be left in the cabin.

As it was, Belle came awake at the faint scraping of the key in the door lock. In the darkness, and with only night-lights on in the corridor, Belle just made out the silhouettes of two of the crewmen in the doorway as the door swung open. As before, one of them stood in the doorway, as one of them entered. They spoke softly in Arabic, which Belle could easily understand. "Did they eat the food?"

"Yes," chuckled the man who was within the cabin, seeing the empty plates. He came over to the bunk, and took hold of Belle's leg. Eyes closed, she regulated her breathing to make it appear as though she was still asleep, making no movement even when the hand slid up the inside of her thigh. "The drugs have put them to sleep. We can have our fun, and they will be none the wiser," he chuckled, fingers running through Belle's silken pubic hairs.

The second man came within the cabin, and he closed the door behind him. "Our captain will not like it if he finds out," he warned.

"Our captain would be in here himself, if the addled fool had any brains. These whores are headed for the brothels of Jakarta. What matter if they start earning their keep earlier than planned?" he scoffed, and he began undressing as the second man moved over to Laura's bunk. The two men chuckled inanely like children with new toys, as they stripped the bedding away from the two women.

Belle's legs were pulled apart, as the Arab climbed on top of her. He was lowering himself into position when Belle's head came up off the pillow fast and hard, slamming into his face as she head-butted him as hard as she could, knocking him out cold. As the second man turned away from Laura to see what had happened, Laura's foot lashed out, catching him in the balls, and as he cried out and doubled-up, she swung her fist, catching him on the side of the head. He smashed his head on the metal bunk-frame, and fell to the floor, stunned, as Laura leapt off the bed and on top of him, grabbing his hair and smashing his face into the floor till he lost consciousness.

Belle was rubbing her own forehead, as she pushed her own unconscious assailant off her. Laura was rummaging through the Arabs' clothes, finding the keys, but nothing else of much use. The two women dressed in the men's clothing, ill-fitting though it was, and they tore up the abeyyas they had been wearing and used them to gag and tie up the two men. They locked the cabin door behind them, and then made their way up the next flight of stairs towards the upper decks.

Only the thrumm of the engines could be heard, as they made their way up the stairs, and finally opened the bulkhead door onto the main deck. They waited there, Belle peering out, until they were sure no one was about. Apart from the running lights, the only other light came from the bridge, which was high above them, and the men inside would be concentrating more on their instruments than in looking out of the bridge windows into the blackness of the night.

The deck swayed lightly in moderate seas, and the two women made their way along the port side of the ship. The lifeboats were at the aft end of the ship, out of the line of sight of the bridge, and they headed there, keeping to the shadows. Belle climbed into one boat, whilst Laura began checking out the lowering mechanism. "There's a radio beacon, hard rations, and a flare gun." Belle announced, as she reappeared, and began helping Laura operate the winch. She helped push the boat out over the side, as Laura cranked, trying to lower the boat into the water. The crank was a lot noisier than she wished.

"This isn't going to work," she warned. "These things were meant to be lowered into stationary water."

"If we both climb in before we hit the water, we can release both lines at the same time, drop into the water, and let the ship leave us behind."

"What about the propellers?" Laura warned. "They'll pull us under."

"The propellers are going to be there, whether we're in the lifeboat or not. The ship's not going flat out, so we should be okay. Which would you prefer?" asked Belle. "We're miles offshore. We might be able to swim it, if the tide's right, but I'd rather be in a boat. Keep cranking. It's nearly dawn, and we need to get away before the sun comes up." Belle warned. "We're not likely to get another chance."

The two women got the boat out over the side, and began lowering it past the handrail. The problem was at least one of them needed to stay on the ship to operate the winch, and then shinny down one of the lines into the boat, before they dropped the last few feet into the water. Belle was just about to climb out into the boat when a cry rang out from the direction of the bridge.

One of the Arabs had stepped out onto the walkway for a breath of fresh air, when the sound of the winch alerted him, and he cried out in alarm. "Fuck it!" Belle swore. She and Laura looked around. The boat was too high to release, and would now be too easily spotted and retrieved. They were running out of options. "Nothing else for it. You ever see Butch and Sundance?" she asked Laura, as she got back onto the deck. "Well, run like hell, and dive deep." She didn't wait for Laura to acknowledge, but turned and began sprinting towards the aft end of the freighter, where the handrail was lowest. Laura was a few yards behind her.

Belle ran as fast as she could in the thirty yards or so she had as a run-up, and she launched herself out over the handrail, trying to arc her dive as far back away from those propellers as she could, plummeting down and finally hitting the waves beneath. Laura had no time to think, but flung herself after her daughter, launching out into space, and then plunging deep beneath the waves. As she hit the water, instead of trying to surface, her legs kicked out, forcing herself deeper and deeper into the blackness. She could feel the faint pull of the propellers from the ship, which was lessening by the second as the ship pulled away from her.

Every instinct told her to surface, to breathe, but she fought against those instincts, knowing that if she surfaced too soon, those deadly blades would pull her back and chop her to pieces. Finally, when she could feel no pull from the propellers, she kicked out for the surface, gasping for air as her head cleared the water. Belle was there, some five yards away from her, doing the same. The freighter was pulling away from them, but a searchlight was now arcing back over the water, following their wake.

"Dive," Belle cried, and the two women ducked back down below the surface, trying to escape the searchlight's beam. They swam sideways, trying to get out of the wake, cursing as they realized the freighter was slowing and turning. They were coming back for them. On the horizon, the sky was lightening. In the dark, they might have had a chance, but with the rising of the sun, the sea seemed too small a place in which to hide.

It took only twenty minutes before the freighter was a mere 100 yards away, dead in the water, as the Arab sailors taunted the two women, swimming nowhere. "Keep swimming," Belle advised her mother. Coarse laughter ridiculed them from high above.

"You ladies would do better to return to the ship," warned the Captain, and he signalled one of his men to begin emptying buckets of offal from the galley, over the side. Even in the pale dawn light, both women could see the clouds of blood spreading out in the water. "You will find us more hospitable than the sharks!"

The sailors jostled them roughly as the two women finally climbed the cargo-nets back onto the deck. "Stupid bitches! Where did you think you were going to go?" the Captain asked, with a sneer. "We are ten miles from the nearest land. Take them below!" he ordered, and Laura and Belle were manhandled below decks, past their previous cabin, and into the hold of the ship. "Remove your clothes, or my men will do it for you," he ordered, and Belle and Laura had no choice but to strip off their stolen wet clothing in front of the leering crew.

Fresh manacles were brought, and put on both women, and ropes and a winch were used to haul their manacled wrists above their heads, so that the two women hung there, barely on tiptoe. The Captain swung a length of knotted ship's rope.

"You women were warned to behave. You chose to be disobedient, and now you must pay the price," and he swung the length of rope at Belle's bare back.

Laura and Belle had been left to nurse their bruises in their cabin. Both had suffered a brutal flogging with a ship's rope, as punishment for their escape attempt. They lay face down on their bunks, still naked, trying to will the pain away from their raw back. Dry mens' clothes had been left in the cabin for them, but they preferred to let their backs heal for now, without wanting to let the coarse fabrics chafe them unnecessarily. "What do we do now?" asked Belle. "Looks like we're stuck on this ship until it docks."

"Guess so. They want us alive though, or we'd be dead already. Wouldn't take all this trouble to just kill us. It'd be easy enough out here on the high seas." Laura pointed out. "They're taking an awful lot of trouble just to spirit two women out of Oman."

"Do you think they'll try drugging the food again?" Belle winced as she tried to lever herself up on one elbow.

"You'll know what to check for, when they feed us. But even if it is drugged, we have to eat. Best we do it one at a time, and the other one stay hungry, till we're sure either there's no drugs in the food, or if it is, then keep guard till it wears off. That way one of us will always be there to fight off anyone coming into the cabin. We don't owe them any favours, and we're both pretty useful at unarmed combat. We can inflict as much pain on them as we want, but they have to limit any response, to keep us alive. That gives us an edge," she pointed out.

"How long do you think we'll be at sea?" Belle asked.

"One of them mentioned Jakarta. Lots of islands in that sea, so not sure how long it would take to navigate. Pirates operate there, too. No sense worrying about it till we get there. Once we're on dry land again, then we can start trying to escape."

"Dad will be looking for us," Belle pointed out.

"Yeah, I bet he's none too pleased, right about now," Laura forced a short laugh. "He won't be far behind. He has friends, and I'm sure they'll be helping him. But we can't rely on him playing the White Knight. If we get another opportunity, then we take it. Agreed?" Laura asked.

"Agreed," Belle confirmed. "Let's try and get some rest. Maybe in the morning, our backs won't feel so sore."

Laura looked across to her daughter. "The bruises are starting to come out. Your back's a lovely shade of purple and yellow," she frowned. "Mine feels just as bad. Get some sleep, love. We'll hear the door if it opens."

In a few hours, their backs didn't feel quite so sore, and the two women dressed in the tee-shirts and coarse linen trousers that had been left for them. The food was indeed drugged again when they brought it, and Belle told Laura to eat it, and then enjoy some drugged sleep while she kept watch. After a while, the smell of the cold food was making Belle hungry too, and so she flushed what was left down the toilet to remove temptation. She settled back on her bunk to wait.

After just over an hour, the cabin door was unlocked, and one of the Arab crew stood framed in the doorway. Some of the other crewmen stood behind him, and his face dropped to see Belle still wide awake, sitting calmly on the edge of the bunk. Only one could come through that doorway at a time, and Belle knew that if she allowed that, then sheer force of numbers would overpower her.

"Let's get one thing clear, boys," she began. "If you'd just wanted us dead, we wouldn't be having this conversation. That means, you need us alive. It limits your options, whereas the first one of you to step inside this cabin is going to die," she said, simply. She wasn't joking, but they didn't believe her.

The first man simply laughed, looking down on her as she sat on the edge of the bunk. Sheer bravado made him step forward, and Belle half-turned, using her hands to push down on the bed and pivot, as her leg came up, foot catching the man beneath his chin and snapping his head back in a fierce and deadly savate kick, which broke his neck, instantly.

Belle was up and standing, before the man's body hit the floor, and a second man jumped over him to get to her. She struck out quickly, slamming her fist against the side of the man's head, and followed up with a knee into his stomach as he closed with her. She pushed him back, forcing him to trip over the dead man's body, and another couple of the crew caught him. She had done her best to refrain from using lethal force on the second man, though she would have, if forced to.

She stayed close to the door, ready for another assault, as the men considered their options. The dead body was pulled out of the doorway, and the door clanged shut and was locked once more. Belle breathed a sigh of relief. She had been brutal, but felt no sympathy for the man she had just killed. They needed to know she was serious. They couldn't get off the ship, but they could influence how they were treated whilst aboard.

*   *   *

An hour later, the Dragon-Lady was called to the radio-room, to answer a call from the Captain of the *Jade Star*. "Who are these women? One of my crew is dead. The black haired one killed him, and fought off some of my crew, all by herself. These are no tourists. What have you gotten us involved in?" asked Captain Alhazred. Feminine laughter was his answer across the short-wave radio.

"My dear Captain Alhazred. Those two women are not tourists, by any means. Perhaps this wasn't explained to you, but they should be treated with caution. They are agents of an organization that is a threat to our own. That is all you need to know. Your job is simply to deliver them to me, and I will deal with them. Is that clear?"

"Yes, it is clear, but what about my men? I am now shorthanded," he explained.

"I'm sure you'll be able to pick up extra crew in Jakarta, but I suggest you minimize the losses and treat those two women a little better. I daresay the assault was not unprovoked?" she guessed rightly.

"You said you wanted them alive. That was the only criteria."

"Captain, I can imagine the circumstances. Two beautiful women, on a ship of lusty sailors? But you'll find that not all women would be keen on that sort of thing. Think yourself lucky you only have one crewman to replace, Captain. I'm sure if you treat them a little better, they'll behave themselves. They have nowhere to go while they're at sea. Once they land, they're my problem, not yours. Have a good day, Captain." She handed the microphone back to the radio-operator, before the Captain could protest further.

*   *   *

That next morning, Gabriel awoke early, showered and dressed, and went down to Reception, handing in his key-card. He knew his way about Muscat, and so walked across the highway towards the Ruwi High Street and the souk, where he knew some of the hire-car establishments were based. He didn't need to use his excellent Arabic, for the desk-clerk launched into good English as soon as he walked in. These days everyone recognized American Express cards, unlike twenty odd years ago when the manager of one establishment looked at the card in wonder when Gabriel had offered it in payment, and then politely asked him 'How much is this worth?'

Eventually, he rented a small Toyota, and drove it back to the hotel, parking it in the lot. Walking back into reception, he was pleased to note that the reception clerk had changed shifts, and he walked straight up to the desk. "Room 247, please." The smiling clerk took the key-card out of its cubbyhole and handed it to Gabriel. "Thank you," he smiled in return. Gabriel sprinted up the single flight of stairs as soon as he was out of sight of the desk, before the clerk realized he had asked for the key of the room next door to his own.

The corridor was empty, and so Gabriel walked straight up to the door to Room 247, slid the key-card in the lock, and as the light flashed green, he turned the handle and quickly opened the door. Pocketing the key-card, Gabriel stepped inside quickly, closing the door behind him.

As he'd expected, the room was currently empty, and the two side walls had small holes in them, which could have been mistaken for recent holes for screws to hang pictures etc, but Gabriel knew better. Similar holes in the opposite wall, where Belle's room had been, also. He might glean information from whoever had been booked into this room, but tipping them off might negate any such advantage. He left the room, and closed the door behind him, making his way hurriedly back down to the Reception desk.

He went back up to the desk with a puzzled look of apology. "I'm sorry, but this seems to be the wrong key. Room 249?" He handed the key-card back to the desk, and the clerk turned around and saw the empty cubbyhole for 247.

"Very sorry, sir. I must have given you the wrong key. My apologies."
He handed Gabriel his correct key, and Gabriel took it. Some of the
porters were taking a special interest in Gabriel, he could tell, as they
muttered to themselves, and sniggered.

"No harm done. Thank you," he smiled, and turned back towards
the stairwell. With luck, no one would realize he had been in Room
247. Now to make plans to head south without anyone being too aware
of his destination. His phone could have been tapped, but he had seen
no evidence of that sort of equipment in Room 247, though somehow
they must have known of the women's interest in Al Raschid.

Later that morning, he came back down to the desk to check out,
asking directions for the oasis town of Nizwa. He asked for a porter
to take his cases out to his hire car, to make sure the staff there got a
look at it, and then drove off down the highway for a few miles, before
turning around and heading back into town.

He parked the hire car, and took out his luggage, leaving the keys
in the ignition, to tempt some thief into stealing the car. He walked
back towards the local taxi ranks, and asked one of them to drive him
to the PDO garage pool at the Mina al Fahal refinery terminal.

Access to the terminal office was quite open, with a lot of traffic
coming and going. Guards were only posted around the oil storage
areas themselves, and so as Gabriel got dropped off, no one paid much
attention to him.

Things hadn't changed much. There were no armed guards near
the office buildings complexes, only the actual entrance to the refinery
itself. Every few months, cars from the interior were driven back or
transported to the coast for servicing, and there was normally a two
week turnaround to get these vehicles serviced and back to the interior.
Land-rovers and Toyota Hiluxes were neatly parked in rows, and
Gabriel wandered about anonymously at the outer edges of the parking
area, trying to keep his suitcases out of sight.

Checking the tags on the wipers, to make sure the vehicle wasn't due
for transportation back to the interior for a few days, Gabriel chose a
Land-rover, as they were the most common, and were not likely to have
any electronic locking devices or immobilizers. The doors were open,
and it would take little effort to hot-wire the car. As it was, he didn't
have to, because the keys were stuffed on top of the sun visor. All the

vehicles were parked with a full tank of petrol, and the two jerry-cans in the back were both full of fuel. The recently serviced engine roared into life as he twisted the key in the ignition. He took off his jacket, folded it and put it inside the cab. Rolling his sleeves up, and donning a pair of mirrored sunglasses, he looked just like many of the ex-pats driving around.

His two cases went into the metal trunk, welded into the rear of the Land-rover. Gabriel buckled up, and drove calmly back out onto the main highway. PDO vehicles were a common sight on the roads of Oman, and with luck, this one wouldn't be missed for the rest of the week, which should give him more than enough time to sort things out in Salalah. When he got there, he would probably have to contact Maddox again, and see if he could run down the Indonesian connection, which by the tone of that e-mail, seemed to be controlling things here in Muscat if not Salalah as well.

The bright green and red conch shell symbol that the local Shell consortium used out here made the vehicle stand out and also camouflaged it at the same time, for it was such a common sight. Vehicle numbers painted on the side and registration plates were innocuous.

He stopped briefly at one of the roadside stores, to stock up on bottled water and some foodstuffs, and then took the highway west, towards Nizwa, but in fact he turned south at Izki, before he got there. The long lonely blacktop ran south for more than another five hundred miles, past Ghaba, Hayma, the Marmul oilfields, to Thamarit, and then Salalah itself. It would be less conspicuous to take the Marmul route, but like the SAS vehicles, he would try and attract as little attention to himself as possible. Once he got there, then things would change.

Avoiding the airlines might give him a slight advantage of surprise in them not knowing his destination, but once he made his presence known, things were likely to pick up speed. Laura and Belle were at least a day ahead of him. He could not think that they would have been transported anyway other than by road. Still, a lot could happen in a day.

All this over a feather? Gabriel couldn't believe it. Al Raschid must be into something much bigger than small-scale smuggling for them to risk kidnapping westerners. Window slid back, Gabriel rested his left arm out of the window, enjoying the feel of the air rushing past. Best watch his speed. He had a long way to go and he didn't want to push the vehicle too far too fast. Desert roads were long and straight, and could lull you into a false sense of security all too easily. Still, blacktops were better than the graded oilfield roads, with their dangerous dust-clouds behind every vehicle.

He would pull off the road, and find somewhere to sleep, once it got too dark. These desert roads were lonely places at night, and you never knew when you would run into a camel. Literally.

Chapter Seven

Gabriel arrived in Salalah mid-morning, the next day, turning left past the airport and heading into the main city. The roads had improved a lot since his last time here, but the souk was in the same place, and he parked by the side of the road. Locking the vehicle, he strolled nonchalantly into the maze of narrow streets that made up the souk, enjoying the sights and smells of stale carpets, fresh coffee beans and a multitude of spices, mingling shoulder to shoulder with Arabs, Indians, tourists etc.

One or two of those tourists didn't really look like tourists, and he turned his face away quickly, pretending interest in one shop's wares. If he could pick them up, there was a chance they might do the same, even though no one in the Regiment knew him by face or name these days, they could tell the type, and Gabriel wasn't here as a tourist either.

Members of the SAS had liberty in Salalah quite regularly, for there was none of the formality of Hereford here on overseas assignment. The blending in amongst the tourists was encouraged, and helped improve their surveillance techniques.

Overseas travel necessitated leaving behind some of his preferred toys, and Gabriel intended to find local replacements. The knives were his first priority, and the old Arab who served him watched with a trained eye as Gabriel handled his offerings. He nodded silently to himself as Gabriel made his purchases. Two six inch stilettos, ex-commando surplus from the Second World War, but well preserved. Not the best for throwing, but he had practiced with such before. He couldn't find his regular type of wrist-sheaths, but found something close enough, which would still work.

The lock-picks were more difficult to find. His Arabic was still fluent enough to talk to the old locksmith, and his manner told the man that he wasn't police. He had sold similar sets to some of the other

SAS, for he had recognized Gabriel's type immediately. Morals and scruples came second to riyals, and so Gabriel made his purchases.

Al Raschid's offices were on Al Najah Street, which ran north to south in the northern business area of the city. It was within walking distance from the souk, and Gabriel adjusted his sunglasses as he took a leisurely stroll first north, and then returned south, walking on opposite sides of the street, and feigning interest in a few shop windows along the way, acting just as any other bored tourist would do.

Their office building was a simple two-floor establishment, with a ground-floor reception, and what seemed like a small warehouse at the rear. A further office appeared at the front of the upper floor. Rounding the corner, Gabriel took a parallel route, then coming back and checking out the rear of the property. It looked like the doors were alarmed, but there were skylights in the roof, which looked accessible for a man of his talents.

It would wait till after dark, and he casually asked a passerby if there was an internet café nearby. He was directed west, towards the industrial parks, and Gabriel continued his walk. The Land-rover would be safe enough where he had left it parked, and he had time to kill till evening. Time enough for him to re-familiarise himself with the city.

A few riyals gave him log-on rights, and he accessed his own e-mail server to check his e-mail. Nothing from Laura or Belle, but then that was hoping for too much. He e-mailed Maddox with his progress so far, and then e-mailed Manuel back at his estate in Buenos Aires. This was the safest form of contact at the moment, albeit far from instantaneous.

This done, he continued his familiarization walk around the city, stopping off at the Hilton Hotel on Sultan Qaboos Street, and enjoying a cold beer. He found a nice quiet corner booth, where he read through some of the complimentary newspapers, two in Arabic, and one in English, whilst he enjoyed the cool refreshing drink and the air conditioning, before wandering through to the restaurant and ordering a light meal. The bar and restaurant were always open to the general public as well as the guests at the hotel, so he remained quite anonymous.

Night in Salalah was like night in most middle-eastern cities, full of strange smells as the heat of the day roasted the refuse and the people who called the city home. Car-horns sounded interminably, as the standard of driving had not improved here over the years. Some of the younger Arabs tore up and down the main roads, showing off in their sports cars. No wonder you never saw Arabs racing in Formula One. Most of them killed themselves on the streets of the Middle East, long before they ever got near a real race-track.

It was still hot and humid, and the night was far too bright for Gabriel's liking as he scaled the fire-escape of the adjacent building to Al Raschid's office block. His white shirt stood out too plainly, and so he was wearing his light tan jacket, but he was still too visible, and he was keen to keep out of sight of the streets below him.

Once he was high enough, with his lighter than normal body-weight, it was a simple enough to leap across the distance to the lower flat roof of the adjacent building, Gabriel rolling with the fall, to deaden the sound of his landing. Quickly, he looked around, and then stayed kneeling for a minute, just listening. Satisfied, he went quickly over to the skylights, looking down into each one. Finally, making his choice, he knelt and drew the set of lock-picks out of his coat-pocket.

The lock was rusty, and perhaps so was Gabriel, but in less than a minute, he had the skylight open, and he lowered himself down onto the desk beneath, taking care not to knock anything onto the floor. The skylight closed behind him, still unlocked, but he wouldn't expect anyone to check. He climbed down from the desk, and took stock of his surroundings. The office had appeared closed from the street, and as he wandered about the upper floor in silence, he was pleased to see that that had actually been the case. He was alone in the building. Quickly, he wiped off any telltale marks from the desk surface.

Two upper offices, one downstairs reception and toilet (westernized), and a door leading back into the small warehouse. Offices first, and Gabriel started with the in and out trays on the desks, reading the contents by the moonlight coming in through the skylights. Filing cabinets came next, which were quite full, and Gabriel didn't have time to go through every single file. He needed to narrow down his field of search. The computer on the desk was in standby mode, and as Gabriel pressed the mouse button, the monitor flickered back into life. Most businesses never switched their machines off at night, not knowing when important communications would come in. He quickly checked the contents of the last few faxes, and then turned his attention back to the computer.

Gabriel quickly accessed the e-mail, and ran his eye up and down the inbox, and then the sent items folder, till an e-mail address caught his eye. The same e-mail address as on the stationery in his hotel room. The contents of the e-mail were vague if Gabriel hadn't already known what was going on. 'Consignment in transit aboard *Jade Star*. Arrive Jakarta in eight days.' Gabriel was too late. He had literally missed the boat.

Gabriel took out his car-keys, and unclipped the small thin USB-stick he always carried with him as a portable data storage device. Most customs ignored it as a key-fob, but it could hold 8Gb of data, and he plugged this into one of the usb ports in the back of the computer. He then copied all of the e-mails from both the inbox and sent items folders onto the usb stick. He could go through them at his leisure once he got access to another computer.

Going back to the filing cabinets, Gabriel quickly found the one detailing the schedule of the *Jade Star*, a cargo freighter, due to dock in Jakarta next week. He had to get there to meet it, but getting out of Arab countries was a difficult as getting in, in the first place. If he did it legally, his name would show up on a manifest, as would his destination. His options were to return to Muscat and leave via Seeb, and then catch a second plane into Jakarta under another alias. Fake passports were just as easy to arrange here if you had the contacts, but Gabriel had no contacts here. He would have to leave on the passport he had arrived in, or waste more time.

He would need help in Jakarta, too, but who could he trust in Jakarta? He sat down and began using the office computer to access the internet and log onto his secure mail server. It was evening in Brussels, and he knew he couldn't expect a reply to his earlier e-mail so soon. He began to write an e-mail to Jim Maddox. 'Jim, freighter *Jade Star* carrying Laura and Belle from Salalah to Jakarta. Not sure if I can get there before the ship docks. Do you have any assets in place? I need to have that ship boarded as soon as it docks. I'll contact you day after tomorrow, when I get out of Oman. I am forwarding e-mail. Please check out identity of sender.'

He pressed the send button, and then forwarded the e-mail from Jakarta. Gabriel then composed another e-mail, this time to Donatello

Grimaldi in Latina. 'Donatello, arriving soon Rome. Will need new documents and onward plane tickets to Jakarta, as soon as you can arrange. Will discuss further with you when we meet. G.'

Donatello was almost 'Family' to Gabriel, as well as being part of one of the oldest families in the world, the Cosa Nostra. His uncle, Luigi Grimaldi, had been a wartime friend to Gabriel, and he had met Donatello at the old man's funeral. Gabriel was an adopted son of Donatello's bigger Family. As he was legitimizing his criminal empire, in emulation of other Mafia Dons that had migrated to the US, Gabriel found the relationship mutually beneficial, more so since he had become persona non grata with a few police forces around the world, himself. Friends in low places could often do you more good than those in high places.

Gabriel then finally booked airline tickets online out of Seeb to Rome for tomorrow evening, and then logged out of his account, before accessing internet options and erasing all entries of sites visited. With luck, they would never check. If they did, they would only know that someone had used their machine, and not the reason behind it. By then he would be long gone.

Gabriel then opened the unlocked door leading into the small warehouse at the rear of the office block, and decided to have a look around the place. The overall smell of wood from the numerous packing crates filled his nostrils. He didn't switch on the lights, afraid that they might be seen from outside, and so Gabriel never noticed the cctv cameras positioned high up on the walls, near the roof-trusses. Motion detectors automatically switched the cameras on, and an alarm sounded next to Ali Bin Wakhtar's bedside table, in his home, some three miles away.

* * *

Ali hurriedly rubbed the sleep out of his eyes as the alarm forced him to wakefulness, realizing there was an intruder in the office warehouse. His wife stirred beside him as he switched on the bedside lamp, and swivelled to sit on the edge of his bed. Luckily, she was a sound sleeper, and he managed to get out of the bed without waking her. Still in his underpants and string vest, Ali picked up the phone, and made an urgent call to some of his staff who lived closer to the office block, alerting them to the break-in, and then began looking around for his trousers.

*　　*　　*

Gabriel examined a few of the open packing cases, seeing nothing more suspicious than antique carvings and statuettes, which was the public face of this trading company. Then his keen nostrils caught the scent of machine-oil from one of the cases, and it was inordinately heavy when Gabriel tried to lift it. He looked around, and found a crow-bar, which he used to lever the top off the crate. Underneath the straw packing, he quickly found his suspicions were correct. AK-47s, the terrorists' right-arm. Such automatic weapons were simple and easy to copy, and were manufactured all over the world these days. Stamps on the crate indicated this one had come from the Far East.

He stiffened suddenly, stuffing the weapon back inside the crate, as he heard footsteps outside. He just had time to pull the lid of the crate roughly back into position, when the rear door creaked open, and Gabriel ducked behind some of the crates. Three voices, speaking in hushed tones in Arabic. "Spread out and find him. I'll stay here and guard the door." Gabriel was already moving, keeping low, as the two men started into the warehouse, and one of them passed within mere feet of him, as he kept to the shadows. They hadn't switched the lights on, so they didn't want to attract too much attention to themselves, either. That served his purposes fine. He had to get out of here quickly, while he had surprise on his side. The more time he took, the easier it would be for the men to find him.

Gabriel rose up out of the darkness like a ghost, one of the commando knives in his hand, and the Arab in the doorway barely had time to gasp before that blade was buried in his chest. He had no time to fire his gun, but it dropped from his lifeless fingers as Gabriel's blade pierced his heart, and the sound was heard by one of the other two men, who called out. No time now for anything other than escape, and Gabriel let the body fall behind him.

His silhouette in the doorway brought a couple of silenced gunshots in his direction, as Gabriel ducked to one side, and began to run. Whether just dumb luck, or he had tripped some sort of silent alarm, he needed to get out of here, and he ran as fast as he could towards the main street, and then forced himself to slow to a brisk walk. He didn't want to attract too much attention to himself. He heard pursuit behind him, as he looked to turn the corner quickly. If he could get back to his car, he could head north.

Another cry rang out, and Gabriel realized he had been spotted, and he threw caution to the winds, sprinting flat out past a few surprised pedestrians who were still out and about. He doubted his pursuers would risk shots in public, and kept to the main streets. He had to outdistance them, and then try for his car.

Behind him, one of the two men was talking into a cell-phone, hurriedly reporting Gabriel's route of escape to Ali, who was even now heading into the city, with more reinforcements. Gabriel ran along Al Jadidah Street, turning south down Al Majd Street, which wasn't as well lit. His pursuers were closer than he thought, and there were less people about. He heard the phutt, phutt of silenced shots behind him, and he staggered, stifling a scream, as a bullet tore through his jacket, creasing his ribcage.

He kept on running, cutting down another narrow street, taking one turn after another and trying to find more pedestrians or better lit areas, but it was late, and there were not many people about. His side hurt, and his shirt and jacket were now red with blood, and he would attract stares the more he remained on the lit streets. He saw two cars approaching at speed from the opposite end of the street down which he was running, headlights blazing, seeking him out, and Gabriel hurriedly cut across the road, running down the first back alley he found. He didn't know how many he had on his tail now, but he had to lose them.

Another silenced shot scored along the wall of the building, as Gabriel ran, thankful for the inaccuracy of silenced hand-guns. He pressed his jacket against his wound as he ran, trying to staunch the blood-flow. It was only a flesh wound, but the pain was slowing him down somewhat.

Gabriel found the Land-rover where he had left it. The PDO logo had saved it from being stolen or vandalized. Once inside the cab, he jammed the keys in the ignition, and the engine fired up. A single shot took out the rear glass, narrowly missing his head, as he gunned the accelerator, and tore off onto the road, leaving a cloud of dust behind him, immediately executing a sharp turn down the first junction to get out of the line of any further shots.

Behind him, the man with the cell-phone was passing on information and directions to aid the men in the two pursuing vehicles, and it wasn't long before Gabriel noticed headlights in his rear-mirror, as he drove north to get out of the city. His fuel reserves were low, and he only had the jerry-cans in the rear of the truck. He couldn't refuel without stopping the vehicle, and if they were hit by gunfire, this could all end rather messily. Such an explosion would draw a lot of attention, though, and he gambled that his pursuers didn't want that.

Land-rovers weren't built for speed, and it wasn't long before those headlights in his mirror got larger and larger. He couldn't outrun them. Once out of the city limits, the road only lead one way, straight and flat. As the first car began to pull up alongside him, Gabriel saw the arm coming out of the window, aiming a gun, and he hauled the wheel over, ramming the Land-rover against the side of the other car. The gunshot missed as the driver tried to take evasive action, and stay on the road. More gunshots rang out, and Gabriel kept his head low as some of the bullets ricocheted off the bodywork of the Land-rover.

The car tried to get alongside him again, veering off as Gabriel tried to ram them a second time, and then the car dropped back, headlights full on in his rear-view mirror, dazzling him till he adjusted it. They kept pace with him, and Gabriel knew they were waiting for him to run out of fuel. It was only a matter of time.

Only one thing for it. Gabriel snapped off the headlights, reached down and punched the button to engage four-wheel drive, and he tore off the blacktop at speed, hoping and praying that there were no rocks or gulleys waiting for him.

The two cars behind were thrown into a momentary panic as the lights of the Land-rover suddenly disappeared, and then they went into the dust-cloud caused by Gabriel's tires as they tore up the soft sand, and realized what he had done. Their cars were not built for off-road use, and so they were forced to pull over, and empty their guns into the darkness towards the sound of Gabriel's engine, in frustration. The search would have to resume at first light, in better equipped transport.

Gabriel drove slowly, by the light of the moon, lights still off, for now. Land-rovers could handle most terrain comfortably, but a high-speed collision with any sort of obstacle, or pothole or wadi, would still do a lot of damage, and so he drove with a lot of care, the darkness straining his eyes. Off-road driving was still dangerous during daylight hours, if you didn't know the terrain that well.

His pursuers would be back there on the blacktop, probably in contact with the rest of the Al Raschid organization back in the city. He had a long way to go, and a Land-rover was not the fastest of vehicles. Worse, his pursuers knew his destination. They would be waiting for him. Returning to the blacktop would be to invite trouble and probable interception by faster cars. Driving off-road would severely delay him. Mentally, he reviewed what he knew about Oman during his time here.

Between Muscat and Salalah, there was barely any civilization, and what there was remained near the coast. Inland, it was left to the oilfields. Marmul was the nearest, and before that, was the SAS Regimental base, which Gabriel had to avoid. There was an airstrip there, as there was at some of the oilfield remote locations. PDO charter flights ran to Salalah and Muscat, but getting on them required company ID and pre-booking. He could fly a plane, and stealing one wouldn't be too hard, but the Sultan's airforce, RAF-trained, would be onto him before he could touch down or clear Omani air-space.

Getting out of Oman was going to be a lot more difficult than getting in had been.

Driving was slow and frustrating. The moon kept hiding behind clouds, and Gabriel was trying to run parallel to the main highway, at a safe enough distance not to be seen. He didn't know if the occasional headlights belonged to friend or foe, or just how serious they were about pursuing him. Twice now he had cursed, and braked sharply as his path encountered dried out wadis and defiles. Yet if he switched on his headlights, he could be seen from the highway. The only other alternative was to drive far enough away from the blacktop that he wouldn't be seen, but that worked against his navigation, using it as a guide-line.

Pain from the flesh-wound across his ribs helped keep him awake, but was distracting his attention. The wound was still bleeding, as he was bounced around by the Land-rover's unfriendly suspension.

All of a sudden, there seemed to be a solid wall directly across his path, and as Gabriel hauled the wheel to one side, he realized he was too late to react, and his nearside wheel hit the wall of compacted sand which covered one of the main pipelines, and the front end of his vehicle was hurled up into the air in a cloud of sand.

The Land-rover rolled over, once, twice, bouncing off a couple of rocks as it tipped over and into the narrow defile, and slid down into darkness. Gabriel followed it, smashing his head against the metal interior, and he lost consciousness.

*   *   *

Later that evening, the Dragon-Lady's mood was not improved with the e-mail she received from Salalah, with the jpeg attachments taken from the cctv footage in the warehouse. Gabriel!

The shots were grainy, but it was him, unmistakeably. Not to be underestimated. He had somehow followed the women's trail to Salalah, and had been searching their offices and warehouse before his presence had been discovered. *Just how much did he know?* she mused? Her reply e-mail was short and swift. 'Find him. His head or yours!'

Chapter Eight

The heat of the day reached the bottom of the defile close to noon, and Gabriel finally regained consciousness. His head hurt like hell, and there was dried blood across his face, though an examination found that this had come from the chest wound, as he had hung upside down in the crashed vehicle, strapped in place by his seat-belt. He felt the wound gingerly, and was relieved to find it beginning to heal now the flow of blood had caked. He found it hard to focus, and his eyesight was slightly blurred, no doubt as a result of the head-injury.

Gabriel unbuckled the seat-belt, sliding down, and readjusted his position to climb higher and wriggle out of the other door, which opened after a few hefty pushes. The vehicle was a wreck, he quickly discovered, and that left him with a few problems. He was now on foot, in one of the most remote places on earth, with no food, and little water. If anyone found the crashed vehicle, it could quickly be traced back to Mina al Fahal. His luggage was in it, and that could be traced back to him. Periodic checks of the pipelines were carried out as a matter of course, and he had no idea when the next one would be. First things first, he had to bury the luggage, for he couldn't carry it with him, and couldn't chance it being discovered.

Managing to open the steel chest welded into the rear of the Land-rover, Gabriel took out his luggage and the shovel that was a standard part of the breakdown gear, in case the vehicle got stuck in soft sand. He wandered along the defile a good distance, till he found a suitable spot, and began to dig. Once he had dug a deep enough hole, he went back to the Land-rover and brought back the items of luggage. Passport, money, plane tickets etc, he kept in his jacket. Everything else would have to go, and so he began covering it up again, tamping down the soft earth with the shovel. Then he walked back to the crashed Land-rover, put the shovel back into the chest and closed it again.

There was only one and a half bottles of water left, and he would have to use them sparingly. He put one in each jacket pocket, as he tried to mentally visualize his location. Marmul was to the north. Salalah to the south. Somewhere in between was the SAS Regimental base (unless they'd moved it, since his time here). He needed to avoid all three. Following the pipeline wasn't really an option, because a PDO vehicle could come along the right of way at any time, and he would be unable to explain his presence there.

Somewhere to the East was the highway, and that was his lifeline, but he would have to approach it carefully. His head throbbed, and he realized he must be concussed. The heat of the day was like a hammer, and he could feel it burning his shoulders through his light jacket, and his short black hair offered his throbbing skull little protection from the heat.

He needed to find somewhere to shelter from the sun, and conserve his water. Night was the best time to travel in the desert, and would certainly be best for crossing the highway. He would see oncoming headlights long before they would see him. He took out his crumpled handkerchief and used it to wipe down the steering wheel and any surfaces he might have touched, for fingerprints. After a while the desert itself would cover his tracks, but best to be sure. He started off following the defile to the north, a hot wind on his back. He had a long walk ahead of him.

Once the sun went down, Gabriel cautiously crept out of the defile. The brilliant red, orange and brown sunsets were quite spectacular out here in the desert, and night came on quickly. Taking advantage of natural cover from the terrain, Gabriel headed East, back towards the highway.

He found a spot behind a low ridge, where he could observe the traffic on the highway. Such traffic was sparse, as not many people drove at night along such deserted roads. Automatically, Gabriel lowered his head, whenever traffic approached.

Southbound was no good, and would only take him back into Salalah. He needed to go North, back to Muscat. After a few hours, he spotted a truck heading north, and crept forward till he could verify the PDO company logo on the side, and Gabriel stepped up to the edge of the road to flag it down. Company vehicles would definitely be safer to flag down than private.

The truck slowed and braked as its headlights caught out the white of Gabriel's suit. The driver opened the door cautiously, clutching a tyre-iron, as he noticed the bloodstains on Gabriel's jacket. Gabriel could see the driver was either Indian or Pakistani, and so used English to speak to him. "Thank God you stopped. I had an accident," he explained. "My car went off the road, and I need to get back to Muscat. Could you give me a lift?" He stood there, in the headlights, making no overt moves to alarm the jittery driver, who was appraising him.

"It is against the company rules to give lifts, Sir, but as it is an accident, I will radio in for permission," he began to explain. Gabriel didn't need that.

"I have money with me. I can make it worth your while to take me. If they say "no", you'll have to leave me here, and neither of us would benefit. The company doesn't have to know, do they?" Gabriel pulled out his wallet, and took a handful of riyals out, displaying them in the headlight's beam. He knew roughly how much these people got paid. Even that handful was more than a month's pay to the man. It didn't take him long to agree to Gabriel's plan, and he indicated for Gabriel to climb up into the cab.

Gabriel saw the cool-flask, and without asking for permission, began refilling his now empty bottles with the cold water, and then he drank some, his throat parched. The driver made no complaint, busy counting the notes Gabriel had thrust into his hand. Buckling himself in, Gabriel sat back as the truck pulled away once more, and headed North along the highway.

"I'm Alex West, by the way," Gabriel introduced himself, falsely. The driver snorted in amusement, and took his offered hand, shaking it.

"My friends call me Prince, Sir," he explained. "It is shorter than my real name," he admitted, with a smile. "I could do with the company on these long night rides. Someone to talk to and help me keep my mind on my driving. Just staring into blackness all night, it is very hard to remain awake."

"Do you make this run regularly?"

"Twice a week, running parts and materials back and forth, from Fahud to Muscat, Marmul to Salalah, and all points in between. It is a good job, but a lonely life. How about you, sir? How did you crash your car?" he asked.

"Silly, really," Gabriel fabricated a story on the spur of the moment. "I had the window open, and one of those shamal winds just sprung up, and blew a load of sand in through the window, straight into my eyes, and I was blinded. Just couldn't see, and I lost control of the car. It went off the road, and I smashed the radiator open on a big rock. Bashed my head, and gashed my side. Fortunately, the bleeding dried up."

"You were lucky, then," the driver commented. Gabriel nodded. The drive continued with small-talk, as Prince revealed something of his life here in Oman. Gabriel was prepared to let him ramble on. He'd rather listen than talk himself, and he just lay back in the seat, resting as they drove, only adding to the conversation intermittently.

They had covered nearly fifty miles, when Gabriel noticed lights ahead. Stationary lights. He came alert instantly. "What are those lights ahead? Road-crews? They don't usually work at night." he pointed out.

"There was no problem with the road on the way down, Sir," Prince agreed. All sorts of things were going through Gabriel's head. There was a chance the Sultan's Army might have set up some sort of road-block for whatever reason, he didn't know. Could he take the chance it was legitimate? The road was the only route North and South.

"Listen, Prince, as you said, it's not allowed to give lifts in company vehicles. I don't want to get you in any trouble. What say you let me out here, and I meet you a couple of miles further north, past those lights? I'll give you more money for your trouble," he offered, and pulled out his wallet again. Prince slowed the truck down, stopping, and eyeing the wallet. He also eyed Gabriel, and the lights ahead. Something wasn't quite right here, but it was none of his business.

"Alright. I will stop and wait for an hour, a mile beyond those lights, whatever they are. I can make up the time once we get moving again," he agreed, and he took more riyals off Gabriel, and let him alight from the cab. Gabriel set off, distancing himself from the edge of the road, and then running parallel with it. Behind him, he heard the engine start up once more, and the truck pulled away, heading towards the waiting lights.

It got to the lights as Gabriel was still half a mile away, close enough to see, but not be seen, and the truck was waved to a halt. Two cars blocked the road, and uniformed men with rifles beckoned Prince out of the cab. The uniforms looked official, but the vehicles didn't. They were just ordinary Mercedes, and not the military vehicles used by the Sultan's Army. Prince was held at gunpoint while the rear and then the cab of the truck were searched.

One of the men found the wad of riyals, and Prince was bludgeoned to the floor with the butt of a rifle. One of the men dragged him to his feet again, questioning him roughly, and Prince was hit again. He began babbling, terrified, and Gabriel couldn't blame him for what he revealed. One of them gave orders, and a couple of them began fanning out into the darkness on either side of the road.

Prince was shoved back in the cab once more, and one of the men got into it with him, and the truck pulled away. Two men were left with the vehicles, two men were roaming the dark desert on Gabriel's side of the road, and another three were on the far side of the road. He remained hiding, out of sight, as he noticed the truck's tail-lights come on, about a mile down the road. They had forced Prince to stop, as agreed, and were baiting a trap for him.

Gabriel set off on foot, heading East away from the blacktop, walking slowly, and silently, trying to put as much distance between himself and his pursuers as he could while it was still dark. There was nothing he could do for Prince, but they had no need to harm him. He was fortunate they had no night-sights, for cover out here was minimal, and he would be easily visible come the dawn. The blacktop was now denied him, and Muscat was a long way to walk. His replenished water bottles might last him two days if he was careful, but he would need more water than that to complete such a journey. He needed to be well away from the road by the dawn, and find some cover from the sun to get through the worst of the day.

He thanked his stars he had gotten news of the *Jade Star* to Maddox. He was going to be a bit late getting to Jakarta, but by the time he arrived, Laura and Belle would be safe and sound.

Smoke from campfires alerted Gabriel to the presence of life out here in the remote wastes of the southern desert, and as Gabriel crested a small jebel, he picked out the small fires in the distance. The light breeze also brought the smell of camels, and picked out their distinctive shapes and silhouettes against the tents of the camped caravan. Many of the indigenous tribes in the interior were too poor to afford modern transport, and such caravans were still fairly common. Although the Sultan shared his wealth out amongst his people, certain tribes were favoured above others, and some tribes not favoured at all. His father had been quite ruthless in dealing with some of them during his reign. Qaboos was not as harsh a man as his father, and for this, his people, even the poorest, were grateful.

If Gabriel could seek refuge amongst this Bedouin tribe, he could easily pass himself off as one of their own, and the journey North would be safer, if perhaps a bit longer. The camels grew restless at his approach, and one young boy standing watch hailed him as he came near. "Salaam Aleikhum."

"Aleikhum Salaam, rafiq," Gabriel replied in Arabic, allaying the boy's fears. In the moonlight, Gabriel could see the scarred hide of one of the camels, revealing patches where a camel-spider had at one time fed on the beast's flesh. The bite of such spiders instantly paralysed the flesh, and the beast was unaware as the spider chewed its way in through its flesh. Gabriel shivered. He hated those fucking things. Some of them grew to quite a size, and the arachnids were ferocious. They never ran away, they always came at you, he knew from experience.

Controlling his loathing, Gabriel made his way through the camel herd, and allowed the young boy to lead him into the encampment.

*   *   *

"Hi, Dad," Julie was in cheerful mood as she answered the phone.

"How's my girl?" Maddox asked, delighted with the sound of a voice, only a year ago, he thought he'd never hear again. She had made a complete recovery from the coma, and was out of hospital within a few months of regaining consciousness.

Since then, the blossoming relationship with Nick Turnbull had resumed its course, and she had recently moved in with him, at his flat in Hereford.

"I'm doing fine, Dad. Nick's been lovely, and a friend of his is getting me a job at the casino. They need a bookkeeper, and my accounting skills are good."

"Glad to see University wasn't a total loss, then," Maddox joked, and Julie laughed. "I'm coming over tonight. Could you ask Nick to pick me up at the airport?"

"He's here now. I'll put him on," and she handed the phone over to her smiling lover.

"Hey Guv, how's tricks?"

"I'm glad you're home, Nick. Ever see that film *Day Of The Dead*?" he asked, and waited a few seconds till Nick mulled the phrase round in his head.

"Something we need to discuss?"

"Yes, but not on an open line. Can you pick me up at the airport, later? Might have something for you, if you have no present plans. Give you an opportunity to pick up a few bob."

"A private job? You know the Regiment doesn't like that sort of thing, Guv."

"I can think up some legitimate excuses to second you for this one, Nick. I don't think they'd have any objections. Details tonight, when you pick me up, okay?"

"Okay, Guv. I'll meet you coming out of Arrivals."

*   *   *

Maddox only had one small case with him, and he carried it himself, as he met up with Turnbull at the airport. Apart from the cordial greetings, they exchanged few words till they got inside Nick's car, and he started up the engine. "Good film that, Day Of The Dead. Plot was about dead people coming back to life, wasn't it? Are we on the same wavelength, here, Guv?" Nick asked, putting his receipt into the automatic machine, and driving out of the car-park as the barrier rose up.

"Yes, good to see you're still as sharp as ever," Maddox chuckled.

"Problems?"

"Yes, our friend has stirred up a hornet's nest in the Middle East. It's somehow linked to events going down in Indonesia, though he doesn't know that. He's not in the loop as regards current intelligence coming across my desk. As you know we've had an upsurge in Al Qaeda activity there in the last few years. The local branch, Jemaah Islamiyah is stirring things up big-time. Laura and Belle seem to have been kidnapped by a White Slaving gang, and shipped to Jakarta. I have a few addresses to track down. Gabriel has his hands full in Oman, just at this moment, so I thought you might enjoy a trip to the Far East, to give him a hand. If the trip pans out, we may uncover the conduit by which the Al Qaeda people are getting into Indonesia. Are you up for it?" Maddox asked.

"Ordinarily, I'd say yeah, no problem. But Julie will kill me. She's been planning this trip to Marbella for weeks."

"Let me talk to Julie. As I explained, we need to keep this low-key to avoid our "zombie" coming into the limelight, so to speak. I don't envisage you getting too deeply into this. Merely provide backup, and assistance where required, while we let Gabriel run this down, and maybe do our work for us. See if you can find the women before he gets there. They're being transported on a freighter called The *Jade Star*. I'll arrange to have Indonesian Authorities meet it when it docks. I've had contact from one of their security people out there, an Angelo Zoro, who you can liaise with, officially or otherwise, I'm sure you'll come to an understanding," Maddox grinned. "He's been working on the Indonesian end of the Al Qaeda problem. So far, no luck in breaking their network. He's almost a counterpart of you, out there. Someone's blue-eyed boy. Special Forces, KOPASSUS, on temporary assignment to work undercover with the Jakarta police, trying to track down the local end of the terrorist pipeline into the country, Jemaah Islamiyah (JI)."

"Absolutely out of the fucking question!" Maddox fumed.

"Could you please moderate your language, Daddy. This isn't a barracks, and if you swear at me again, I'm going to start swearing back. We already had the holiday to Marbella booked, and we'll have to cancel. If Nick goes, then I go, too. That's final!" Julie was as stubborn as her father.

"Listen, babe," Turnbull began, trying to act as mediator, "this whole thing will only last a week or so. I'll just be there as backup and to offer a little behind the scenes assistance and intelligence support. No danger. I promise."

"If that's the case, then there's no reason I couldn't go along," Julie pointed out. "If you step on that plane without me, Nick Turnbull, don't bother coming back." Nick wrung his hands. He felt like tearing his hair out. Like Father like Daughter.

Why did he have to fall for someone just as pigheaded as her old man? He looked at Maddox. Maddox looked back. The two of them were desperately trying to think of an argument that would work.

"What about your new job?" Maddox hastily interjected.

"Won't start till the end of the month. You'll have to do better than that, Daddy. A couple would be less conspicuous than a single man on his own, surely? You said there's no danger."

"She has a point, there, Guv," Turnbull agreed. Maddox glowered at him.

"Oh shut up, Nick." Maddox didn't like his own daughter turning the tables on him like this.

"It'll be just like a Honeymoon," Julie beamed, already planning the trip in her head.

"You're not bloody married!" Maddox retorted.

"If he leaves without me, we never will be. I warn you, Nick Turnbull." Julie was leaving them little choice.

"Oh Christ!" Nick looked again at Maddox. "Guv? Look, having Julie there gives me an excuse to break away from this Zoro, and do my own thing, away from eyes n ears."

"Alright," Maddox was being out-manoeuvred by his own daughter, and he didn't like it one bit, "but when Nick has work to do, you stay in the bloody hotel, or go shopping. Don't get in the way, okay?" His daughter was already nodding, that wonderful smile beaming across her face. *This is going to cost me a fortune*, he was already thinking to himself . . . "I'll talk to you tomorrow, Nick. In private, and we'll go over the details together, okay?"

Nick nodded. "Sure, Guv."

"Right, I'm starving," admitted Maddox. "Couldn't stand that crap they call food on the airline, and buggered if I'm gonna pay for it. Pass the phone and let's order a Chinese."

Chapter Nine

The *Jade Star* rendezvoused at sea with a small fishing vessel, and the two western women were escorted out on deck. They were forced to climb down some cargo nets, and make the jump onto the deck of the smaller vessel in choppy seas. They were only too glad to get off the larger ship and its unpleasant crew. Shortly, once they made landfall, they would see what this was all about, and then be in a better position to make their escape.

As Laura jumped down onto the heaving deck, one of the deckhands swatted her with a sand-filled cosh behind her ear, and she collapsed instantly. Belle jumped down, half-turning as she thought she saw Laura fall, and reached down towards her, when another deckhand swung a similar cosh at her, missing as she darted to one side, and tried to grapple with him, but sheer numbers overwhelmed her, and she too was rendered unconscious. "Collar them both," the Captain said to his crew, as the two women were dragged off the deck.

Knitted-metal collars were snapped into place around each woman's neck. The one inch square by half inch thick semtex charges were securely fastened to the knitted metal collars, and covered by their hair. This done, the two unconscious women were placed in a crate, and a top loosely nailed in place, till they docked.

*   *   *

Some time later, Belle started to come around. Her head was splitting, and she groaned as she slowly regained consciousness. Her eyes had a problem focusing, as a face swam in front of her. She thought she was dreaming momentarily, fantasizing, as the face came into focus. The hair was now jet-black and cut thai-style, square, a few inches below her shoulders, but the face she remembered all too well.

83

"Hello Precious. How's the hand?" An evil face smiled malevolently down at her, then the woman sprang back quickly as Belle rolled over, and pushed herself upright, realizing she was not tethered in any way. Angelica glared at her, daring her to make a move, and Belle snarled as she came up off the floor, hands reaching out towards her. "Ah, ah, ahhh . . ." Angelica gleamed, holding her own hand out in front of her, so Belle could see the device she was holding. "Take a good look, Precious, before you do something you'll regret. Take a good feel at that collar around your neck. I suggest you do it gently," she advised. Belle realized it was there for the first time, and reluctantly did as she was told, feeling the braided metal, close-fitting around her neck. The tiny lock, the bulky square object at the back of her neck. Angelica was holding a device no bigger than a mobile phone, with the same sort of tiny aerial, but Belle knew it wasn't a phone.

"What have you done to me?" she demanded. Angelica smirked, relaxing slightly now that Belle was getting the idea.

"A couple of ounces of semtex at the back of your neck. Try and force the lock, or the semtex, and BOOM. Conversely, I depress my finger on this little remote, and the same thing happens. I needed a way to control you and Laura, and a friend of mine suggested this one. Works very well, don't you think? Right now, the frequency of this transmitter is adjusted for the collar around Laura's neck. You misbehave, I press a button and blow Laura's head off. The opposite is true for her. Her obedience keeps you alive, and vice versa." She smiled as she let Belle absorb her predicament. "Now I want you to tell me how you tracked me down. I've taken great lengths to stay out of Solomon's way since Borgia died."

"I didn't track you down. I didn't know you were here," Belle replied truthfully, as she thought about the predicament she now found herself in, at the mercy of this sicko vampire bitch. "Laura found a feather. It turned out to be an angel-feather, and my Father wanted us to track it down. He thinks there's another angel out there somewhere." Angelica looked dumbfounded for a few moments, and then burst out into hysterical laughter.

"That's what this is all about? A feather?" she scoffed. "I haven't the faintest idea what you're talking about, girl. Is that the best you can do?" She raised the transmitter once more, in threat.

"We bought it in Cairo, and the old shopkeeper told us the Al Raschid organisation was responsible for the strange curios in his shop. They smuggled them in from all over the Far East, legally and illegally. We were just asking a few questions till Gabriel got there, when we were drugged and kidnapped from our hotel and brought here," Belle explained. Angelica shook her head in disbelief.

"You really knew nothing about my presence here? It was all some wacky wild-goose chase for a stupid feather?" Belle nodded. "Well, well, well . . . A fine mess we have, don't we? Daddy is on his way, and determined to cause me problems again, all because of a little misunderstanding with a feather. We export and import many things, Belle. Some far bigger and more important than stupid feathers. Yet all this is responsible for delivering you into my hands once more, lovely girl, so I shouldn't be too ungracious. The situation is already being salvaged, and Daddy-dearest will be walking right into my hands. In the meantime, I have you and your lovely sweet-tasting mother in my clutches." Angelica smiled broadly, revealing those sharp elongated canines, reminding Belle of her vampiric abilities. "Whatever shall I do with the two of you, eh?" she laughed.

Belle was watching Angelica closely, waiting for an opportunity, but she held the transmitter close, and it would take only a fraction of a second to press one of those buttons. If it were only her own neck at risk, Belle would already have tried for the device. The bedroom was small enough. Angelica didn't have room to manoeuvre. If she got in close enough, Angelica might hesitate to press the button for fear of being too close to the explosion, but only if the frequency was set for her own collar, and not the one around her mother's neck.

Angelica watched the lithe young woman, prowling impatiently back and forth, just a few steps away from her. She knew exactly what was going through Belle's mind, but Angelica had thought this through well.

"As long as I have this little device, you'll do everything I ask, won't you, Belle, dear?" she taunted.

"Yes," Belle grudgingly admitted, through gritted teeth.

"Well, my dear, The Jade Gate is a brothel, albeit a very exclusive one, and you're going to earn your keep while you're here. You will be showered, and given fresh clothes. Then you will be put to work," Angelica promised, "and if I get a single complaint from any of my clients, I blow your mother's fucking head clean off. Do you understand?" she grinned.

"I understand." Belle replied.

*　　*　　*

Laura was prowling her own secure bedroom when the door finally opened, and she recognized the woman standing in the doorway, in the green cheongsam, black hair or no black hair. "You!" she accused, one hand going to her neck, though not to the collar she had already examined before deciding to leave it well alone. Her hand went to the area where teeth had once punctured her flesh. Angelica's teeth, which the woman now flashed to remind her of her vulnerability.

"Hello, Laura," she greeted her.

"What are you doing here? Why this?" she pulled at the collar around her neck, though not too hard. She could smell the semtex.

"Control," Angelica explained, showing Laura the transmitter. "Keyed for either you or for Belle, with just a flick of my thumb. One misbehaves, the other dies. Simple but effective, don't you think?" she smiled, cruelly. "Now, tell me how you found me. If your answer doesn't match your daughter's, I press a button, and you'll hear the BOOM all the way up here," she warned.

"We didn't know you were here, I swear. We didn't even want to be here. Honestly." Laura tried her best to sound convincing. "We were just looking for a feather in Oman. Next thing we knew, we were drugged and brought here. You're as much of a surprise to us as we are to you, I assure you." Angelica looked at her, tilting her head sideways for a moment, as if deliberating.

"That's what she said, too," Angelica admitted. "So that means probably true. Still, it's opened a fine can of worms, and that's the truth as well. But we'll have to make the most of it, won't we? At least I now have you and Belle to play with once again. I examined the hand while she was unconscious, Someone did a marvellous job. It was my idea to keep it on ice, you know. You should thank me."

"Belle wants to thank you herself," Laura warned. Angelica laughed.

"Yes, I bet she does, poor girl!" Angelica's eyes flashed. "But back to you. We never really got much chance to become well acquainted last time we met, did we dearie?" she smiled, seeming to somehow glide closer, as Laura stared. Laura backed away, but got only as far as the wall of the small bedroom. Angelica's eyes seemed somehow brighter, as she got closer and closer to Laura. Her red lips got closer, too, as Laura felt gentle hands on her shoulders. She was close enough for an attempt to wrench the transmitter out of her hand, but somehow Laura couldn't think of anything but those lips, as Angelica's eyes burned into her own, and that deadly white smile widened to reveal sharp canine teeth.

Laura's blood was pounding in her veins, and Angelica was watching the thick vein in the side of her neck slowly pulsing, as she drew closer. Laura felt flushed, somehow filled with desire. Angelica's eyes seemed to bore into hers, mesmerising, and Laura couldn't break eye contact. She wanted to kiss those ruby red lips that were coming so close to her own. Angelica laughed sweetly, tongue snaking out and tasting Laura's lips so lightly, making her gasp.

"My dear Laura, I remember you tasted so sweet, and now I get to taste you again. This time we'll get to know each other so much better than before. I promise!" Angelica's face brushed aside Laura's long blonde hair, and Laura gasped at the feel of her hot breath on her neck. She gasped once, at the slight nip against the soft flesh of her neck, and then Angelica's arms tightened around her as she pressed her mouth hard on the vein, teeth puncturing and then worrying at the new wound, sucking and drawing her lifeblood from her, as Laura swooned in Angelica's arms, lost in a rapture more intense than anything she had ever experienced before.

*　　*　　*

Belle was given over to the auspices of a big fat ugly Mamasan, brandishing an electric cattle-prod. Her false smile showed discoloured yellow teeth, and her thick make-up failed to disguise her age. Belle was shown down to the basement, or a section of it, anyway, where there were some cages. A couple of those cages were occupied by naked women, who stared blankly out, their eyes clouded with drugs.

Beyond the cages was a shower-block, and Belle was made to disrobe and shower, while the Mamasan picked out a few outfits for her to wear, from a large selection of clothing hung from more than a dozen labelled clothes-racks.

The Mamasan had a good eye for size, and the evening dresses she chose for Belle looked a reasonable fit. Then she was shown to a set of drawers, wherein was a selection of underwear, all rather filmy and falsely erotic, still in individual plastic bags. Seemed like she wasn't getting much of a choice, so Belle shrugged her shoulders and chose a selection. At least they didn't appear to be second hand. She put on one set of underwear, and one of the evening dresses, as the Mamasan watched, nodding approvingly.

Then, carrying the rest of her clothing in her arms, it was back upstairs to the main room, where a passageway led behind a series of glass-fronted booths. Most were currently unoccupied, as it wasn't yet opening time, but Belle was shown her new home, and the door was locked behind her. The Mamasan pocketed the key. "You be comfortable, PrettyPretty. You new girl. You get plenty customer tonight," she smiled. She turned and went away, leaving Belle to settle into her new accommodation.

*   *   *

Angelica drank her fill from Laura, moaning in sensuous pleasure at the taste of hot blood in her mouth. Not enough to drain her, as that wasn't her intention at all. She had special plans for Laura, and they began with her ravishment. Laura lay on the bed, in a daze, as she felt the other woman stripping off her clothing.

It wasn't long before she was naked, and she watched through half-closed eyes as the other woman also began to disrobe. Off came the cheongsam, and then the bra, to reveal her breasts. There was something slightly unnatural about them, but Laura had little time to dwell on them, as the woman then shoved down her briefs, and something even more unnatural caught her attention, and caused her eyes to open wider.

The snake tattoo writhed along her belly, disappearing into her pubic hair, and from within that pubic hair an even older serpent appeared. Angelica handled her erection proudly, working it back and forth as it caught Laura's eye. It wasn't very big, but it was stiff, and getting stiffer as she handled it.

"Surprised, Laura? There's a lot about me you don't know, and a lot I want to share with you," Angelica smiled, approaching the bed once more. She put a knee on the bed, leaning over Laura. Her wide eyes bored into Laura's own once more, as she reached out to caress Laura's breasts, tweaking the nipples, which sprung to attention under her touch.

Leaning down, she put her mouth over one of those nipples, suckling tenderly, and Laura groaned with pleasure. One hand dipped between Laura's thighs, gently stroking, finger penetrating, as her sex got wetter.

Laura shuddered as the other 'woman' made love to her. Weak and under Angelica's spell, she found she could offer no resistance as she was pressed down onto the mattress by the other woman's body lying on top of her. Then the nudging at her labia, and Angelica's face beaming with pleasure as she thrust into her. "Can you feel it, Laura? Does it feel good?" Angelica taunted, hips beginning to hump up and down, working up a slow sensuous rhythm.

*   *   *

As the brothel opened for business, the main room soon began filling up with clientele. Belle watched with a show of disinterest from the confines of her Perspex glass-fronted cell, though she was taking in as much detail as she could, for a possible breakout whenever the opportunity presented itself. She didn't fool herself. Unless the collars could be dealt with, she had to be on her best behaviour, and it looked like she would have to rely on her father making an appearance to perform any rescue.

Both men and women seemed to be customers in this brothel. More men than women, but only a few of the women were with male friends. Some were single and obviously predatory, by the way a few of them eyed her up through the glass.

Many of the customers came to give her the once-over, her being a new face, new body. Some of them leered openly through the Perspex, while others looked and moved on. It took about an hour for the door to her cell to be unlocked, and the fat Mamasan beckoned her out.

She followed her to the end of the passageway, where a nervous looking teen male awaited. The Mamasan gave him a ticket, and turned to speak to Belle. "Upstairs. Numbah Four room. You give good time, long time," she smiled, revealing crooked teeth.

Resigned to her fate, Belle began to climb the stairs, and heard the man follow her. On the first floor landing, there was a series of room, all numbered. She opened the door to Number Four, and went inside, leaving the door open behind her for the client to enter also.

The room was small but functional for purpose. Nice big queen-sized bed, with fresh sheets by the look of it. A shower and basin to one side of the room. On the bedside table were a selection of sex-aids. Various vibrators, butt-plugs, handcuffs, even condoms. Whatever the customer wanted.

She turned to face the man, and was surprised to find him almost cowering against the wall with nervousness. "I've never done anything like this before," he began to explain. He looked young, less than twenty certainly. "My friends paid for this as a birthday present."

"Happy Birthday," Belle forced a smile, trying to reassure the man. "Come and unwrap your birthday present, and let's get this over with," she suggested. He was far from being ugly, but obviously inexperienced. Belle realised she would have to lead proceedings.

$*$ $*$ $*$

Angelica relaxed, smoking a cigarette, as Laura lay in a fetal position, curled up beside her on the bed. "My father's name was Hector Maggio, and he worked in the Foreign Office. During the War years he managed to wangle himself a posting to Bangkok," Angelica explained. "It was safe, and out of the way of all the hostilities. Widowed, he took just his only son, Enrique, with him. It wasn't an easy relationship between father and son, for the boy was not as manly as his father had wished. Effeminate in his ways, and unsure of his sexuality in those formative years, perhaps Bangkok was not the best of places to take the boy, but it made him into a man eventually, well, as much as I am today," Angelica laughed ironically.

"I was supposed to finish my education with a private tutor whilst I was there, but the tutor wasn't available fulltime, which left me plenty of time to familiarize myself with the fleshpots of Bangkok, and became enamoured of the colourful glamour of the ladyboys, and the transvestite shows. It was true what they said about Bangkok. The most beautiful women were not women, but men in disguise, some just in drag, others undergoing surgical changes to turn their men's bodies into their female equivalents. I wanted to be just as beautiful, but the medical techniques at the time were very basic, and not guaranteed to work with everybody.

I first met Bird, when my Father employed him as a guide. He was a likeable and handsome young man, of a somewhat striking appearance, with similar tastes to my own, and we hit it off almost immediately. We socialized together most of the nights of the week, in bars, taking in shows. It was part of his duties as a tour-guide to organize the evening's entertainment, and he was well-known in many establishments. He helped open many doors for me. Realizing my sexual preferences early on, he arranged for my first experience with one of the local lady-boys. It was something I had never yet dared to do back in my native Italy," Angelica reminisced, fondly. "It was a long time ago, yet, somehow, it seems like only yesterday . . . ."

*   *   *

Hector Maggio was a diplomat in the Italian Foreign Office, when his wife gave birth to his son Enrique. Maria was left in ill-health after the difficult birth, and eventually died when the child was still two. Although still an infant, Hector could not find it in himself to love the boy, somehow blaming him for taking away the wife he had loved so much. Hector despised himself for his failure to love his own son, but every time he saw the boy's face, he also saw the face of Maria, the wife he had loved so much.

Much of Enrique's childhood was spent in the company of Nannies, and then when he grew older, he was sent off to boarding schools, where he found life difficult amongst the other children, forever teased because his parents never visited him. Children could be as cruel as only children could. Enrique soon began to hate his school, and his work suffered as the bullying continued. He was not a physically strong person, of rather frail frame, and an easy target for some of the more muscular boys.

When he was thirteen, Hector accepted a posting to the embassy in Bangkok, thinking the change of scenery would do his son some good. Private tutoring was available, though limited to two hours a day, but

Hector also managed to secure the services of a local guide to take the boy around the city and show him some of life in Thailand.

Enrique gawped openly at the teenage boy who was introduced to him by his father. The name was unpronounceable to anyone not familiar with the language. The youth laughed as he watched Enrique attempt to twist his tongue around his name. "Just call me Bird, everyone does. Most people prefer shorter nicknames here than the ones we were born with. Foreigners can't pronounce them, so they call us something they can associate with. I'm tall and lanky, gawky almost. People say I look like a Heron, so they call me Bird," he smiled, and offered his hand. Enrique took it, gladly.

"I'm Enrique."

"Yes, I know," Bird grinned. "I've been a guide here for three years now, and your Father wants me to take you out and familiarize you with the city and surroundings. There's a lot to see," he admitted.

"My tutor is only here for two hours in the morning, so I guess we have plenty of time," Enrique enjoyed the offered friendship of the strange tall teenager. His previous life in Italy had been spent friendless. Bird spoke good enough Italian, English, and was working on his German and Dutch. Enrique was looking forward to learning Thai.

*　　*　　*

The first few weeks of their time together, Enrique was shown around all of Bangkok and some of the outlying districts, and he took in the colourful surroundings, strange smells and exotic scents. Bird advised him to learn the layout of the place carefully during the day, because Bangkok by night, was a totally different environment, and once they had permission from Enrique's father, Bird organized trips to some of the clubs and shows that were so famous in that part of the world.

Enrique had noticed the differences between the men in Thailand and those back in Italy. The men here behaved in a much more "feminine" way, often walking together, holding hands, and once Enrique saw his first Ladyboy show, he understood that the best looking women in Bangkok weren't usually women at all. He fell in love with the theatre, and the gaudy lights and colourful costumes. This was a totally different world from what he had been used to, and Bird was enjoying being his tutor. Bird soon began guiding Enrique around by the hand himself, and Enrique soon thought nothing of it.

*   *   *

Hector noticed a welcome change in Enrique's outlook after a few weeks. The boy's work with his tutor was progressing well, though he wished the tutor was available more often, but Italian-speaking teachers were in high demand here in Bangkok. Enrique was picking up a bit of Thai, which he practiced with the houseboys, and that pleased Hector. He had thought the boy might not take to foreign climes, but it seemed to be panning out quite well.

The post here in Bangkok was a good one, coming with perks such as the villa and the car. The salary also was nothing to be sniffed at, and the guide he had hired for the boy was cheap enough. So an arrangement that everyone seemed to be happy with.

*   *   *

Enrique's fourteenth birthday came and went, when Bird took the young man-boy into one nightclub, and eventually, after negotiating a fee, brought a beautiful young woman back with him, and the three of them went up to one of the higher floors, and one of the secluded bedrooms. "My birthday present to you, Enrique," Bird laughed, as the woman leaned forward to kiss him, the first kiss he had ever had. As Bird watched, Enrique let the woman dictate events, accepting her sweet-tasting tongue into his mouth, and doing his best to respond as she expected.

Bird took a seat across the room, as he watched the woman slowly remove Enrique's jacket, and push him back to sit on the edge of the bed. Enrique sat there, letting her unzip his pants, which revealed a stiff erection. He was strangely unembarrassed, as the woman's head dipped and she took him in her mouth, and he gasped at the marvellous wet heat and suction as she fellated him. Bird smiled as he watched with amusement.

Enrique groaned, one hand on the back of the woman's head, stroking her hair, though trying to resist the temptation to force her head down further. He wanted more, but did not want to dissuade her from continuing the intimate act. He looked across to where Bird returned his stare, and grinned. Bird gave him a silent thumb's-up.

The woman's hair seemed to move in his hand, as her head dipped slowly up and down, and at first Enrique didn't really notice. When he did, finally, he stiffened, one hand holding onto the wig, while the "woman" kept on sucking his dick. He looked wide-eyed across to Bird, who was laughing, and suddenly Enrique was laughing along with him, groaning as the Ladyboy continued the loving blowjob. Enrique groaned as he came in the hot sweet mouth.

Then, as he watched, Bird got up from the chair, unzipping his own pants, and pulling the Ladyboy up from behind, he rucked up the silk dress, pulled the panties to one side, and eagerly sodomised her from behind, letting Enrique watch as the Ladyboy accepted the rough sex, moaning as Bird pumped away behind her.

Enrique didn't know what to say or do. He just sat there, wet dick still out of his trousers, whilst he watched his friend bugger the Ladyboy. Enrique felt that a watershed had been crossed tonight. He had somehow matured from a boy into a man in that dingy hotel room.

*   *   *

"From there, Bird let me in on his scams of blackmailing the local tourists, the paedophiles, who came to Bangkok looking for underage sexual experiences. He quickly showed me how the game was played, and often picked out my targets for me. Picking them up was easy, and the hotel rooms were already set up with the hidden cameras, taking discreet photos of the sexual acts some of those tourists performed with me. I was along for 20% of the profits from blackmailing them, so had little sympathy for their plight after Bird had milked them dry. The money was put to one side, to help pay for my surgery, though I waited till after the death of my father before I first went under the surgeon's knife. Bird arranged that, too, my father's death, I mean," Angelica chuckled. "I stood to inherit everything from my father, though lately he had talked of being dissatisfied of me, and possibly rewriting his will. Bird and I gave him little opportunity once he had mentioned the idea," Angelica chuckled at the memory. "I was a wealthy man after that, and I let the publicity of my father's death die down before

I visited a surgeon who re-structured my face, and I dropped out of the public eye shortly afterwards. It took another two operations, over a number of years, to turn me into the "woman" I am today, though I was reluctant to have the final operation. Surgery then wasn't as skillful as it is today, and I received no guarantees that I would end up with a working vagina, so I stuck with what worked best for so many years. My dick!" Angelica/Enrique chuckled, penetrating her once more, and slowly moving back and forth, thrusting in and out of Laura's body, as she moaned softly beneath him, half-asleep with the drugs he had given her.

Laura laid there, half-conscious, as Angelica's words washed over her. She felt Angelica's body pressed up against her on the bed, and gentle fingers stroked her shoulder. The slow rhythmic sex kept her highly stimulated and sensitive to the other woman's tender caresses.

"I came back to Italy to consolidate my father's estate, and while I was there, I found it hard to live as a woman. I had an early breast augmentation, but the surgery was not available at the time for a full sex-change, even if I'd wanted it, and so I joined a nunnery, learning to live amongst women, learning to *be* a woman. Eventually Father Patrick Ryan took me under his wing for a while, recruiting me into Solomon, until your daughter came along. Then we had a sort of falling out", she reminisced, smiling ruefully, "and I was ordered back to Rome where I met Borgia for the first time. Borgia also liked boys as well as girls, and once he found out my unique physiology, I became his protégé, and he eventually made me into the same creature as he was himself, a vampire. It was a mutually beneficial arrangement. When Borgia fell, I realized a coup had taken place within Solomon, and knew I had to make myself scarce, having hitched my wagon to a falling star so to speak, so I came back to Asia, and found Bird once more. We had kept in touch, and he offered me a place within his own organization. Which brings us right up to date. To here and now, and you lying in my arms," she leaned closer and lightly kissed the still raw wounds on Laura's pale neck. "I've only taken a little blood this time, Laura," she reassured her, "and I'll go on only taking a little bit of blood here and there, till I have you on the very threshold of life and death, and then I'll take you over that edge, and what a wild ride that will be, Laura. One you'll never forget till your dying day. A walk on the wild side of forever," she promised.

*   *   *

No one paid much attention to the flat-bed Toyota truck as it drove into the old port area of Muscat. Four Arabs were squatting in the back of the flat-bed, holding onto the framework, as another two of them sat in the cab. The truck stopped near one of the open-air markets, and the men all got out of the truck. One of the men, slightly taller than the others, said his Goodbyes, hugged a few of his compatriots, and started out towards the Diplomatic District, which wasn't too far away.

Gabriel's eyes scanned this way and that, under his hooded djellabah, though his head didn't move. He strolled slowly, letting himself get a feel for his surroundings. Underneath the Arab dress, he still had his passport, and his wallet still contained credit cards and money. After more than a week under the hot desert sun, his already olive skin had darkened, and the black beard, roughly trimmed, and shaped, now made him indistinguishable from many of the Arabs around him.

The caravan had provided a needed refuge, and, although travelling slowly, kept him out of the way of the people who were looking for him. Muscat was a Danger-Zone, but he needed to be here. He had flown in on an Argentine passport, and without good contacts, that was how he had to fly out again.

Once he got to the Embassy, he could count on assistance from the staff there, to get him some clothes, and book his flight out of Seeb. Most of the Embassies were close to each other in the Old Quarter, and some of them even had Armed Guards outside. Plenty of Omani nationals visited many of these embassies for visas, planning foreign trips etc, and Gabriel joined a small queue inside the Argentine Embassy, wanting to draw no untoward attention to himself.

Once he got to the counter, Gabriel showed his passport, and spoke to the staff there in English, requesting to speak with the most senior official present. He was asked to wait on one side of the room, whilst inquisitive eyes glanced his way, from other people queuing. After a short wait, Gabriel was ushered into one of the side offices by one of the day to day Embassy staff. More senior officials did not usually arrive until later in the day, but Gabriel had wanted to get here as early as the Embassy opened, to avoid as many eyes as possible.

"Mr Angell? My name is Da Silva. I understand you wanted to speak to the senior attaché? He doesn't normally arrive before lunch. Is this something I can help you with?" the small thin man asked.

Gabriel had thrown back his hood now, and the man could clearly see his features weren't Arabic. The passport had also probably been scanned through their computers by now, verifying his identity. "Yes, Mr Da Silva, you may. I was in a car accident. No one else involved. My luggage was destroyed, and I was miles from anywhere when it happened. It's taken me a while to get back to civilization, and I missed my flight out of here. Would it be possible for me to stay here for a day or so, whilst someone from your staff obtains some fresh clothing for me, and book me on a flight to Rome, at your earliest convenience?"

"Why, certainly, Mr Angell. We are always here to help. We keep a couple of small rooms available upstairs, in case of need, but wouldn't you be more comfortable in a hotel?" he asked, curious.

"I'm sure your rooms will be comfortable enough. I'm afraid my business trip was a bit of a disappointment, and I can't wait to get out of Oman, so I don't want any more hassle with the hotels. Don't worry, I didn't leave any unpaid bills," he reassured him.

"Very well, Sir. If you'd follow me, I'll show you up to one of the rooms," he led Gabriel out of the small office, and they crossed the floor to the flight of marble stairs. Gabriel's sandaled feet found the going a little slippery, but he held onto the banister as they climbed the stairs. The room itself looked out over the rooftops, away from the main streets. The room was only slightly smaller than a standard hotel room, with a single bed, lushly carpeted, and sufficient furniture to be reasonably comfortable. Bathroom and shower off to one side, behind the door. There was a phone by the bed, but Gabriel didn't want to risk his calls being intercepted. "Can I get access to a computer?" he asked Da Silva. The man nodded.

"I'll send someone up with one of the laptops. There's a socket next to the phone. It's secure. He'll show you how to set it up. Once that's done, if you give him the details, he'll go about organizing a new set of clothes, and your plane tickets to Rome."

"Thank you, Mr Da Silva. I'm indebted to you," Gabriel shook the man's hand.

"Merely doing my job, Sir. Your name is not exactly unknown back home. It caused quite a flutter when we sent your passport details through.

I was told to give you every possible assistance." As he left, Gabriel headed into the bathroom to wash off the desert sand and sweat. His alias was indeed well known, as a millionaire, and beneficiary to many needy charities in Argentina. He kept things as sweet as he could for himself back home, whilst trying to maintain as low a profile as possible.

Gabriel showered, but decided to leave the beard. He merely trimmed and shaped it a little. In this part of the world, many wore beards, and they certainly served to hide individual faces and blur them into the background. Freshened up, he put on the complimentary bathrobe that was hung up inside the bathroom. He went back into the bedroom and switched on the TV, to scan through the news channels. CNN usually gave the most unbiased reporting, so he settled for that, and caught up on events while he waited.

It was a mere fifteen minutes later when there was a knock on his door, and Gabriel opened it to find a young man there with a laptop and some cables. Once in the room, he quickly set up and connected the laptop for Gabriel, logging him on to the Embassy's secure network, and then he asked Gabriel for his clothes and shoe sizes, before leaving him to it.

Once Gabriel was alone, he logged onto his secure website and checked his e-mail. What he found didn't please him. Two e-mails from Maddox, the first dated two days ago. '*Jade Star* boarded by Indonesian Port Officials as soon as she docked. Only minor contraband found on board. Main cargo must have been offloaded in International Waters. Further enquiries ongoing. Will be in touch. Jim.'

The second e-mail was dated earlier today. 'Indonesian authorities making enquiries. Will assist. Contact me. Jim.'

Gabriel started typing a reply. 'Weather here has been hot. Resorted to using sun-block, and staying out of the sun. Disappointing news. In transit to Rome. Will contact again from DG. Gabriel.'

The White Slavery Ring was slick and well-oiled. He should have expected they had the means to avoid the Customs in Jakarta. Corruption was a way of life out there. Jim would understand the terminology he had used in his reply, and realize why it had taken him so long to respond. He was sure Jim was pulling all the strings to find both Laura and Belle, but he would be happier once he could take charge of that search himself. It took precedence over his search for the source of that angel-feather.

Chapter Ten

"No, it hasn't gone well in Oman," Angelica, the Dragon-Lady, confirmed in her telecon with Bird in Bangkok. "Gabriel evaded our men, and eventually caught a flight to Rome, where he will doubtless meet up with his Mafia friends. The *Jade Star* was searched by Customs as she docked, so they were expecting to find our cargo. Gabriel will be coming here next, I'm sure. He knows more than is good for him, and too much for my liking. I don't have anyone here good enough to take him out. What do you suggest I do about the situation? I can't very well let the women go, now that they know about this organization. That by itself wouldn't be enough to divert Gabriel. If I have them killed, it will only enrage him more."

"My dear Angelica, our friend Gabriel is still a wanted man. I suggest a dropped word here and there to the Indonesian Security Services, and let them prepare a warm welcome for him. They have more than enough resources to get him out of our hair." Bird was nothing but pragmatic. "They already have their hands full dealing with our friends from Al-Qaeda, so they won't want another terrorist running around loose on their territory."

"Yes, that might work," she agreed, musing.

"No might about it. With Gabriel's reputation, they won't take any chances. No need to dirty our hands ourselves when the Indonesians can do it for us, eh?" he chuckled. Angelica did the same. They thought alike, as always. It had been many years since their first meeting, as Bird, still a tour-guide in those days, had shown the new Italian Ambassador and his son around Bangkok and its environs. Both had changed greatly in the years in between, Bird seeking power amongst the elite of Bangkok, and Angelica climbing the inner rungs of power with the Sword of Solomon organization, until Borgia's demise, anyway. Now

Bird provided a fallback, and a refuge, a place where she could once again climb the ladders of power in Bird's own criminal empire.

*　　*　　*

Gabriel managed to sleep on the plane, fatigue finally catching up with him. The slight jolt from the wheels as they hit the tarmac awoke him from his slumber, and a half hour later, he had cleared Customs and was welcomed by Donatello Grimaldi who had come to greet his friend.

"You look like shit," was all Donatello could say, laughing, as he embraced Gabriel. "Come, my car awaits. Let's get you back to my villa where you can freshen up. I have your new papers ready for you, and your connecting flight doesn't leave till tomorrow."

"I could do with a good shower," Gabriel admitted. "Then I'll need to use your computer to contact Maddox. If I use the phone again, I'll probably get my ear chewed off." Gabriel joked. He allowed Donatello to take one of his new cases, and they went out of the Arrivals Hall to where his chauffeur awaited.

Donatello looked to have put on a few pounds since Gabriel had last seen him. Still dapper, and still waxing his moustache, he looked a good advert for a typical Italian middle-aged playboy. Marianne was feeding him too much.

During the drive south towards Latina, Gabriel filled in the details of his current predicament to his long-time friend. "Jim's official contacts there may be able to help us further with regard to this Al Raschid company, if it still operates by the same name over there. Things were always rather confusing in Jakarta, and the place has changed somewhat since the last time I was there. I have an e-mail address and an ISP to track down. Jim's organizational contacts should help there, too," he added.

"You do not live a quiet life, do you, my friend?" Donatello mused. "All this over a feather, and then your women get mixed up in some white-slave trade."

"They're connected somehow, Donatello. I can't believe this is all coincidence."

"If I can help in any way?" he offered.

"You are helping enough, Donatello," he assured him.

"Marianne has been cooking again. Some of her delicious pasta awaits you," Donatello grinned.

"How do you keep so slim on her cooking, Donatello?" Gabriel chuckled.

"With a woman like Marianne? Plenty of sex, my friend. Plenty of sex." He punched Gabriel's arm lightly, as both of them laughed.

After freshening up, Gabriel joined Donatello and Marianne in the dining room, where servants actually served the meal Marianne herself had cooked earlier. A nice red wine complimented the pasta and spicey meat sauce. Gabriel restricted himself to just two slices of garlic bread, though he loved the stuff. "It's a pity you can't stay with us for longer," Marianne mused over her wine.

"If I could, I would. You know that." Gabriel apologized. "Even with the current truce between me and Solomon, I still don't feel safe being too close to them. I wouldn't be here now if I had a choice," he admitted.

"I'm sure your friend Maddox is doing all he can. He has influence in his position," Donatello added.

"As long as the girls are alright. I don't know what's happening to them right now, and I'm worried," he admitted. "They're both capable of looking after themselves, but they don't seem to have done too good a job of that, so far. Once I've found them and made sure they're okay, I've got to send them packing, while I follow up on the trail of that feather."

"It is real, then?" Marianne asked. Gabriel nodded.

"As far as can be told. Real and freshly plucked. So I have to track it down. Lucifer and Michael were both killed in England. Matthias died in Madrid, many years before. I thought I was the last of my kind, but it seems not. Whoever it is, I need to find him."

The three of them finished their meal, and Donatello and Marianne left Gabriel at his computer, where he plugged in the usb-stick, and started going through the copied e-mails. He was at it for over an hour, before he finally rejoined his hosts. Jakarta was the next link in the chain. It had undergone much change since Gabriel's last visit over twenty years ago. Sights, sounds, and smells kept flashing back in his mind.

"I'll need a laptop with an internet account set up. Can you organize that for me before my flight tomorrow?" he asked Donatello, who mused for a moment, before nodding.

"Yes, that should not be difficult. I will have one ready by noon for you, and I will run you to the airport myself," he assured Gabriel. "Try to relax till then. Let your friend Maddox worry about things. There is nothing you can do till you get there, anyway, and I daresay Laura will try and find some excuse not be sent home." He laughed, and Gabriel gave a wry smile.

"Yes, she can be a pain in the ass at times," he admitted, only half-joking.

"Men can be a pain in the ass, too, but we love you, regardless," Marianne pointed out, smiling.

"Assuming you can persuade the lovely Laura and Belle to return home, what will you do?" asked Donatello. Gabriel shrugged his shoulders.

"Follow down the leads I have from the Al Raschid corporation's e-mails. They have a conduit in Jakarta, somewhere. Once I find it, I can follow the trail back from there. There's been a lot happening in Indonesia lately, a lot of unrest, the tsunami, and Al Qaeda has been blowing up the tourist industry. Lots of extremists making their feelings known. My gut-feeling tells me this is more than just a minor smuggling operation. If they're into white-slaving, they have a conduit set up, which other organizations could make use of."

"You think there's an Al Qaeda connection there?" Donatello's eyebrows raised, remembering only too well the campaign those fanatics had recently launched on the Italian Mainland.

"They're getting into the country somehow," Gabriel pointed out.

After a restless night, Gabriel got up and took another shower. He found Donatello out on the terrace, watching Marianne as she swam in their pool. Gabriel sat down at Donatello's computer, and logged onto his server to check his e-mail, and found a communication from Maddox waiting for him.

'Gabe, ISP says that e-mail address is registered to an R. Dwiputro, address given as 34 Jelan Kendal, Jakarta. There's a club at that address called the Jade Gate.' Gabriel wasn't too surprised. Jelan Kendal was in the heart of one of the city's many Red-Light districts. But at least he had a name and an address to track down, now. 'Indonesian Customs Authorities were tipped off about the *Jade Star* and boarded as soon as it docked. No sign of the women. They must have been unloaded whilst the ship was in international waters, and brought ashore in something smaller. We can't get involved too closely with internal Indonesian affairs, but Nick is ready for some vacation time. Can you recommend anywhere nice?' Gabriel mused over the last couple of sentences.

It seemed like Maddox and Turnbull were offering him their help. He debated whether to accept, as it might cause further problems with the Regiment. He would have to think about it. Who else could he ask for help? The only person he knew in that part of the world was Denny, and he hadn't spoken to her in years. Didn't even know if she was still alive, and he still felt bad, even admitting that to himself. She deserved better treatment than he'd given her, even though he had little choice in their breakup, those many years ago. After all this time, could he ask for her help in this? She might be his only hope, and so he typed a reply to Maddox, asking him to track her down, and find him a contact phone number.

Maddox's reply came with a phone number. N.D.Zoro. After all this time, Gabriel hesitated to make the call. It had been an awkward relationship, with the ill-feeling towards local women who socialized with western men. Leaving, and leaving her well-provided for was possibly the best thing he could have done for her, under the circumstances, though he doubted she had thought that way at the time. Still, the run-in with Borgia in Singapore left him with little choice. It was evening in Jakarta now, and he slowly picked up the phone and dialled the overseas number.

*   *   *

Denny Zoro was settling down for the evening, after enjoying a light meal. Her maidservant had already cleared away the table, and Denny was sipping on a light cognac as she sat out on her veranda. She heard the phone ring, and also heard her maidservant answer it. Calls in the evening were unusual. Even Angelo knew she liked her 'quiet times'. The girl came out onto the veranda. "Madame, a gentleman is asking to speak with you." Denny turned to regard her.

"Who is this gentleman?" she asked.

"So sorry Madame, but he would not give his name." Denny looked puzzled, and put down her glass. She got up out of her easy chair, and followed the girl inside, to where the phone waited off the hook. She certainly wasn't expecting any calls.

She picked up the handset and held it to her ear. "Hello?" she asked the mysterious stranger. She heard a strangely disquieting sigh at the other end of the phone, before a male voice spoke.

"Denny?" the voice asked, as if unsure to whom he spoke.

"Yes, this is she. Who am I talking to?" she asked, a strange chill going through her. The one word, and the voice, and the way it spoke her name were setting off all sorts of alarm bells throughout her very being. Somehow, she knew that voice, and the hand holding the phone began to tremble slightly . . .

"Denny, it's Gabriel." There was silence at the other end of the phone, and then".

"Aiieee!!!" she dropped the phone as if it were on fire. Her mouth opened and closed, but no words were coming out. Her maidservant looked at her in alarm, as she bent to retrieve the handset. Her weak heart began to thump against her ribcage, and she felt herself growing faint. Quickly, she sat down, fanning her face.

"Madame? Are you alright?" she asked, concerned, and offered the handset to her once more. Denny looked at it for a moment, staring at it as though horrified, and then she reached out a thin trembling hand, and despite her own now pounding heart, took it from her. She brought it to her ear, slowly.

"Yes?" she paused. "My bastard finally phones," she almost sobbed down the phone, but managed to control her tears in front of her maidservant, who realized the personal nature of the call from the state of her mistress, and she excused herself.

On the other end of the phone, Gabriel heard the emotion welling up in Denny's strained voice, and he hated himself for all the years in between, when he had not felt it right to contact her. "Denny, I know it's been a long time," Gabriel tried to explain, but the awkwardness of the situation was affecting him as well. "I couldn't call you back then. People were looking for me. People are still looking for me. I had to leave Singapore suddenly, and I couldn't go back to Jakarta. My life was in danger, and yours would have been in danger if I'd stayed and the people who were looking for me learned about our relationship. They would have used you to force me into their hands."

"There's no need to explain." Denny sniffed back a tear, so happy just to hear the sound of his voice once again. "I know you wouldn't have hurt me if it could have been avoided. I was very grateful for the money you left behind. I used it well. It changed my life greatly, and for the better."

"Denny, I never knew when you were lying to me back then, and I don't now. I wouldn't have interfered in your life again if it wasn't important. I'm coming back to Jakarta. I'll be using another name, and I'll need to keep a low profile, because of events related to my forced departure those twenty five plus years ago. Jakarta has changed a lot since I've been gone, and I need to keep away from the authorities, so I need someone on the ground with local knowledge, to help me find two missing women. One blonde, called Laura, one with black hair called Belle. They were kidnapped in the Middle East, and shipped aboard the *Jade Star* to Jakarta. Customs couldn't find anything when they boarded her at the docks, so I'm thinking the women were offloaded onto a smaller boat whilst still in International Waters. All I have so far is the name of the Arab end of this affair, the Al-Raschid Trading Company, and a possible link with Jelan Kendal, one of the red light districts. A club called the Jade Gate. I need you to act as my ears and eyes till I get there. Can you do this for me?"

"I'd do anything for you, my bastard, you know this. You always have," Denny sighed. "But I must see you, talk to you. Twenty five years is a long time, and people move on, but we still have things to discuss. Promise me we will have this conversation, my darling. Do this for me, and I will do what I can to aid your search."

"I promise, Denny. It will be good to see you again. I will be there in a few days. I'll phone you again once I arrive and check into a hotel."

Denny heard the soft click as he hung up, and she cradled the receiver against her cheek, warm salty tears beginning to flow, finally, as she sobbed softly. The memories that came flooding back were too painful for her.

*　　*　　*

A nice Pollo Freschetta was served for lunch, cooked by Donatello's chef this time, and the promised laptop arrived shortly after the meal was over. Gabriel checked it over, though did not upload any of the files from the usb-stick.

Laptops had a habit of being examined or going missing through various customs in the Middle East and Far East, and he wanted to take no chances. Universal adaptor for the power-pack was in the bag, so he wouldn't have to buy one at the airport. Battery-life was good for a couple of hours, but best to run on mains electricity where possible, as you never knew when you'd get the time or opportunity to charge the damn thing up again. Batteries were also very susceptible to climate and temperature.

He plugged the phone card into the slot, and checked the gps internet connection. It was working fine, though might alter once he changed continents. He hoped the cell networks worked over in Indonesia these days.

Donatello had also organized a tropical wardrobe for Gabriel, and the luggage now filled the two medium sized cases supplied by the Argentine Embassy in Muscat. He didn't know how long he'd be over there, so best prepare for a lengthy trip. He carried the cases out to the limousine himself, and Marianne gave him a farewell hug before he got into the back of the limousine with Donatello. The chauffeur set off on the hour long journey to the airport, and Donatello tried to engage him in conversation, but his mind was elsewhere. He hated the enforced inertia of air-travel, being forced to just sit there for hours on end, waiting till you got to your destination. He preferred to try and sleep through such journeys, but often had no choice. As Donatello had pointed out, there was nothing else he could do till he got there.

*   *   *

Angelo Zoro was still in the office, trying to put names to the faces of the men he'd been running surveillance on over the last few days. Police computers had links to other agencies around the world, and he was hoping one of those links would come up trumps on this.

Fresh news on the streets today was word that a terrorist named Gabriel was on his way to Jakarta. The name rang bells with Angelo, who ran it through his computer. He found references to a foiled Al-Qaeda plot in Italy, with a notification that the man was now dead, killed during the final shootout with the Arabs. How could he be on his way here if he was dead? Angelo put in a request for a full file download, which would probably take till tomorrow, if the Italians were holding onto it. He would at least read through the file, before dismissing it as a false report.

*   *   *

Angelo Zoro's request ended up on Jim Maddox's computer, and it resulted in an immediate "Oh, shit." Such requests for closed-case files were not uncommon, but this one mentioned Gabriel by name, and its source was Gabriel's next destination. The name of the requester caught him by surprise. A common enough name in that part of the world, or so he'd thought when Gabriel asked for the phone number of that woman, but too much for coincidence now this Angelo Zoro was asking for information on Gabriel. Was this Angelo Zoro related to Denny Zoro?

He couldn't deny the request, but he could at least give Gabriel a heads-up that someone out there was very interested in him. Jim quickly put together an urgent e-mail, warning Gabriel that the Indonesian authorities were enquiring about him. He left Zoro's name out of the e-mail for now. Best be sure before alarming him unnecessarily. Time to check up on Nick Turnbull.

Already on his way, and currently out of touch, he would check in at the Embassy once he got to Jakarta, so best leave word there. He would be able to check out any connection between Denny Zoro and Angelo Zoro before Gabriel got there.

*   *   *

The next day, Angelo opened up the file sent to him from Europol's Brussels office. Maddox had no alternative but to respond to the formal request between security forces. It contained edited details of Operation Osprey, against the Al Qaeda cells headed by Torquemada, and the involvement and subsequent 'death' of the former terrorist Gabriel, who was acknowledged as helping the Italian Authorities against the Arabs. Convinced of the veracity of the report, and the probable false information they had received concerning his imminent arrival in Jakarta, Angelo was about to dismiss it, when he finally noticed the photo likeness of Gabriel contained in the report.

It was the fake I.D. used at Porton-Down, and showed a blonde and bearded Gabriel. Something about the man's eyes bored into his own, and Angelo looked closer, beyond the beard, beyond the blonde hair, and saw the face of the man in the photograph that hung on his mother's wall. The hair style and colouring may have been different, but his training taught him to look beyond that, and he knew that face. A face his Mother had never once, in all the years, even given a name to. Gabriel. Was this man his father?

As he mused this, he instantly scoffed, realizing it must somehow be a mistake. The man would be nearly sixty by now. The likeness was just coincidental. It had to be. Besides, the man was dead. Or was he?

Angelo had enough on his plate already with home-grown terrorists such as Jemaah Islamiyah, who were active across the whole of S.E Asia now. Kopassus had had some success in attacking some of their training camps, but since the tsunami, word had it that they had relocated some of their training camps onto the Malaysian Peninsula and beyond.

The Indonesian Islands themselves were home to more than 231 million people, and predominantly Muslim, though other religions were tolerated, and up till recently, extremism hadn't been a problem, as the Muslim community had lived and worked hand in hand with the western cultures and companies who helped fund Indonesia's economy. Since the War on Terror had begun, it had stirred up a veritable hornet's nest of ill-feeling towards the West.

Extremists were now on every street corner, agitating and fomenting hatred against the western companies the country had come to depend upon for its livelihood, hence Angelo's sudden secondment from Kopassus, to work the streets, on undercover assignment.

*   *   *

Nick Turnbull and Julie were settling into their room at the Garden Hotel, in the Kebayoran Baru district, tired from the long flight. A porter collected their luggage and showed them into the grand reception hall. Nick went over the reception, whilst Julie's eye was caught by the delightful garden area over to the left, behind the plate glass doors.

There were two messages waiting for Nick at the desk, one asking him to check in at the Embassy the next day, and another asking him to present himself at Security Division HQ to meet with Angelo Zoro. Tomorrow was tomorrow, and tonight was tonight. A quick shared shower took longer than he'd originally intended, but once the two lovebirds had towelled themselves off, they dressed and went downstairs for a late dinner in the restaurant.

This was Julie's first time in the Far East, and the first time Nick had been here unofficially. She was excited and enervated by the noticeable differences in the climate, the humidity, the strange exotic smells in the air. The faint smell of smoke in the air was a residue of the forest-burning that the hill farmers persisted with each year, but he didn't let on to Julie about that.

A bit of comfort was a relief to Nick, more used to sleeping out in the jungle during his SAS training. He was giving life a lot of thought, since Julie had come out of that coma, and their relationship had blossomed.

Marriages never seemed to last long in the Regiment, and although he loved the life, he couldn't do that to Julie. He had another year to go, and then he could opt out. Maddox, her Dad, had hinted he might be able to provide employment for Nick, though unofficial, and it would pay well, though not without a few risks, as a sort of James Bond type, working direct from Brussels, though with H.M. Government's best interests at heart, obviously. Nick didn't like the EEC, and even to Maddox, it was a necessary evil he had to work within.

So, similar work, but able to spend more time with Julie. This current secondment was a taster of things to come, Maddox had intimated. A 'civilian' often had less trouble getting around than a soldier, even one of the SAS. Less red tape, and the SAS were well known for their dislike of the bureaucracy that Governments seemed to love, in these politically correct days.

He had heard of other ex-members of the Regiment being approached by Five and Six, but you couldn't always trust Whitehall. At least he 'knew' Maddox, well as much as anyone could. One advantage he had, was that if he was married to Maddox's daughter, there was less likelihood that Maddox would send him out on something suicidal, as long as kept on his good side, he thought to himself, grinning. Of course, if he pissed Julie off, that was something that could well be arranged, he chuckled to himself.

He was currently unarmed, and that didn't feel right, but Maddox had assured him that he had made arrangements with the Indonesian authorities for him to be kitted out with suitable weapons, and that would happen after his meeting with Angelo Zoro tomorrow. Tonight, it was just him and Julie, and he would make the most of it.

Chapter Eleven

Denny's enquiries into the Jade Gate began with some casual-sounding phone calls to some of her former business associates and board-members, pretending boredom. She knew that a lot of businessmen were at pains to maintain an appearance of respectability, but once the sun went down, many preferred the fleshpots of the city to a sedentary life at home with their wives.

Joseph Yeng was pleased to receive her call. One of her many admirers at 3M over the years, he had tried to seduce her on many occasions, and Denny had always let him down lightly. He was not unattractive, though his wife was a very good friend of hers. This was no barrier to Joseph, though he kept his flirting a secret from his wife, and so did Denny.

"Ahh, my dear Denny. To what do I owe the pleasure of hearing your sweet voice once again?" he began, charming as always.

"I take it Yeti is out?" Denny chuckled, knowing Joseph would not be so bold if his wife was in earshot.

"Ahhh, but you know me too well." Joseph chuckled. "Come now, tell me, is it Yeti you wish to speak to, or to me?" he said hopefully.

"Oh, to you, you flatterer." Denny chuckled, and heard Joseph too laugh at the other end of the phone. "You forgot my birthday, and I rang you up to chide you about it."

"I did? How ill-mannered of me, my dear. Yeti normally remembers such things." Yeti did indeed, and already had, but Denny knew such mundane events were above Joseph, who was still involved on the Board of 3M.

"Never mind, I've decided to forgive you. You can make it up to me by taking me to dinner, and then out on the town."

"This evening? Ahhh, no, it is Yeti's bridge night with her friends. Tomorrow night would be better. I'll tell her I'm working late at the office."

"Do you do that often, Joseph? Yeti is not a forgiving woman, I know."

"Yeti has her regime, and I have mine," he replied. "I like my nightlife a lot more than she does, as you know. I thought you were the same?"

"I've decided I might as well grow old disgracefully, rather than wither away. After dinner, you can show me some of the fleshpots you normally go to with the other Board members. What was the name of that place in Jelan Kendal again?"

"The Jade Gate? Yes, still a popular place. A good floorshow, and the girls are second to none," Joseph laughed.

"I no longer have a reputation to worry about, Joseph. It's different for us women than for you men. It's almost expected of you, but you'd frown upon Yeti staying out all night, wouldn't you."

"Alright, yes, double-standards as you say. But it is a Man's World, my dear, and we are allowed to make our own rules," he chuckled.

"Only for as long as we let you," Denny retorted, giggling. "Tomorrow night at eight, then. Our little secret. I won't tell Yeti if you won't," she promised, and heard a chuckle from Joseph.

"Eight it is, then. I'll pick you up, and then we can try that new restaurant on Blok M, the Bamboo Garden I think they call it."

"It's a date, then," Denny agreed.

*　　*　　*

Laura's head was swimming. Naked limbs intermingled as they rolled around entangled in the silk sheets. Hot flesh was pressed against her own. Those sharp teeth were nipping at her neck again, and she cried out softly as Angelica's hot mouth fastened down, sucking her blood. The rush was fantastic, then, when she'd taken her fill, Angelica used a nail to cut into her own neck, drawing blood, and pressing Laura's mouth against her own wound.

"Your turn to drink now, Laura. Just a few sips, till you get a taste for the stuff," she laughed, and Laura found herself drawing on Angelica's neck, the hot coppery taste in her mouth, as Angelica moaned softly in triumph and pleasure . . .

Gasping, Laura found she did not want to relinquish her hold on Angelica's neck, and struggled as the more powerful hands pulled her bloody mouth free. She could already feel the blood being absorbed into her own system, setting it afire in a way similar to that which Gabriel's own blood had done, the first time she had drank it.

"Now, I've got something else for you to suck on, Laura," Angelica chuckled, forcing Laura's head down, towards the hairy groin. Her soft belly was tattooed with the tail of a snake, the body of which disappeared into her dark pubic hair, and then the body reappeared, tattooed along the length of the small but stiff penis, transforming it into a fleshy colourful snake. The bright colours amazed her, and she opened her mouth in awe, when Angelica's hand on the back of her head forced it down, and Laura suddenly found her mouth filled with the fleshy shaft, and as Angelica's strong hands held her head there, she began to suck obediently, and Angelica moaned softly with pleasure. "I'm going to make this last as long as I can Laura," Angelica moaned, enjoying the fellatio. "The passing on of the Dark Gift, as they call it, is special, and not done lightly. When you're ready, and when you're thirsty enough, I'm going to leave you alone with your lovely daughter again. I'm sure you'll both enjoy that reunion. The urge can be resisted, once you're used to it. But you'll be new to it, Laura, and you'll be ever so hungry," she laughed.

Chapter Twelve

Angelo Zoro stood up as Turnbull was shown into his office, and he came around a messy desk to shake hands with him. "Mr Turnbull, I've heard a lot of positive things about you," he smiled, warmly, in greeting, as he shook the offered hand firmly.

"Just call me Nick, please," Turnbull didn't like formalities. "I assume we'll be working closely together?"

"Then Angelo will do fine for me, and yes, I could use a little help here. You're Special Forces, too, I believe?" he asked. Nick nodded, though didn't elaborate further. "Experience with Al Qaeda in Italy, and also with this man Gabriel?" Nick shrugged.

"All dead, now. Past history. We did a clean sweep in Italy," he lied. Angelo smiled.

"Maybe not, if my contacts are to be believed. I have word this Gabriel is on his way here to Jakarta," he revealed. Nick continued to play dumb, trying to allay the man's suspicions.

"I think your contact is mistaken," he said, straight-faced.

"Tell me what you know about the man," Angelo asked.

"Not much to tell. I've met him only briefly. Former ties with the Regiment, and then he got mixed up with ETA for personal reasons for a time. Dropped out of circulation until he offered assistance against Al Qaeda when they moved into Italy. There was a big shoot-out, and he got caught up in an explosion when we took out the terrorist cell." At least, that was the official version.

"Did you see the body?" Angelo asked, studying him. Nick paused before answering, not wanting to be caught out in a lie.

"No. I was wounded in the takedown, and I left the cleanup to the Eyeties." Nick was becoming more aware of something behind the man's words, some sort of special interest, though he couldn't put his finger on it as yet. "What have you heard?" he decided to ask.

"Gabriel turns up in Italy, supposedly acting against Al Qaeda. We have an Al Qaeda problem here, too, in Indonesia, and I hear on the grapevine that this man is headed here also. What would you make of that, Nick?"

"Assuming he is still alive, what reason would he have for coming? He was once a wanted terrorist, then he dropped out of sight for years. He shows up to help us, maybe to make up for past sins, and then 'apparently' gets killed for his trouble. If he's alive, why show his face again? If it were me, I'd let Al Qaeda look after itself."

"Perhaps he has an axe to grind with that particular organization, or perhaps it was all a ploy to make contact with them, and resume his terrorist activities?" Angelo suggested.

"I met the man. Believe me, he's no terrorist. Whatever he did in the past, I'm sure it was for good reasons. Ones we'll probably never know. But don't go slagging him off without proof."

"I think we touched a nerve there, didn't we, Nick?" Angelo smiled. "You liked him, didn't you?" he accused.

"I guess you could say so. He was straight with me, and dependable during the operation. When you work with someone on an operation of that sort, you find out a lot about them."

"Perhaps not everything, Nick. The file your boss sent me is quite extensive, though hard to fathom in places. He seems to be still rather sprightly considering his age, and yet the photo used in the Porton Down I.D. doesn't make him appear to be that old." Nick didn't respond as Angelo leafed through the file. "Gabriel aside, I've been trying to track down these insurgents for the last couple of months, working undercover on the streets. They're coming into the country from the Malaysian Peninsula somehow, probably using fake IDs. We've tightened up our searches of shipping, but they're still getting in. It's been hard to keep track of people since the tsunami. A lot of the people we pick up are using assumed identities of people who were drowned. How did they infiltrate Italy?" he asked.

"Posing as tourists for the most part. They're well-backed with oil money, and can afford good fake papers. They came in bold as brass, from what I could make out, and used different entrance points. They met up at two locales, from what we gathered. Their plan was good, and would probably have worked if we hadn't had a Mossad mole, and help from Gabriel."

"We can't expect any help here from Mossad. As for your friend Gabriel, I have my own reasons for wanting to meet him, and he is still technically a wanted man," he reminded Nick.

"You still keep warrants out for dead men?" Nick tried to make a joke of it, but the younger man wasn't buying it.

"You don't believe he's dead any more than I do, Turnbull. Do you?" Nick bit his lip. "Come on downstairs to the firing range, and we'll get you kitted out. Something small and compact, I think. You'll be helping me on the street tomorrow, so don't bother shaving tonight. The scruffy look is in this year." Nick followed the man out of the office. Mr Zoro, well-intentioned though he was, was going to be a problem!

The rest of the morning followed pretty much as Nick expected. Going through case-files, and photo-fits of likely candidates, including some spotted by Angelo himself while working the streets. He didn't like to think of himself as racist, but they all did look alike. Perhaps it was the uniform manner of dress or facial hair, but it was harder to differentiate between individuals of foreign races.

Once you got to know them, or study them, then the distinctions would make themselves known, but photographs alone weren't much help. You looked for mannerisms, the way they walked, all unique signatures which you couldn't spot from photographs.

Tomorrow he would accompany Angelo out onto the streets of Jakarta, suitably scruffy as Angelo had suggested. If he dressed like a tourist, he'd get fastened onto by all the beggars and urchins, and he'd never get away.

As Angelo gave him a lift back to his hotel, Nick began to steer the conversation. "My girlfriend is mad keen to go out and do some shopping. She promised her Dad she'd bring him something back. I don't have any family myself. How about you?"

"Just my mother," Angelo admitted. "I never knew my father."

"What's your Mum's name?" Nick asked, nonchalantly.

"Denny," Angelo revealed, and Nick realized he'd struck pay-dirt, though his attitude didn't show any change.

"Nice name, but a bit unusual for a woman, isn't it? Denny is a bloke's name back where I come from."

"Nevy Denny Zoro, but she's always used just Denny. I suppose it's the same in your country, where your parents give you a choice of names, and you just use the one you like the most?" Nick chuckled.

"Yeah, I suppose you're right. I've just been stuck with Nickelarse, ever since I was a kid. Had the mickey taken out of me God knows how many times." Just at that second, Angelo turned his face away, checking for traffic, as he pulled out of a side-street, and the light caught him just right. There wasn't too much of a resemblance when you looked the guy straight in the face, but a half-profile caught the same bone structure. Unless he was wrong, Angelo Zoro was Gabriel Jnr.

Nick called in at the Embassy to contact Maddox, not trusting communications from the Security Building in case the Indonesians were monitoring calls and e-mails. He drafted a veiled e-mail about his impressions so far. 'Introductions made. Contact 'relatively' interested in Lazarus. Looks the bulldog type. Any further intel, or advice on how to play him? He's no mug. Will accompany our friend on surveillance tomorrow, and get a first look at the potential location. Tomorrow night, I may pay the place a visit, in an unofficial capacity, but you'd best back me up with Julie, in case she gets wind.' That would have to do for now. Julie would have been lounging by the pool and getting adjusted to the local time. He had promised to take her out and show her a few of the local sites around Blok M, though he might be better off organizing a proper tour-guide to take her out and about during the day, if he was going to be busy with Angelo Zoro. Not telling how soon, or even if, he could get a handle on the two missing women. He knew them by sight, and so would recognize them, but they might not even be there. No way of telling till he got into the place.

*   *   *

Dinner had gone well. The Bamboo Garden was a neat outdoor restaurant, on the fifth floor terrace of one of the hotels. It looked out over the city, and the noise from the streets drifted up, occasionally interrupting the piped music. The balcony was small and exclusive, yet all the tables were occupied.

Truth to tell, it was good to see Joseph again, and the expected hand on her knee was removed without protest, easily enough. Though it was repeated throughout the evening, and she insisted he *keep* removing it. Joseph didn't give up easily, and his attentions were as flattering as ever.

Fifty-seven years old, Joseph was still as spry as a forty-year-old. Middle age hadn't been traumatic for him. A slight paunch, and a few more notches on his belt, were the only signs that he was no longer as young or as fit as he used to be, but gossip had it he was still as active sexually as he had ever been, though not with his wife.

Denny's request to visit some of the raunchier fleshpots of Jelan Kendal hadn't really come as too much of a surprise, for just as many women went there as men. All ages, all nationalities, the Jade Gate was a melting pot, and anything was permitted beneath its roof. Whores from all over the world plied their trade there. The Management provided quite a variety, and customers, if they didn't like what was on offer, often paired off with each other. There had been lots of rumours about Denny while she had been on the Board, though none could be substantiated, as none of the other male members had ever admitted sleeping with her. Rumours were easily spread by jealous people. Joseph had always been discreet in his affairs, but Denny had always eluded him. Even now, as he sat here with her, with her thigh pressed up against his own, he wasn't sure how the evening would pan out. She was too complex a woman to try and second-guess.

Joseph took Denny's hand as she alighted from the taxi. He would have preferred to use his own car, but parking was a problem in this part of the city. Roads too narrow, and not many safe places to leave a car. Taxis were more convenient. Almost 11.20pm, and the Jade Gate was just coming to life. Strident music could be heard out here on the street, and the two big bouncers nodded in recognition as Joseph escorted Denny inside, where she suddenly stopped as the narcotic incense assaulted her nostrils. Not unpleasant, just strangely intoxicating. Joseph took her coat, and handed it in at the cloakroom, accepting a ticket in return.

Subdued light illuminated only what was necessary, and most of the secluded booths remained in darkness, unless their occupants, turned up the wick on their own table-lamps. All the booths were in good sight of the glass booths, where some of the establishment's girls paraded themselves when not with a client.

The clients' needs were paramount, and it was entirely up to him or her what they did with the girls. They could fuck them, in any number of delightful ways, or they could simply pass the evening away with dinner, drinks, conversation. They were given a time-stamped ticket, and the cost was calculated when the girl was returned. The management dealt quite severely with anyone who attempted to abuse the system. Abuse of the girls was permitted, provided there were no lasting marks. The girls became the clients' property for as long as they held those tickets.

Joseph nodded to Madame Eve, as she chatted to other clients at the bar. They called her the Dragon Lady, because of her penchant for those long elegant cheongsams, with the dragon motifs, that she liked to wear. Also because of her temper.

He had once had occasion to witness her disciplining one of the girls, who had refused to carry out the wishes of her client. It had started as a vocal argument, and then the girl had grabbed a bottle off the bar, smashed it open, and lunged for the Madame with the jagged edge. Obviously well-trained in the martial arts, Eve had disarmed her easily, effortlessly, and then proceeded to give her a thorough beating, where everyone could watch. She broke no limbs, and the girl's bruises disappeared after a couple of weeks, but the girl never again rebelled.

Denny had never been into an establishment like this. It was a strange new world, and so far was living up to her own expectations. Not like one of the cheap brothels, this place was more cosmopolitan, and much more high-class.

She cruised down the line of glass-fronted booths, that allowed the customers to see in, and she studied the girls within, all of them beautiful in their own way. Each of them different from the next. Asian and Caucasian, dark and light-skinned, blondes, brunettes.

There were many Russian and Kazakh women here, if the names on the glass were anything to go by. Westerners were rare, but not unknown. Denny studied their faces, the way they held themselves. They posed, they preened, knowing they were being watched. Their faces told one story of availability, and desire, but as Denny looked deeper, in some eyes she detected resignation, and even despair in others. Some knew their place as cattle, as commodities.

Joseph pressed a glass into her hand, and himself up against her. "See anything you fancy, my dear?" he joked. Denny smiled back at him as she raised the glass to her lips.

"It's all so strange to me, Joseph. All these girls, paraded like cattle."

"It depends on our viewpoint, Denny. None are here against their will. They sell themselves willingly, and everyone makes a profit out of the arrangement. Management even provides healthcare for the girls. No lasting harm is allowed to come to them, and they suffer no more abuse than they might receive at the hands of a harsh husband, but here, they generally get treated far better."

"And anything goes?" she asked. Joseph laughed at her naivety.

"But of course. We leave the world's rule-book at the door. In here we can be free, or relatively so. We don't invite monsters in here. Some disturbed people exist in all societies, but here they can indulge their foibles, within reason. Men with women, women with women, men with men, and that's just the tip of the iceberg. Anything can be arranged for a price," Joseph explained.

"Will you hire a girl for me?" Denny asked, shocking him into silence for a few moments.

"My dear, that wasn't quite what I had in mind for this evening, but if it is your pleasure, then yes, I will indulge you. Has anyone caught your eye?" he enquired.

"That one, there." She pointed to the glass booth which held the nameplate "Belle". Inside, a sultry sulking raven haired beauty sat on a small bed, reading a book. She deliberately did not look towards the glass, though she must have known that she was being observed. Well made-up, and wearing a wine-coloured evening dress, she looked all set for a night out. The steel choker around her neck looked slightly out of place with the rest of her ensemble.

Joseph admired Denny's choice. A new addition to the Madame's stable. Caucasians were not his personal taste, though many of his friends found them delightful. He nodded, and went away to negotiate with the Main Desk.

Denny stared in through the glass. This had to be one of the two women, though there seemed no sign of the blonde, Laura. She had other friends than Joseph, some of them moved in different circles, and they could be counted on to help Denny extricate two women from this place. But first she needed to talk, and introduce herself, and make plans. The two women must be ready when the time came.

Looking more closely at the woman, a sudden chill came over Denny. There was something about her. As she raised her head and moved it slightly to one side, the profile reminded her of her own son Angelo. The more she looked and studied, the more similarities she found. The skin tone, the raven hair.

Gabriel had told her little except a description and names of the two women who had been kidnapped. *Oh my God, what I am getting into?* she thought to herself. The girl was Gabriel's daughter! There couldn't be any mistake. A half-sister to Angelo. And if Belle were his daughter, then what was Laura to Gabriel? Could she go through with this?

She jumped suddenly, startled, as Joseph returned and lightly took her arm. "Come, we need to go into the rear of the establishment," and he led Denny back to where a beaded curtain sparkled and parted to reveal a narrow corridor which led to the rear of those glass-panelled booths. Further, a staircase led to the upper floors, where a variety of bedrooms awaited selection by the clients.

Joseph handed the ticket to the small old woman who looked like a cross-gendered sumo-wrestler, who had overdone his makeup. She stood just over five feet tall, and bulged out of the seams of her dress. Her eyes widened slightly when she took note of the number of the ticket, and she disappeared momentarily, before reappearing with an electric cattle-prod.

Denny and Joseph were told to wait, and the woman disappeared down the corridor. She came back shortly, pushing Belle before her. The old woman stayed well behind Belle, cattle-prod at the ready. Belle stopped, suddenly, observing the man and woman in front of her. "A tag-team?" she queried, and then shrugged. "Which room?" she asked.

"Numbah fourteen," the old woman told her, and Belle reluctantly began to climb the staircase. Joseph kissed the back of Denny's hand politely, and allowed her to follow Belle up the stairs.

Belle turned the handle of the door, and opened it. She stepped inside, noticing, as she looked back, that the man had remained downstairs, and only the petite older woman had followed her up. She left the door open as she walked over to the bed. She heard the door close behind her, as the woman followed her inside.

"What's it to be?" Belle asked.

"What do you mean?" Denny asked.

"I'm yours for the night. I'll do whatever you want. So what do you want?" she asked, simply, resigned to her situation.

"I just want to talk," Denny blurted out, unsure as to how to begin this conversation.

"Makes a change," Belle shrugged. "Usually they fuck first, and then want to talk. It's your money," she stated. Belle was aware the woman was staring at her, but it wasn't a sexual stare. She had known the attentions of lesbians in the past, but this woman wasn't behaving like one.

"You're his daughter, aren't you?" Denny suddenly blurted out, frightened of the expected answer, yet she had to know. Instantly alarmed, Belle regarded the woman in a new light.

"Is this some kind of trick?" she began looking around the room, for the possibility of hidden cameras or microphones. "Did Angelica put you up to this?" she asked.

"I don't know any Angelica. But I did know Gabriel, a long time ago," she admitted. Belle saw tears begin to well up in Denny's eyes, and then her hand clutched her chest, and her legs gave out from under her.

She fainted dead away, and Belle rushed to catch her, just managing to cradle her head as the rest of her body hit the floor. She lifted Denny's small and light body easily onto the bed, and went over to the small sink to run some water. She took some tissues and dampened them, before using them to mop Denny's forehead, till she slowly came round again. Denny had always had a weak heart, and any emotional stress sometimes caused her to have fainting spells.

"Are you okay, now?" Belle asked, moving back to let Denny sit up.

"Yes, thank you. I'm sorry. This is a shock to me."

"You said you knew my father. Is he here?" Belle asked.

"No, but he's on his way. I haven't seen him in over thirty years. Yet I recognized his voice on the phone instantly. He asked me to try and find you and Laura."

"My mother, have you seen her? They're keeping us apart. I only see her at mealtimes. I think she's being drugged. I get less sense out of her every time I see her." Belle began to explain, but then paused at the pained expression that came over Denny's face.

Her worst suspicions had proved true. Gabriel's wife and daughter. She reached out a hand to the metal-braid collar around Belle's neck, as if noticing it for the first time, and Belle explained.

"The collar contains an explosive charge. One of us misbehaves, and the other one has her head blown off." Denny raised Belle's long dark hair, examining the collar, and the small lump of metal at the rear of the collar.

"I could pick this easily enough with a lock-pick," she said.

"So could I, but I don't have one. If I try and force it, it blows." Denny was nodding to herself.

"I can come back tomorrow with lock-picks. We need to get you both out of here. Can you talk to your Mother and explain things to her? It has to be both together. If I just break you out, then that means the other will suffer for it."

"I'll try and talk to her at breakfast. Get this collar off, and I'll shove that cattle-prod up the old woman's arse," she promised. "They don't keep any hard weapons inside the club from what I can see, and if we can get the other collar off Laura before anyone knows there's any trouble, then we can handle ourselves. I owe that bitch Angelica. What she's put me through this last week has been bad enough, but God knows what she's doing to my mother."

"How did you get caught up in all this?" Denny asked, curious. Belle shrugged.

"Wrong place at the wrong time, I guess. Some people didn't like us making enquiries about how they did their business. Some sort of smuggling ring was all we thought at first, and then it turns out they're into white slavery, and an old 'friend' of mine is behind it. They call her the Dragon-Lady here. We knew each other a long time ago. She killed a friend of mine. We're not exactly bosom-buddies. She must have ordered our abduction when my name was mentioned to her in Oman. Now she's had me fucking for my supper, ever since I've been here. With this collar around my neck, I can't cause too much trouble. My mother is being forced to wear one too, and I've hardly seen her since we arrived. All I can do is bide my time, and wait for an opportunity. I knew Dad would track us down. It was only a matter of time," she said, with a hint of pride, which Denny recognized in her eyes.

"Yes, he would," she admitted, sadly.

"In the meantime, Angelica has been keeping her distance for some reason. I'd have thought she'd be keen to rub my nose in my own degradation. That's her bag. But she's keeping away from me. It's not like her. She must be planning something really nasty for me."

*   *   *

Julie wasn't too keen on Nick not shaving, though kept the complaints to a minimum, as she understood the reasons for it. He restricted the evening's tour to strictly bona-fide tourist traps, and deliberately didn't take her to a few of the other nightspots he had visited on his earlier trip to Jakarta a few years back. Need to know, and all that.

After the meal, as they finished off the wine, Nick brought up the subject of tomorrow evening. "I may have to go out later. Something I have to do, and I can't do it while young Angelo is tagging along. He's taking an unnatural interest in our mutual friend, and he makes me nervous," he admitted.

"I've never met our 'mutual' friend, but if he was a mate of Dad's he can't be as bad as some people think. You're not a bad judge of character, either, Nick Turnbull, and you've obviously taken a liking to him," she pointed out. Nick smiled.

"He's likeable enough," he admitted. "We even look about the same age, but I believe he has a few years' more experience than I do," he went on, not wanting to reveal his and Maddox's suspicions. Gabriel's perpetually young appearance had never been explained by him. "I don't know all the answers about him, but I'd trust the guy with my life, just like your Dad did. When you go on these type of ops, you become a good judge of character very quickly. I met his wife and daughter, too, and if they're here, I'll find them. In the meantime, I need to know just what our Mr Zoro intends. He doesn't believe the official line of Gabriel dying in Italy. Someone's tipped him off, and I wish I knew who. He could be walking into a trap by the Indonesian Authorities if he's not careful."

"Can't you or Dad warn him?" Julie asked, reaching out and taking his hand.

"I'm not in contact with him. Your Dad can only reach him by e-mail, and there's something about all this he's not telling me. Wish I knew what it was, and why not. I don't like playing games in the dark. Well, not these kind anyway," he chuckled, squeezing Julie's hand. "I gather Gabriel is in transit, and it's up to me to sort this mess out before he gets here. Hope I'm up to the job. I don't like leaving you on your own so much, but it's a job, not a vacation, really, though I'll try and spend as much time as I can with you," he promised, apologetically.

"I understand. It's not just a mission either, if you're personally involved with these people. You wouldn't be doing it if you didn't consider them friends, and friends look out for friends where they can. You're up to it, Nick Turnbull. No worries on that score. Just be careful, won't you?" Nick smiled again, and squeezed her hand once more. "It's been a nice night, but I can't wait to get back to the hotel," she admitted.

"Oh, can't you?" he chuckled.

Chapter Thirteen

The streets of Jakarta heaved with an undulating sea of bodies, amid a veritable cacophony of sound. The tide of human flesh ebbed and swelled, miraculously avoiding contact with the individual entities which made it up. Thousands of people always seemed to be out on the streets during the day, all jabbering away. Nick tried to turn it into background noise, but it was difficult, and Angelo spoke in soft tones as they walked side by side towards the area where he had last seen those suspicious contacts.

"I have men stationed on a few street-corners around the area. Nothing too overt. Today, I am wired, and in contact with them. If anything comes off, follow my lead. You memorized the faces?" he asked. Nick nodded. "Good, if you see them before me, let me know. I assume you've done this sort of thing before?"

"A few times, yeah. Just box-work," he intimated.

"Too many people here for that simple an operation, I'm afraid. Perimeter back-up is all we can hope for. If anything goes down, it'll go down fast, and we won't have time to organize much in the way of support."

"I'm up for it, don't worry," Nick reassured him. Truth to tell, Nick probably had more experience in this sort of thing than did Angelo, but it wouldn't do to undermine his authority, and this was Angelo's home-turf, so to speak. Let him take the lead, if he wanted.

For the rest of the morning, Angelo reprised his role as a street-dealer, and Nick took on the role of his minder. He dealt small amounts of drugs to a few dozen punters, some regular, some new. It was just ordinary day to day petty crime on these streets. They took lunch at one of the street-side stalls, and Nick was persuaded to try the Cows' Brain Soup, which he did reluctantly, enjoying it till the large bluebottle floated to the surface after he had consumed half the bowl.

Nick suddenly lost his appetite. He managed to keep down what he had swallowed, though left the rest, amidst Angelo's laughter.

Later in the afternoon, Angelo dug him in the ribs, and he followed the man's eyes to a figure hurrying along the crowded street. Nick instantly crossed the road, keeping both him and Angelo in sight, as Angelo let the man go past him, and then followed slowly, at a distance. There were plenty of other bodies about on the streets to hide behind, but the mass of them made it difficult to keep the man in sight, and still follow him discreetly. Angelo was speaking into his throat-mike, alerting the other members of his team.

Angelo was directing his team, trying to keep them ahead of the man, trying to predict his movements, and then correcting directions as his quarry changed his route. He was leading them out away from the centre of the Blok, to more secluded streets. Secluded here meant not actually rubbing shoulders continually with the rest of humanity, so it was still not a problem to follow him discreetly. A second man caught Nick's eye, now paralleling the route of the first, and Nick flashed a glance across at Angelo, to make sure he had seen him, too. Angelo nodded in confirmation, passing on the news into his throat mike.

There were other people walking in the same direction, some with the same sense of cautious energy, but no telling if they were connected or not. Angelo had only gotten the two descriptions during his previous attempts at surveillance.

As the two men converged, and paused to talk to each other, Nick kept walking, going past them, trying to catch the snippets of conversation, but the dialect escaped him.

He continued down the street, before pausing momentarily to stoop to tie his shoelace and risk a glimpse behind him, where he found the two men walking towards him once more. He let them pass him, noting Angelo's position.

Eventually, the pair led him and Angelo to a town-house, and Nick watched as the two men were allowed entrance through a door into a white-walled compound. There were no upper floors visible, and so he had no idea what or who was beyond that wall. He crossed the road to Angelo, and they both continued walking as Angelo spoke into his throat microphone, seemingly pleased with the way the operation had gone.

"Now we have an address, which was more than we had yesterday. We can get proper surveillance set up on it, and anyone who comes and goes."

"Well, nothing doing immediately then, so I'll leave you to it. I promised the girlfriend I'd take her shopping, so I'll get back to the hotel. I'll check back in with you tomorrow morning, and review the results of any observations," he promised.

"Okay, enjoy your day," Angelo thanked him, continuing to talk down his throat-mike, as he co-ordinated operations. Nick reversed direction, and headed back towards the centre, where he was more likely to catch a cab.

Chapter Fourteen

O f course, Nick didn't take the taxi back to the hotel, but directed it towards Jelan Kendal, correcting the driver with a clip on the ear as he tried it on, and deliberately started driving in the wrong direction, as though he thought Nick was a tourist who didn't know his way about Jakarta too well. Nick hadn't been here recently, but Jelan Kendal was still in the same place, and he knew the way.

He got the driver to drop him off, and completed his journey on foot, taking his time and making use of available cover, though the Jade Gate looked dead during the day. He walked the street slowly, taking out his pocket camera and taking the odd snap, as though he were a tourist off the beaten track. He got a couple of shots of the place, as he noted what security features he could see from the main street. Then he did a reverse at the end, and went to see how close he could get behind the buildings. There was a closed-off alleyway, walled by corrugated tin, but he could hear a low growling dog behind it. "Nice doggie . . . ."

The best way in was going to be as a paying customer. Getting out would be on a wing and a prayer, depending on what he found. He hoped Julie was in an understanding mood. He might be able to keep his promise of a shopping trip in what was left of the day, which hadn't been a total lie to Angelo. Nick headed back out onto the main street again, in search of a taxi.

*　　*　　*

Belle was roused from her slumbers by the fat bitch of a Madame. They let the girls sleep through the morning, to get over the exertions of the late nights, and they set them to work cleaning the place up during the afternoon, using them as slave and drudge as well as whores. She followed the rest of the girls into the kitchen, where a long table was laid out for them. She saw Laura already seated, and eating her food listlessly, just playing with it, really, and Belle moved to sit down next to her.

"Listen to me," she began, in hushed tones, "Dad may have sent someone to help us." There was no reaction from Laura. She simply continued to use her spoon to move the soup around in her bowl. "Are you listening to me?" Belle nudged her. Laura turned to her, and Belle was shocked to see the vacant expression in her mother's face. "My God, what has she been doing to you? You look so pale."

"What?" Laura asked, as though she didn't understand the question. Belle reached out a hand, moving aside Laura's blonde hair, studying her neck, and then gasping as she noticed the small trickle of blood which the braided metal collar couldn't quite conceal. Her fingers moved it aside, and the puncture marks could be seen quite clearly. Angelica had been feeding on her. No wonder she looked so pale.

"Mother, can you understand me?" Belle asked, once more, but Laura had lost interest in the conversation, and had returned her attention to stirring her soup around the bowl once again. "We've got to get you out of here before it's too late," she promised her.

That was why her mother hadn't been put in one of the booths. Angelica had been keeping her for herself. Belle had no real idea what had been done to her mother, but it wasn't good. She hoped it wasn't fatal, but the first thing to do was to get her away from the 'thing' that was feeding on her.

She hoped that woman Denny kept her promise and came back with those lock-picks. They needed the collars off, before attempting to break out of here.

*   *   *

That evening, Belle was placed in her customary booth, all dolled up as the clientele liked to see the women (all the better to undress you, my dear). She paid little attention to the thick plexi-glass, or the punters' faces leering in through it. She could blot the sex-acts out of her mind, like she had done with old man Cannucci, though she admitted to getting two half-decent fucks out of a couple of the clients in her short time here. The rest weren't so memorable.

*   *   *

Nick Turnbull was one of the punters currently peering in at her, but she showed no signs of paying any attention. He was reluctant to rap on the glass to draw her attention, in case anyone else noticed, or saw the recognition that would undoubtedly dawn on her. He moved around the lower floor, inspecting all the other girls, but there was no sign of her mother/sister. Nick had had his doubts about their relationship. They looked too close in age to be mother and daughter. Perhaps Laura was already at 'work' upstairs with a customer.

He had already seen how things were conducted. The fat Madame over in the corner was selling the tickets, and you paid by the hour when you returned the ticket. It was the simplest way to see her, and so he went over and suffered her pidgin English (better than his Indonesian, he reluctantly admitted) and indicating which girl he wanted.

"Five thousan rupiah an hour. You pay latter. Okay?"

"Yeah, okay. Fine." He took the ticket, and she led him behind the row of cubicles, through a glass bead curtain, to a corridor which ran behind the small rooms.

"She new girl. Not know all rules. Any trouble, you yell. I fix. Okay?"

"I get the picture, yes. I should be able to handle her by myself. No problem," he smiled, as though cocksure of himself. Perhaps that wasn't the best metaphor under the circumstances, but he tried to put on an air of bravado as the Madame unlocked the rear door to Belle's booth. She opened it, beckoning the girl out. "You got customer. Come now," she beckoned, and Nick turned away as Belle came out of the door.

"Which room?" she asked, surly, as she brushed past the fat bitch, careful to keep on the good side of the electric cattle-prod she carried.

"Numbah six is free. Go earn some money for me, Pretty-Pretty." Her smile revealed yellowed teeth. If looks could kill, she'd have dropped on the spot. Belle did not like the woman. Saying nothing, she brushed past the punter, and started up the staircase. She heard his footsteps behind her. He was probably looking at her ass, but nothing she could do about it. The sooner he came, the sooner she could get back to her book, or another customer.

At the top of the stairs, she turned left, and walked down a long corridor. Nick had seen from outside that the building was much longer than the frontage indicated. She tried the handle of room number six, and it opened as she went inside. She was already reaching behind her to unzip her dress when Nick walked into the room, and slowly closed the door behind him.

He gave the room a quick scan, though couldn't see anything apparent. As Belle let the dress fall, he went up behind her, and slowly lowered his head appearing to kiss the nape of her neck, but actually whispering in her ear. "Is the room bugged?" Belle stiffened as his hands touched her shoulders, gently. That wasn't the usual sort of talk she got from the clientele.

Slowly, she turned around, doing her best to hide her surprise as she recognized the SAS man from the operation in Italy. "Not in this room," she replied, in hushed tones, after a few seconds. "As far as I know, only Room Eight is set up for surveillance and blackmail tapes. You're a long way from home, Nick isn't it?" Nick nodded, picking up her dress and handing it back to her. Belle shrugged, and hung the dress over the back of a chair as she sat on the bed, and drew a sheet around her. "If we get interrupted, it's better if the dress is off. So tell me, Nick, what's going on? Is my Dad here?"

"He's on his way. I managed to get here ahead of him, to give him back-up. He had a bit of trouble getting out of Oman, so I hear. Though another day or two, and he'll be here, I reckon."

"Forgive me, but the sooner I get out of this knocking shop the better."

"If you know where your mother is, let's go now. I came armed," he explained, pulling the gun out from beneath the rear of his jacket. "I don't think anyone will object too much once I go waving this around."

"You'd be surprised. This isn't just a brothel. It's a front for a smuggling operation, people as well as commodities. They have armed guards throughout the place. We attracted too much of attention to ourselves in Oman, and next thing we knew we were on our way here. An old acquaintance of mine seems to be running things, and she wanted to renew our 'friendship'."

"Not one of your fan-club, then?" he chuckled.

"Not exactly, no. She's a psycho bitch from Hell. Also, she's a vampire," she said, matter of factedly, though Nick scoffed. "No, seriously, she is."

"Give over, luv. She might be a blood drinking Goth, but vampires don't exist," he scoffed.

"She's got my mother somewhere. She's feeding on her. I saw her only today. She looks terrible. Whether you believe me or not, you've got to find her for me. I can't leave without her."

"I think we should just waltz out of here right now, and force that fat old tart at gunpoint to tell us where Laura is," he explained simply. Belle pointed to the collar around her neck.

"This isn't here for decoration. There's an ounce of semtex attached, and another one around Laura's neck. If the right button is pressed, a signal gets sent, and one or the other goes boom. We need to get the collars off, or both get out of range at the same time." Nick came forward to examine the collar.

"I'd need tools, but shouldn't be difficult," he admitted.

"I've already organized tools," Belle revealed. "Another friend of Dad's turned up last night, and she's bringing some lock-picks as soon as she can organize some, maybe tonight, maybe tomorrow."

"This 'she' you're referring to, wouldn't be a Denny Zoro would it?" he asked.

"Yes, did Dad tell you about her?"

"Via Maddox, yes, I suppose so. There's a few things you don't know about her. I gather he knew the woman from previous visits here. But I can't quite grasp just what's going on here, Belle. I gather the woman and your Dad knew each other quite well, but that would be a long time ago. As far as I know she's in her fifties. Allowing for the fact that your Dad was in the Regiment at the start of the Eighties, say in his twenties, he'd be around the same age as her, but we both know he isn't. He only looks a little older than me. We also have you and your "mother", who look too close in age to really be mother and daughter. You care to tell me what's going on, before I explain further? There is no Fountain of Youth that I know of, yet I can't think of a logical explanation," Nick admitted his puzzlement, and Belle deliberated before answering him.

"Your friend Maddox knows as little as he does for a reason. The more people who know how special my father and his bloodline are, the more dangerous it becomes for him. People who know, are at risk from people who want to know. Are you sure you're ready for that knowledge, Nick?" she asked.

"I'm the last one you should be asking that question to," Nick shrugged his shoulders. Belle seemed to deliberate for a few moments, and then loosened the sheet from around her body. Nick tried not to look, but he was a man, and she was a half-naked woman. He looked. Belle didn't mind. Lack of interest, to a beautiful woman such as herself was an insult.

"You say you don't believe in vampires, well that's understandable, but there's a lot of things go on in this world, that most people don't know or don't want to acknowledge. If something isn't public knowledge, it doesn't mean it's not true. Take me, for example," she smiled, sweetly, invitingly even. "How old would you say I was, Nick?" He was surprised at the question.

"It's never polite to talk about a woman's age. Usually gets me a slap," he joked. "I'll take a wild guess at 28-30?" he half-asked, quizzically.

"I was born in Mussolini's Italy, Nick. I'm old enough to be your Grandmother." Nick's mouth dropped.

"Come off it," he scoffed. Belle extended her leg, and reached down to press a nail into her thigh. As he watched, she drew the nail along the skin, pressing deeply enough to draw blood, and he was about to step in and grab her arm to stop her harming herself, when she raised the nail and brought it to her mouth, licking the blood off it.

"Looks like blood, doesn't it?" she asked, amusedly. "It's a very special kind of blood, and it's kept me and my family alive and in the best of health, for a lot longer than we could have expected. Take a good look, Nick," she used the sheet to wipe the surface blood off the recent wound, and Nick gawped as he saw the wound had already stopped bleeding. He could hardly see the puncture in her thigh. "In a few minutes, my leg will bear no trace of that wound."

"I saw something similar to that with your Dad in Italy. Freaked me out, then, too," Nick interrupted her momentarily, and then allowed her to continue.

"The blood flowing in my veins is courtesy of my Father, and that's why he's been hunted over the years. It can't be reproduced, but when ordinary humans ingest it, it can prolong their own lives. I don't know how to scientifically explain it, but somehow it's absorbed, and stimulates the body's regenerative systems, so that cells don't die out as rapidly, and it can promote healing as you've just seen. My mother got her long life from ingesting such blood, before I was born. The Church calls such the

Chosen, and they nickname the blood as Blood of Christ. I was born with it," she explained. "My Father has been around for a lot longer than people would think, and he's been hunted all his life for the secrets he's carrying in his veins. If we can exist, and I've just shown you evidence of that, then why not vampires? Once you take that One Step Beyond the barriers of the Known, you enter the realm of the Unknown, Nick. It's just different, there's no need to be afraid of where your mind is now taking you," she tried to reassure him, as his face revealed a plethora of emotions currently running through his body, as the ramifications of what he'd just seen and heard were sinking in. "The vampire I'm talking about is nothing supernatural, if anything she's a lot like me, although I hate to say it. She gets her power from blood, prolonging her own life, and she's been drinking the blood of a Chosen, so that must make her more powerful than normal, and believe me, she was a handful before that."

"That's quite a tale, Belle," Nick admitted, still unsure of what to believe, but there was no doubt that Belle believed it, and he knew of no reason why she would lie to him. "All tales of ghouls n goblins apart, we need to get you out of here. I need to find out where your mother is, and then we can work on breaking the both of you out of here."

"Together, or not at all. Just watch out for Angelica, Nick. She's a mean piece of work," Belle warned. "Her quarters are up on the third floor, but I've never been there. There's also a basement. They have holding cells for some of the new girls down there, and I gather that's where they keep the munitions, drugs and stuff they market. I don't know where my mother is being held."

"I'll find her, and once I do, I'll let you know. How we're going to synchronise things, though, I don't know. What have you got planned with Mrs Zoro?" he asked.

"Maybe tonight, maybe tomorrow, she's coming back with lock-picks so I can get this damn collar off. The same problem applies, though. I need to find out where my mother is being kept. I'd guess upstairs, if Angelica is feeding off her. She'd want her close."

"I'll take a look," he promised. "One other thing, did Mrs Zoro tell you anything about her relationship with your father?"

"Not a lot. But I guessed they were lovers at one time."

"They may have been a bit more than that. She has a son." Belle's mouth half-opened at the revelation. She had guessed the old woman wasn't telling her everything, but hadn't realized the possible implications at the time. "He looks more like you than your father, though. It took me a while to understand the resemblance, why he looked so familiar. His age is about right for the time Gabriel would have known the woman, but if he's like you, he could be older I suppose."

"I guess that's not that surprising, considering the amount of time my Dad's been alive, and the women he's probably had relationships with over the years. There may have been a number of half brothers and sisters through the years, but he certainly wasn't aware of any, at least that he's mentioned to me, or my mother, though it's not the sort of thing you'd bring up in conversation with a new partner or child," she smiled. "What is his name, my half-brother?"

"Angelo. Angelo Zoro. He's in Special Forces with the Indonesian Army, doing surveillance work on Al Qaeda with the police, and I'm supposedly over here to help him out. He's been making enquiries, and, I may be wrong, but I think he's showing an unnatural interest in your Dad, though obviously I haven't been able to ask any direct questions. Your Dad IS supposed to be dead, after all. Once he shows up here, if the authorities get a glimpse of him, all that hard work in Italy will have been for nothing. Maddox hasn't advised me of his arrival plans yet. I check in with him every night at the Embassy. Out of contact like he is, I can't warn him. He's playing his cards too close to his chest on this one."

"With good reason," she explained. "Solomon came after him the last time he was out here. Almost got him, too, from what he told me. They tracked him to Singapore, and he had to leave in a bit of a hurry. In the SAS, I'm sure you know what that's like? I've been trained too. Drop all contacts. Your first priority is your own life. Everything else is secondary to survival, unless there's a mission to accomplish. If you're compromised, and you can't complete your mission, you get the Hell out of Dodge. Dad's coming to the rescue, and he's putting his life on the line for me, and not for the first time," she admitted, proudly. "I appreciate your own help, too," she smiled, to avoid hurting Nick's feelings, but there was mischief behind the smile as well, and Nick couldn't help but smile along with her.

Was it his imagination, or was she letting the sheet slip just a little bit on purpose? He was all too aware that Belle was a very attractive woman, a half-naked very attractive woman, but there was something about her alleged age-difference that disturbed him. Grab a Granny nights he usually avoided back home, when he was growing up, and if she really *was* old enough to be his Granny, it didn't bear thinking about.

"You'd better get dressed," he suggested, and Belle did indeed pout. She was enjoying his discomfiture, he was sure. Women could sense things like that. She stood up and let the sheet drop, and Nick did his best not to gasp. The silk underwear didn't conceal as much as accentuate her charms. She reached for the dress, and began to step back into it. Nick helped her with the zipper. Her perfume was intoxicating this close. He hadn't noticed it before. If only he wasn't here with Julie. "I'll take you back downstairs. When I do, pick an argument with the fat cow to distract her, and I'll do some checking out upstairs." Belle nodded, and checked her hair in the mirror, mussing it up a little, and using the back of her hand to smudge her lipstick. She turned and quickly kissed Nick before he could object, and as he registered surprise, she admired the smudge of lipstick on his face,

"We're supposed to have been fucking," she laughed. "Maybe next time, Turnbull?" she smiled. "Do I shock you, Nick?" Belle asked, amusedly. "Let me give you a woman's perspective. Sex and lovemaking 101. Sex is physical, whilst lovemaking incorporates a mental intimacy as well as the physical. You can enjoy sex by yourself, with another partner, male, female or animal etc. It's still sex. It might not be the sex you want, and it might not be the most enjoyable, but you can still get some pleasure from it. Women are capable of sex, even when they don't desire it. A quick dollop of KY jelly and away you go. Sometimes it's easier to sleep through it," she joked. "A woman's lack of desire isn't always appreciated by some members of the opposite sex. It's not always possible to find someone to make love with, but a woman only has to smile at a man to get sex if she wants it." Nick regained his composure enough to open the bedroom door for her, and he let her go out first, pausing in the corridor to get a closer look at the place. "The stairs to the next floor are at either end of the corridor. You can go either way. Angelica's room could be anywhere up there. Likewise my mother's."

"I'll find her," he promised, and then he and Belle walked back along the corridor, passing another girl and her punter, before heading down the stairs. The fat Madame had a small booth just inside the beaded curtain, and along to one side were the toilets which the girls used, as opposed to the more public ones out front. A good enough excuse as long as Belle provided a distraction. Belle nodded. She was ready, and as they got to the foot of the stairs the older woman took the offered ticket from Nick as he asked "Where's the toilet, luv. I'm busting for a piss." He looked in discomfort, and turned away from the woman as she rose from her chair.

"Keep your hands to yourself, you fat bitch!" Belle cried out, shoving the woman, and as she turned to deal with her, Nick took his cue, and bounded back up the stairs two at a time, as softly as he could manage on the carpeted treads. He heard the discharge of the cattle prod below, and Belle's scream, and a loud stream of Italian expletives, as the woman must have connected, but he had no time to dwell on that. His absence would be noticed before too long.

He turned left at the head of the first stairs, making speed while there was no one about. On the top floor, he paused looking along the corridor. He could try the door-handles, but if they opened, there was no way of knowing what was on the other side. The safest way to handle this was to play peeping tom, and he dropped down to peer through the first keyhole as he listened intently for noise coming from inside the door. No one home in the first one. Someone's bedroom. The next three were the same. The fourth contained a small radio room, and someone was in there talking down the microphone. Nick couldn't understand the conversation. The next room was a small office, and looked empty. Chancing his arm, Nick found the door unlocked, and he opened it and slipped quietly inside.

There was an adjoining door to the Radio Room, but it was currently closed. The computer on the desk was switched on, and Nick quickly went to it, and began accessing files. He grabbed a floppy disk from the container on the desk, and began copying what he hoped were relevant files. It took him less than five minutes, but already he was sweating more than he would have been had he joined Belle in that bed. Pocketing the disk, he listened at the door, and then opened it to step out into the corridor once more.

More rooms followed. One of them contained a naked blonde on a bed. She was lying on her side, so Nick couldn't see her face. He tried the handle, and found it locked. Peering again through the keyhole, he saw the woman had turned at the slight noise. It was Laura. No doubt. She looked awful, like she hadn't slept in days. She too wore one of those braided metal collars. Time to go.

Nick backtracked to the stairs and was about to start down them when he heard someone coming up, and he backed away, quickly disappearing around the corner and heading for the other staircase. He didn't want to be seen. Quickly, he descended, passing no one on his way down to the first floor, but as he descended down to the ground floor, a stunning beauty in a black cheongsam passed him on the way up. She was no hooker, and from her looks, she matched the description of Angelica that Belle had given him.

Nick tried not to stare, but it was difficult. She was indeed beautiful, but there was something mesmerizing about her. She noticed his stare, and flashed him a brief smile in return. Nick's blood chilled instantly at the sight of those white teeth. He had noticed the slightly enlarged canines immediately, and for one horrible moment, he realized Belle hadn't just been winding him up.

He forced himself to turn his gaze away and continued down the stairs, to find the fat Madame haggling with another customer. His absence hadn't been noticed. He pretended to zip himself up as he approached her, and she turned.

"So how much was that worth, then? Can't grumble about what I got for my money," he leered deliberately.

*   *   *

Back in her cubicle, Belle nursed her side, where the fat cow had used the prod. It hurt like hell, but she knew from past experience that by morning all trace of the marks would be gone. At the glass of her booth, Nick Turnbull suddenly appeared, weaving slightly as though he'd had too much to drink, and he put his hand on the glass to steady himself. The palm pressed flatly against the glass, and Belle saw the rough map which Nick had drawn on it with his pen. She nodded silently as she digested the details. Nick turned away, holding his stomach, apparently about to be sick. Belle was formulating plans in her mind. Now she just had to wait for the old woman to return.

Chapter Fifteen

ick didn't know it, but he had been followed to the Jade Gate. One of Angelo Zoro's people was asked to watch his movements, more for his own security than anything else. When he had been spotted entering the Jade Gate, a phone call had been made, and Angelo himself soon turned up to relieve his man. He couldn't believe the man would bring a beautiful woman out to Jakarta, and then abandon her to visit a brothel. There were rumours about the Jade Gate, and its name had cropped up in his own investigations. Putting two and two together, Angelo decided it needed his personal touch, and a little off-duty chat with Mr Turnbull wouldn't hurt.

Angelo entered the smoke-filled establishment, his nose rankling at the acrid mixed aromas of tobacco and marijuana, being smoked openly. He went over to the bar, and ordered a drink, just a beer, to blend in with the rest of the partygoers in the place. He leaned back against the bar and slowly surveyed the surroundings, checking out the occupants.

It didn't take him long to pick out Turnbull, peering drunkenly through the glass at one of the girls, hardly able to stand by the look of him. Beer in hand, Angelo started across the crowded room, as Turnbull stiffened up and stepped back from the glass, walking towards him, though not seeing him for the moment. "Hey, Nick, good to see you," Angelo blurted out loudly enough to be heard, and as Nick looked up, surprised, Angelo linked arms with him, and directed him to a quieter corner of the room. Angelo found Nick a lot more sober than he looked.

"Good to see you, too, mate," he answered less than enthusiastically. "You been following me?"

"Not me, but my people. Wouldn't want you to get up to mischief, on foreign soil, now would we, Nick?" he forced a smile, though was ready for trouble if Nick acted out of turn. "This is the last place I would have expected to find you, if you were up to something legitimate. Does the lovely Julie know you're here?" he asked.

"You know damn well she doesn't. I have my reasons. Best you go home. You don't want to be here, or be involved with what's going down," he warned.

"Listen, Turnbull, this place is rumoured to be a clearing house for all sort of illegal activities, though we've been able to prove nothing to date. You being here means you know something, and I want to know what that is." All of a sudden, Angelo paused in mid-sentence, his jaw dropping as he didn't want to believe what he was just seeing over Nick's shoulder.

Nick half-turned, casually, and noticed the elderly couple coming into the place. He didn't know the man, but the woman matched the description he had of Denny Zoro. Oh Christ, it was going down *now*!

He knew what a firebrand Belle was, and once that collar was off, all Hell was going to break loose, and he and Angelo would be right in the middle of it.

As Angelo gawped, his mother spoke to the fat madame, and disappeared through the beaded curtain with her. Now it was Nick's turn to pressure Angelo, and he blocked him off as he attempted to move. "Listen, mate, I know it's a shock, but you have no idea what's happening here, or maybe you do, I don't know how much you've guessed. Your Mum's here to help a couple of friends of mine. They've been kidnapped, and sold into the white slave trade. They're being held here against their will, and your Mum said she'd help them."

"You've involved my mother in something like this? Are you mad?" Angelo's eyes flashed. He obviously shared the same temperament as Belle. "She has a weak heart. Do you know what this could do to her?" He started to push Nick to one side, and Nick had no option but to grab his lapels, and twist into a choke-hold, pinning him against the wall.

"You interfere, and my friends could end up dead. I didn't involve your mother. She involved herself." Angelo fought himself to avoid responding automatically to Nick's hold on him. If the two of them cut loose in here, who knows what would happen. If his own suspicions were right, then there would be weapons on the premises, and if they thought they were being raided, they would use them.

"Let me go. Now!" Angelo's eyes burned into Nick's own. Reluctantly, and cautiously, Nick released his hold, whilst Angelo regained his composure. "Are you armed?" he asked. Nick nodded. "Two guns against the Dragon-Lady's crew won't be much. At the slightest hint of trouble, I'm going up those stairs," Angelo warned.

"You'll be behind me, don't worry. I have a stake in this as well, remember? I'm sorry your mother got herself involved. It wasn't my doing, and I didn't know about her heart condition, I swear," he explained apologetically.

"But why did she get involved, Turnbull? As far as I know she has never been inside a place such as this." Angelo was asking for an explanation, and Nick owed him one.

"Friends of friends. That's all I can say."

"How does my mother know two foreign women?" Nick remained silent. Angelo's head was nodding silently as he weighed things up. "Funny how Europol only offered assistance after I made enquiries into this Gabriel, wasn't it, Nick?" he stated rather than queried. Nick's silence confirmed his suspicions. Angelo was bright enough, and starting to piece things together. "Why does his face look like the photo on my mother's wall?" Angelo demanded. "For God's sake, that was a recent photo they sent. It can't be him!"

"You're a clever boy, Angelo. I think you've figured most of it out for yourself," Nick confirmed. "But there's a lot more to this than meets the eye. There's a lot you don't know about the guy. A lot I don't know either, but I know enough not to cross him. Don't you make that mistake," he advised.

"Is he my father, Nick?" Angelo asked.

"It looks like it," Nick agreed. Angelo's mouth dropped open at the sudden confirmation.

"Then why? Why did he do it, Nick? Why did he abandon me and my mother all those years ago?" Angelo was looking for the answer to a question he had been asking himself all his life.

"I can't say for sure, only what I know. People were trying to capture and possibly kill him back then. He fled so they wouldn't link him with your mother, and put her life at risk. He was trying to protect her. I don't think he knew she was pregnant at the time."

"That's still no excuse for the lack of contact all these years. I can't believe my mother would keep something like that from me."

"Sorry, but that's all I can tell you."

"He's coming here, isn't he? That's what all this is about, and the real reason you're here isn't to help me against Al Qaeda, it's to help him free those women. Who are they?"

"One of them is his current wife or partner. The other is your half-sister." The news hit Angelo like a bombshell, and he was lost for words momentarily.

*　　*　　*

Upstairs, Belle sat impatiently on the bed, whilst Denny used the delicate lock-picks on her collar's tiny lock. Finally, a soft click was heard, and the deadly collar fell away from her neck, and she sighed with relief. She took the collar and put it under the mattress. "This might still go off," she warned. Denny backed away from the bed, instinctively. Her small frame looked naturally timid, and she was dwarfed by Belle when she stood up. The two women were so different in physique and attitude, and Belle realized the woman was not used to this sort of clandestine behaviour. "We have to move quickly now. My mother is on the next floor."

"I'll be alright. It's nothing." She seemed about to say something, and then forced herself to remain silent, though Denny was dreading meeting the woman who had won Gabriel's heart. Belle opened the door and quickly checked the landing was clear, and then she beckoned for Denny to follow. The older woman did her best to keep up as Belle moved swiftly along the landing, the map from Nick's palm fresh in her mind.

"It might be best if you give me the lock-picks, and go back downstairs," Belle suggested.

"If I go back downstairs without you, the Madame will be suspicious," she pointed out. Belle had to admit she was right, and as much as she didn't want to hazard the old woman any more than she had to, she allowed her to accompany her up the next flight of stairs. They met no one on the way up, and Belle counted off the doors. She could hear snippets of conversations behind some of them, and then she finally came to the door she wanted, and found the door locked. Denny was quick to crouch down and apply her lock-picks to the task as Belle stood impatiently by.

Just at that second, one of the doors opened further down the corridor, and a man stepped out. Quickly, Belle put her body between him and Denny, so that he could not see what she was doing. He looked at Belle curiously. "Why are you up here?" he asked, suspiciously. Most of the girls were not allowed on this floor, apart from the Dragon Lady's latest paramours.

Belle shrugged, flicking her long black hair back seductively as she began to walk slowly towards him, hips swinging. She smiled as she closed the distance between them, and he smiled at her approach. Belle's lips puckered invitingly as she reached for him, and as he went to return her embrace, Belle brought her knee up savagely into his groin, forcing the air from his lungs, and as he doubled up in agony, she followed up with a sharp elbow down on the back of his head, knocking him out cold.

Lifting him was a struggle, but she needed to get him out of sight, and she opened the door he had just vacated. Another man looked up from a desk as she stood framed in the doorway, with the unconscious man propped up against the door jamb. "Help me, I think he's fainted," she asked quickly, reacting on first impulse. Not thinking, the second man got up from behind the desk to help her with his friend, but as Belle shifted her weight to throw the dead weight at him, he became alert, and sidestepped.

Belle flung herself at him, not wanting to give him time to call out and alert anyone else. He reacted in time to block her first blow, his head weaving out of the way to let her fist sail past, but then Belle brought the elbow of that arm back against the side of his head, as she took a hit to her own ribs. Grunting, she brought her knee up into his stomach, as he attempted to grapple with her. Grabbing his arm, Belle pivoted, swinging him into the desk hard, and papers and computer fell to the floor with a loud crash. As he whirled back round, Belle chopped him across the throat, and as he grabbed at his injured larynx, she followed up with a savate kick in the chest which slammed him back against the wall. Another kick to the head followed as he collapsed on the floor, rendering him unconscious like his companion.

Unsure if anyone had heard the brief combat, Belle went back outside quickly, and found Denny getting to her feet. She was already turning the handle, and the door swung open as Belle joined her. Both women gasped at what they saw.

Laura was still naked, lying listlessly on the bed. Her eyes were trying to focus on the two women who now entered the room. "Mother," was all Belle could gasp, as she rushed to her side. Laura didn't seem to know who she was for a moment, only making a sound as Belle made her sit up.

"Belle? Is it you?" She reached a hand to stroke Belle's face, wiping away the tears that Belle found herself crying. Dear God, what had that bitch been doing to her? Forcing herself to remain in control, Belle brushed aside her mother's long blonde hair, revealing the braided collar, and the livid bite-marks on her neck.

Denny was hesitant to approach the woman who had replaced her in Gabriel's affections, and when she saw the marks on her neck, her eyes went wide with fear, for she had always believed in magic, which was still a part of life for many Indonesians. "Quickly, we have to get this collar off," Belle beckoned her forward, till she forced herself to overcome her fear, and approach the bed.

Concentrating on the task in hand, she began to apply the lock-picks, more proficiently now, after having already opened one such lock earlier. The thing fell from Laura's neck, and Denny grimaced at the still livid wounds on Laura's neck.

Belle grabbed the collar and gently took it out of the room, going back along the corridor, and back into the office, where she left it on the desk. Returning to the bedroom, she found Denny staring at Laura intently. Her mother did raise her head this time, and seemed to recognize her. "I'm sick, Belle," she moaned, weakly.

"We have to get you out of here, Mother. Help me get her dressed," she asked Denny, as she opened the wardrobe to find clothes. Angelica was almost the same size, so something in here was bound to fit her.

*   *   *

Downstairs, Angelo was just getting over the shock of Nick's words, when Angelica put in an appearance, coming up from the basement with two or three seedy looking characters. They were engrossed in conversation, and ignored Nick and Angelo as they moved towards the bar. Nick drew Angelo to one side. "What do you know of that woman?" he asked him.

"Madame Eve? Not much. They call her the Dragon Lady. I think she's Italian. Been running this place for the last two years. She doesn't look much, but seems to generate respect or fear from her employees. We pulled a couple over the last few months, once our suspicions were raised, but nothing we did to them made them talk about anything to do with her. She's put the fear of God into them, I think."

"I'm sure she has," Nick commented.

"Apart from that, she pays her bills on time. We have no legal reason to pester her, just too many rumours for me to believe she's as clean as she makes out. Jakarta is a corrupt city, and Jelan Kendal is one of the worst areas. She's too clean, in fact. Is the Italian connection anything to do with this?" he asked.

"Partly, from what I can gather. I'm as much in the dark with some of this as you, believe it or not. I'm just trying to help a friend. But that woman is a lot more dangerous than she looks, believe me," he assured Angelo.

*   *   *

Laura struggled into a tight-fitting evening dress as the two women helped her. "Oh, baby, I'm so glad you came. I couldn't resist her. Those eyes of hers. You don't know what she wanted me to do to you," she was crying herself now. "Another few days," she sobbed. It hurt Denny to see the woman like this. She was having trouble reconciling her feelings towards her, but she wished no harm on the woman, and she had obviously suffered abuse whilst in this room. The bite-marks were not unknown, and the room stank of recent sex.

"Let's get you downstairs and out of here," Belle insisted. "Then I'll deal with that bitch once and for all," she promised.

"No, you don't understand, Angelica isn't a she . . ." Laura blurted out.

"What are you . . . ?" The question was left unspoken as Denny butted in, understanding.

"She's a banshee, a lady-boy, she-male, a chick with a dick, I think you call them in the West," the old woman explained.

"Ohmigod!" Belle gasped, realizing the truth about what had been done to her Mother, and the previous fights she'd had against the 'woman'. She had been fighting a man, not a woman, and now a male vampire. She would not underestimate her/him again. "Alright, can you walk?" she asked, and Laura nodded, slowly regaining independent movement. Half-supported by Belle and Denny, she managed to walk out of the room and along the corridor towards the stairs.

*   *   *

As Nick and Angelo tried to remain inconspicuous in the back of the room, they heard raised voices beyond the beaded curtain, and then a short scream that failed to disguise the sharp electrical discharge. "How do *you* like it, you fat bitch?" a raised female voice could clearly be heard, Belle to be sure. Then a second electrical discharge, and the fat madam came hurtling through the beaded curtain, carrying it with her as she fell heavily to the floor, and everyone in the establishment looked on at the debacle.

Nick was paying more attention to Angelica, who calmly reached under the slit of her cheongsam, to take a small remote device from out of a garter, where she kept it close to hand. A grim smile highlighted those white teeth once more, as Belle stumbled into the room, half-supporting Laura with the aid of Denny. Angelo started to move forward upon sight of his mother, but Nick held him back, aware that quite a few of the people he had previously thought patrons, were now pulling guns, and were obviously in Angelica's employ. "Take it easy. We're outgunned here," he cautioned the younger man.

Angelica held the remote out in front of her, where the women could see it, and then scowled as she noticed their bare necks. "Well, well, you've been busy, haven't you? Who's your new friend, Belle?" Angelica indicated Denny, who shuddered pointedly as she felt that malevolent gaze fall upon her. Angelica placed the now useless-detonator on the bar, and she stepped forward, indicating her cronies should fall back. "Everyone else, out of the club. This is a private matter."

As she indicated, the heavies began herding and then shepherding the regular clientele out towards the main doors. Nick and Angelo ducked under one of the rear tables in a secluded booth, pulling guns, and hoped for now they weren't noticed. They were outnumbered six to one. Not good odds at all.

"Now what do we do?" Angelo whispered.

"Stay quiet, and wait for now."

"Wait for what?"

"How the fuck should I know? Just wait, till we get an edge. Plan B. We 'wing' it." Nick quickly assessed the situation. All attention was on the three women. He and Angelo might be able to reduce the odds to three to one before they could expect a return of fire, but they were sitting ducks where they were, and their ammunition was limited to a couple of clips. "How good are you with that thing?" Nick asked. "You seen combat before?"

"I'm good enough. Don't worry about me."

"When I give the word, we take down as many as we can. Kill-shots, don't fuck about trying to play this by the book and just shooting to wound, okay? Shoot and move, 'cause they'll be shooting back. Surprise will only buy us seconds."

"It's my mother's life we're talking about here, Nick. Theirs don't matter to me," he assured him.

Angelica appraised the three women. The old woman was no threat, terrified in fact. Laura was still out of it, and under her influence. There was only Belle to deal with, and she had had other plans for her, but plans had a way of changing. "I see you got reacquainted with your mother again, Belle. She and I have been having so much fun this last week," she taunted. Belle stepped in front of Laura, protectively.

"Come to me, Laura," Angelica beckoned, showing off her power and control, and Laura took one step forward, crying out, as though she couldn't control herself. She didn't want to, but Angelica's voice was so compelling. Eyes flashing, Belle whirled and punched her mother hard on the jaw, taking her by surprise, and knocking her out, cold. She and Denny caught her before she could fall. Angelica laughed. "She wants to be with me, Belle. Would you keep two lovers apart?" she chuckled.

Denny and Belle sat Laura down in one of the booths, two down from where Nick and Angelo were hiding in fact. Belle turned to face her long-time nemesis. "I'm going to make you pay, Angelica!" she swore. The woman just laughed.

"Remind me, again. How many times have I kicked your scrawny ass, Belle?" Belle remembered those times, and now she understood why she had been beaten, underestimating her opponent, but now she knew her true nature, this time they would be on almost equal terms. Her one advantage lay in the fact that Angelica might hesitate to reveal her true vampiric nature in front of so many people, henchmen or not, she doubted whether they knew they worked for a vampire, and old folklore survived out in this part of the world. One flash of those teeth and they would know exactly what she was.

"Bring it on, Vampirella!" Belle snarled, clenching her fists by her sides. Angelica appraised her, and then appraised her battleground. There was about twenty feet of clear space along the length of the bar, and tables and chairs were set back about ten feet from it.

"Give us some room," Angelica urged her men, and they stepped back into the shadows, a couple of them coming close to where Nick and Angelo were hiding. Everyone was concentrating on the two women now squaring up to each other. Angelica sidestepped slowly to her left, as Belle moved closer, keeping the bar-rail at her back.

Angelica lunged forward, one leg snapping up to take Belle under the chin in a deadly savate kick, but Belle caught the leg, holding it as she slammed a knee right up into Angelica's crotch, and then head-butted her in the face, viciously, breaking her nose for a second time, causing blood to pour down her face. Angelica screamed as she tore herself free, and staggered back, her tongue coming out to taste her own blood as she glared at Belle.

"Careful, dear. Your 'Dark Side' is showing," Belle warned her. "Does it hurt?" Belle mocked. "Good!" Now she launched at Angelica, screaming her hate at the woman, closing her down before she could back away, and a high kick from Belle caught her in the chest, just below the sternum. Angelica grunted with pain, and fell back, dragging one of the chairs in front of her to block Belle's follow-up attack.

As Belle paused to clear the chair, vaulting it, Angelica body checked her, using her own momentum against her, and twisting to slam her back into the bar-rail, hard enough to almost crack her spine.

Belle cried out in pain, and Angelica chopped her across the throat as she tried to bounce back away from the bar. A second blow to the midriff followed, and then Angelica grabbed Belle's hair, dragging her head down to meet the rising knee which she managed to take on her forehead.

Around them, Angelica's henchmen were cheering on the action, getting visibly excited by the girl on girl fight. "There's something about a cat-fight . . ." Nick whispered to Angelo. "Let's move closer while they're all preoccupied," he suggested.

Belle tried another savate kick, but her own dress didn't offer as much freedom as the slit thigh cheongsam that Angelica wore, and she blocked the attempt easily, then crouching and using her own outstretched leg to sweep Belle's standing leg from under her and down she went. Angelica dropped on her eagerly, snarling, and blood dripping from her face, as her elbow smashed down onto Belle's ribcage, making her scream as she felt a couple of ribs fracture if not break altogether.

Belle's hand lashed out, nails raking for Angelica's eyes, and drawing more blood from her cheek as she tried to avoid the blow. She grabbed for Angelica's crotch, squeezing hard enough to make her cry out, and then the two women were rolling around the floor now, smashing into tables and chairs as each tried to get in a vital blow, and Belle determined to protect her injured ribs. Her bodice was torn, allowing one breast to hang free, as Angelica clawed at her. Legs flailed, hands clawed.

Another kick to Angelica's injured nose, made blood flow once more, and Belle prayed Angelica would be hesitant to reveal her vampiric powers in front of her henchmen. Long legs, bare flesh, and flashes of panties, made this a typical cat-fight, and the men were revelling in it, and getting excited, though of course wanting Angelica to win.

All eyes were on the two women, and Nick chose that moment to make his move. Signalling silently to Angelo, the two of them crept out of concealment and crawled closer to the two nearest men, before rising suddenly behind them, and snapping both men's necks as effortlessly as the other. Nick was glad to see that Angelo was no boy-scout. He had indeed done this thing before. Their action went unnoticed as they lowered the two bodies silently, and dragged them behind the table, out of sight.

Belle rose to her feet first, but Angelica sprung up off the floor, tackling her high, and both women went back over the bar this time, in a loud crashing of glasses and bottles. The watchers crowded closer as the fight went out of their sight, and then Angelica suddenly was flung back up into the air as Belle got both feet under her and thrust her backwards.

This was no true "cat-fight", more like a traditional Thai-Boxing match, all elbows, knees and punches, as onlookers quickly realized. The two women were both really trying to kill each other, and it was as brutal as it was frenetic. Devoid of weapons, and restricted in manoeuvring room behind the bar, both women fought hard and dirty.

There was little room for any leg moves now, and it was upper body strength that both women had to rely on. Belle was finding it hard to protect her injured ribs, and one eye was rapidly swelling up and closing, hard to see out of, after a head butt from Angelica had landed on her.

Angelica had her own preternatural strength to rely upon, whereas Belle was now injured and tiring. Belle couldn't let this fight go on too long. She grabbed a bottle and smashed it against the bar, leaving her with the neck and a sharp glass edge. "You'll need more than that to kill me!" Angelica scoffed.

"I've no intention of trying to kill you, but it's time for a little payback." Belle clawed at Angelica's throat, forcing her head back purely as a distraction, then quickly stabbing low with the broken bottle, slicing at Angelica's groin and staining the cheongsam with dark blood. Angelica screamed in pain. Belle dropped the broken bottle and punched her in the face, knocking her back, and she followed up, punching repeatedly as Angelica dropped her guard to try and stem the flow of blood from her crotch. Belle punched Angelica in the face, and forced her back, ramming and then holding her head back down on the bar. Belle's fist hammered down again and again and again, to make Angelica's mouth a bloody mess. "The only way you'll be fucking biting anyone is with false teeth from now on, you fucking whore!" Punch after punch rained down, as teeth and blood flew, until Angelica could stand no more and Belle let her fall unconscious to the floor. Breathing hard, and flushed with victory, Belle turned to survey the watching gunmen.

"Kill her," one of them cried, levelling his gun, but then Belle held up her hand, and let them see what she was holding in it. The radio transmitter that Angelica had discarded on the bar-top.

"Don't think so. Look what I found, boys!" A simple switch with an L and a B on opposite sides, Belle flipped it to the L and pressed the button. A large explosion was heard overheard, and the walls and ceiling shook, as the men ducked for cover. "Next one literally brings the house down," she warned. "Your choice, boys. Let us go or I push the other button," she warned. The men looked at one another. Without Angelica, none of them knew what to do. As the men hesitated, Nick and Angelo were working their way towards Denny and the unconscious Laura.

Denny cried out, "Angelo!" as her son suddenly became visible to her, and the noise and movement caused eyes to whirl around, and one gunman took aim on Angelo as he stood up and ran to protect his mother. Denny's eyes widened as she realized the danger, and pushed her son in the chest, knocking him out of the way, as the gunman pulled the trigger, and the bullet zipped narrowly past, missing it's intended target, but hitting the frail old woman centre-chest, and she flew back against the fabric of the seat, a surprised expression on her face.

Angelo screamed as he realized what had happened, and it was up to Nick alone to return fire, and with just one magazine and one spare clip, that return fire wasn't going to last too long.

Belle thumbed the transmitter a second time, and the ensuing overhead explosion brought the ceiling down across one end of the bar, flattening four or more of the gunmen. Belle dove over the top of the bar, rolling as she hit the floor, and then suddenly bounding to her feet in front of a surprised gunman. Belle grabbed him and turned him around in front of her, to accept two bullets that were meant for her, and then wrested the gun from his dying fingers, to return fire herself, holding his dead body up in front of her as a shield.

The barroom quickly filled with the smoke of burning timbers, dust and gunpowder, as the remaining frightened and stunned henchmen didn't know what to do. Two of them threw down their guns and ran for the exit, whilst the last of them tried to shoot it out, and Belle and Nick between them made their shots count. As the gunfire ended, Angelo remained sobbing over the dead body of his mother.

"It's your fault she's dead," Angelo accused. "If she hadn't been here, she wouldn't have been killed." He was in shock, and overcome with grief. He cradled his mother in his arms, gently rocking her back and forth. Belle tried not to take his comments personally.

"A lot of people are dead because of me," Belle admitted, sadly. "Some intentionally so. Some otherwise. I didn't ask your mother to get involved, though I'm grateful for her help, and I'm sorry she's dead. She took a bullet meant for you. You didn't ask her to do that, either. It was her choice. People sometimes do the right thing without being asked to, regardless of the consequences." Angelo rocked away, seemingly oblivious to her attempts to comfort him.

"You didn't ask her, no, but *he* did, and *he'll* pay for that," Angelo swore, before returning to his grieving.

There was nothing else Belle could do to ease his pain, and so she turned to her own mother, who was still unconscious, laid back on the seat. She turned again to Turnbull, who seemed preoccupied with her own semi-nudity. "Stop gawping, Turnbull, I've shown more on the catwalk, and this outfit is hardly Versace. But be a gentleman and offer a lady your jacket."

"Sorry," he looked away embarrassingly, as he took off his jacket and handed it to her. While she was putting it on, he lifted Laura from the booth, and found her starting to stir in his arms. "I think she'll be okay to walk," he said, as he pulled her to her feet. Belle walked back to the end of the bar, as the flames from the explosion were spreading. Angelica's bloodied leg was sticking out from under some of the rubble. Flames were already licking up one of the fallen beams.

"Burn in Hell!" she cursed, and turned to help Turnbull walk her mother out of the place. Outside in the street, they found a crowd gathering to watch the place catch fire, and in the distance they could hear sirens. Flames were now breaking through the roof of the Jade Gate in places, lighting up the night sky.

"Transport. We need to get out of here," said Nick, as he left Laura with Belle and began speaking to some of the onlookers. He offered money to anyone who would drive them, and quickly found a willing punter, eager for some rupiah. Laura and Belle were soon sat in the back of a battered old Daihatsu, while Nick sat up front with the driver. "Where to? I think maybe the Embassy is best. It's where Gabriel will look for you, I guess. He's due here today, I think." Laura's eyes went wide at the suggestion.

"No. Please, no. I can't let him see me like this," she began to sob into Belle's shoulder as she allowed her daughter to comfort her.

"We can't go to the Embassy, but I may know some people I can contact. I need a phone. Do you have a hotel room, Nick?" Belle asked.

"Yeah, but . . ." he was thinking how he was going to have to explain all this to Julie, let alone turning up unannounced like this with two women, one of them wearing his jacket. Reluctantly, he began giving the driver directions to the Garden Hotel.

As it was, the presence of the two women took Julie's mind off the ear-bashing she was ready to unleash on Nick, for him being out most of the night. "Ohmigod, what's happened?" she gasped upon opening the door, still in her nightgown, and Nick ushered Belle and Laura inside the hotel bedroom.

"Julie, this is Belle and Laura. Friends of friends. They're in a jam, and I'm the only friend they've got here, so please bear with me," he pleaded.

"Sorry for the imposition," Belle assessed the situation quickly, and decided to put the girl at her ease swiftly. "We just need to use a phone, and get cleaned up, and then we'll be out of here in an hour or two. Do you have a medical kit, Nick?" Belle asked.

"Just a small travel kit, but it has antiseptic and bandages etc."

"Can you clean out those neck wounds while I use the phone?" she suggested, and Julie took Laura into the bathroom, whilst Nick found the kit. He joined the pair in the bathroom where Julie was trying to use a flannel and hot water to clean the blood away from the livid teeth-marks.

"My God, what have they done to her?" Julie was horrified. Nick didn't feel like elaborating. Instead he handed the medical kit to Julie, and let her use it to clean up the wounds as best she could. In the bedroom, Belle was making calls to previous contacts in the Sword of Solomon organization. The truce still held, and she could still call upon the resources of her former organization when required.

By the time Laura walked back out of the bathroom, neck wrapped around with a bandage, Belle had managed to arrange a safe house. "We'll leave you now, Nick. Sorry for all the trouble, but it's for the best. Tell Dad we'll be in touch," Laura was still sobbing, and allowed Belle to cradle her in her arms. "She's been through a lot, and just isn't ready to see him again. I'm sure he'll understand," she hoped. "I'll send your jacket back in a day or so," she promised.

Nick insisted on walking them down to Reception, and out to the entrance, where a private car had pulled up, and a solitary male figure waiting, holding the rear door open. Belle got in first, and Nick helped Laura get inside with her. "Thanks aren't good enough, Nick. But they'll have to do for now," Belle smiled as he closed the door. The driver got into the vehicle, and drove away.

Nick mentally cursed as he remembered the floppy disk in his jacket pocket, and made a mental note of the license plate. He was sure Gabriel would want it. He could also get a record of the number Belle called from his room from the hotel switchboard. As for Gabriel 'understanding', he didn't know. Coming halfway around the world to find someone, who now didn't want to be found, would tend to piss most people off.

When he got back up to his hotel room, Julie was watching the local News on the television. Outside, dawn was just breaking. Footage showed the fire-fighters bringing the fire at the Jade Gate under control, and various body-bags being taken out of the building. Brief footage appeared of Angelo Zoro, arguing and pushing against the medics, over the handling of one such body-bag, which obviously contained the body of his mother.

What looked like the local Chief of Police was interviewed against a backdrop of illegal arms and munitions, apparently discovered in the basement of the building, before the fire could gut the place. He looked pleased with himself. Nick didn't feel in such a good mood. The whole evening hadn't exactly gone to plan, and Angelo Zoro's presence there was obviously going to cause some future problems.

"Well? Are you going to tell me what happened tonight?" Nick didn't need this, but he was going to have to make an effort.

"Well, luv, it started like this . . . ."

Chapter Sixteen

abriel disembarked from the Garuda Airways plane without incident. The papers provided by Donatello were expert forgeries, and they, combined with the typically Muslim facial hair he now sported, made him look quite innocuous. Eduardo Corpuz, a native Filipino, was in transit back to the Phillipines, and stopping off for a week in Jakarta. His connecting tickets could always be changed.

He passed through Customs & Immigration without incident.

*   *   *

As he did so, Nick Turnbull was still at Police HQ, answering questions, and unable to meet him at the terminal as arranged. There was nothing Turnbull could do without attracting too much attention now. The fallback was for Gabriel to call on him at the hotel, but Julie hadn't been briefed on the job, and only knew what he had explained in the early hours of the morning.

*   *   *

As Laura was receiving medical help in the doctor's surgery of the private clinic that Solomon agents had call on in this city, Belle changed into the fresh clothes that had been purchased for her, from one of the local malls. As she hung up Nick's jacket, she found the floppy disk in the side pocket, and being naturally curious, used the doctor's computer to examine the files that were contained on it.

She found them very interesting, obviously obtained by Nick while he was searching for Laura. They gave details of shipments of both goods, munitions and personnel, that the Al Raschid Organisation acted as a front for. Belle wasn't interested in the Al Qaeda angle, as much as the source of some of the exotic curios.

Laura didn't want to go back and face Gabriel so soon. She needed to recover from Angelica's feeding, regain her colour and let the wounds heal somewhat, though Belle remembered only too well how long that single bite had taken to heal previously. She was getting a complete transfusion of a mixture of group O and plasma. Her body should be able to process that, and eventually produce its own replacement blood, but only after whatever she had been injected with was out of her system.

Gabriel wouldn't care what she looked like, as long as she was alive, but Laura was vain, and blamed herself for the mess they had ended up in. Belle placed a personal call to Marco Falcone. "Marco?"

"Belle, so nice to hear from you," he began, but Belle cut him short.

"Let's not make the mistake of thinking this is a social call," she set the ground rules straight away. "I daresay you've already been told where we are, and why we're here?"

"Yes, I was told. How is she?" he was genuinely concerned.

"She'll live, no thanks to you."

"Belle, I swear, I had nothing to do with this."

"Angelica was *Solomon*, Marco. You knew her, and she ran when Borgia was killed. She was your responsibility," she accused.

"The world is a big place, Belle. If it wasn't, we would have tracked your father down a long time ago," he pointed out.

"You may have heard, I've been having some CCTV footage studied," she teased. Silence was her only response. Falcone was saying nothing. "I know it was you, you bastard!" she swore. "But I need a favour, and you can grant it to me. My mother needs to disappear for a while, and I want you to organize tickets for us both to Cambodia."

"I have no idea what you're talking about," Falcone finally responded. His voice was calm and betraying none of the nerves she had expected. He was a cool operator, and no mistake. "But why for Cambodia?" he asked.

"Never mind. Arrange it. We need to leave no later than tomorrow. As a reward, you get a choice," she said, enigmatically.

"What's the choice? Though you know I'll help your mother anyway," he admitted.

"The choice is simple. I owe you big time for that firebomb!" she hadn't had conclusive proof yet from the study of that tape, but her instincts were rarely wrong. "Do you want me to deal with you myself, or should I tell my mother, and let her do it?" There was silence on the other end of the phone for a few moments.

"Don't tell Laura," Falcone finally spoke, admitting what Belle had suspected for some time. It was he who had planted the firebomb under the catwalk, not Al Qaeda. The Church had tried to convince Gabriel to help them and he wouldn't, so they had forced his hand. "The doctor will take you to a safe house. Stay there overnight, and I'll have the tickets organized and delivered to you tomorrow. First available flights, and I'll arrange bookings at a hotel in Phnom Penh. I'll also arrange access to a bank account there. Anything else?"

"It's a date, then. Ciao!" Belle hung up on him.

*　*　*

Gabriel checked into The Garden Hotel, handing over his Filipino passport. He had others hidden in a secret compartment inside his luggage, if he needed them. Once in his room, he called the desk to connect him to Denny's home phone number. But all he got was a worried maid on the end of the line, whose mistress hadn't returned home last night. He plugged in his laptop to the hotel broadband service, and began checking his e-mail, but nothing new from either Donatello or Maddox. Nick hadn't yet been able to update his boss on overnight events.

He phoned the desk and got Nick's room number, next floor down. So he hung up, and went to pay a call. He knocked, and waited, and eventually a young blonde woman, in a light green two-tone dress, opened the door. "Yes?" he looked like a local, all facial hair, long shirt, baggy trousers. It was only when he spoke that she realized he was something else entirely.

"Is Nick in?" Her eyes widened, and her jaw dropped.

"Ohmigod, you're 'im. 'Lazarus'." Gabriel's bearded face broke into a forced smile.

"Is that what he's calling me these days? Listen, it's important I see Nick. Do you know where he is?" he asked.

"Please, come in," Julie ushered him into the room, then theatrically checking the corridor in both directions before closing the door.

"Really, I don't think that's necessary. I just need to speak to Nick and then I'll let you two get on with your holiday, though I do appreciate the help. You must be Jim's girl? I'm an old friend of your father's." He offered his hand, and Julie shook it, still a bit dumbfounded.

"Nick's been at Police HQ all day. They let him ring me once, but I've no idea when they're going to let him leave."

"Is he in trouble?" Gabriel asked, worried. He didn't need more problems.

"No, it's just, after last night, they want him to answer a few questions, debrief him, like. He's quite pally with the Special Force's guy that's running the investigation, so it'll just be paperwork, I'm sure. Just no idea when he'll be back, is all," she apologized.

"What happened last night?" Gabriel asked, as innocently as he could. Julie was reluctant to answer him.

"Your wife and daughter are fine, at least as far as I know. They did a runner early this morning. Your wife was injured, though the wounds weren't deep," she didn't elaborate. "I cleaned the wounds myself and bandaged her up proper like."

"Okay, do you know where they went?"

Julie shook her head. "No, sorry. Your wife was a bit shook up, and your daughter, Belle, was it? was very protective of her, and said she needed rest. She made a few phone calls, and a taxi collected them. She said she'd be in touch in a few days." Okay, nothing he could do till she got in touch. Knowing Belle, she'd call in a few favours from Solomon in a situation like this. She had a sound head on her, and could be relied upon to look out for Laura.

"What else happened?" he asked.

"Some nightclub called the Jade Gate got burned down. It was a front for a smuggling and terrorist organization, to hear Nick tell the tale. A few people got killed there last night in a gunfight. I gather Nick was involved, and that's why he's down at Police HQ now" she admitted. Gabriel's stomach was beginning to churn, uneasily. Denny hadn't come home last night. He had asked her to get involved, though not that closely. He needed to make further enquiries.

"Tell Nick I'll call on him later tonight. For now, I need to make some more enquiries of my own." He stood up, and let himself out.

Julie gave him a small wave, and closed the door after him. Not at all like she had expected.

Gabriel left the hotel. It was best he used a public phone for this next call, and he walked a considerable distance from the hotel to make the call. He rang up the various hospitals, one by one, pretending to be a reporter for one of the English-Speaking Newspapers, asking for information on any dead and wounded people from last night's incident at the Jade Gate.

It took him four calls, before he finally got the news he didn't want to hear. But he had to be sure. Nevy Denny Zoro, DOA. Her body released to her family for burial in the Family Plot at a local cemetery in Bandung. The funeral had already been arranged for tomorrow, as with the heat and humidity out here, morgues didn't like to keep bodies too long.

He lost track of how long he stood in the phone booth, just staring at his reflection in the cracked mirror, clutching the handset that toned dully in his hand after the line had gone dead. It was only when someone rapped on the glass, that he finally got a grip on reality, and hung up the handset. "Sorry," was all he could say, as he stepped out of the booth, though he was saying it to Denny, and not the impatient caller.

He had only asked her to make enquiries, not involve herself this closely. What was it about women and their damn curiosity? Of course, he blamed himself. Who else could he blame? If he had not called her, she wouldn't be dead right now. Another death on his conscious. He had lost count, over the centuries. Hard to believe, and cynical, but it was the truth.

Gabriel didn't go back to the hotel. He spent the night in a bar, drinking, doing his best to get thoroughly drunk, which was difficult as his unique blood didn't absorb the alcohol as readily as human blood, but he tried really hard. He was so drunk in fact, that he had merely laughed as two men accosted him in the back alley while he was pissing up against the wall. He couldn't be bothered to defend himself, perhaps not wanting to, deeming the beating a punishment deserved. They only roughed him up enough to rob him, and God knows he had spent most of his money on the booze. They left him lying there, still laughing, as they took what few bills were left out of his wallet, and threw it back at him, cursing.

He walked the night, a lone and solitary figure, sobering up. By dawn, his aches and pains were easing, and he was heading out towards Bandung, though it was too far to walk all the way. His recovered wallet still had his credit cards, and he used an ATM to draw out more money, to pay for a ride on one of the little Betchas, the enclosed scooters, that the locals tended to use. Not as fast as a taxi, they could often go where a taxi could not, and by mid afternoon, he found himself at the cemetery.

Gabriel went inside, a strangely cheerful place, with ornate headstones, and fresh flowers from loving relatives. He had forgotten to buy some on the way, and cursed himself a second time. He walked around till he found the fresh grave that had been dug, and the hastily carved headstone. Tears came unannounced, for a few seconds, and then he looked around for a safe and secluded place to observe the ceremony, without being seen himself.

He watched the funeral from a distance, as the afternoon wore on. It was a small gathering, and a sombre affair as he'd guessed. Not many family left at her age, although some of the younger relatives could have been kept away from the graveside on purpose. The tall, athletic looking, young man made a speech which he couldn't hear. He would have liked to have heard it.

Gradually, the small crowd left, the tall young man the last to go, and eventually all there was left was the filled grave, which Gabriel was drawn to. Slowly, he walked down the small hill, the headstone getting bigger and bigger, till it was all he saw, and Gabriel knelt by the graveside, and bowed his head. He was crying again.

He had loved Denny at one time in his life. He had left her to save her life, to keep her safe from Borgia and Solomon, who could have used her as a lever against him, as they had tried to do with Lucifer. Now, one phone call from him, and she had thrown her life away in an attempt to help him. He was just letting the tears flow, and they slowly trickled down his face.

"Whoever you are, go away!" he warned, suddenly sensing the approach of someone from behind him. "This isn't the time." He spoke calmly, though through clenched teeth. The figure who had silently approached Gabriel from behind, though not as silently as he thought, stood stock still. He had expected to get much closer before the kneeling figure could become aware of him. He raised his gun and cocked the hammer. Gabriel stood slowly to his feet, and turned, facing the tall young man who minutes before had been making a speech at this very graveside.

"Gabriel Angell, you are under arrest. My men have this cemetery surrounded. Lie down on the ground and place your hands behind your back." He ordered, in a voice which was used to being obeyed. His face was as black as thunder, his eyes a mirror of Gabriel's own, dark and undetermined.

Gabriel appraised the man, his peripheral vision noting one or two figures spotted around the cemetery who may or may not have been part of the man's team. Why have this cemetery under surveillance? How much did they know of his relationship with Denny? How did they know he'd be here now? Too many unanswered questions.

Angelo studied the man who stood before him. He noted the wet cheeks and the tears. He had loved his mother alright. The remorse was genuine. If he had loved her, then why did he leave her? Why abandon her? Was he his father? Despite Turnbull's ridiculous tales, the man looked far too young. But if so, why did he abandon him?

Gabriel complied, all too readily, laying down, and allowing Angelo to approach him, one hand going behind his back to unsnap his handcuffs from his belt. As he began to kneel down, shifting his weight, Gabriel rolled and struck out at the man's gun-wrist, the gun going off even as it dropped from slack fingers. Taken by surprise at the sudden resistance, Angelo still reacted quickly, swinging a punch which Gabriel leaned forward to take on his head. Savagely, he brought his knee into Angelo's side, as he tried to force him back down on the ground, and Angelo cried out, as Gabriel broke his hold.

Not following up on his attack, Gabriel simply turned and fled, running as fast as he could. Escape was all important and best achieved quickly. Two other men were running towards the altercation, and it seemed the younger man had not lied when he had said he had men in the cemetery, though just how many remained to be seen.

Gabriel needed cover, and people and traffic. He needed to immerse himself, hide and evade as they had taught him in the SAS. Get out of the immediate danger zone, and then blend in, become invisible, and God knows he was dressed for the occasion.

He hadn't as yet had time to change from his flight, and last night's run-in with those two bruisers had left him suitably soiled to pass for just another typical citizen out on the streets. The cemetery wasn't too far outside the teeming centre of Bandung, and he ran as fast as he could for the streets and relative safety.

No shots followed him, and for that he was grateful. It meant they wanted him alive rather than dead. He risked a glimpse behind, and spotted only three pursuers, though there could indeed be more scattered about if this was an organized police operation. But Denny had died less than 48hrs previously. How did they know he'd be here? Where was the connection? It didn't add up.

Gabriel legged it flat-out. He needed as much distance between himself and those men before he hit the teeming streets, where the mass of bodies would slow him down, but also enable him to use what cover there was, to get out of sight. He ignored the initial shortness of breath, soon getting into his second wind, avoiding the main gates to the cemetery where there was surely someone waiting to take him down. Instead he headed towards the right, where the surrounding wall was much shorter, and he went up and over in seconds, his light body mass and musculature enabling him to reach the top of the 12 ft high wall and flip himself over to the other side, in one easy movement.

On the streets, he quickly looked right to left, and made a decision, heading into the thickest of the crowds. He heard frustrated cries behind him, and yet as he looked, he saw one man scrabbling over the wall, either athletic indeed, or given a boost up by one of the other men.

Gabriel started weaving in and out of the crowd, using the odd street vending stall to take himself out of sight. He needed a change of clothes or a refuge. His progress was now down to a brisk walk through the crowds, as he didn't want to attract attention to himself and risk any brave souls deciding to tackle him themselves, and make a citizen's arrest.

As the street narrowed, he was hampered further by the mass of bodies, and he decided to take the first street junction he came to, now moving at ninety degrees to his original path. Just as Gabriel was about out onto the parallel street, around the corner came the young man who had accosted him at the graveside, running flat out, and out of breath, but he pulled up short with a grin on his face as he saw the surprised Gabriel. He drew his gun again as he approached.

"That's far enough, I think," he announced, pleased with himself. Gabriel had nowhere to go. The cop must be local, and had second-guessed Gabriel's movements. That meant trained in surveillance, and he looked too young for normal police work. That also meant Special Forces, and therefore trouble. He'd pissed somebody off, for sure.

He stood his ground as the man approached. "We both know you're not going to use that," he pointed out. "You had ample chance to shoot me in the cemetery. You're certainly not going to do it here, in public, with so many witnesses. I'm not going to surrender myself, so let's get down to it!" He launched a high swivel-kick at Angelo's upper body. Angelo dropped the gun to block the kick, grunting as it hit home, but found it carried considerably less force than he had expected.

He took the attack to Gabriel, launching a kick himself, though more Thai than Savate. Gabriel knew many different forms of unarmed combat. He didn't want to kill the younger man, and so was restricting his reactions, but he had to escape. He couldn't afford to be embroiled in any local law enforcement issues. The police shouldn't even think him alive. What had changed?

The two men jockeyed back and forth, trading blows and blocks, as a crowd began to gather. This wasn't what Gabriel wanted at all, and his blows became more savage, drawing blood now as he moved inside Angelo's own blow to land one of his own, rocking the younger man's head, and yet he came back, ignoring the blood which now streaked his face.

"It's your fault she died! Yours!" he cursed, as he slammed a fist into Gabriel's ribcage, and then a second. Gabriel grunted with pain, trying to block the blows, as one of them made him wince. He grabbed Angelo's arm, pivoted, and threw him against a parked car, giving himself a breather as the younger man painfully got to his feet. The surrounding crowd were now hampering any sort of quick getaway by Gabriel. He had to finish this before they would let him move. Yet the man's words were personal. He hadn't just been a police plant at the funeral, as Gabriel had first thought. He was related.

"What was she to you? I loved the woman. Why do you think I was at the grave?" he panted, getting his breath back, and readying himself for the next attack, which he knew wouldn't be long in coming.

"You put her there!" Angelo accused. "She was my mother! I don't understand what I've been told about you, or how you could be my Father, but I do know that if it is you, you abandoned her when she needed you the most." Gabriel stood looking Angelo over. He was momentarily stunned by the man's words. Physically, there was a good resemblance, and he would be the right age, if not for one thing.

"Your mother had one child before I met her, and he died when he was three. She couldn't have children after that. She told me so."

Angelo sneered. "My mother said a lot of things she didn't mean, but she was my mother nonetheless. Your photo hangs on the wall in her house. The same damn face, though it should be a lot older now in the flesh. She's never discussed you with me in all the years, and you never contacted her, as far as I know. I grew up without a father," he accused, "yet my mother was all that mattered to me. But now you did finally call, and it's cost her life. I can never forgive you for that, Father or not!"

Angelo came at him once more as the crowd surged around them, cheering on both he and Angelo, as they took sides in this contest they knew so little about. Gabriel contented himself just with blocking the blows that came, and they were many, letting Angelo tire himself out, as he deliberated on the younger man's words.

Denny had sometimes been a scheming little bitch, though he had loved her for it at the time. Many local girls had done their best to get pregnant by a foreign boyfriend as a way of getting out of Jakarta, and poverty, and he supposed it was feasible that she might have lied to him, hoping for a happy ending when she finally announced she was pregnant. Though she had never gotten the chance to tell him, had she?

Once Borgia had tracked him down in Singapore, Gabriel had to make himself scarce, and, fearful for Denny, he had severed all ties, so as to avoid Solomon tracking her down and threatening her life as a lever against him.

The hate seemed genuine, for this certainly seemed personal. If it had happened to him, would he act any differently? Suddenly he was reminded of the similarities between the man and Belle, his daughter.

So much anger inside. Blocking the blows hurt, careful not to meet them directly and chance his hollow bones, he let them glide off his arms, and yet he was reluctant now to fight back.

"Fight, damn you!" Angelo roared, lashing out with yet another kick. The noise from the crowd was changing, and it took Gabriel a few seconds to realize it. Looking up, beyond Angelo, he could see the crowd parting in fear, and his lack of concentration let Angelo's next blow hit home, and his head rocked, blood spurting from his mouth.

The cheers were turning to screams of fear. Bodies trying to run, to flee, but caught up in the mass of watching the impromptu street-fight. Gabriel saw the turbaned figure that was suddenly causing the panic. His linen overshirt was now hanging open wide, revealing the sticks of homemade explosive that circled his waist, and he was frantically fiddling with the contraption around his waist.

"Down!" Gabriel flung himself at Angelo, avoiding the first, and taking the second blow, as he forced Angelo back off his feet, and Gabriel fell down on top of him, covering him as the huge explosion ripped the crowd apart, and Gabriel's breath was lost as the explosion hit him, lifted him, and smashed him into the wall. Everything went black, and Gabriel lapsed in and out of consciousness amid a world of pain, his nostrils full of the smell of smoke, and burnt flesh.

Chapter Seventeen

Gabriel awoke out of a maddening dream, the details of which he couldn't remember. His mouth tasted of blood and drugs, and his eyes opened slowly to take in his surroundings. The leg strung up in a protective cocoon in front of him must be his own. Both his hands were bandaged and the bandages felt as though they extended all the way up to his elbows. He was in a hospital bed, though in a private room.

The pain hit him as he tried to sit up, and he then took it slowly, exploring his body, trying to estimate the extent of his injuries. His leg hurt, obviously, though whatever they'd shot him full of was dulling the pain. It didn't feel broken, probably elevated just to reduce the blood-flow. His head ached, and his vision was blurring a little, probably concussion from the explosion. There was salve and protective bandages across one side of his face, probably for superficial burns. He felt a lot better than he looked.

Gabriel reached out and managed to press the call-button by the bedside, and a minute later, the door was opened by a policeman, to admit the nurse. Gabriel noted the chair outside the door. They obviously wanted him to go nowhere, till the hospital released him. The nurse smiled as she came into the room, obviously pleased to see him regain consciousness. "Hello, Sir. I'm so pleased you're feeling better," she announced, checking his chart from the foot of the bed.

"Would you mind if I looked at the chart, nurse?" he asked, trying to sit up. She rushed around the bed to help him, elevating the end of the bed, and settling a pillow under his back, before she handed over the chart, and made him take a thermometer in his mouth. Gabriel complied. It was better than getting one shoved up his arse. He acted the perfect patient, as he read the doctor's notes, the physical damage to his body, which wouldn't take long to heal by itself, and the drugs they had tranquilised him with. "When was I admitted, nurse?" he asked.

"Yesterday, sir. Your injuries aren't too serious compared to some of the other poor people, but we thought it best to tranquilise you, and keep you in for a few days to check on your concussion. The police insisted in placing a guard outside your door, sir. I'm terribly sorry but the Administration could do nothing about it."

"No need to apologise," Gabriel reassured her. "What about the young man? Tall, dark suit, black hair? He was with me when the explosion occurred."

"That would be Mr Zoro, sir. I understand he's working with the police trying to track down these suicide bomber fanatics. That's the third one we've had this month. Mr Zoro escaped with just a broken arm. We set it, and allowed him to discharge himself. He said he had things to do," she explained. "Are you hungry? We are still serving luncheon. I'll get you a menu." Gabriel smiled in response, and waited patiently till she returned.

The food was good, and he was certainly hungry enough, having eaten nothing since the plane, though difficult to eat with his bandaged hands. As he digested it, he was trying to think of his next move. Was the man his son? It looked that way. He was certainly Denny's son, and yet the likeness to Belle seemed unmistakeable. A son who blamed him for his mother's death.

He had shed his tears yesterday. He couldn't afford any more. He had other more immediate problems, such as finding his current partner and daughter, finding out if there was one more angel still alive out there. Someone to share the loneliness and isolation he still felt, even in a relationship as satisfying as the one he had with Laura, and a reconciled prodigal daughter. Could he reconcile with Angelo, if he accepted him as his son? Would the angry young man allow it?

His current position was not one of strength, and the chart had him down as requiring another three or four days of this hospitalization. He needed to escape from here before that time had run out; else the police would have him in custody.

It was later in the afternoon, after the nurse had cleared up the remnant of his meal, and offered him a bedpan, which he'd tactfully refused, for the time being anyway, that Turnbull came to see him. The policeman outside the room allowed him in, and resumed his seat as the door closed.

"What happened, Nick? How did it all go so wrong? Have you heard from Laura or Belle yet?" he had many questions for the younger man.

"Too many cooks, I guess," he shrugged his shoulders. "I'd found the two of them, and was working on getting them out of there, when who pops up but your old girlfriend."

"I didn't ask her to get this closely involved, Nick," Gabriel interrupted him, but Nick waved him quiet.

"She was of great help in freeing the girls, but unknown to either of us, Angelo had had me followed there, and decided to show up himself. When the shooting started, he ran protectively to his mother, and as he did so, he drew fire from one of the opposition. He didn't see it, but she did, and pushed him out of the way of the bullet. She wasn't so lucky." Gabriel was shaking his head, slowly, eyes closed.

"What about Belle and Laura?" he eventually asked.

"Physically, they're okay, at least I think so. Laura looked like she'd gone through hell, and those bite marks on her neck looked nasty. Julie cleaned them out with antiseptic as best she . . ."

"What bite-marks?" asked Gabriel, coming suddenly awake.

"That woman, Angelica."

"Angelica???" Gabriel was stunned at the news of her involvement here.

"Look, Belle's told me about the vampire thing. I don't believe it, and I don't disbelieve it. But I've seen the bite-marks, and the woman gave me the creeps. Whatever those bites are, Laura didn't want you to see them. She wanted to go away somewhere and stay away until they healed."

"I'm afraid those bites won't go away so quickly by themselves, Nick. I've had experience before, and so has Laura. The bite injects a sort of toxin that reacts with your bloodstream. It's best she had a full blood transfusion, though Belle will probably understand that. She's more of an expert on toxins and poisons than I am myself," he complimented her. "She'll probably seek Solomon's help in obtaining medical aid and transport. If that's the case, there's nothing more I can do here unless she gets in touch, however long it takes."

"I got the license number of the car they left in, if that's any help?" he offered, but Gabriel shook his head.

"If Belle doesn't want to be found, she won't make it that easy."

"How long are you going to be in here?" Nick asked, trying to change the subject, as he felt partly at fault for the mess.

"Not as long as they think I am, that's for sure," he answered. "What time is it? They took my watch," he explained. Nick checked his.

"About twenty past four."

"Give it till seven, and it'll be dark. Does your car have a sunroof?" he asked. Nick nodded. "Well make sure it's open when you park underneath my window. I can see the treetops, through the window, so this room is only on the first floor, and it should be an easy drop."

"What about your injuries?"

"Mainly superficial, and the concussion will take care of itself. Seven o'clock. Don't be late. Honk the horn once, and give me a couple of minutes to get out of this bed and out of the window. Any more than that, and I won't be coming, so make yourself scarce. If you've got any spare clothes, I think we're about the same size. I'll change in the car."

"You sure you're up for this?" Nick asked.

"I'm a fast healer, remember?" Gabriel smiled reassuringly.

"Okay. It's your funeral."

"Not for a few years, yet, I hope." Nick left, and the police guard closed the door, leaving Gabriel alone with his thoughts. The drugs and the strapping would help until he got back to the hotel and assessed the damage for himself. His metabolism would quickly heal anything which wasn't too serious. Getting out of Jakarta could prove more of a problem than Oman, though, with the authorities involved.

They'd have someone watching the airports, now Angelo had had a look at him, beard or no beard. They didn't know his travelling identity though, so he should be safe overnight in the hotel. Then, tomorrow, he needed to make himself scarce. There were always small boats looking to make some money by something not too illegal. One of them could take him over to the mainland of Malaysia, or one of the other Indonesian islands.

Gabriel tried taking his leg out of the sling. It was awkward, but manageable, so he left it there for now. As he stared out at the skyline through the window, he wondered how much Belle had revealed to Turnbull. If he knew about the vampirism angle, what else had she told him? Gabriel trusted him but there were degrees of trust. He had gone out on a limb to rescue Belle and Laura though, on no more than a friendly request from Jim Maddox.

Was friendship and trust so far gone now from his makeup? How alienated did he really feel in this modern world? He was certainly feeling it more lately, with everything that had happened to him since finding Laura again. Lucifer's death in England, finding his daughter in Rome, and now it looked like he had a son, one who blamed him for his mother's death. Under present circumstances, he couldn't even hang around to discuss it with him, without the risk of imprisonment.

*   *   *

Two floors above Gabriel, in another private ward, another patient was having a phone brought into her room, now that her drug intake had been reduced. She could move and think coherently. A metal cage covered the lower half of her body, and one arm was heavily bandaged due to burns. The bandages around her head were mainly cosmetic, as most of her hair had been burned off in the fire. When the nurse left, the patient picked up the receiver painfully with her bandaged hand, and used her uninjured hand to dial.

"Yes?" a male voice answered impatiently. Angelica paused before responding.

"This is an insecure line, so I'll be brief. There was an incident, a fire at the club. The authorities are investigating," she paused, letting the import of that statement sink in, before continuing. "Our two friends left. They had help."

"What are you doing about it?" was Bird's reply.

"Not much I can do from a hospital bed. I was injured, badly, and I need an operation. I won't quite be the same "woman" ever again," she sighed.

"Very well, I have their photos. My people will be informed. Phone me again when you can." Bird hung up.

There was nothing more to say on an open line. She could sense the displeasure in his voice about the threat to his operation, particularly if the police managed to retrieve anything off the computer's hard drive. All paper records would have gone up in the fire, and she hoped the heat would have damaged the hard drive too, but no way of knowing until the police actually charged her or let her go. In the meantime she had more pressing matters to contend with.

Belle had used that broken bottle well. She'd grown more ruthless and savage since their last encounter. Angelica had underestimated her, and she now would need to go through with the full sex-change operation she had been unable to face those many years ago. It would make a new woman of her. Maybe Belle had unwittingly done her a favour? One for which she would have to thank her, sometime in the future.

*   *   *

Seven pm was slow coming, and Gabriel waited until the nurse cleared away his meal tray before removing his leg from the elevated trapeze. It was well strapped, but he could stand on it, though walking was awkward. He lay back down on the bed, with his legs under the sheets, in case the police guard decided to pop his head around the door.

He heard a single honk of a horn just below his bedroom window, and finally made his move. Throwing back the sheets, he went over to the open window and looked down. Turnbull had parked half on the grass verge to get the roof of his car directly below the window. The sunroof was slid back as he'd asked for. Gabriel pulled at the bandage on his leg, loosening it somewhat. He couldn't drop straight into the seat, and that meant bending the leg to land on the rear part of the roof first. Flexing the leg, he removed enough of the bandages to allow him to bend the knee, and then he sat and swivelled on the window frame. Once his legs were out, he levered himself out of the window, dropping and grabbing the frame with his hands as he checked beneath him. He pushed out, and dropped the ten feet or so, onto the roof of Turnbull's car, the suspension rocking as his weight suddenly was added.

Crouching and sliding, he slid into the passenger seat through the open sunroof. It had taken only a few seconds, and Turnbull was now pulling off from the verge, and heading towards the main gate as Gabriel buckled up. The rear of the hospital grounds were dark and no one had seen him dropping from the first floor window.

Once they were out of the grounds, he pulled over, and Gabriel climbed in the back to change his clothes. He bundled the pajamas up, and threw them into the nearby bushes. He did the same with the bandages he removed from his head and arms. His face looked a bit red, but he now looked respectable enough to get back into the hotel.

As they drove, Nick began to talk. "While I was doing a recon, I came across an office with a computer, and had a look through a few files. I copied them off onto a floppy, but I screwed up and left the disk in my jacket pocket when I loaned the jacket to Belle, so she's got it. I still remember some of the details though," he apologized. Gabriel let him continue. "Most of the e-mails came from Thailand, from a character who calls himself 'Bird'. Leastways I assume it's a he, you can never tell in this part of the world. Anyway, not sure if it's a real name or a nickname. I can get Maddox to look into that end. A lot of the consignment notes seemed to come out of Cambodia. Blue Elephant something or other. A place called Kampong Thom, or something similar. I think its north of Phnom Pehn, near the Mekong River. I can maybe wangle an extended "holiday" out of this and check out the Thailand angle if you like?" he suggested.

"Leaving me to check out the Cambodia angle? Could be a plan. I don't like the fact that Belle has got her hands on the disk, though," he frowned. "No telling what they might do. Women can be so predictable in their unpredictability."

"A bit like football teams. I have a mate who's a Middlesbrough supporter. Poor bastard," he chuckled. "What are you going to do about Angelo? What do you want me to tell him'"

"I don't have time to do anything about Angelo, Nick. If I hang around, the police will catch me eventually, and once inside, I doubt I'd find it so easy to get out. I'll have to put that problem off for a future time. As for what to tell him, as little as possible obviously. If you have to, tell him I'll be in touch, but only when I'm a long way from Jakarta." The rest of the drive was conducted in silence. Gabriel wouldn't be missed at the hospital for a couple of hours, and Nick needed to establish an alibi for the questions that would surely come with the morning.

Gabriel left him to park the car, and entered the hotel lobby by himself, asking for his key at Reception, and then going quickly up to his room to change, and remove the rest of the bandages. Half an hour later, he called on Nick's room. Nick opened the door, looking surprised as he saw that Gabriel had shaved off most of his beard, now leaving just a moustache. "You need to show your face downstairs in the restaurant or somewhere," Gabriel suggested. "But before you go, do you have any bleach or something similar in your make-up kit?" he asked Julie. "I need to change my appearance a bit more. Make it look as though I have a few grey roots under a bad dye job. That's how a lot of the locals here treat their hair."

"I've got something for adding highlight streaks, if that's any good?" she suggested, and Gabriel nodded as she rummaged through her bag. "Come into the bathroom, and I'll do it for you," she suggested, and Gabriel accompanied her into the bathroom, while Nick got changed. Gabriel quickly showed her how to do it, and she got the hang of it easily enough. "Tell me something, I'm curious. Looking as young as you do, it kinda spooks me to think of you as my Dad's friend. How did you meet him?"

Gabriel let her work on his hair, as his mind flashed back through the years. "I needed to lay low for a time, and I also wanted some military training," he began, though without explaining his need for it. Every so often, as the world changed around him, Gabriel felt the need to try and play catch up with technology, politics and the military. "It's easy to get lost in the Military, like a single blade of grass in a field. I looked around and plumped for the British Army. I had a few specialist skills, and was sent to Norway for a while. Then I got put forward for the SAS, and eventually got a transfer to Oman where I met Jim."

"Why the British Army? Why not the Americans?" she wondered. Gabriel smirked.

"The Brits were always better organized, disciplined, better soldiers," he revealed. "That's what I wanted to be, a better soldier."

"What nationality are you?" she asked, touching up his sideburns now.

"Truth to tell, I don't know. My earliest memories are in and around the Mediterranean. I honestly can't remember."

"So you and my Dad palled around for a few years in Oman?"

"Yes. Best mates and best rivals, me and your Dad. We fell in love with the same girl, and I ended up a poor second," he admitted.

"I've met Rebekah. She's a nice woman. I hope she and Dad will get married. They're good for each other."

"Yes, Rebel was some woman, and she eventually ended up with the right man, though a few years got in the way. I hope I get invited to the wedding," he revealed. Julie switched sideburns as Gabriel turned. This close, he could see some resemblance to his old friend, mainly in the eyes and cheekbones, though her mother, whom Gabriel had never met, must have been a beautiful woman.

"There, how does that look?" she asked, indicating the mirror above the sink, and Gabriel turned to admire her handiwork, turning his head this way and that. Not too overt, and would appear typical in this part of the world. He nodded.

"Damn good job. Thank you, Julie." She opened the bathroom door, and Gabriel called out. "Nick, could I have a quick word?" he smiled at Julie to reassure her, and she vacated the small bathroom to make way for Nick. He took the hint and closed the door behind him.

"What's up?"

"Probably nothing, I'd just like to know what Belle told you about me, about my 'Family'," he smiled, reassuringly.

"She confirmed a few things about you that have been bugging me. Though I still can't believe half of it, yet I can't think of any other explanation. Your special blood, and about how it keeps you alive, and prolongs the life of anyone who drinks it. Why it's the reason so many people are after you." Gabriel appeared to be considering his words carefully.

"Don't take this the wrong way, Nick, but my secrets remain secret for a good reason. I'm sure you can understand that. Even Jim doesn't know of them, though I know he has his suspicions. I trust you as a friend, but even friends can only be trusted so far. What you don't know, you can't tell, right?"

"I know the drill. Don't worry." For a second, just a second, Nick was suddenly wary, as if unsure what Gabriel's next move was going to be. All at once, Nick found himself being more aware of his surroundings, taking in distances, clearances, the same automatic things he did before going into a fight

"I'm not worried Nick, but you should be. Anyone who knows that much information about me is in danger from those that seek that knowledge. How much does Julie know?" he asked.

"Only bits of it," Nick revealed.

"Best keep it that way, and do the same with Jim. I don't like my friendship putting my friends in danger. I'd rather Belle hadn't told you as much as she had, but now you know, so the weight of that knowledge now lies on your shoulders." Nick was beginning to appreciate the full import of what Gabriel had just explained.

"I can be trusted."

"Belle has good judgement. I don't doubt it," Gabriel smiled, reassuringly. "But you'd best know what you've just let yourself in for. For instance, let me tell you what I know about 'vampirism', Nick," Gabriel went on. "It's not your standard 'Bram Stoker' tale, though I'm sure his novel was based on fact, probably second-hand, and exaggerated a bit to suit the popular beliefs of the times. They're not really un-dead, as far as I know. There is no aversion to sunlight, crucifixes or anything supernatural. It's some sort of disease, purely physical. The bite injects some sort of stimulant or paralytic toxin, rendering the victim effectively helpless to allow the vampire to feed. Some animals, reptiles and insects adopt similar methods, as you're probably aware. There's also some sort of enzyme that gets into the bloodstream to infect the wound. Laura's first experience was just a single bite, and it took months to heal. As for how the infection is passed on, as it must be, for Borgia and then Angelica to have gotten infected, I can only assume it must be some sort of ritualized drinking of the vampire's own blood, which carries some sort of parasite. The bite alone obviously isn't enough to pass the infection on. I can only hope Angelica contented herself with merely feeding off Laura's enriched blood. Otherwise, we're in uncharted territory," he frowned. "Belle would know more about the effect of these toxins than me, and she's with Laura, so can check for herself, and I'm sure she'll ensure Laura gets the best possible treatment, if she needs it. But yes, I'm worried, obviously," he admitted. "She wouldn't be staying away if she wasn't worried, herself. She'd be with me, letting me help her. Nothing I can do for now but trust Belle to do the right thing."

"You know, Belle thinks in some strange way, you and this 'vampire' are related. She's right, the blood-drinking sounds somewhat similar to what happens when people drink *your* blood. It prolongs their lives to a degree, according to her."

"I have my own theories about that. The similarities *are* obvious. But I'll keep those theories to myself, if you don't mind?" Gabriel was already thinking back to all the legends of strange creatures that supposedly roamed this planet at some time in the distant past. As the years advanced, such tales grew less and less.

History has a way of obscuring the past where no evidence remains to the present day. It doesn't mean things never happened, or such creatures didn't exist, just that no evidence had been found to support such theories. If such evidence could indeed be found one day, then parts of history would have to be rewritten.

His mind kept going back to Malevar, the alien Genetic Scientist who was responsible for creating Gabriel and his hybrid race. His own DNA had been a mixture of human, avian, faery and elf. What else could Malevar have created in his laboratories and unleashed on the world? The known world of that time contained many legends about strange creatures in both Greek and Roman Mythology. Were they all really myths, or simply some of Malevar's creations?

"It's time I went. My absence from the hospital is going to be noticed soon, and it's better if you were in plain view when that happens. It's best you don't know how I'm going to leave the country, and I'll head for Cambodia. Let Jim know he can expect to hear from me, and we can liaise through him, okay?"

"I'd be happier contacting you direct."

"Wait till I get to Cambodia. Once I pick up a local cell-phone, and a few spare sim-cards, I'll let Jim have the numbers to pass on to you. One time only calls. Cell-phones are getting too easy to trace, almost as bad as landlines. Just try and get some enjoyment out of the trip to Bangkok with Julie, and look after her. Jim Maddox is a very protective Father since his wife died."

"Don't worry, I plan on looking after Julie for a good few years yet," Nick grinned.

*　　*　　*

Angelo was dumbfounded by news of Gabriel's disappearance from the hospital, and after initiating a search and organizing roadblocks and extra security at the airport, he called Nick in to his office first thing the next morning, obviously in a foul mood, partly due to the lack of sleep, and partly due to having his prisoner escape from under his nose. "He was badly injured. How did he escape without help? You must have had a hand in it, Turnbull!" he accused. "I've already checked at the hotel, and they confirm you were there visiting him yesterday, but something's not right." His instincts were usually correct.

"Prove it." Nick smiled. "I visited him in the afternoon, yes, but he was still there for his evening meal, wasn't he? I didn't go back inside the hospital, or the cctv cameras would have picked me up, even if your man had missed me, wouldn't they?" There was something phony behind Nick's smile, but nothing Angelo could disprove, although he had his suspicions.

"I'll find him, Turnbull. However long it takes. I'll find him," he warned, frustrated.

"Enjoy the search. Now if there's something else I can help with? This trip was only supposed to be for one week, and we made some progress on tracking down that cell. Anything on the surveillance?" he asked, trying to get Angelo's mind focused on something else other than Gabriel.

"Forensics will have some news this afternoon, about the latest bomber. If we can identify him, and tie him in to any of the surveillance photos, we'll be organizing a raid on the place before the day is over. I'd like to go in now, but my hands are tied."

"Yeah, I know what that's like. Your gut tells you you're right, and more times than not, you are, but that's what the justice system is for. It makes the decisions, not you. We all wish the red tape would go away, or at least not take as long."

"You interested in taking part in that raid, or has your interest evaporated now Gabriel has come and gone?" Angelo asked, pointedly.

"My plane doesn't leave till tomorrow. I came here to help you as well as him, so yes I'm up for it. Police, or Special Forces?" he asked.

"You, me, and the police. Our Special Forces aren't as readily on call, as are your own. We have all the main islands to cover, and that's difficult enough. Many areas of pure jungle offer lots of hiding places for these insurgents. Plus they don't call this the Sea Of A Thousand Islands for nothing," he pointed out. "Our police are well trained, though, and with you and I leading, well, we're not expecting an army in there," he explained.

"You sure you're up to it?" Nick asked, pointing out the left arm which was securely strapped in a sling.

"I only need one hand to operate a gun. I'll manage. I'll let you lead, though, if it makes you feel any better. Wouldn't want you thinking I was a liability," Angelo added.

"Just out of curiosity, how is your health generally?"

"Normally fine. Had a couple of childhood illnesses, but nothing lasts for long. Fit as a fiddle, isn't that what you say in England? This is the first serious injury I've had," he admitted.

"Keep an eye on it. I think you'll be surprised at how fast it heals," Nick advised.

*   *   *

It was indeed a Sea Of A Thousand Islands, and small boats were almost impossible to track, if the captain knew his navigation well. It had taken Gabriel only a few hours scouring some of the bars near the docks, till he had found the right man. A few thousand rupiah later, Gabriel followed the man to his boat. He carried only a small rucksack, the laptop and papers stuffed inside. He had left most of his luggage at the hotel. It was a small fishing boat, and Gabriel offered to help with the work, which the captain seemed glad about, as he was always short-staffed. Working as one of the crew would help his cover in case they did run into any of the patrol boats. Once they had made their catch for the day, they would drop Gabriel off at one of the other larger islands, and he could make his way to the Mainland from there.

*   *   *

Later that day, after escorting Julie around some of the congested malls in the various Bloks, Nick checked in with Angelo by phone as promised, and was relieved to find the raid was now going ahead. Anything to save his poor feet. He didn't know how women could do it, particularly in those high-heels, but wandering around from shop to shop was wearing out his shoes. He gave Julie the 'bad' news, and dropped her off back at the hotel, then directing the taxi driver back to Police HQ.

Two minivans were already being kitted out in the walled car-park, with officers in riot gear stowing equipment, and checking weapons. Angelo was on the radio to officers in place near the building, getting a sit-rep on current events. He gave the headset back to the driver as he saw Nick approach. Angelo looked funny with his bad arm now under the oversize flak-jacket, but it meant he didn't need a sling, and it held his arm securely enough.

"Come with me and get kitted-out. Pretty calm at the house, and we reckon there are only three people in there. Should be an easy takedown. We go in hard, stun grenades and light weapons. Do you concur?"

"Yep, that's pretty much how we'd do it back home, as long as we were happy with the intel. Your men on site good? Reliable?"

"Yes, experienced men."

"They gone up against terrorists before?"

"No. Police often only deal with the aftermath of terrorism. But they'll have to do. This seems to be just a low-key cell. No smarts, just idiots stupid enough to follow a Mullah's directive to enter Paradise. They never question why the Mullahs aren't stupid enough to join them."

"Yeah, I've been up against Al Qaeda recently myself. Grunts are expendable. It's the boys with the brains we need to catch, but they rarely pop up long enough to snatch. Okay, you and me lead the way. I'm point, and I'll advise if I see fit, and if I do, you fucking well listen to me, okay?" Nick insisted. "No grandstand heroics. I know you're currently pissed off with Gabriel getting away from you, but don't try and make up for one perceived failure by screwing up. Being alive at the end of the day is a victory. The best type."

"Don't worry, Turnbull. I know my priorities. Let's do this," and he handed Nick a flak-jacket. The equipment looked more SWAT than the gear the SAS used, but it would have to do. Jacket, helmet, combat knife, automatic, throat-mike personal comms. All tuned to the same frequency. No time to organize anything else. Nick checked the magazine of the gun, to ensure it moved nice and smooth, dropping out the clip and reinserting it.

Accuracy was less important in close quarter combat, else he would have insisted in practicing with it first. Just point and pull at close-range. TV and movies didn't really tell it like it was in a fire-fight. All those bullets flying, and hardly anyone got hurt. It was more brutal than that in real life. Gunfire was usually a lot more accurate than tv ever made out, at least when professionals were doing the shooting, instead of actors. The van held six people, nothing too big; else they might have difficulty navigating some of the narrow streets.

During the drive, Nick was checking out some of the surveillance photos, when something caught his eye. One man in the background of the photo, half turned away as he entered the adjacent compound in the background, and slightly out of focus. He nudged Angelo. "Check this out. Does that guy seem familiar?" Angelo studied the photo.

"It could be one of the men," he admitted. "Hard to tell, in profile."

"This adjacent building, would it be anything like the one we've been watching?" Nick asked, as he studied the blueprint of the house concerned.

"Probably near enough identical," Angelo confirmed.

"Then it's likely they'll also have a basement here, near the bordering compound wall," he pointed out.

"Are you thinking they might have tunnelled through"'"

"Houses aren't really big enough to hold a number of men, arms etc. They need to be ready for a search, so where better to hide stuff than an adjacent building, as long as no one knows of the connection. Also an easy escape route."

"We may have more on our hands than we thought," Angelo frowned. "We can't be sure, so can't go in all guns blazing, and we don't have a warrant for the adjacent property," he pointed out.

"Get back on the radio, and see if your men have noticed anyone entering or leaving the adjacent property today," Nick suggested. "Looks like we'll have to split the men. Go in hard and fast in the compound as planned, and while we're making a lot of noise in there. Let them think they're safe in the other house. Second team goes in more covertly. Takes 'em out while they think they've got away with it. How does that sound?"

"As good as we can manage in the time we have. We'll worry about the legalities of the warrant later."

Nick smiled. "Now you're thinking more like the SAS." Angelo liked the compliment. "Better if you let me handle the illegal end. That way, any comebacks will be on me, and my flight is leaving tomorrow anyway," Nick suggested.

Angelo agreed. "I'll flush them out, and you take them down. Sounds good to me. Try not to get any of my men killed in the process."

"I'll even try not to kill any of these insurgents, as I know you need information. But if they're fanatics, and insist on it, I'll be shooting to kill, rather than let them have a pop at me. Fair enough?" Angelo nodded. "Right then, let's get moving."

The two vans parked a couple of streets away from the houses currently under surveillance. Angelo made contact with his team of watchers, and split them up between his and Nick's squad. Nick quickly explained the game-plan, and then everyone moved to put it into action, Angelo holding off, until Nick and his team had gained entry to the property.

A mirror on a pole was used to give a quick view of the property beyond the metal doors. The lock was wired into an alarm system, so it looked like over the wall. The mirror revealed nothing obvious in the yard, not even a dog. Rubber mats were quickly thrown over the broken glass on top of the walls, and Nick and his men boosted themselves over with a minimum of fuss, dropping quietly and assuming positions close to the wall, where the shadows lay from the streetlights. Only a few windows of the house showed any lights, and heavy curtains revealed no detail of what was happening within, or allowed those inside to see outside. The occupants must have felt pretty secure. Nick spoke into his throat mike. "Two minutes, and it's a GO."

"Roger that. Two minutes, on my mark," replied Angelo. Nick was quickly directing his men by hand signals, and they approached the building, crouching down by the windows, and fixing up numerous sucker-microphones to the glass panes, monitoring the conversations within. Det-charges were quickly laid along the ground floor window frames, and others on the hinges and lock of the front door. He wasn't sure they would be needed, hoping the occupants would rush blindly out as the neighbouring house was raided, but better safe than sorry. The men assigned to him were taking his orders smoothly enough, and seemed as though they knew what they were doing. He hoped Angelo's men were just as well-trained.

Mentally, Nick was counting down. He rarely looked at his watch at times like these. His own internal clock was more reliable. He felt the adrenalin rush, the hairs standing up on his arms, as the time approached. On the other side of that wall, Angelo and his men were making the same preparations as Nick and his men. Surprise and confusion was what they wanted. Enough explosive to deafen and confuse the hell out of anyone inside the house. All they needed was the first few seconds to make their entry, and then one on one, better training and better weapons should decide the outcome.

BOOOOOOMMMMMM. All the explosions seemed to go off simultaneously, and they lit up the sky, the flashes reflecting off the low clouds that hid the moon. Gunfire, some static, some on auto, cries from within the house, and answering gunfire now from within. Angelo was under orders not to immediately storm the house, but to give the occupants time to realize they were in a no-win situation, and let them look for a way out, in the tunnel they thought no one else knew about . . . Nick and his men were waiting to spring the real trap.

He was listening to the feed from out of the suction microphones on the windowpanes, as the conversation inside got agitated moments after the explosions were heard from next door. He always had trouble with the many dialects they used here, so it took a few moments to grasp the heated conversation. He recognized one word "explosives". More voices added to the cacophony of sound, as Nick gathered people were funnelling through the tunnel. He struggled to make any sense of the snatches of conversation he overheard. The tunnel. It suddenly struck Nick that the best place to hide their explosives was where they would easily be missed, in a tunnel which wasn't on any of the official house plans.

Instantly, he thumbed his throat mike. "Angelo!!!! . . . . Angelo!!! . . . ." No reply, just gunfire, and more gunfire. The terrorists were withdrawing down the tunnel as expected, but it looked like the tunnel was going to blown up as their pursuers came down it. No time. He turned to one of his own men. "Blow the doors, now! We're going in." A quick hand signal to the rest of his squad to take cover, and BOOOOOOOMMMMM the charges went off, blowing doors and windows in this side of the compound wall.

Nick was through the doorframe, before the door fell. They had seconds at most. His squad were right behind him. The stunned terrorists were shocked and stunned into immobility for a vital few seconds, long enough for the 2nd string of police to get into the room, and they showed the stunned men little mercy. Guns chattered, spraying lead about the room. Nick grunted as he took a round in his flak-jacket, but that was what he wore it for. He didn't look back, just charged for the back room, shooting one man as he raised to a kneeling position from behind an overturned table. He kept going, down the stairs to the basement, shooting one man at the bottom of the stairs.

With all the smoke and noise, he barely spotted the second man, and a bullet whistled past his cheek as he fired back, double-tapping the guy, and slamming him back against the wall. Wires were everywhere on the floor, coming out from under the door, as he looked around frantically. Too many wires to cut. Where did they all go?

He dropped to the floor as a robed man flew down the stairs behind him with a Kalashnikov. Nick fired as he dropped to one knee, hitting the man in the leg, and as he dropped, and fell painfully down the stairs, Nick took him out finally with a head shot, before he had time to recover. He staggered to his feet, shooting through the basement door, before shoulder charging it open, raising his gun as he rushed into the room, rolling as shots were fired at him.

Two men, one with a gun. Nick blasted him with a gut shot, one more to the head. Out of bullets as the second man tried to attach the wires to a detonator, Nick pulled his knife, and leapt up off the floor, grappling with the man as he was forced to drop the detonator and half-attached wiring. He was big and he was strong, but still grunted with pain as Nick drove his knee up into the man's groin, once, twice, then head-butting him as he spun him around, tripping him and falling down on top of him, both hands behind the knife, forcing it down, into the man's chest. Nick took a knee in his own groin, grunting, as the man fought for his life, trying to force back Nick's hands, but the blade bit as he gasped, and then Nick forced it home, burying it in his ribcage, sawing to the side, as he had been taught. The fetid air rushed out of his ribcage and into Nick's face, but he was well-used to the stench of death.

Rolling free, Nick grabbed the wires, pulling them loose. He had been lucky they weren't pre-wired for such an eventuality. A few seconds more, and there would have been a few more virgins getting shagged in Paradise.

He grabbed his gun, reaching into his pocket for the spare clip, and reloading, before he left the room once more. Gunfire was only sporadic now. "Angelo!!!" he tried the throat mike once more.

"I'm clear. I pulled my men back when I spotted the wiring. I've got men guarding the house, and I'm coming round to help you. We'll keep out of your way, and just watch for stragglers, if that's okay. Less chance of any friendly fire that way."

"Roger that. Mopping up in here. 2nd assault took them by surprise." As he cautiously came back up the stairs and showed himself, giving hand signals to his men, there were only three terrorists left alive. One insisted of getting himself shot. The other two obviously weren't keen on virgins, and gave themselves up, finally. Nick took charge of checking the dead, to make sure they were actually dead, and left the police to bind the two captives. "We have two live ones. Everyone else preferred Paradise. Two police slightly wounded."

"Only one wounded my side. Leg wound, bleeding badly. I think his femoral artery caught it. We have him strapped up. Ambulances shouldn't be long. Bring 'em out and we'll keep them inside the compound till we can secure the area. We need to get Bomb Disposal in here to make sure those explosives are rendered harmless and then taken away from here. We'll get men in to search the place in the morning. Good work, Nick."

"Sounds like you did alright yourself. Not bad for a cripple," he laughed.

"Fuck you, Turnbull," Angelo chuckled in return. He found it strange that he could manage that laugh, albeit briefly. Inside he was still hurting, though managing to do his job as good as he had ever done it. Training, all else put to one side, while the job was there to do. Just as he'd been taught.

*　*　*

The next day, after the fuss had died down, and Nick had filled in some pertinent paperwork, leaving the bulk of the explaining for Angelo to take care of, Angelo insisted on taking them to the airport himself, though requesting a driver from the official pool.

As Julie queued with their cases at the check-in, Nick took Angelo aside for a last minute chat which he didn't want Julie to hear.

"Listen, mate. Let me give you some good advice. His blood is in your veins, just like it's in your sister's. You're more alike than you know. We can't always choose our family, and he might not be the father you were hoping for, but my advice is don't make an enemy of him. I know you're hurting, and you blame him for your loss, but he loved your mother at one time. I'm sure he never meant for her to come to harm."

"Intent counts for nothing, Turnbull," Angelo pointed out. "He asked for her help, and in giving it, she lost her life. His fault, and it doesn't end here," he insisted. "I have work to do, mopping up these Al Qaeda cells. I don't know how long it will take, but once it's finished, I'm coming for him. Tell him that. Tell him to keep looking over his shoulder. He'd better hope to see me, before I see him," he warned. Turnbull was close to losing it, and he grabbed Angelo by the lapels, using his weight to shove him back up against the wall, out of sight of where Julie waited with their luggage. Angelo struggled, but Nick's skilled hands twisted the lapels into a choke-hold, leaning on the injured arm, and taking advantage of the younger man's injury, as he pushed him back, keeping him off-balance.

"Listen, you young stud, and listen good. I've been with the SAS for 5 years. The roughest toughest bunch of men you'll ever hope to meet. There's nothing we're afraid of, but I'll tell you this now in confidence. Gabriel scares the shit out of me. I haven't known him that long, and in that time he's always been my friend, and a friend of a friend. But I know things about him you don't. Things I shouldn't know, and you never will. I've seen him in action, and I've heard stories from my boss. You do not want this man as your enemy, believe me. He's a good man," he emphasised, "but killing is as natural to him as breathing. He's had more combat experience than you'd ever believe. I'm good. In fact, without blowing me own trumpet, I'm fucking good, but I just have to look at Gabriel, and I know he could take me. It's something you learn over the years, summing up the opposition. He knows it, and I know it. Neither of us needs to say it. He knows how good I am, so it would be quick, dirty and final. In any sort of a fair fight, he'd win. I've no doubts in my mind about it. He wouldn't give me a chance, and that's how he'd do you, too, if you push him to it. So just leave it, if you've got any sense, or if not, make sure your will is up to date." He let go of Angelo's lapels, and the younger man pushed him away with his good arm, face flushed.

"I have no one to leave anything to, now she's dead. Tell him, Turnbull. Tell him he doesn't frighten me."

"He should," Turnbull said, with finality, and turned to walk away, back to where Julie waited with the cases, a concerned look on her face.

Chapter Eighteen

Belle was worried about her mother. Laura looked tired, drained even, by the ordeal Angelica had put her through, and then the blood-transfusions. The wounds were still ugly on her neck, and she changed the dressing daily, using a scarf around her neck to disguise it. Through the thin adjoining wall, Belle could hear her cry out occasionally in her sleep, beset by nightmares.

She was driving herself, trying to keep her mind off her own situation, by trying to help Gabriel with his. Belle regretted sharing the information with her, but once learned, there was only one way Laura wanted to go. Track down the consignments notes to Cambodia, and that meant flying into Phnom Penh as tourists, and using that cover to get close to the source of the mysterious feather.

Fortunately there were many tourist holidays in Cambodia since the Khmer Rebellion had been overthrown, and even allowing for the fragments that still caused trouble on the northern borders with Thailand, excursions to famous ruins like Angkhor were still plentiful. Personal tour-guides were abundant, and they all offered a variety of pre-set tours, or were willing to take the tourists anywhere they wanted to go, for a price. They needed to go into central Cambodia, the South of Kampong Thom district, east of the Mekong River. Lots of jungle, and not many inhabitants. A few scattered ruins here and there, and somewhere within that district, was the source of the Al Raschid shipments.

Belle had already checked the phone book here, to find the address of the local conduit for Al-Raschid, a little Import/Export Agency called the Blue Elephant Exporting Company. The old man in the curio shop hadn't lied. She had checked it out that morning, as her mother rested up to regain her strength. She had posed as a tourist, interested in possibly shipping some souvenirs back home, and had come away with brochures, phone numbers, and shipping lines it was possible to use. She had gotten a look at the invoice tray while the helpful secretary had busied herself digging out the pamphlets and such, and had found a few which pointed to one isolated location in South of Kampong Thom. All they had to do was get there.

She had checked out the official tours, and it should be easy enough to tag onto one of them till they were close enough to their real destination, then veer off and make their way there themselves. Some guides would be required, as it was probably a couple of days trek through the jungle, maybe more, depending on conditions. They would need camping supplies, and possibly some weapons. The jungle was full of threats, from crocodiles in some of the rivers, tigers, not to mention a number of species of poisonous snakes and insects. Belle had no jungle experience, and as far as she knew, neither did Laura. They needed guides.

*   *   *

Laura was soaking in a hot bath, lying back and watching the steam slowly rise. The water was as hot as she could stand, and her skin tingled under the water. The neck wound was still tender, and so she kept it above the surface of the water. She would clean it and apply fresh dressings once she finished her long soak.

It was hardest for her at night, and she tried not to sleep, for as long as it was possible. What dreams she remembered were dark and awful. That woman had gotten right into her soul via the hypnosis, drugs, and the blood-taking itself. It was hard not to dream of those penetrating eyes. She had lost count of the days she had been held captive, a plaything to the transsexual's jaded whims. She thanked God that rescue had come before Angelica had succeeded in turning her into a thing like herself, and turned her loose on Belle.

Still, she couldn't allow herself to dwell on what might have been. She had survived the experience, and no matter how long it took, she would recover from it. She needed to keep busy, and stay away from Gabriel till she had regained some of her colour. He had been worried enough by the single bite she had received earlier. She had lost count of the number of times Angelica had now fed on her. It was all a blur, fortunately. An experience best put behind her.

She needed now to prove herself, to Gabriel and to herself. She felt lessened by the ordeal, somehow, as though she had failed. She didn't want to be a liability to anyone, let alone to the man she loved. She and Belle could find the source of the feather, and the truth as to whether there was another surviving angel or not.

They were close now, and only a couple of days away from their destination. She could do it. She would do it. She had to do it.

The next day, Belle and Laura joined up with the other tourists. The minibus picked them up in front of their hotel, and they joined a small convoy, which included armed guards, for Cambodia was still lawless in many regions, and the government did their best to ensure the safety of tourists, provided they organized themselves into controlled groups. Anyone venturing out on their own was literally *on* their own, so to speak.

It was a typically hot humid day, and both women wore loose dresses, with the necklines unbuttoned, and just briefs underneath, to keep as cool as they could on the journey. Large brimmed hats, to keep off the sun, handbags and the usual cameras, were their only other attire, along with canvas flat-soled trainers, trying to blend in with the rest of the tourists. The trip away from the city led off the main roads, and onto very bumpy back-roads, which, although kept clear to make it easier for the tourist industry, were hardly passable in places. A couple of hours saw the first set of ruins, and although scattered and broken by the centuries, overgrown in places, were still impressive. The Khmer must have been marvellous architects in their day.

Cameras snapping away, as expected, the two women listened to the tour guides avidly, though striking up conversations with some of the armed guards, sounding them out. Neither of the women had jungle experience, so guides would be essential, if they were to navigate their way off the beaten track. South of Kampong Thom was not on the approved tourist sites, and could not be guaranteed as safe for foreigners.

Laura and Belle found the guides easy to talk to, in their pidgin English, eager to practice it, and to talk to the foreign women. Not all of them were keen on the idea of a private excursion trip off the beaten track.

Two brothers, Dwi and Rama, eventually agreed to consider the proposal, though insisting that they may need to recruit another couple of men, to ensure the women's safety in the area the women wanted to visit. They didn't really look like brothers, apart from both having the same dark thick red hair, which was a throwback to some mixed breeding in the past. Dwi looked to be in his early twenties, and of medium height and build. Rama looked a few years older, and had a few inches on his brother. Both were clean-shaven.

"It bad place, Missy. Not on approved list for good reason. Still bad people there." Rama told them. "It maybe two, three days. More if rains have washed out the roads. Then couple days more by foot to the highlands. Too muddy to use cars this time of year. Larger trucks would be too visible. Too risky."

"We've camped out before, so no problems," Belle assured him. "You good jungle guides, yes? We need to go there. Plenty money, and plenty guns. We can use them, also. Short time, quick trip, minimum risk. No problem. We will pay you well, I promise," explained Belle. Dwi and his brother agreed to contact them at their hotel later that evening, once they had considered the deal more closely, and spoken to some friends of theirs whom they thought may be needed to assist on this trip.

"What do you think?" Laura asked Belle, as they huddled together privately in one part of the ruins. "Can we trust them?"

"Pay them well, half in advance, half when we get back. Maybe offer a bonus. I don't see why not. They won't see that much money too often out here. With the two of us, that's six guns. More than enough to handle anything we might encounter, I should think. We're not trying to fight a war."

Later that night, Dwi phoned Belle at the hotel, to confirm that he had found two more men, Pak and Dong, to help with plans, and that he would source vehicles, provisions, and weapons for the intended trip. It would take a few days to organize, and then they would accompany an official trip to Angkhor, breaking off on their own, once they got close enough to their intended route. Till then, they could play tourist in Phnohm Penh and soak up the sun.

Chapter Nineteen

ulie beamed as they took a taxi from the airport into the city of Bangkok. The exotic East was something she never got tired of. She had a lovely smile, thought Nick, as he squeezed her knee. "We'll get checked in, and then I'll have to pop down to the British Embassy. Your Dad's sure to have left word for me there," Nick assured her.

"I wish we could have spent a bit more time in Jakarta," she regretted.

"Maybe not that wise, at present, luv. Indonesia is the biggest Muslim country in the world, and they have more troubles with fundamentalists, and insurgents than most. I wouldn't have taken you there if you'd given me a choice," he reminded her.

"I'd rather be with you somewhere dangerous, than knowing you were there without me," she put her hand on top of his own, and squeezed.

"I'd rather you stayed safe. I'm trained for all this. You're not," he reminded her.

"You'll keep me safe. It's not as if I'm running around after you. I'll stay in the background and let you get on with what you've got to get on with, but I'll be there for you when your day-job is over. Besides, this is a great way of squeezing a damn good holiday out of my Dad, seeing a bit of the world, and whatever you've got to do is still going to leave you plenty of time to spend with me, isn't it?" she asked.

Nick smiled, "I hope so, doll. I really do. Should take no more than a few hours a day, asking questions, maybe seeing a few people, and then passing the information on. Piece of cake," he assured her. "Let your Dad and Gabriel take it from there. Between Jim and the Embassy, they should have run down a few contacts for him to chase up here on the ground. This Bird character shouldn't be too hard to trace."

Later, at the Embassy, Nick was allowed access to a secure computer, and he checked his e-mail. Maddox was up to speed, as usual, and Gabriel had obviously been in touch with him, as a couple of cell-phone numbers were listed, with dates when they would be active. Nick took out his own phone, and entered them in as speed-dials. The background info on this Bird character was sketchy enough. No photos existed, and it was all pulled together from a brief by the local resident chief of staff, based on word on the streets.

The Bangkok underworld was run by a mix of informal Asian Mafia, Tongs, Triads and even Yakuza. Quite an Asian mix. But the underlying core of the people here was still Khmer. Modern criminals had moved in, and were exploiting things, but the Khmer, since the fall of their empire, were used to such exploitation. Word had it that Bird was Khmer, and seeking to regain control of his country from such foreign influences. What he couldn't destroy himself, he hoped to control. He had visions of a 2nd Khmer Empire. How would he attempt to do that? An ordinary man couldn't do it. He needed to be someone with influence, power. Governments held the real power, backed up by the army, so it was either someone in or around the fringes of government, or some idealist army officer with an agenda, Nick made the assumption.

Local elections were organized for the end of the year. That was a good time for changes to be made. There was a lot of civil unrest at the moment, with the army fighting a constant war along the northern borders with remnants of Pol Pot's outlawed Khmer Rouge brigades, who were scattered far and wide across the Cambodian Highlands. The current government was getting a lot of flak for these ongoing attacks and their failure to put a stop to them.

Nick picked up Julie back at their hotel, and the two of them travelled by taxi to some of the tourist spots. Julie was enjoying the experience, the sights, sounds and even the smells. Nick bought her some local delicacies off one of the street-side stalls, cooked over a well-used stove. It looked like someone had chopped lengths off a broom handle, but it tasted like salted potato. Nick told her the name, but Julie couldn't pronounce it, much to the old vendor's amusement.

"Come on then, where's the Red Light district? This is Bangkok, after all," Julie laughed. Nick looked slightly ill at ease. "Look, I know you've been here before. You must know where it is, so spill the beans. I don't mind. It's what men do, and it was before we got together."

"It's not that," Nick started to explain. "There's a couple of districts, some refined, some less so, and some you're certainly not going to see. They're dangerous, even for people like me. Have you heard of Soy Cowboy?" he asked. Julie shook her head. "Well, it's not as blatant as some of the others, though everything is available. You just have to be a bit more discreet about how you ask for it. It's generally safe for tourists, or at least it was, last time I was here," he explained, and they hailed another taxi.

The huge red and yellow neon figure of a cowboy straddled the entrance to the street, swinging its lariat, and Julie guessed rightly, that 'this was the place'. She and Nick alighted from the taxi, and Nick was careful to walk just a half step behind her, guiding her by the elbow. If any pickpockets tried their luck, he would see them coming, or they would have to get past him first. Julie was a bit of a novice in this part of the world. He intended she stay that way, though without spoiling her enjoyment of the place.

The two of them wandered along the teeming street, trying to ignore the many touts who were trying to persuade passing punters into the various exotically named establishments. Julie couldn't pass up on the one called the Kitten Club, and she went in, dragging Nick after her. It took her a few seconds to get used to the lighting inside, and then she gawped at all the working girls moving around, or sitting at tables, sometimes with a man, or otherwise sat talking amongst themselves. A few men were stood at the black vinyl bar, which was weathered now with age, drinking as they surveyed the available girls. An old Mamasan sat at the end of the bar, smoking a cigarette out of a holder, and sipping on a small cup of coffee. "Wow, so this is what it's like out here?" Julie marvelled, pulling Nick to the bar to order drinks.

"Err . . .not exactly. They're not all like this. I mean to say, the one's I've been inside. Just a few," he tried to explain. "Two beers, mate, please," he ordered from the bar. "Singha will do for me, and a Fosters for the lady?" pleased to see they still had a few imported beers on tap. Julie wasn't too adventurous when it came to sampling foreign foods and beverages, so best stick with what she knew.

Some of the working girls were eyeing Julie up, as though deeming her competition. He would have to watch that. Some of them could be hellcats if their mood turned. There were a couple of shifty looking dudes sitting in a booth towards the back, that Nick had noticed on the way in, keeping their eye on the people inside the place. They would need watching too.

The bartender brought them beers over to him, and Nick paid the man, leaving a reasonable tip. "You tourists?" he asked. Nick nodded. "Unusual for guy to bring his own girl in here," he commented.

"Just tourists, seeing the sights," Nick confirmed. The bartender nodded, took the tip, and began mopping down the bar-top as Nick handed Julie her beer. She was staring at everything. He couldn't tell, but her eyes looked a bit red, either from the cigarette smoke or the overlying happy-baccy fumes which some of the working girls were using. It wasn't that strong, but Julie wasn't used to such.

The music from the jukebox was loud, but Nick could still hear raised voices, and he noticed the two shifty guys pointing and gesticulating to the arguing couple in one of the booths. Nick followed the direction of their gaze, and did a slight double-take when he saw who was doing the arguing. "Fuck me!"

"What, here?" Julie laughed.

"No, over there. It's an old mate of mine," he explained. "Better wait here while I go say hello. Okay?" Julie shrugged her shoulders.

"Okay, but don't be long." She watched Nick cross the floor towards the booth, where one of the working girls had now stood up, obviously not happy with something.

"JayJay, you old cunt, what are you doing so far from home? I thought you got demobbed last year? Uncle Sam still got you on a retainer, or are you here on holiday?" The big black American looked up from the table, and his face lit up when he recognized Nick, but the smile couldn't disguise the bruises.

"Nick, man! Nick, Jeesus, it's good to see you again! Go on, scram then," he dismissed the girl, and pulled up her seat to offer it to Nick.

"You look like you've been in bother?" he commented. Then indicated Julie at the bar. "I've got my girlfriend with me. Mind if she joins us? She's Jim Maddox's daughter," he explained. JayJay's eyes widened as he eyed the blonde looker at the bar.

"Hell, no. Invite her over to join us, by all means," he smiled broadly, and Nick beckoned Julie over.

"Julie, this is an old mate of mine from Delta Force, Jesse James III, so we called him JayJay for short. JayJay, this is Julie, the light of my life, and if I see your hand on her knee, or on her anything, you're in deep shit! Keep your hands off the white woman," he warned, only half in jest. Both Julie and JayJay laughed.

"Damn fine to meet you, Julie. Nick tells me your Daddy is Jim Maddox? I know Jim. Worked with him a couple of times." He reached to shake her hand.

"Is that where you two met?" she asked.

"No," said Nick. "We met up on the yearly Special Forces meets, where we all go at each other. Sort of unofficial Olympic Games. The Delta Boys always used to finish runners-up," he grinned. "They're good to know in a pinch, though," he joked. JayJay avoided taking the bait. "So what's with the black n blue makeup, Jayjay?" he had to ask. "Woman trouble?" JayJay frowned.

"You could say something like that," he admitted ruefully. "Last time I was over here, I met a sweet little thing called May-Lee. Sweetest thing you ever saw. Most of the girls here don't like us black boys that much. They take our money, but there's a lot of racism here. May Lee was different. Me and her had a real nice thing going. My plan was to take her back to the States and marry her, but then one of her parents fell ill, and we had to postpone plans, and I went back home alone so to speak. We kept in touch, and made plans for me to come fetch her. Then when I came back over here, she's disappeared. People haven't taken kindly to me asking too many questions," he admitted.

"Did you contact her parents?" Julie asked. JayJay nodded.

"First point of call, but as far as they knew, she'd returned back here to Bangkok. She used to work at one of the places up the street, so I keep trawling and asking people if they've seen her. Lots of the girls haven't, but one or two have clammed up on me real tight, with a frightened look on their face, and the heavies like those two over in the corner usually move in once they see a girl getting upset. They don't want any trouble. Neither do I. I'm just trying to find my girl. Hey, my round. I'll get some more drinks," he pushed back from the table.

"Go steady, JayJay," Nick cautioned.

"Hey man, with you here, this'll be just like old times. Might help me take my mind off things for a while." He sauntered over to the bar.

"Do a lot of men do that sort of thing? Marry these working girls I mean?" Julie found it hard to believe.

"Yeah, quite a few. Asian women aren't as pushy as Western women, and they do look after their men-folk. Despite what you might think about their backgrounds and their careers, as long as they look after themselves, it's just another job to most of them. They do it for the money, most of which goes to support their families. Finding a nice man to take them away from all this isn't something any of them would run away from. I have the feeling May-Lee's intended absence might have upset a few people," Nick explained, before JayJay returned with another round of drinks.

"Here you go, guys. Drink up. The night is young." He raised his own glass to his lips, and took a good sized swig of the cold beer.

"I can't promise we'll be here all night. Got other things to do, you know?" Nick tried not to be too brusque.

"Don't worry, Nicky-boy. I won't cramp your style with the lady, but I do know my way around more than you, so let me show you and Julie a few of the other nightspots along the way, and then I'll let you finish off by taking the lady back to your hotel. I'd welcome a break from my own troubles. How's that?" Nick was happy enough with that, even thinking on his feet, as he was. JayJay would indeed know more about the local scene than Nick himself, so it would be good to pick his brains.

The next two hours were spent going from one club to the next up and down the crowded street. Julie ordered non-alcoholic drinks, though Nick ordered halves to JayJay's pints. It was rare to meet an American who could handle his beer so well. Julie managed a few discreet nudges in Nick's ribs, with a friendly smile, to keep him aware of his alcohol intake, and Nick was indeed watching it. He knew how fast and how much his body chemistry could process the alcohol, and as long as he didn't drink too much too quickly, he'd remain sober. Besides, you always needed to drink a lot of liquid in these sort of climates. The heat and humidity made it worse. If you took too long drinking your drink, it would end up warm. So you necked it while it was still cold.

JayJay often nipped off to one side, to question a few of the working girls discreetly, getting a few daggers drawn looks from some of the Mamasans, and once a couple of the bouncers headed in JayJay's direction till Nick joined him, and discreetly led his friend away by the arm. JayJay was feeling the alcohol by now, and Nick tried to persuade him to return to his hotel.

"Hell, no, Nicky-boy. The night is young. You and your good lady head off back, and I'll see you back in the Kitten Club about lunchtime tomorrow, and I'll show you a few other places off the beaten track. Okay?" he slapped Nick on the back, and made a show of kissing the back of Julie's hand, and called for one of the rickshaw taxis that touted for the tourists. Nick and Julie got in, and JayJay waved them off, as Nick gave directions back to their hotel.

"That's some friend of yours, Nick. He's a bit over the top, but I like him," Julie complimented.

"Most of the Yanks are over the top, but they're good people underneath. He's one of the good guys. You enjoy the little tour tonight?" he asked, hugging her to him as the rickshaw rattled along.

"Yes, it was an eye-opener, though I can't wait to get you back to the hotel. You haven't drunk too much have you?" she asked cautiously, as her hand slid down onto his crotch and stroked him, feeling him hardening under her palm, and chuckling. "Well that part of you still works, anyway. The night is still young, as your friend said," she giggled.

*　*　*

The two women were dressed more like soldiers than tourists, when the four men came to pick them up from their hotel. Cam-pants, sturdy boots, tee-shirts, neck-scarves, though still using the broad hats, both women carried rucksacks filled with a couple of changes of clothing, and essentials. Laura had a portable Garmin GPS, and her mobile phone was tucked away in one of the pockets of her rucksack. Belle had her own little survival kit. As well as her own phone, she had a couple of tailored throwing knives, and a hunting knife was attached to her belt.

Two beaten up old Land-rovers were well packed with tents, water and foodstuffs, and on checking further, Laura found, under the tents, half a dozen AK-47's in serviceable condition, complete with three banana clips of ammunition each. She nodded in appreciation. Should be more than sufficient for what they needed. Introductions were made to Pak and Dong, two men of middle age. Pak was small and skinny, and looked a trifle undernourished. Dong was of medium height, but broad, and heavily muscled. A small scar on the side of his neck looked recent, but neither of the women asked about it. Belle got into one car with them, whilst Laura got into the other car with Dwi and Rama. They then set off to rendezvous with the official excursion coaches to Angkhor.

The trip to Angkhor went well, though the two cars kept to the back of the convoy, and slipped away as the rest of the tourists headed back towards Phnohm Penh. They headed East as dusk fell, the roads becoming narrower and more overgrown by the jungle, as their speed dropped and they looked for a suitable place to stop for the night. Such roads were rarely used by day, and almost never by night, but they wanted to find a spot off the road to set up camp, just in case.

Settling on a spot, both vehicles turned off and forced their way through light undergrowth to where there was almost a clearing, and Pak and Rama set about fully clearing it with parangs, while Dwi and Dong began assembling the tents. Laura and Belle examined the weapons, loading the magazines and checking the mechanisms, to ensure they were in good working order. The four Cambodian men watched the women's expertise with the weapons, nodding in appreciation. They knew what they were doing.

Once the tents were up, and the sleeping bags moved inside, a small fire was started with some chemical firelighters, and Rama broke out some provisions. Basic stuff, beans, and soups, but it all cooked up quickly enough in some small pans, and was enough to put a warm glow in their stomachs. Then as the fire was allowed to die down, darkness enveloped everything, and they retired for the night. One of the guides would remain on watch, alternating throughout the night, and allowing all of them to get some sleep. They were not expecting trouble, but best to be alert. Tigers were not uncommon in these jungles, and other wild animals. It wasn't just Man they had to worry about.

Belle zipped up their tent, making sure not to leave any gaps, to let creepy-crawlies inside the tent. There were dozens of poisonous snakes and spiders in these jungles. Many were nocturnal. If she needed to pee during the night, she would do it into one of the emptied plastic water bottles. She had no intention of going outside again until it was daylight, unless she had to.

In the morning, a secluded bush or some such could be used as a toilet, but not usually in the dark. Both she and Laura had carried along a toilet roll in their rucksacks, thinking of the essentials. She and Laura crawled into their sleeping bags, and settled down for the night, hearing the occasional night sounds from the jungle all around them. It took a while for both of them to get to sleep, as the varied sounds melted eventually into background noise, and somehow were reassuring.

Belle woke up before Laura, and pulled on her clothes. They stank of yesterday's sweat, but there was nothing she could do about that out here. There were no four-star luxuries where they were going. Taking her AK-47 with her, and a toilet-roll, Belle unzipped her tent and went outside. The four guides were already up, and Dong tended the small fire, boiling a kettle of water for coffee, whilst the others were dismantling their own tents in preparation for continuing with their journey. They gave her nods as she passed, and Belle disappeared into the undergrowth. She didn't want to go too far, yet far enough to remain unobserved, as she used the barrel of the AK-47 to stir the undergrowth to disturb anything that might be lurking there. She had no intention of baring her bum, just for something to bite her on it.

The four guides grinned as they watched Belle root around in the distance, debating whether to try and spy on her, as they mumbled away together. Just then, Laura came out of the tent, awoken by the smell of coffee as Dong poured out mugs for them all. He handed her a mug which she sipped at, graciously, squatting down to stare into the small flames of the fire, which they had kept going throughout the night.

She had found the night sounds soothing, and had slept better than she had hoped. The jungle was all around her, limiting visibility, yet strangely she was not overawed by it all. Rama was cutting some slices off a haunch of pork, and throwing them into a small frying pan where they began to sizzle and spit as they cooked in their own fats. Nothing fancy for breakfast under the circumstances, just bacon and bread. She didn't know whether it was wise to try more beans, as she had had a couple of gas attacks during the night. It wasn't so much a problem for men, but definitely not ladylike to let one rip.

In the jungle, Laura and Belle were feeling the effects of a couple of days without a good shower, so when they came upon the river it was too good an opportunity to miss. They quizzed the guides about crocodiles and piranha, and the reply was that piranha, like sharks, usually only attacked when there was blood in the water. Crocodiles were best treated with more caution, and the two women decided to stand guard for each other, with one of the AK-47's, while one of them bathed in the shallows. The four guides did their best to sneek a peek at the two women, though never managed to get too close because of the one on guard, atop one of the big rocks, her position letting her watch the river and the surroundings as well. There were tigers, and other dangerous wildlife to consider in this jungle, also.

Laura bathed first, enjoying the flowing waters, though careful not to get too much out of her depth in the fast-flowing waters. She washed herself, and then did some of her clothes and underwear, before laying them out on the stones to dry in the hot sun. Once she dressed, she took the AK-47, and took up the same position Belle had used, while her daughter took a cleansing dip in the river.

Progress was slow, as the rough tracks they were using were partially washed out, and full of potholes. Another day or two should see them getting close, and they set off again after a brief lunch. The vehicles' air-conditioning was a blessing in the tropic heat. They made slow progress, rocking back and forth, as the guides navigated through the jungle, ever Eastward.

A mud-slide brought them to a complete stop. The recent rains, as well as flooding the river, had caused mud slides to come down from the hills, and one such now completely blocked their path. "Now what?" asked Belle.

"Looks like we walk," Laura shrugged, and the guides began sorting out the gear they could carry between them.

"Two, maybe three days by foot," Rama advised Laura, which meant tonight and tomorrow night camped out in the jungle. They had no option but to leave the two vehicles where they were, in the hope of collecting them on the way back. Laura hid the keys under the front tire. Shouldering their heavy packs, the two women and four men set off while there were still a few hours of daylight left.

The guides carried their weapons across both arms, and constantly scanned the undergrowth. Every half mile or so, they called a brief halt, to listen to the jungle sounds. They were a lot more wary now that they were on foot in the jungle.

They made camp while it was still light, as the sun went down rather quickly, and set up their tents. After eating a small evening meal, one of the guides produced a bottle of Scotch, and proceeded to hand it round. Both women took a hefty slug, feeling the warmth as it went down into their stomachs. It would help them relax from the tensions of the day. The four men continued to pass it around, though, shared between them all, it wasn't enough for any of them to get really drunk on.

The four men were laughing and talking amongst themselves in some unknown dialect, after a few drinks from the bottle. They kept offering the bottle back to both Belle and Laura, but the two women deferred after taking just a couple of neat shots each. That was enough for them.

Laura disappeared into the undergrowth with a toilet roll and her AK-47, as discreetly as she could, but she knew the men were watching her. Dwi nudged Pak. He nudged Dwi, who in turn nudged Dong, and then Rama, and the four men tried not to snigger. There wasn't much modesty to be had in these conditions. She didn't go far. When she came back, Belle decided to follow suit, and taking the toilet roll and the AK-47 from Laura, she too went off into the foliage.

A few minutes later, a shrill scream erupted from the undergrowth, followed by a white-faced Belle, eagerly trying to draw up her trousers. "Something bit me," she blurted out, and Laura rushed to grab her.

"Get in the tent. I'll have a look."

The four guides stood back as the two women went into their tent, and Belle dropped her trousers and lay on her tummy as Laura took the medical kit out of her rucksack. Its contents were limited. By the light of the small torch, Laura examined Belle's rump. One buttock showed a raised swelling, and what looked like two distinct fang-marks. "It looks like a snake bite. Small one. Did you get a look at it, and see what it was?" Belle shook her head.

"I don't have eyes in my ass, Mother. I was concentrating on something else at the time. Whatever it was, bit me, and then slithered away before I got a look at it."

"Hold still!" Laura bent and fastened her mouth over the bite marks, doing what she could to suck out the poisoned blood. She spat out one mouthful, and then bent again to take a second. Laura took out the single ampoule of anti-venom, from the medical kit, and filled the plastic syringe with it. "This is all we have. Just a generic. It should help, though without knowing the exact snake, we don't know the exact nature of the toxin." She stabbed the needle home in Belle's rump, and pressed the plunger. Belle grimaced. She was an expert in toxins herself, and she knew there were a lot of extremely poisonous snakes in the jungle. She had a strong constitution, but even that wouldn't save her if the venom was too toxic. She rubbed the injected area, to get the anti-venom moving through her system. "Better get some sleep. I'll watch over you." Laura promised. The one-time use syringe, was put back into the kit, and Laura put it back into her rucksack, as Belle got into her sleeping bag. She closed her eyes, and tried to sleep. Laura sat down beside her, watching her breathing to check if it became erratic.

*   *   *

Outside the tent, the four guides sat, talking in low voices amongst themselves. The bottle of scotch was almost empty now. "Two more days on foot," Rama spoke. "Maybe longer if she slows us down."

"Will the woman survive?" Dwi questioned.

"Depends what bit her," shrugged Pak.

"We should help keep her alive. They are expecting us to deliver both of them," said Dong

"What does it matter? They'll only kill both of them eventually. Might be easier for her if she dies now?" Dwi mused.

"We might not get paid full money if we only deliver one of them," Rama pointed out.

"Good point," chuckled Dong, taking one last swig to empty the bottle. "Best see how she is in the morning. I've seen those medi-kits before. Just basic stuff. We're too far away from civilization to get more anti-venom, but we know the right plants and roots to brew up something just as effective, against some of the milder toxins anyway. If she got bit by something really venomous, she won't last the night."

The four men watched the glowing embers of the fire slowly begin to cool. Away from the glow of the fire, the jungle waited, in darkness. Within that darkness, a variety of creatures wandered, and some watched the men around the fire. A nocturnal game of hunter/prey was going on all around them, amongst various species. The men were playing their own game, unknown to the two women.

Belle was running a temperature by morning, shivering and shaking occasionally, and Laura found it hard to rouse her from her sleeping bag. She went down to the river for a fresh bottle of water, and used that to help clean Belle, and cool her down. She checked the medical kit again. No more anti-venom. They would never get back to civilization in time to get more. Their only hope was that there might be something in the place they were headed for. Otherwise it all depended on Belle's naturally resistant constitution to fight it off herself, if she could.

Laura roused the four guides, and explained Belle's condition. She organized the building of a travois, using two lengths of bamboo, and lashing the sleeping bag to them, with ropes, with Belle still in it. They would have to drag her along with them, for she was too weak to walk. Pausing only for a quick breakfast, they started off early, and at a brisk pace, with a slight distribution of their luggage amongst them all. Laura insisted on taking a turn with the travois, after Dong had pulled it behind him for the first hour, then Dwi took over from her, when her shoulders started aching.

At midday, they stopped for a short lunch, and Laura examined Belle, giving her water, though noting no change in her condition. As she ate, one of the four men also examined Belle, taking a careful note of her condition, and softly discussing it with one of the other men when Laura was out of earshot. He had recognized the symptoms enough to know Belle was seriously ill, though he didn't expect her to die. She was in fine health otherwise. The other woman wasn't as well-versed in the ways of the jungle, and was extremely worried by the woman's condition.

The odd chuckle came from the two men as they discussed their options, and how best they could take advantage of the situation. Their progress was slower now, and it would take longer before they reached the settlement. Once they got there, the two women would be taken away, and their lives made just as miserable as the enslaved priests, forced to serve new masters such as the Khmer and their Al-Qaeda trainees.

Chapter Twenty

It had taken a while to get in Cambodia, and Gabriel had used the time to plan his strategy. To track down the girls, he was going to have to make enquiries with all the hotels and tour agencies in Phnom Penh. Maddox had thoughtfully gotten the local Embassy to make discreet local enquiries, and a pair of women, answering Belle and Laura's descriptions had taken a tour to Angkhor a few days ago, from which they had not returned.

The tour agency had no information on their whereabouts or their intended destination. They would be travelling under aliases, he assumed. Gabriel placed a call via one of his cell-phones to his arms supplier in Wales, asking to be put in touch with a local weapons dealer here he could trust. By evening, Gabriel was tooled up with handgun and ammunition, as well as some appropriate knives and forearm sheaths.

He also visited some of the local stores, stocking up on jungle clothing, boots, light tent; survival gear etc, as he had a feeling his search was not going to end here in Pnomh Penh. The type of operation he expected to find would need to be away from public eyes. Next thing was to find that location, and that meant tracking down the two women.

He began a series of phone-calls to the freelance guide agencies in the phonebook, asking if two women had requested any private tours. He struck lucky on the fifteenth call, advising him that two women had requested a private tour of the Highlands, but no specific location was specified. They had been accompanied by four armed guards, so they should be safe enough, provided they didn't find what Gabriel expected them to find, a training ground for Al Qaeda recruits.

Blue Elephant Imports was going to have to give Gabriel the information he needed, and Gabriel cased the place, walking around the building, though appearing to pay no undue attention to it. The office fronted onto the south side of the main street of Samdach Preah Sokun Meanbon, a right mouthful. There didn't appear to be any second floor, or any other visible entrance to the place, apart from the front door, which a security camera covered. Deciding to keep it simple, Gabriel noticed the cctv camera moving to cover him as he approached the front door.

It was inconspicuous as offices go, and there were no attached warehouses to the property. They operated strictly as a front, or so it seemed. He had a number of ways he could play this. Making standard enquiries would take time he didn't have. He had to assume Laura and Belle were ahead of him in this game. He didn't trust them to stay out of it. He needn't to make things happen, and sooner rather than later. Making his mind up, he crossed the street, opened the front door, and the jangling bell announced his presence to the office staff inside.

A second cctv camera behind the front counter, turned to pick him up as he closed the door behind him, feeling the chill from the AC a welcome relief from the sweltering heat outside. "Yes sir, can I help you?" a pretty young thing with the nametag of Margaret asked him.

"I'm looking to catch up with a couple of friends of mine, who may have been in here a few days ago. Two women. One blonde, one with black hair. They were heading into the Highlands in search of some rare bird, whose feathers I believe you have been exporting as curios?" Gabriel studied her face, and she seemed truly puzzled by his information. The cctv camera's lens was zooming in on his face, and the phone on the desk rang. As the second woman picked it up, she turned to study Gabriel, who was still engaged in conversation with Margaret. "They were doing research for the Smithsonian Institute, Ornithology Division," he continued, watching the second woman out of the corner of his eye, as she hunched over the phone, talking softly so he could hardly hear her. He saw her reach under her desk, obviously pressing some sort of alarm device. He sensed he was now in a Red Zone. Not unexpectedly. Someone on the end of that cctv camera had recognized him, and was giving orders over the phone.

As Margaret struggled to remember the two women Gabriel described, and quite honestly, he thought, the older woman put the phone down. "Excuse me sir, I couldn't help but overhear your conversation. That was my Manager on the phone. He is on his way here. He may be able to give you the information you seek, when he arrives" she smiled, obviously trying to stall his departure and give whoever she had called, time to get here.

"I'll call back later. I have a few errands to run, just now." Gabriel smiled, as he turned and quickly exited the place. He let the cctv camera follow him along the pavement before taking the first side road, and then quickly doubling back to watch the front of the building from a discreet distance.

Five minutes later, two men pulled up in a car, outside the building. They both got out and hurriedly went inside. Through the mirrored glass, he could make out gesticulating arms, as it soon became apparent they had been too late to make Gabriel's acquaintance.

The two men came back outside, and decided to split up, hoping to catch sight of Gabriel still nearby. Gabriel melted back into the shadows of a shop awning, pretending to window-shop, and then entering the shop, a Jewellers, to examine some of the wares inside, though really more interested in events outside. He watched the man approach, scanning both sides of the street. There was too much glare coming back from the windows of the shop Gabriel was in for the man to see inside the shop too well, and he went past, eyes glancing from side to side.

Gabriel stepped out onto the street, closing the door silently behind him, and he followed the man in quick strides, timing his approach to catch up with him near a small alleyway off the main street. The first the man knew of Gabriel's presence was a tug on his sleeve, and as he turned, Gabriel hit him hard, one punch low in the pit of his stomach, to knock all the breath out of him, and as he doubled up, Gabriel swung him by the arm, slamming him into the wall, before pushing him into the alleyway.

The man's hand managed to dip under his jacket, but Gabriel hit him again before he could draw the gun, and he removed it himself, before the man could recover from the sequence of blows. He looked up into the barrel of his own gun, as Gabriel aimed it at him and cocked the hammer.

"Time for a little chat," he smiled grimly. "I'm looking for two women. Tell me where they are, and I'm gone. No one will need to know we had this little chat," he promised.

"I don't know, mister," the frightened man swore. "I don't know what you're talking about." Gabriel sensed he was telling the truth. Small fry like him wouldn't necessarily know everything about this sort of operation.

"Second question then. Somewhere in the Highlands, you have an operation, either to assist in your smuggling operations, or to aid foreign insurgents in getting into Thailand and Indonesia. I want to know where it is."

"I don't know what you're talking about. Honest, mister, I'm just hired help. I do a little clean-up work. Nothing too heavy. They don't tell me any more than I need to know." Gabriel weighed the man up. In truth, he had expected nothing more. But at least now he had let them know he was here. They just needed to know what a thorn in their side he intended to be until he had the information he needed.

"In that case, give your people a message from me. I want names and destinations. Until I leave here with those names and destinations, I am going to bring a lot of unwanted attention towards your employers. Now strip!"

"What?" the smaller man cowered under the threat of the gun, which had not wavered by so much as an inch during their conversation.

"Your clothes. Take them off!" Gabriel's face was set in stone. The man began to undress at gunpoint. Gabriel watched him, slowly, impassively, till at length the man was stood there naked and cowering, covering his genitals with his hands, in the hot sun.

Gabriel gathered up the man's clothes, and simply turned and walked off, leaving the squealing man to call out after him, as he rounded the end of the alley, and went back onto the main street. Thirty yards down the street was a small dumpster, and Gabriel upended the clothes into it.

He continued walking back in the direction of Blue Elephant Import/Export, and walking past on the far side of the road, he aimed and fired the gun, shattering the plate glass window. Screams from pedestrians, and alarms from the office itself, soon caused panic, and no one attempted to stop Gabriel as he walked calmly along the street, people rushing past him to see what all the commotion was. A few blocks away, he hailed a taxi to take him back to his hotel. That was enough excitement for one day.

He was travelling under a false passport, so they would not be able to readily trace him. That should allow him to use the hotel as a base for a few days. He would use those few days to cause as many problems for the people behind Blue Elephant Imports as possible.

*   *   *

Later in the week, when he picked Nick and Julie up from their hotel in a taxi, JayJay had acquired a few more bruises. "Don't worry about it. You should see the other guy," he insisted, laughing the incident off. Nick and Julie swapped looks in the back of the car. Julie could tell Nick was feeling awkward about this. It wasn't something he was likely to discuss in front of her. She knew her man well enough by now. This was boy-talk, and she made it easy for them.

"Why don't you drop me off at one of the shopping centres, and I'll meet you back at the hotel for lunch, say around two o'clock?" she smiled, and JayJay gave directions to the driver. When Julie had waved them goodbye, Nick turned to JayJay more seriously.

"Does he know the way to the British Embassy?" JayJay shrugged.

"If not, we'll get the grand tour, unless we give him directions," he chuckled. "Why do you need to go there?" he asked.

"I'm not here purely to see the sights, JayJay. I'm looking for someone too, and that someone may be connected to the person you're looking for. Then again he may not, but I have contact with Jim who's running down some intel for me. We can add May-Lee's name into the pot, and see what Jim can find out," he suggested. JayJay perked up instantly.

"Gee, Nick, I'd sure appreciate that sort of help right now. A little help from the boys upstairs might go a long way in a place like this," he admitted.

Later, at the Embassy, JayJay read Maddox's reply, as Nick downloaded file attachments and printed them out. 'Evidence so far indicates that someone wealthy is operating behind the scenes to help facilitate movement of Al Qaeda personnel into S.E. Asia. This would take money and contacts. The name "Bird" has been associated with this man, but no use without a real name to work with. Research into the Import/Export of Al-Raschid in Oman goes no further than a local businessman there, obviously a cut-out. But news from Gabriel about the Blue Elephant end of the franchise has brought up some names. Once we had Angelica's name in the frame, Eve Maggio was easier to track. There was a diplomat called Maggio in Bangkok during the war. He had a son, but no daughter. The son had a tutor hired, who was a tour-guide. Wihok Hongrugipon. That tour-guide is one of the leading businessmen in Bangkok today, rumoured to have his fingers in all sorts of pies. He is a frontrunner in current elections that are to be held later this year. Check out the photo. It's the only one on record that shows him full body. He's taken great pains to only have head n shoulders shots published, since he came into the public eye. If he's involved in as much as is rumoured, then he'll want to keep a low profile. Remind you of anything?'

Nick and JayJay both looked at the spindly heron-like figure, shown in his youth, standing next to another two male acquaintances. They were head and shoulders shorter than him. "Looks like we've found our Bird," Nick exclaimed.

After examining the accompanying reports, Nick and JayJay took a taxi to Chinatown, to check out first the man's business address, and then the penthouse flat over the river. CCTV cameras were in plenty of evidence in both locations. The cameras swivelled to view the two of them, as they approached, obviously set up to detect motion and observe what was causing it. Nick and JayJay kept on walking as the cameras followed them, not appearing to pay undue attention to either place, though both of them had done enough surveillance work to know how to case a place without appearing to.

"Won't be easy getting into either place," Nick discussed, over a cold beer in one of the bars. JayJay preferred a shot of vodka, followed by a larger shot, which he nursed. "We could follow someone into his building through the security doors, but no idea of the layout of the place, or how much security he has installed in there. Rooftop might be best, but getting up there would be a problem. No neighbouring buildings, and we don't have any outside help here. We're on our own."

JayJay nodded, scowling. "His office building is similar, though a daylight approach might just be worth a try. Just turn up and ask to see the man? He won't know who we are, till we tell him," he suggested. Nick noticed it first, the slow clearing of area around them. Then, JayJay followed his gaze to the four shifty looking characters who were stood observing their table. Hard to tell who they belonged to. Their eyes met, and Nick nodded slightly.

Nonchalantly, JayJay walked back up to the bar, and took a straw from one of the dispensers. He came back to the table, and put the straw into the vodka, to take a sip. The four locals came over, and one of them leaned close to the table as he addressed JayJay. "Hey, Yank, you still here? Not got message yet? May-Lee not interested in you, no more," he grinned. "Time to go home," he advised. "You, mister?" he turned his attention to Nick. "You keep your nose out of other people's business."

"He's a friend," Nick met the man's stare, his eyes cold and steady. The other man broke the eye-contact.

"I have friends, too, mister. Maybe it's time you meet them, eh?" he motioned with his hand, and the other three began to move forward quickly, hoping to take them while they were still seated. JayJay's hand quickly came out of his pocket, holding and flicking his lighter, applying it to the end of the straw, and he blew out the vodka he had just taken into his mouth. It ignited like a mini-flamethrower, spewing liquid fire into the faces of two of the heavies, as Nick overturned the table to gain a bit of breathing room.

The two burning men were screaming as they tried to claw at their faces, patting at the flames. One of them grabbed a drink from a nearby table and inundated himself. While this was going on, the other two men attacked Nick and JayJay. One pulled a knife, flicking it open, and holding it low. He knew how to use it, and Nick took him on, grabbing a bottle, and smashing it against the table, hoping he wouldn't be left with just a shard of glass in his hand, but the glass was thin enough to break properly, and left him holding the bottle by the neck, as he avoided the first lunge.

JayJay grabbed for the second man as he tried to draw a gun, using his greater weight and whirling him around, slamming him into the wall, where he rammed a knee into the man's kidneys as he went down, groaning in pain. JayJay kicked the gun away as the man dropped it.

He turned as one of the other red-faced men tried to get back into the fight. Both went down together, rolling on the floor, each clawing at the other, using knees and punches, seeking to get an advantage.

Nick swayed and weaved about, as the sharp blade ripped his jacket. He scored himself with the broken bottle, gouging the man's arm, causing him to cry out, and drop the knife, though attempting to switch hands with it. Nick dropped the bottle and delivered a swift uppercut, snapping the man's head back, and laying him out on the floor. He turned just in time to avoid being hit on the back of the head by a raised chair from the remaining man. Nick raised his arms, blocking the chair, and kicking out at the man's kneecaps, his toecap catching him on the shin, and making him howl. A swift kick into the man's stomach took the wind out of him, and made him drop the chair, which Nick used himself, breaking it over the man's head.

JayJay was throttling his opponent on the ground, pinning him in a choke-hold, when Nick kicked the man savagely on the side of the head. Fight over. Fearful patrons stood well back for the time being, and Nick helped JayJay to his feet. "Time we weren't here," he said, and JayJay agreed, both of them exiting the building and putting space between then before any of their four assailants recovered.

"Guess we outstayed our welcome?" He and JayJay started laughing uncontrollably as they walked off down the street, attracting amused stares from passers-by, well-used to see drunken westerners staggering along, arm in arm.

Later that afternoon, when he met up with Julie back at the hotel, he and JayJay had agreed to meet up the next day, and try and get an official audience with Hongrugipon. With a mouthful of a name like that, no wonder he preferred a nickname. "Nick, what's happened to your jacket?" she asked, spotting the tear. Nick shrugged it off.

"I caught it on one of the street-stalls as me and JayJay were doing the rounds. I'll see if the front reception desk can recommend a tailor to fix it for me. They're good with a needle and thread out here. So, how much money do we have left?" he asked, seeing the large carrier bags under Julie's table, putting her on the defensive, and taking her mind off his jacket rather neatly, as she went on the defensive.

"Don't worry, things are a lot cheaper out here. I've got some marvellous stuff, for absolutely bargain prices," she assured him, forestalling any argument, with a time-honoured woman's excuse. "Now what do you want to order for lunch?"

*　　*　　*

Gabriel surveyed the street through dark sunglasses. The beard was growing back, so he let it. Just enough to alter his basic appearance. A work-crew were installing a new plate glass window. Very efficient, Gabriel thought. Shame.

Two streets away there was a shop, selling beers and spirits, and Gabriel popped inside. He bought some cigarettes, and a disposable lighter. He also bought a bottle of cheap brandy. He popped the bottle in his pocket as he left the shop. He used a parked car to shield what he was doing from the other side of the street, as he opened the bottle, and took out his handkerchief from his pocket. He poured the brandy onto the handkerchief, soaking it well, and then stuffed it partway down the neck of the bottle. He then put the bottle back into his pocket and retraced his steps till he was across the street from the Blue Elephant offices.

One of the workmen looked up as Gabriel crossed the street. Gabriel smiled, turning up to look the roaming cctv camera full in the lens. He wanted them to know who was doing this. All the workmen stopped as Gabriel drew the gun from inside his jacket. "Out. All of you. Now!" He waved with the gun. They didn't need to be told twice. Gabriel popped inside the office, to make sure no one was lingering or hiding in there. Satisfied, he took out the bottle, and then the lighter. He lit the end of the handkerchief, and it caught flame easily, as he stepped out through the door, he threw the Molotov cocktail into the office, and as he stepped to one side, he saw it burst into flames, and the sudden explosion of heat and resulting fireball blew out the brand new window, so that it lay in tiny pieces on the road and pavement.

The workmen were running like hell away, whilst pedestrians stopped to stare at the burning office. It was only a small explosion, and of no real danger to adjoining offices, but would certainly cause some disruption and some gossip where Blue Elephant was concerned. Gabriel made his way along the street. No one was trying to stop him. He had almost cleared the end of the street, when a car screamed around the corner, almost passing him before screeching to a halt, and four men hurriedly getting out of the car, and running at him. They must have had men on standby, watching the cctv footage. Gabriel turned and ran, with the four men in pursuit.

Pedestrians scattered out of the way as Gabriel ran through them. No gunfire followed, so they were either very circumspect about collateral damage, or they wanted him alive. The latter, he guessed. At least until they were satisfied as to the level of the threat he posed. Gabriel was fit, but so were the four men pursuing him. Slowed down partially by the milling pedestrians, they were slowly gaining on him. The longer the chase went on, the more tired he would be when they caught up with him. Making a decision, Gabriel took the next alley he came upon, whirling instantly, and pressing himself up against the closer wall.

The first man to run around the corner, caught Gabriel's boot in his midriff, knocking the wind right out of him, and doubling him up. A karate chop on the back of the man's head put him down for the count, and Gabriel backed off as the remaining three men approached more warily. Weapons appeared in their hands. No guns, one knife and two of those extendable metal-spring mugger-sticks. They spread out, closing off the exit from the alley, and intent on coming at Gabriel from all angles.

Instead of backing off, as they expected, Gabriel suddenly ran at the middle man, leaping from the ground with incredible speed. His lighter body weight made the seemingly impossible leap possible, and he shot out his foot, taking the man just below the chin, and snapping his neck. He was dead before he hit the ground.

As Gabriel dropped, he flexed his forearm, and a slim blade dropped into his hand, and he lashed out to one side as one assailant tried to rush in and catch him. The blade bit into the man's leg, slicing through the trousers and drawing blood. The man screamed, and Gabriel turned his attention to the other man, who also had a knife.

KCHINGG . . . . their blades met momentarily, as Gabriel blocked the man's lunge, and they both began circling, feinting, and striking. The other man recognized Gabriel's skill as being greater than his own, and he called frantically for the bleeding man to rejoin the fray.

Cursing, the wounded man picked up his steel club, and limped forward, only for Gabriel to turn, and throw the knife backhanded. The blow stopped the man in his tracks, and he stared down, blankly, at the knife protruding from his chest, before his legs gave way under him, and he collapsed, dead.

Seizing his moment, the knifeman lunged at the unarmed Gabriel, who suddenly flexed his other arm and released a second knife into his other hand, quickly enough to parry the blow, and then slash at the arm holding the knife, scoring deep, and making him drop his weapon. He tried to back away, but Gabriel closed him down quickly, forcing him back up against the alley wall, pricking his throat with the tip of his knife.

"I want to know where you got the feather from." He saw the man's eyes go wide. He didn't know what Gabriel was talking about. "Tell Bird! Give me the location, and I'll go away. If it's the wrong location, I'll be back. Next time I ask, I'll expect an answer. Until then, you and your organisation are going to get a lot of unwanted publicity." Gabriel punched the man suddenly, his head snapping back and hitting the wall, and he let him slump to the ground, unconscious.

Gabriel withdrew the other knife, and cleaned it on the man's jacket, before re-sheathing both knives in their forearm sheaths, Dusting himself off, he stepped back onto the main street, and began to put distance between himself and the dead and injured men.

* * *

Next day, Nick met with JayJay in the lobby, and JayJay confirmed he had made an appointment to see Mr Hongrugipon. Supposedly to discuss a possible export deal. "We can ask him straight out if he can help us find May-Lee, or tell us why we can't find her. He won't dare do anything while we're inside the building, and he may answer some questions for us."

* * *

As Nick and JayJay left by taxi, there was a knock on the hotel room door of the suite occupied by Nick and Julie. Julie was always a late sleeper, and the knock roused her. It was only a little while since Nick had left her, and she wondered if he'd forgotten anything. She grabbed for a robe, and pulled it on loosely, as she moved towards the door. She opened it on the safety-catch, as Nick had always warned her, but as she did so, someone threw his shoulder into the door, and it burst open, slamming her backwards as she screamed.

Two men entered the room quickly, one of them closing the door again behind him, and holding it closed. Julie started to scream anew, but was quickly forced back, and a hand pressed over her mouth as she was pushed back and down onto the bed. The man half on top of her was small, but stocky. He was far too strong for her to break his grip, and she tried to remain calm and control her breathing. The other man, taller, but just as heavyset, grabbed her with one hand, pulling her back onto her feet. He had a knife in his other hand, and Julie forced herself not to scream or lose control as he brought the knife closer, so she could see it's sharp edge. "Missy Maddox, yes?" he asked. Julie nodded, terrified. The man smiled. He pulled her closer, and she could smell his rancid spiced breath as his face neared hers. He pushed her back up against the wall, pressing the cold steel to her throat, and she shuddered as his other hand crept inside her loosened robe, grabbing her left breast roughly, hefting and squeezing it as he chuckled.

Julie tried to pull away, but the cold blade prevented her from doing anything more than averting her gaze. The hand slid down her body, over her sleek belly, which she sucked in, trying to avoid the touch of his hand, and she gasped as she felt fingers sliding between her sucked-in belly and the elastic of her panties.

Grinning into her face, his fingers clenched and ripped the panties from her body, as she screamed anew and tried to kick out at him, panicking now, remembering the horrific attack she had undergone back in Hereford. His fist still gripped the torn flimsy garment as he punched her, knocking her back on the bed, and he threw himself on top of her, as she struggled anew. "Quiet!" he warned, pressing the knife to her throat. "When I let go of you, you will get dressed. Pack a suitcase. Then you will leave the hotel with us, as though we are your friends. If you try and alert anyone, I will use this knife, and people will not think you so pretty anymore," he warned.

*   *   *

When Nick and JayJay made their entrance, the secretary in Reception checked her appointments books, verified their names and appointment, and asked them to wait. She kept them waiting for almost an hour, before four men in business suits came to escort them to the lifts. They had the look of ex-military, of indeterminate middle-age, all fit, slim and trim. A small scar down the side of one man's neck was the only distinguishing feature between the four of them.

"Gentlemen, Mr Hongrugipon will see you now. If you'd come with us, we will escort you to his office floor." The smile seemed genuine, but neither he nor his three associates looked like genuine businessmen. Nick and JayJay got to their feet, and allowed themselves to be escorted to the lift, which one of the men called with a key-card.

The six men entered the lift, and it began to rise as they all stood silently. On the fourteenth floor, the doors opened, and all of them exited. One of the men prevented Nick and JayJay from going any further momentarily. "Sorry gentlemen, but Mr Hongrugipon values his security. Just a standard pat-down, if you don't mind. Just a formality." Nick and JayJay remained motionless while skilled hands carried out a brief but thorough body-search. They were unarmed. One of the men waved them on, and they were escorted deeper into Hongrugipon's sanctum.

Another waiting area was revealed, and JayJay was asked to wait, whilst Nick was admitted through the panelled door. "Mr Hongrugipon will see you first, Mr Turnbull," one of the bodyguards explained. Nick shrugged, and as JayJay seated himself patiently, Nick entered the adjoining room. Hongrugipon was seated behind a long table. It was obviously a room used for meetings, and there were papers scattered across the desk which the man had obviously been pouring over moments before. He was studying a clipped report as Nick entered, and looked up to meet Nick's gaze.

Hongrugipon was old, even by Asian standards. He looked frail, yet the tightened skin showed none of the usual liver-spots associated with the onset of old age. He still looked pretty fit, and his eyes had lost none of their sharpness. "Please sit down, Mr Turnbull," he waved a hand towards one of the chairs on the opposite side of the table. Nick took the offered chair, noting that two of the bodyguards had remained in the room with them, as the door had closed.

The skeletal hand put the report down on the table. There was a small photo attached to it. Nick's photo. From the quick glance, he recognised the background as one of the bars he had visited with JayJay.

Hongrugipon smiled as he saw Turnbull's gaze, and his attempts not to register surprise. "My people are rather thorough," he smiled. "I take it you have made your own enquiries into myself and my business, therefore I thought it only fair to return the compliment," he added. "I would rather you made no further enquiries into my business enterprises, Mr Turnbull. The same goes for your friend," he warned.

"My friend is just interested in finding his girlfriend, nothing more," Nick reassured him.

"That may be so, Mr Turnbull, but your own enquiries are rather more substantial, are they not? They are also connected to another individual who is proving to be a bit of a thorn in my side, also. I believe you know each other. You are currently with the British S.A.S., and this man is former S.A.S." He moved the first report, to reveal a second one, with another photo attached. It only needed a quick glance to identify Gabriel's photo on that report. "You are both connected to enquiries currently being orchestrated through Europol, and you yourself are on 'leave' from the British Special Forces, are you not?" he asked. He didn't need the question answered. He obviously had all the answers already.

"So why did you agree to see me?" Turnbull asked. "You obviously knew this wasn't a real business meeting," he accused.

"Ah, but it is, Mr Turnbull. We still have business to discuss," he smiled. "Your friend there is causing me some embarrassment in Phnom Penh. I could have him killed, but that would only bring more unwanted attention to my interests. I need him removing with a minimum of fuss. He has already caused too much unwanted publicity for my organisation. Currently, I have no one individual skilled enough to tackle this Gabriel. He comes with quite a reputation himself. I want him removed from Phnom Penh. I want him taken to a location in the Highlands. Once he gets there, what happens to him is of no concern of yours. I want you to deliver him there." Nick's eyes widened.

"Dream on, squire," he smirked. "I'm not your man."

Hongrugipon shrugged. "I disagree, Mr Turnbull. I have studied your background, and I think with the right incentive, you are just the man I need for this. You're a friend of his, so would be able to get close to him, without attracting suspicion. You also have the physical skills needed to take him down. I want you to employ those skills on my behalf."

"No." Hongrugipon shrugged his shoulder. He had expected this reaction from Turnbull.

"One of my men is going to put his hands on your shoulders, Mr Turnbull. Please remain calm. It is for your own safety. We don't intend any harm to you." The two bodyguards came up behind Nick's chair, and, standing to one side of it, one of the men pressed his hands down on Nick's shoulders. That's all he did, applying pressure to prevent Nick rising up out of the chair.

Nick could feel the adrenaline rushing through his system. Something was going down, but as yet he wasn't sure what was happening. Hongrugipon put his hand in his pocket, and pulled out what Nick thought at first was a handkerchief, till he laid it down on the table in front of him. Then Nick could see it for what it actually was. A pair of panties. A torn pair of panties. Julie's panties.

The action was instinctive, and Nick attempted to lunge across the table, but the hands on his shoulders forced him back down.

"I see you recognize them," Hongrugipon smiled. He lifted the scrap of cloth to his nose, inhaling the musky fragrance, and sighing contentedly, as Nick's blood boiled. "Your fiancé is very beautiful. You are a lucky man. I need a lucky man to help me capture this Gabriel. If you do this for me, she will be returned to you unharmed. If not, then you will likely not see Miss Maddox again. There is a market for beautiful western women in the Far East. I am sure she will make me a lot of money. Turnbull, if I wanted you dead, we wouldn't be having this conversation. You're more useful to me alive at the moment. It's Gabriel I want dead, and I'd like to ensure that personally. I have no interest in any harm coming to you or to your girlfriend, except where necessary, to ensure you do as I ask. Do this and you get her back unharmed."

"Let her go. You're asking the impossible." Nick was trying hard to retain his temper. "Gabriel is out of my league. I can't take him, he's too good."

"Who do you want to marry, Turnbull? The delightful Miss Maddox, or your friend Gabriel? You'd better think of a way, or I'll have Miss Maddox marry someone else. Maybe marry a lot of someone else's?" Nick was set like a stone, muscles all locked, as he was held down in the seat, trying to analyse everything that had just happened in the last sixty seconds. The man and his organization were more thorough than he had thought. A pre-emptive strike had been made, and now Nick was on the defensive. Not the first time he had been in a fuckup, but this time there was more than his own life on the line. "My men will put you in place. All you have to do is take him down, and deliver him for me. Once he gets there, you and Miss Maddox can go on your way. I'll deal with Gabriel myself," he promised, menacingly. "Good help is so hard to find these days, so forgive the method of recruitment. I'll have your girlfriend waiting for you at the rendezvous point. My men will help you deliver Gabriel to me there in four days time. If you want to see your girlfriend alive again, you'll do as I say. Use your friendship to get close, and then take him down. No permanent damage. I'll take care of that myself. Do we have a deal?"

"How do I know I can trust you? If I do this my friend is dead."

"I'll give him a chance in a fair fight, Turnbull. I promise you that. As for your friend outside, please inform him that he has one week to leave Bangkok, or he won't ever leave. His girlfriend is no longer a subject for discussion. He will never find her without a shovel. Please impress that upon him." Hongrugipon's eyes stared coldly into Nick's own. May-Lee was dead. Nick understood that all too well. Hongrugipon took a plane ticket out of his inside pocket, and pushed it across the table towards Nick. "That flight leaves for Phnom Penh tomorrow night. I will expect you to be on it. You will be met, when you get there. This meeting is now over," he announced.

The pressure on Nick's shoulders was now removed, though the two bodyguards remained close to Nick's side as he collected the ticket off the table. Hongrugipon calmly took the torn panties off the table, and put them back into his pocket, smiling back up at Nick, enjoying his helplessness. The tables had been turned well and truly. All thoughts of investigating any further links with Al Qaeda or the man's organization was now well and truly on the backburner. Julie had to come first, and he had to sort this mess out himself. He couldn't tell Jim Maddox what was going on.

The two men escorted him out of the meeting room, and JayJay stood up when he came out, noting the blood n thunder expression on Nick's face. "Didn't go too well, then, I guess?" he asked.

"You guess right, JayJay. I'm in the shit, good and proper. Let's go. I need a drink."

Later, in one of the many bars that were scattered about Soy Cowboy, Nick broached the delicate subject of Jayjay's girlfriend. "I don't think you'll find May-Lee, JayJay. The way he discussed the subject, she's already dead," Nick announced, sadly, to his friend. JayJay sighed as he studied the small shot-glass in front of him. Whatever emotions were going through him, he disguised them well.

"I kinda guessed that a week ago," he revealed. "The girls were giving me funny looks, trying to tell me, without putting it into words that might be overheard." He shook his head resignedly, and took another shot of vodka. "Most of them live in constant fear of the Mamasans, the pimps, and the heavies, the people that control them. It doesn't do for any of them to step out of line too far. May-Lee must have confided her plans to someone, and that someone made an example out of her. Mr Bird is going to pay, one way or another," he promised.

"My first priority is to get Julie back alive. After that, I'll join you in anything you want to do against him, but she comes first. My boss is her Dad," he reminded JayJay.

"What you gonna tell him?" JayJay asked.

"Fuck all!" he forced a brief laugh. "He can *wait* to kill me." Nick took another mouthful of Singha. "If I can pull this off, he might never need to know. There's a few other people in the queue before him, and I have enough to worry about at the moment, without the knowledge of impending doom waiting for me when I get back to the UK, with or without Julie. Right now, I have to figure a way of doing the impossible." JayJay looked puzzled, before Nick explained. "We SAS always used to take the piss out of your Delta Boys, you know. Well, Gabriel is in a whole new league. My own personal bogeyman. Someone I've looked up to, and respected, even modelled myself after, in a way. Somehow I've got to take him down. I'll only have surprise on my side for a few seconds. He's being watched, so I can't chance contacting him, and tipping him off. When I go for it, there'll only be seconds, and then he'll be trying to kill me, assuming I'm trying to do him."

"Hell, let me get word to him, for you," JayJay suggested. Nick thought about it for a few seconds.

"No, same reasons. They'll spot any attempt to contact him." JayJay mulled it over, and then his eyebrows raised.

"Hey, I know a guy. A local CIA contact. He might be able to help me rig something for you. I did a few covert numbers for them, while

I was on active service. Shouldn't really be telling you this. They were takedowns, and I needed to be discreet. If you can get close, a couple of seconds is all you'll need with the gadget I have in mind. Should give you a good edge." Nick's curiosity was piqued. "Let's go see the man. Have to get you measured up for it," JayJay smiled, not giving anything further away. Nick followed him as he got up from the table and headed off out onto the street.

*   *   *

Gabriel phoned Luis Montalban from his hotel room. "Luis, it's me. I'm in Cambodia, and getting close to the source."

"That's wonderful. How can I help? I have a medical team standing by." Luis knew what would be required of him. He and Gabriel had already discussed possible options before Gabriel had left Argentina. If another winged angel did indeed exist, it would be almost impossible to spirit such out of the country. Money only went so far, and bribes might get people to look the other way, but eyes remembered what they saw, and sooner or later, lips talked.

"Fly into Bangkok, and once I have accurate co-ordinates, you can bring the chopper in to pick us up. Make sure you have all the necessary forged paperwork, and medical forms to transport him back out of here," he advised his friend.

"The best forgeries your money can buy. I've already looked into hiring the medical helicopter. My team and I will fly in, pick up something suitable, and persuade the pilot to file the necessary flight-plans. A couple of days and I'll be on site," he assured Gabriel.

Chapter Twenty One

Once they made camp for the night, Laura ensured that Belle was comfortable inside the tent, and then joined the men for a hot meal. A second bottle of scotch was produced, and handed around the fire. Laura took a healthy swig. "I think your friend will not survive the night without more medicine," Dwi started the conversation.

"We don't have any more medicine," Laura stated, grimly.

"We may be able to make some, from plants and roots,"

"Make your potion," she answered simply. "I'll pay you hefty bonuses when we get back," she promised. Dwi said something she couldn't understand, and Rama and Dong got up and went off into the jungle, presumably to forage for the right plants and roots to make their potion.

Dong administered the potion to Belle, as Laura held her head up, encouraging her to drink, and within an hour or so, her fever subsided. The potion was apparently working. The four guides had kept their side of the bargain

The next morning, Laura woke up with a bit of a headache.

Dwi was cooking breakfast, but over another pot, Pak was stirring another concoction with a stick, adding a few leaves and roots to it occasionally. They left the brew to cool, whilst they ate their breakfast, and then Pak went back to it, pouring the contents of the pot into a small bottle, and insisting Laura get Belle to drink all of it. They would need to make a fresh potion again tomorrow, though Belle was expected to show signs of improvement by then.

Laura took the bottle into the tent, holding Belle's head up, while she forced her to drink from the bottle, though spluttering a lot of it.

Once Laura cleaned her up again, they took the tents down, packed up their gear, and put Belle on the travois once more. Another long day's trek was ahead.

During the day's journey, Laura found she was constantly checking on Belle, and pleased to discover the shivering had stopped, and her temperature was starting to go down. The herbal potion was doing her some good it seemed. The guides hadn't lied to her.

By evening, Belle was strong enough to get to her feet, and Laura washed her down with water in their tent. More of the potion was offered, and Belle forced down some solid food. She managed to keep it down, with difficulty.

The next morning, Belle managed to walk under her own steam, though feeling the worse for wear after the workout the four guides had given her. Laura shouldered her portion of the baggage, not wanting to overstrain her daughter until she was sure she was fully fit once more. "How far now?" she asked Dwi.

"Tomorrow, we should reach the village. The priests there still live in a ruined temple by the river. They will have more proper medicine for your daughter." Laura was very much reassured. It had been a near thing.

The four guides seemed in higher spirits throughout the day, as though glad to be nearing the end of their trek.

They broke camp early the next morning, and Laura found Belle awake, weak but aware of what was going on around her. Laura helped her up, washed her, and helped her change her clothes. Rama went on ahead to alert the village of their impending arrival. The rest of them took it slower, letting Belle set the pace.

Their eventual arrival in the village brought out many of the villagers to stare at the newcomers. Laura and Belle smiled at all the inquisitive faces, though they were puzzled to see many such faces turning away, once the novelty had worn off. Other faces were mixed with the villagers, some priests in their red robes, and others dressed in black. Many of them carried weapons.

There was fear on the faces of the few priests in the crowd. Laura was at a loss to guess the reason behind it, when a few of those carrying guns, levelled them at her and her party. Pak and Dong quickly darted in and seized the weapons carried by Laura and Belle. "What's the meaning of this?" Laura asked, as she automatically stood back to back with her daughter, as they realised they were now surrounded.

"The women are delivered, as promised," announced Dwi. "Where is our money?" he asked to one of the men in the black pajamas.

"You bastards!' cursed Belle, lunging forward, still weak. Laura pulled her back, only too aware that they were outgunned. If looks could kill, all four guides would now be dead, but the four men just grinned brazenly in response to her glare. Dwi accepted the thick wad of notes handed to him by one of those men.

"Take the women away, and put them in separate huts," ordered the obvious ringleader. At gunpoint, Laura and Belle were disarmed, and then frogmarched off through the village.

Chapter Twenty Two

Gabriel had now turned his attentions to the port authority offices used by Blue Elephant to organize their shipments in and out of the country. Security was tighter, so he contented himself with some mischief concerning their trucking, blowing the odd tire out here and there. Smashing windscreens. All relatively minor stuff, with no casualties, but still causing enough problems to hamper their operations.

They had by now traced Gabriel to his hotel, the Sunway, on No 1 Street 92, but were cautiously shadowing him instead of seeking to apprehend him, either wary of what he had done to the first set of assailants, or under orders just to keep tabs on him. It was hard to find an inconspicuous hotel in Phnom Penh, as most had been built in grandiose style for the expat community. If he'd been here longer, he would have looked around the back streets for something smaller, but beggars couldn't be choosers for the moment.

Gabriel kept alert, but was intent on continuing this game until they found it easier to give him the information he wanted.

He had asked his friend Luis Montalban to fly to Phnom Penh as soon as he could get a medical team together. Luis had access to one of Gabriel's accounts which was used to fund the medical facility in Cordoba, and this meant he had funds on standby to charter a chopper for medivac once he got here. Somewhere in those Highlands, was one of Gabriel's kin, and if he was still alive, he would probably need help to get him out of the country and home. Gabriel couldn't do that on his own, taking into account what he expected to find.

*   *   *

Gabriel's call, days earlier, was not unexpected, and revealed an urgent need for a possible medi-vac out of Cambodia. Luckily, Luis had permanent access to a privately funded account, set up by Gabriel, and funds were always available to deal with emergencies, when found necessary.

Luis was checking available facilities, and assessing requirements, based on Gabriel's instructions. Anywhere in Cambodia meant a helicopter would be needed for extraction. That helicopter would need to be fitted out with suitable medical facilities, and such would not be found inside Cambodia. Bangkok was a better bet, and so Luis began contacting various medical organizations to see about chartering such a helicopter. Flight plans would have to be filed, and cross-border co-operation for an emergency medi-vac of a wealthy client would need a lot of paperwork. Such paperwork was often expensive, but went faster when it was indicated the client was wealthy, and organizations applied whatever price structures they thought they could get away with. Gabriel could afford it, and so Luis put the wheels in motion, before selecting a small team to accompany him, and then setting off for Ezeiza airport. By the time they reached Bangkok, the fitted out helicopter and pilot should be waiting for them. Then it would only be a case of waiting for Gabriel's call, and direction to a suitable rendezvous point.

Luis was quite excited about the possibility of finding a live winged specimen of Gabriel's race, though what state he would be found in was anyone's guess, and Luis had to prepare for all eventualities. He was under no illusions as to what would be required to move such out of Cambodia and back to his facility in Cordoba.

The team he had chosen to assist him was trustworthy, and had worked with him for a number of years. They were all familiar with Gabriel's physiology, which up until now, they had thought unique. Maria Acosta, Esteban Ruiz and Osvaldo Varela. All experts in their fields, and fascinated with Gabriel as a test subject.

*   *   *

Julie woke up as the truck pulled up in the settlement. Whatever they had drugged her with had left a horrible taste in her mouth, though had meant she had been unconscious for most of the journey.

She had no idea of where she was, only that she was still a captive, and they hauled her down roughly from the back of the truck as she tried to get her bearings. Jungle all around in three directions. Looked like a river and a waterfall to the south. A hillside to the north and west contained traces of an ancient Khmer temple, which vanished up into the tree-line, leading up to where the falls spewed out from above into the river below.

The village was a scattering of old native huts, and a series of newer tents. Belligerent men were ill-treating a couple of what looked like holy men, beating them with lengths of thin bamboo. Julie had no idea what it was about. The beating stopped, with the two holy men almost unconscious. They were allowed to be helped to their feet, by other men, wearing the same coloured robes, obviously subservient to the men who had been doing the beating.

The men giving the orders wore black pajamas of some sort, backed up by others in more ethnic garb. Some wore typical Muslim head-wrappings. They were very obviously of a different breed than the holy men. The men in black pajamas, stood side by side with these Muslims Smaller men, no, make that children, were also in evidence.

Some of these black-clad men soon gathered around her, as her captors pushed her forward, jabbering away in a language she couldn't understand. They took possession of her, and the men who had brought her here, were moving back to their truck as Julie was marched towards one of the mud buildings. She was forced inside, despite her protestations, and found the interior contained a few trappings of civilization, such as furniture and a bathroom. The door was closed and locked behind her, which was a relief as Julie desperately needed to use that bathroom, and she hurried inside, dropping her trousers on the way.

*   *   *

No amount of yelling throughout the day brought Julie her freedom, though she was fed twice, once at midday and again at dusk, with a thin soup, bread and fruit. She was thankful for the one piece of luggage they had allowed her to bring, with toiletries and essentials, but she had no idea what she was doing here, or why she had been taken captive in the first place. She could only assume it had something to do with Nick, and she had to trust him to find her, and rescue her from whatever this situation was. "How long I stay here? How long?" she tried to converse with one of her captors as he collected the remains of her meal.

"Two days. Maybe Three days. Then you go home. You behave, or you not go home," was his only response, and he took the food bowls and left her alone again. She had not been ill-treated since her capture, merely drugged and transported to wherever this place was, somewhere in some anonymous jungle in Thailand, she guessed.

The only door remained locked from outside, and the few windows had been recently fitted with rough barred grilles. She was here for the duration, or until Nick did whatever they wanted him to do.

She had no clues where she was from the dialects of the men around her, as everyone spoke a gobbledygook mishmash of different tongues, and she couldn't understand anyone, unless they spoke pidgin-English to her. Her surroundings were better than she had imagined they might be. Not up to the standards she was used to, but a lot better than most people had out here, away from the cities. The single bed smelled, but at least it was soft, and Julie settled down on it, trying to sleep.

*   *   *

Across the small clearing, Laura and Belle had noticed the arrival of Julie, earlier in the day, and both had recognized her, though they had remained silent as she had been put into the neighboring hut. They waited till early evening, and there were less people about before trying to make contact.

"Julie . . . ." Belle shouted/whispered as loudly/quietly as she could. She needed to get Julie's attention and no one else's, so it was hit and miss. She repeated the call four times, before Julie's face appeared at the barred window, and her eyes opened as she finally recognized Belle at the window opposite.

"What the fuck are you doing here?" Julie asked, incredulously, as she recognized Belle.

"Ditto. How did you come to Cambodia?" asked Belle.

"Cambodia? Is that where I am?" she asked. "I don't know. I was in Bangkok with Nick, and these men broke into my hotel room. Then they drugged me, and the next thing I know, I woke up here," she recounted, gripping the bars tightly.

"Someone must have made Nick's connection with us or Gabriel. Sorry, but looks like our fault you're in this mess." Laura was looking out of one of the other windows, and quickly hushed her daughter, as she spotted one of the Khmer approaching. "Talk later," was all Belle had time to say, before pulling her head back into the room.

*   *   *

Turnbull was collected from his overnight hotel on Sihanouk Plaza around midday, by two of Bird's men, who were to arrange his meeting with Gabriel. They were under orders to hold back, after Gabriel had easily turned the table on four of Bird's operatives. To take him down with what he had available locally, would end in a bloodbath which would attract the authorities. Best to keep this as low-key as possible.

He had flown in late the previous evening. JayJay had been on the same flight, though seated apart, and the two men kept their distance. It was hard for JayJay to blend in, at his size, and with his colouring, so he had gone the opposite route, bright flowered shirt, and pretending to be African.

After clearing Customs, the two of them took individual taxis to separate, but adjacent hotels, and early morning, JayJay was out there renting a car, and making contact with an arms dealer of his acquaintance, after a phone call the previous day to make arrangements. The haul wasn't a lot, but still extremely illegal. He hoped it would be enough for the work he had in mind.

The car ran more sluggishly, with the load in the trunk, and he was glad to see Turnbull waiting for him on the corner of the street. He climbed swiftly in, as JayJay pulled over, and they drove quickly off again, heading for a car showroom, specialising in off-road vehicles. You couldn't rent one of these, unfortunately, so that left them with only one alternative.

Turnbull stayed in the first car, while JayJay went inside. After about half an hour, JayJay came out with the salesman, brandishing a set of keys, insisting on taking it for a test-drive. JayJay got in and fired up the ignition, as the salesman pointed out the controls.

JayJay gingerly drove the vehicle off the lot, and out onto the streets of Phnom Penh, which were starting to liven up by this time. Instead of once round the block, JayJay drove to a car-park which he had spotted earlier, and Turnbull followed him in, parking so that their two open boots would obscure what they were doing as they transferred the ordinance and tracking equipment. Turnbull drove the off-road, as JayJay returned the first vehicle, and then both men sat in the off-road discussing tactics.

"This is the main road out of town, heading up towards the highlands," JayJay pointed out on the map. "I'll wait out there. The tracker is good up to ten miles, and that's only about five miles outside of town. I should be able to spot them if they take a different route, and still be able to catch you up. If all goes as planned, I'll eyeball their vehicle as it passes, and follow at a distance."

Both men studied the relief map, memorising it, assessing possible destination points, access to water and to roads. Turnbull nodded absentmindedly, trying to keep his mind off Julie, and wondering what was happening to her? It was best not to think about it. He forced his mind back on to the job in hand, letting JayJay kit him up with the device he promised would give him an edge against Gabriel.

He would need that edge. He would have no chance to warn Gabriel of what was happening, and it would be pure instinct, adrenalin and luck that decided the outcome from thereon in.

*   *   *

JayJay dropped Turnbull off back at his hotel, and drove off. By the time the theft of the vehicle was realised and notified to the police, he would be in the Highlands. They'd have a job catching him out there, if they could be bothered, that is.

The main highway ran north, splitting to go east to Kampong Cham or further north to Kampong Thom, and Sisophon in the far North West of the country. There were many obscure side roads in between. Most of the country to the west of the highway was unmapped, and many isolated communities lived in apparent anonymity. It was a good place in which to get lost.

*   *   *

Gabriel had left his own hotel around eleven, after a late breakfast, first paying another visit to the docks, before heading back into town, wondering what mischief to get up to today. He had picked up the usual couple of tails, but Bird's men kept their distance, just prepared to watch rather than intervene. He didn't mind them reporting his movements, in fact he wanted them to tell their employer of all the problems he was causing for them. It was in their best interests to give him the information he wanted, and move him on. They weren't good enough to take him out.

As he walked down the street, Gabriel noticed a recognisable face in Nick Turnbull, approaching from the junction near the traffic lights, and Nick acknowledged him with a nod as he approached. He made his way closer, as the pedestrian traffic allowed, and he put out his hand in greeting as two men met. "All roads lead to Rome, Nick?" Gabriel queried, wondering why Nick was suddenly here in Phnom Penh and not Bangkok.

As Gabriel went to shake hands, Nick's hand didn't grasp Gabriel's own, but raised up to point the small metal tube sticking out from under the cuff of the jacket sleeve into Gabriel's face. Taken by surprise, Gabriel cried out as the ejected vapour stung his eyes. Gabriel's hands raised, trying to protect himself from whatever it was being sprayed at him, but the liquid was atomized, under pressure, and it clung to his face and hands, stinging instantly. "Bastard!" he cursed, trying not to rub his watering eyes, knowing it would only make matters worse.

Nick admired the mechanism. It had worked exactly as it was supposed to. The flex of his forearm muscle triggered the device, a miniature aerosol, spraying the chemical irritant in Gabriel's face and eyes. Surprise and treachery were the only way he was going to win this fight, so best not think about it, and just get it over with. He could do it. He could do anything for Julie, even betray a friend.

Gabriel lashed out with his foot, as Nick kept coming on, and Nick grunted as he turned, letting it glance off the pit of his stomach. Gabriel's eyesight was failing rapidly, disorienting him, but he still lashed out with a couple more blows, rocking Nick's head with the second, which came at him almost before he had managed to block the first. The third blow missed, as Nick weaved. He couldn't drag this out, but getting in close was going to be dangerous. The skin on Gabriel's hands and face was now turning rapidly pink as the chemical spray did its worst. The eyelids were puffing up. Nick struck out himself, and Gabriel could only partially block the kick.

Instinctively, the flex of a forearm dropped one of his knives into Gabriel's hand, and he lunged for the blur that was Turnbull. The blade ripped Nick's shirt as he stepped forward, turning into the blow, grabbing the wrist, twisting and backing up hard to slam Gabriel into the alley wall. Gabriel grunted as Nick's head snapped back into his face, and the pressure on his wrist forced him to drop the blade.

Bird's men were holding back the pedestrian crowd, eager to see what was going on. He had to finish this quickly. Dodging past another wild blow from Gabriel, Nick slammed him back against the alley wall again, wrapping his arms around Gabriel's own momentarily. "Trust me . . ." Was all he had time to whisper in Gabriel's ear, before he head-butted him, and Gabriel's head snapped back, colliding with the brickwork behind him. Nick followed up with another couple of blows to Gabriel's stomach as the blinded man tried to defend himself. Nick hated himself for this. An ordinary man would be totally helpless by now, but still Gabriel fought on, and Nick knew he still couldn't afford to take a chance with him.

Gabriel lashed out desperately twice more, but failed to connect. His eyes had closed completely now, and he was fighting blind. As Nick moved, Gabriel still managed to move with him, as though his sensitive hearing could determine Nick's own movements almost as well as his eyes. Nick stepped in, allowing Gabriel to block the first blow, as though by instinct, then landing a good solid punch to Gabriel's jaw and his idol went down, knees sagging, and Nick followed up with a heavy blow to the back of his skull, pole-axing him.

Gabriel collapsed on the ground, unconscious. Nick stood over him, still hardly believing he had achieved the impossible. He felt cheapened that he had had to resort to this betrayal, but as much as he liked and admired the man lying before him, he loved Julie, and she came first.

Then, as he debated his treachery, one of Bird's men appeared beside him, drawing a black PVC body-bag from under his coat and rolling it out. Another of Bird's men knelt down, pulling a syringe form inside his coat, and injected Gabriel in the neck, to keep him sedated. Nick knelt to help him roll Gabriel into it, feeling the second blade still in the forearm sheath, which Gabriel had not drawn against him. Had his message gotten through to him? Had he understood what was at stake here?

Nick helped them lift and then lower Gabriel into the body-bag, which would keep him immobile, though ensuring the zip was not closed altogether, to give him air, and two more men were suddenly there to help lift the immobilised Gabriel, as others dispersed the crowd of people who had tried to witness the fight.

Nick stayed with Gabriel, as his body was carried away from the scene, over one man's shoulder. A short distance away, a small minivan stood waiting, with its rear doors open, and Gabriel was bundled inside. Nick and two men clambered in with him, and the doors were closed, leaving the pedestrians to puzzle over what they had seen.

As the van pulled away, Nick put his hand in his pocket and pulled out a partially opened packet of Starburst sour-chews, and offered them to the men in the van with him. One declined, the other accepted, unwrapping the chew, and popping it into his mouth. Nick also took one and did the same, before giving the bottom of the packet a surreptitious squeeze, activating the tracer, and then putting the packet back into his pocket.

The CIA contact had been full of all sorts of useful little gadgets, straight out of a 007 film. The Americans were real whizzes at the miniature electronics stuff. The watch was supposedly good to transmit sound up to five kilometres, and kept reliably good time, he was assured. There were a few other items Nick would have loved to bring along with him, but realistically, that was all he thought would pass a cursory search. Communication was going to be a one-way affair, and he just had to hope JayJay would be able to keep up with him.

If Bird kept his word, they were now both of them on their way to a rendezvous deep in the Cambodian Highlands, where he would be reunited with Julie. If not, then before long, the two men sat across the van would try and kill him. It wouldn't be too hard, seeing as they hadn't trusted him with a weapon, but they had seen his skill in unarmed combat against Gabriel.

In close quarters such as the interior of this van, the odds were about even, two to one. They didn't look military trained, and he saw no outward signs that they carried any weapons themselves, so it looked as though he could relax for the moment. Gabriel was unconscious for the time being, and he would be sightless till the swelling went down. A couple of days. The body-bag would keep him immobile in the meantime. He hoped he got the chance to talk to him privately, and explain the situation.

An hour later, on the outskirts of the city, they transferred into a flatbed truck, which was loaded up with Turnbull's luggage, and also Gabriel's, cleared out from their hotels. Bird was leaving no trace behind.

*   *   *

Bird had men in most of the government departments in Bangkok, and word was already out about his interest in a man called Gabriel Angell, so when Luis' flight plan was filed, the information was passed along to Bird, along with details of the flight Luis and his team would be arriving on. He mused over the information for a while, for he had already been told of Turnbull's success. Gabriel was now a captive, and on his way to the Khmer camp in the Highlands. So why was this medical team on its way there? Gabriel must have arranged it before his capture, so the medi-vac must be for someone else. Who? Gabriel's women? He had no idea what condition they were in. It was a mystery, and one Bird wanted to get to the bottom of. He picked up the phone, and began making a call to one of his contacts at Airport Customs.

*   *   *

Luis and his team were tired after their long flight, and were keen to check into a hotel and catch up on some long overdue sleep. Their passports were noted as they checked through Customs and Immigration. Taxis took them to a hotel, where they all checked into separate rooms, to settle down for the night.

Once Luis had a refreshing shower, he took a half bottle of wine from the mini-bar and poured himself a drink, as he began going through Gabriel's medical file and case-notes to familiarise himself on the physiology he would be seeing in the flesh so to speak. He would have a limited time to study such, and so brought with him portable digital video cameras, in addition to his medical tools and drugs.

It was getting late, when there was a polite knock on Luis' hotel room door. Fastening his robe around himself, Luis went to open the door. Three men were stood in the corridor, one of them unnaturally tall and obviously of advanced years. "Doctor, we need to talk," the grinning skull spoke.

Chapter Twenty Three

The three women settled down for the night, though, by pre-arrangement, Laura and Belle took it in turn to stay awake, and take note of the movements of their guards, which were infrequent. Every half hour, someone came by to take a cursory check. Apart from that, there was nothing else to worry about. The doors to their confinement were sturdy, and securely locked. She had no lock-picking equipment, and brute force wouldn't work against the sturdy frame, so Belle worked on the bars of her window with the spoon. The mud was not much of an obstacle, though she used her plate to catch the scrapings. She would need to use saliva or the remnants of her soup to congeal the scrapings to paste back over her work by morning. Two bars and she could squeeze through. It was slow going, and would take more than one night to achieve.

*   *   *

In one of the commandeered temple cells, the Khmer lieutenant Anjin was talking to Bird on the radio. "We now have all three women. My men are restless, and tiring of the village women," he warned.

"Miss Maddox is not to be harmed. Do whatever you like with the other two. I have no interest in them. If all goes well, you will have another visitor shortly. You will need to take special care of him till I get there. Keep him safe. Miss Maddox's boyfriend will be bringing him. She may be released once he arrives. I keep my word, but once she is released, you may recapture her again if you wish," Bird chuckled.

"You are coming here?" Anjin asked, incredulously, for he knew the low profile Bird liked to keep.

"I wish to greet my new guest personally," Bird chuckled. "His death will be personally satisfying, and serve as an example to you all," he promised himself. "My contacts with the civil aviation authorities advised me of a logged flight plan, which was of interest. It seems as though my friend had other people en route here. They have been intercepted. I will keep you advised," Bird promised.

*　　*　　*

The next day, the women were roused early, and fed with a bowl of rice soup and some bread. There was an air of expectation in the camp, though neither of them had any idea what it meant. The men came for them shortly before noon, unlocking the doors and beckoning them forth. Laura and Belle were released, whilst Julie remained in her confinement, wondering what was happening.

The men made no threatening moves towards either Laura or Belle, though they could kill them at a whim, for they all still carried their weapons. Best go along with things for now, or so they thought.

The men formed a line on both sides of them, and one or two prodded the women with their rifles to get them to move forward, through the camp, up into the tree-line, where the ground rose up a steep hill. They could hear the falling water through the trees, from the falls that fed into the river, and eventually they all came out past the trees, onto a small plateau halfway up the mighty falls, which gave a good view out across the treetops, and, looking down, into the cascading waters of the falls where it met the river below.

One of the men pulled two knives from out of his belt, and offered them hilt first to both Laura and Belle, while the rest of his men laughed and made what they assumed were crude comments in dialects neither woman understood. First Belle and then Laura accepted the knives, cautiously, as the man quickly backed up, his arms coming up and beckoning the two women together, pointing at the blades, and then mimicking, he brought his thumb up to his own throat and sliced it across.

The roar of water crashing down on the rocks below made it hard to hear conversation, as Belle leaned in close to Laura to whisper to her. "Looks like they want us to put on a show for them. One of us is going to die here," Belle surmised. "They won't settle for half measures. If we chicken out, they'll just kill one or both of us." Laura turned to her daughter, her face hardening. "I'm better with a knife than you, so this fight will only go one way," Belle stated the obvious. "They'll recognize if I hold back, so there's only one way out." Laura looked puzzled at her daughter's words. "You have to trust me. I'm the only one who can make this work. Make it look good for a minute or two, then give me an opening. I'll make it quick . . ." Laura was studying Belle, trying to work out in her own mind what her daughter couldn't fully explain.

"The one who lives is going to end up as a camp-whore. You really expect me to let that be your fate?" she asked her daughter.

"If we play this right, we'll end up with an edge. Trust me." That was all Belle had time for, as by then, the men were growing impatient. The natural stage was set for this duel to the death. As the men crowded around the edge of the plateau, both women were keeping one eye on the other, and trying to study their surroundings at the same time.

It was a small plateau, less than twenty feet across and now hemmed in by more than two dozen men, laughing and jostling, and all still armed to the teeth. Belle and Laura stared at each other, not wanting what was to occur, but being given no choice.

Laura had never faced off against her own daughter before, but Belle was right. She was better with a knife than Laura. The only way out of this situation meant the death of one of them. She had the choice of killing her own daughter, or being killed herself. Sacrificing herself to give Belle her life would mean she would spend the rest of her days warming the beds of these animals. Not much of a choice. Daresay Belle was thinking similar thoughts, though her face was set like a mask.

"Fight!" one of the men ordered, and Belle lunged forward, eager blade aimed for Laura's heart, and Laura used her own knife to parry, stepping to one side, and using her right leg to trip and raise Belle's own. A quick lunge of her own caused the off-balance Belle to fall, throwing herself back, rolling and coming up just short of the edge, as Laura tried to press her advantage. Belle cried out as she met Laura's charge, and the two women struggled, one grasping the other's knife-hand, as they teetered on the brink of the falls.

Belle's slight height and weight advantage forced Laura back, as her foot slipped on the wet grass and Belle fell on her, her knife stabbing into the ground by her head, as she rolled to one side. Belle's leg lashed out, catching Laura in the midriff, as she tried to take advantage, and she cried out, rolling back and away to catch her breath. All around them, the laughing and shouting men urged the two women on, each of them choosing their own champions, as the combat surged back and forth.

Laura cried out as Belle's knife ripped through her shirt, gashing her waist, and leaving a bloody stain on her shirt. It stung, but wasn't that serious. Belle was nodding slightly to her, her waving knife backing Laura towards the falls. What was she trying to do? Laura still was not sure. Belle's eyes implored, but implored what? Laura lunged forward herself, but Belle's knife caught her own, flipping the blade back, and she had to dance back out of the way of Belle's knife as she came forward once more.

The men were crying out for blood, and unless they saw more than was currently seeping from Laura's shirt, they would be intent on spilling some themselves. Laura pretended to slip, but her knife came up as Belle lunged forward to take advantage, and the tip of the blade ripped through Belle's shirt, between her side and her arm, as Belle twisted to avoid the blow, falling. Laura came after her, but Belle's legs drew back, and then snapped out, catching Laura on her shins, and she too took a tumble.

The two women were rolling on the ground again, struggling to keep the other's knife away from their bodies. "You have to trust me . . ." Belle whispered in Laura's ear. "Do it now before you're too tired. When I lift up, get a foot into my stomach and push me back. Then give me an opening. If you don't we'll both die . . . ."

Laura was starting to feel an unnatural blood-lust, the more she fought. Always competitive from her tomboy days on the farm, it was hard not to give her best in such a situation. She did indeed trust her daughter, but failed to recognize how Belle could turn this situation to their advantage.

Snarling, Laura's foot fitted nicely into Belle's stomach, as she raised herself for better leverage, and then Laura kicked her back and away, and both women got to their feet once more.

The men were baying for blood, enjoying watching the two hellcats fight. Every survival instinct within Laura was telling her not to drop her guard, but that's what she did, feigning that the injury in her side was troubling her more than it actually was, and her movements began to slow, just dancing out of the way of Belle's blade by millimetres, instead of inches.

"Now, do it now." Belle mouthed, though Laura couldn't hear the words for the noise of the roaring waters. Whatever she had planned, it had better be good, Laura thought to herself, as she pretended to slip on the wet grass, her knife hand dropping.

Laura's eyes widened, real fear there, with the speed of Belle's attack, as she lunged forward faster than Laura would have believed possible. The sudden impact to her chest stunned Laura, still gasping into her daughter's face for a second, and then, as Belle withdrew her bloodied blade, Laura's jaw dropped as she looked down at the blood seeping from her chest.

The watching men were stunned momentarily, and then roared their approval, as Laura staggered, one hand clutching the useless knife, the other clutching at the reddening stain on the front of her shirt. As she looked back up at Belle, her daughter lunged forward once more. The watching men heard her scream a hateful "DIE!" as she delivered a tremendous savate kick to Laura's chest, which knocked her back over the edge, and she instantly vanished into the flowing torrent of the falls, without even time for a scream. Celebratory gunfire rang out around Belle, as the men celebrated the outcome of the fight, and the winners of bets goaded the losers.

One of the men came to collect the knife from her, warily, as others held their guns on her, and Belle's hands were re-tied behind her back. She knew what her own fate would be. She just hoped her mother's would end up better.

*   *   *

The truck bounced wearily along, its suspension rougher on Gabriel in his rubber cocoon, than it was on Turnbull. He peered off into the jungle, hoping that JayJay was managing to keep up with them. This wasn't something he fancied doing without backup. He was confident of his own abilities, but one bullet was all it took. He had gotten little sleep overnight, and one of Bird's men had administered another injection to Gabriel, to keep him unconscious. He was going to be pretty dehydrated by the time he woke up.

Chapter Twenty Four

"DIVE!" Belle had screamed, as she ran forward and kicked Laura back off the edge into open air.

Laura barely had time to recognize the words for what they were, still stunned that she was still alive from the blow which even she had thought was fatal, before she twisted and turned as she fell, turning the fall into the dive that she hoped Belle's kick would cause her to clear the waiting rocks below.

It was a brilliant plan, providing it worked. Laura merged with the falls about halfway down, and lost sight of what was below, till all of a sudden she hit the water, and thankfully no rocks. She plunged deep, bottoming out, and looking around to get her bearings. The clear water flowed one way, away from the falls, shallowing out, where she might be seen if she surfaced. The men had to think she was dead, and truthfully, she found it hard to believe she wasn't.

At the last second, Belle had palmed the knife, letting the blade cut, but not penetrate too deeply, before letting it slide up within her fist, and it was the fist hitting the chest that had made the sound of the impact so convincing. The suddenness of it all had fooled everyone, even her. For one horrible second, she thought Belle had really killed her.

Fearful of crocodiles in the water, Laura needed to get out of it, yet she couldn't afford to be seen, so she swam into the deeper water, holding her breath as she worked her way along the bottom, through the rocks, behind the falls, hoping to hide there until nightfall. Any crocodile would find it more difficult to swim upstream, against the full force of the falls.

As she cleared the roaring waters, to the calm behind, Laura surfaced and took a grateful breath. As she levered herself out of the water, she stuck her knife into her belt, and brushed her hair back out of her eyes, wringing it out as best she could, and then smoothed down her shirt and pants, trying to get as much water out as she could.

The two shallow wounds stung, but were not serious. It was while she was doing this, that she noticed a small worn pathway coming out of the jungle, and onto the rock shelf at the base of the hillside. Following it in the poor light, she noticed a dark shadow, which at first she thought just looked like being caused by a projecting part of the rock face. Going closer, Laura found the opening into what looked like a small cave. It would be a good place to hide until nightfall, and so she decided to enter.

She had taken no more than three steps inside, when she realized she was not alone, jerking the knife back out of her belt, as she heard a faint sound, as though someone had taken a hesitant step. The one sound she heard, indicated a depth to the cave, and she remained motionless, forcing herself to breathe very shallowly, as she let her eyes accustom to the dark.

There was a bowl of half-eaten fruit on the floor, and a jug of what was probably water, next to it. Someone was hiding out in here. One of the priests that had escaped the slavery the Khmer imposed on his brothers? The cave went on for about twenty feet, before making a turn, and the light from the falls behind dimmed, the further into the cave she went. Laura moved very slowly, as she didn't want to frighten anyone unduly. There was a slim chance any scream may be heard from outside, though the noise of the falls would taken some getting through.

As she turned the corner, her feet felt the carpet on the ground. Some semblance of comfort, and in the gloom, she made out an alcove, which had been fitted out with more rugs and pillows. A man lay there, either resting or asleep, as he seemed to be huddling under blankets. She didn't want to wake him, but best she did it gently so as not to alarm him.

She got closer, and began to reach out to him, to gently shake him awake, when she gasped, pausing in mid-stretch. "Oh my God . . ." The figure on the bed roused himself, raising to a sitting position. The 'blankets' did not fall away from his shoulders. What she had mistaken for blankets, were in fact wings! She had only ever seen Michael from a distance, and to see such at such close proximity was a shock.

Not alarmed, the 'angel' spoke, querying her in one of the local dialects, as if expecting someone else. When she didn't answer, he spoke again.

"I won't hurt you . . ." she blurted out, and the angel whirled towards her, standing, his wings flaring out behind him as far as the confines of the cave would allow, presenting an imposing figure, even allowing for the sorry state of those wings, and the few feathers that even now dropped out of them, as a result of that action. The wings looked crooked, somehow, though she had never seen real angel wings close up before. Her remembrances of Michael were fleeting and vague. She had the impression those wings had not been used in a very long time.

"English?" the angel queried. "Speak more." His wings folded back in of themselves, as he seemed to calm down.

"I'm a friend." She wasn't sure what to say, how to keep him calm.

"Only priests friends. Bad men come. Hurt friends." It sounded like he hadn't spoken English in a very long time. How long had he been here? "Who you?" he asked.

"My name is Laura. I came here to find you. My daughter and a friend are held captive by the bad men. I intend freeing them, and you," she stated. The angel scoffed. "What is your name?" she asked, reaching out, to gently touch his face, and he didn't recoil from the touch of her fingers, tracing the bone structure which was so like Gabriel's own.

"Nathaniel. That was my name." Laura looked him full in the face, from close range now, as he sniffed the air, smelling a mixture of sweat and faint perfume. She looked at the clouded eyes. He was blind. Cataracts.

"How long have you been blind?" she asked. Nathaniel answered first with a faint shrug of his shoulders, wings flexing.

"My eyesight was failing after a storm over the great mountains, and I flew south, separated from my people. The natives here thought me a God, and treated me well, so I stayed to get well, but once they saw my sight was failing, they determined I could not be an imperfect God, and so imprisoned me. My eyes failed altogether, once I was confined, and I haven't flown the whole time I've been in this cursed land," he explained. "Over the years, the people stopped imprisoning me, and started to care for me, but even though I was allowed relative freedom, without eyesight, I could not fly. I still remain a prisoner of sorts," he sighed.

Nathaniel reached out with his own hand now, touching her face, and Laura let him examine her as she had done him. Then his hand moved down onto her chest, over the swell of her bosom, though not in any sexual way. She gasped as he touched the still raw wound between her breasts, shallow but stinging. "You are hurt." Nathaniel pulled back his hand.

"It's not serious. It will heal in a few hours."

"The bad men?" he asked. Laura gave a short laugh.

"Sort of. They were responsible, anyway."

"You must have travelled far from your own land? I visited Britain once, many centuries ago."

"My people hail from there, but I was born in a land called America," she explained, though Nathaniel didn't recognize the name. "It's across a great ocean, a different land mass," she tried to explain further, but Nathaniel seemed to lose interest.

"I have some food and water, if you wish it. One of the priests keeps me fed, when he can steal away. I have been down here since the bad men came. My friends fear for my life, should the bad men find me." Laura nodded silently to herself. The Khmer Rouge, at the height of their power, were infamous for slaughtering mindlessly anything they didn't understand or didn't agree with. "You say you came to find me, from your land so far away? How is this? How did you know of me? Why would you want to help me?" Nathaniel queried.

"I found one of your feathers, in yet another land. I didn't recognize it, but a friend of mine did." Nathaniel's head turned, half to one side, quizzically. "His name is Gabriel." Laura spoke his name, wondering what sort of reaction it would cause.

"Gabriel? The wingless one?" he seemed puzzled for a moment. "Do more of my people still live on this cursed Earth?" he asked, voice raised slightly.

"He is all that is left," she admitted. "Lucifer and Michael died a few years ago. I know of no others," she replied truthfully, and Nathaniel bowed his head in sorrow.

"I was there when we abandoned Gabriel and Lucifer, though it broke Michael's heart. We left them to a life among the humans, while we sought refuge from mankind amongst the mountains and high places. We never found any such refuge. They hunted us everywhere," he stated, bitterly. Laura noticed tears streaking Nathaniel's cheeks, as he recalled the painful memories, and she used her fingers to try and brush the tears away. "This existence, for what it is worth, is the most peaceful I have known in centuries. I have grown accustomed to it. Leave me and go your way," he implored. "I am blind. My wings are useless. What good am I? Leave me to my self-imposed misery. It is all I have."

Suddenly, Nathaniel stiffened, turning his head slightly to one side. "What is it?" Laura asked, for obviously, he had heard something.

"Someone comes," he warned. Instantly Laura whirled around, ready to repel an attack from the only entrance to the cave. Sensing her concern, Nathaniel reached out a hand in her direction to calm her.

"Radna, the priest, brings me food. Do not harm him," he asked. Laura stepped back, though remained on guard, as she could now hear the soft pad of bare feet approaching.

The priest stopped in his tracks as he saw Laura stood there with Nathaniel, so surprised he almost dropped the small parcel of food, wrapped in green leaves.

"I know you," he said, in heavily accented English. "One of the women those guides brought to the village. If you have escaped, they will hunt for you," he warned, concerned.

"I went over the falls. That's how I found this cave," Laura explained. "They doubtless think me dead by now. It gives me a chance to try and rescue my friends. They hold two other women up there, one of them my daughter," she explained.

"Those are bad men, the Khmer. They killed many people, and would do so again. These young foreigners they train, they are keen to learn from them, how to kill. Even if you did free your friends, what would you do? Where would you go? We are miles from civilisation here," he explained.

"I need access to a phone or a radio. I have friends out there who would help me. But if that's not possible, then we'd have to take our chances in the jungle. If we stay here, we'll be raped or worse." The priest could only nod. His eyes had seen more than he wanted, since the Khmer had come here and taken over the village.

"They are bad men. They have hurt many people since they came here. But they have guns, lots of guns, and we cannot fight bullets," he explained.

"Then we're going to have to get some of those guns," Laura stated.

Radna handed over the small package of food to Nathaniel, apologetically. "I will return with more food," he explained, as he turned and left. Nathaniel sat back down on his rough bed, and began opening the small parcel of food, offering to share it with Laura. Fruit, and some portions of cooked meat. Laura took some, politely, though she wasn't that hungry at present. She used the small jug to refill it with water from the river at the cave entrance.

Radna returned less than an hour later, with more food for both her and Nathaniel. Laura couldn't stay here for long. Her presence may draw the Khmer towards the cave. She needed to plan, and act, soon.

The priest began talking, whilst he attended to Nathaniel's needs, cleaning and grooming him with a skill and devotion Laura could tell was out of respect and awe. Nathaniel wasn't a captive here, by any means. He was being protected from the Khmer and their Al Qaeda trainees. "He has always been here, in my village, though housed in what parts of the temple remain habitable, now taken over by the Khmer. They came almost two years ago, and enslaved my fellow priests and the neighbouring villages. We are fearful of what an outright battle would bring, and so we prefer to suffer, that no one else may suffer, least of all Nathaniel. He has suffered enough. My people tell that he fell from the sky and has been revered as one of the gods ever since, but I have heard his own tale, of how my people captured him, and confined him to prevent him leaving. My people have a cruel history, and his tale is first hand knowledge, not the stuff of legends. Blinded as he is, he cannot fly, and his wings have atrophied too far to be of any real use to him. They mark him as different, and the Khmer kill anything different or beyond their own knowledge."

"Can I count on your help to take down these evil men?" Laura asked. "If I can free my daughter, and get hold of some weapons, we can free your people. It's not something I can achieve on my own."

"I cannot organize such in one night," Radna protested.

"Then help me get weapons. I can cause them a few problems, free my daughter at least. It will give you time to talk to the rest of your people. Together, we can defeat these men," she assured him.

"Tomorrow, I can get you a weapon. I can only slip away during prayers. The rest of the time they make us work, and they watch us too closely," he explained.

"Tomorrow is a long time. I can't wait that long. Get what weapons you can tomorrow, and give them to some of your people, but tonight I'll make do with this," Laura made her mind up, brandishing the knife. "If I can obtain my own weapons, I will," she promised.

Chapter Twenty Five

*L*aura waited till just after dark, when she left Nathaniel in his cave, placated and quiet now with the few words and phrases she knew, and the priest explaining the situation to him. She pitied him his captivity, but the modern world was no place for such a physical oddity.

Now she had seen such wings with her own eyes, she understood more of Gabriel's feelings and viewpoints. She couldn't imagine what it was like to have such, but she could understand what it felt like not to have them anymore.

She followed the tiny worn path, into the jungle, and towards the faint sounds of the encampment below the temple ruins. If this had been a Solomon camp, then the weapons would be stored in the centre, apart from the individual guns that the Khmer might have. Their sentries would certainly be armed, and that's where Laura intended to make her mark. The Khmer and their trainees had to be alarmed enough to keep their minds off Belle and Julie. She needed to cause enough mayhem to get them searching the jungle all night, and still avoid their search herself.

Unused to jungle warfare, all Laura had to go on was her own experience, and a new found relationship with the night. She moved slowly, her eyes becoming more accustomed to the dark with each light step. Her hearing and sense of smell also seemed heightened. The knife was gripped firmly, and held low at her right thigh. Within sight of some of the campfires through the foliage, she began moving sideways, trying to seek out one of the sentries.

Her jaws were aching, and her own teeth now felt unbelievably sharp against her tongue, slightly more pronounced, and she shuddered as she realized what was happening to her. The tainted blood she had ingested from Angelica had infected her system, and it was making changes to her body, rewriting her DNA, her musculature. She was both terrified and thrilled by the new sensations she felt. Juliana had hinted that somewhere in Laura's ancestry, her genes were mixed with magic, presumably from the days when the people of Faery crossed over frequently into the Human world. It made her all the more susceptible to Angelica's power. A new Laura was waiting to be born.

She spotted the first sentry from a distance. He looked bored, leaning against a tree. Her nose caught the faint whiff of tobacco from a hurried cigarette, though he must have stubbed it out by now. Closer, and she could smell the stale sweat on his body, hear his shallow breathing as he was close to dozing off. Laura circled her prey, keeping the foliage and trunks of trees between them. It was ridiculously easy. She readied the knife.

The man didn't know anything about Laura's approach until the last seconds, when she came out from behind the tree he was leaning against, grabbed him by the mouth with one hand, and then slid the knife between his ribs with the other, sawing sideways as she ripped through his ribcage. She let him fall, still alive, but unable to do more than croak with his punctured lung. His death wouldn't take long, and she had already begun examining the AK47, checking the magazine.

The pooling blood on the jungle floor reflected the moonlight coming down through the foliage, and Laura paused to look at it, as it caught her eye. She reached out and poked it with a finger, holding the red-stained finger aloft in the moonlight, as she studied the way the liquid trickled down her digit. She brought it to her mouth, lips automatically opening to taste it, and then, feeling those teeth of hers, now seemingly more pronounced than before, she forced herself to stop, and wiped the finger against her pants. She brought the hand back up to her jaw, feeling the structure. It didn't feel normal at all. It ached, and felt like it was somehow almost rearranging itself. She could taste blood in her own mouth, as though suffering from pyorrhoea. It was seeping out around the base of her teeth, as though they were growing faster than her gums could allow for.

Sheathing the knife back in her belt, she took the AK-47, and went looking for another of the sentries. Now she was armed, she needed to make this kill more noisy, and deliberately alert the camp. If she kept the men busy looking for her, they'd have less time to think about their captives.

*   *   *

Belle could do nothing but wait. She had no idea if Laura had even survived the plunge over the falls. It was dark now, and one of the guards had laughed as he had warned her to be ready for a lively night. They had separated her and Julie just before dusk, and the two women were now housed in separate guarded huts once again. They seemed to be more wary of taking care of Julie than they did herself, for some reason. More interested in her welfare, whereas they had told Belle what she could expect as her lot. Many of the grinning, drug-chewing boy-soldiers had passed by during the day, saying little, just smiling knowingly, and looking forward to the night.

Cambodia was one of the world's capitals for both child prostitution and STDs. The children that tagged along with the Khmer were the remnants of families they had destroyed along the way. They had nothing else to live for, and it was either join or starve. The young girls were used as camp whores, and the male children joined as soldiers, being taught to use a rifle and a woman or girl, before they reached puberty. The male children had first dibs on Belle tonight. The older guards had been joking to her since earlier in the evening.

She stirred her plate of cooling food, thoughtfully. Once everyone had eaten and digested their evening meal, she would be entertaining visitors, over a dozen of them, Sex-Education 101, unless her mother came through with the hoped-for diversion. It was hard to look upon what she had seen so far as children. All of them carried weapons, and had the same mad glint in their eyes from all the addictive roots they chewed, same as the older Khmer. They had grown up too soon, had their childhood stolen from them, yet somehow she could not find it in her heart to pity them.

*   *   *

As she stalked her second kill of the night, something was also stalking Laura. It had caught her scent, and moved slowly and powerfully through the dense foliage, keeping downwind of her, the way she was trying to keep downwind on the sentry-line, as she skirted the camp at the same radius that she had found the first unfortunate man.

Laura's heightened senses made her hackles rise. She stared about her in the dark, seeking for whatever was causing the goose-bumps. Something was out there. The jungle around her was quieter than it was supposed to be. Her head jerked back slightly in its traverse, as the moonlight glinted off one huge eyeball peering at her though the foliage. It stared straight at her, body held motionless, waiting for movement before it decided whether to strike. Asian tigers are ferocious beasts, capable of killing with one bite, and their claws were just as infamous as their long teeth. The moonlight revealed those teeth to her now, as the huge beast took a half pace forward, mighty jaws opening wide, as its huge head came into view.

Frozen motionless only for a second, Laura reacted instinctively, ignoring the sudden pain, her own sharp teeth now gleaming in the moonlight as her jaws opened wide, and her own mouth filled with fresh blood as her teeth strained forward, the new musculature distending, and revealing a bite almost as deadly as the tiger's own. She hissed a low challenge, barely audible within a few yards of their position. "You want a piece of me? Come and get it!" she crouched low, knife readied in her hand, blade catching the moonlight. At no time did she even think of trying to bring the AK-47 from behind her back. She'd never have had time. It was the knife or nothing.

As it was, she didn't need the knife. The tiger appraised a fellow predator, held her gaze for what seemed an eternity, and then melted back into the undergrowth, in search of easier prey.

As Laura got her breath back, she could feel her mouth changing back again, as the teeth receded to a more normal position in her mouth. She could still taste her own blood, and she shivered, more at the thought of what was happening within her own body, than the close call with such a deadly jungle beast.

She forced herself to resume her hunt for another sentry, and eventually found one, urinating up against a tree, his AK-47 propped up against the trunk. Laura slid in behind him, knife readied for an easy kill, but that wasn't what she wanted. She reached out with the knife, and sliced deep down the man's back, lashing out with her foot and kicking the weapon to the ground, as the man screamed loudly into the night, and flailed about, whirling to face his attacker. Laura lashed out again with the knife, allowing the frightened man to block, as the blade sliced the palm of one hand. Beyond, within the camp, she heard the first cries of alarm, as she forced yet another scream from the wounded man. Voices, alarmed, began getting louder, as men came out from their tents and huts.

Laura flung herself at the wounded man, hooking one leg behind his knee as he tried to hold off the blade, and he fell back beneath her. Instantly, she straddled his midriff, forcing the knife home into his chest, breathing the fetid air that was released from his ribcage, and then raising the knife to stab down a second time, finding his heart this time. Then, quickly, she grabbed the second AK-47, and began to run back along her previous path, firing a quick burst towards the noise of pursuit, and then headed back toward the river, and the hidden cave. As she ran, odd shots ran out blindly, as frightened men came to find out who was attacking them, firing blindly.

She was almost at the river when she heard another bloodcurdling scream, and a mighty roar which she knew was the tiger. All those men stumbling blindly around in the jungle at night had proved too tempting a target, and the tiger had chosen one. Automatic gunfire rang out, as the men concentrated their fire on the huge beast. Laura kept on running, as a second scream was heard. The tiger was seemingly winning the fight, but then the gunfire increased, and the night became quieter once more. Laura heard concerned voices, shouting orders, but she soon put them behind her, following the path along the fast flowing riverbank, and other sounds were soon deafened by the roar of the falling waters.

*   *   *

Belle had been as alarmed as the rest of the camp, by the sudden commotion and automatic gunfire. Whatever her mother had done, it had had the desired effect, with the whole camp too busy to think of her, and so she huddled down against the wall for the rest of the night, waiting for the dawn of a new day.

Chapter Twenty Six

ayJay fought against the steering wheel as the terrain under him rocked the vehicle. Trying to keep one eye on the sat-nav, and the relative position of the tracking device Turnbull had activated, once Bird's men had loaded them into the truck. But the truck was running along a comparatively smooth stretch of road, whereas JayJay had to follow and keep out of sight, which meant maintaining a distance of between two and five miles, and driving through the jungle occasionally, avoiding places of habitation where there might be people reporting his presence.

He followed behind, generally, though where their route was obvious he tried to take what shortcuts he deemed advisable. From the map, they were heading between two tributaries of the great lake, which was also fed by the mighty Mekong River, and their road seemed to roughly follow one of those tributaries. JayJay knew their general direction, and any camp needed a water supply, so it was logical their camp would be close to one of these tributaries.

*   *   *

Gabriel had been awake only for a few hours before the truck had finally arrived at its destination. The drugs they'd obviously injected him with, were finally wearing off. His immediate panic at finding himself tightly enclosed in blind darkness was stayed by a calm hand resting on his chest, and then the tap tap tap of a seemingly casual drumming finger in Morse code, letting him know what was happening and where he was going.

He could guess by the blackness and texture that it was some kind of body-bag he was in, but there was sufficient air to breathe, though soaked with his own sweat. He was manacled, but could still feel the knife-sheaths on the inside of his forearms, one of them still occupied. They hadn't bothered to frisk him once Turnbull had taken him down.

Under him, the bucking floorboards of the truck told him they were on a rough gravelled road. Turnbull's tapping finger let him know that he had a plan. Best to let him run with it. Gabriel just lay there, conserving his energy. Time enough to use it once they let him out of the body-bag.

The truck delivered Gabriel to the training camp midway through the morning. Turnbull came alert by the sudden downshift of the gears, and the noise of voices outside, more regimented than the normal shouting villagers from the small towns they had passed through on their way here. Wherever 'here' was, they had arrived.

Gabriel's back was aching from the long road journey, and he was sweating profusely, dehydrated from a mix of the drug and the confinement in the rubber body bag, which they had left only partially unzipped to provide him with air, and the occasional sip from a water bottle.

He felt himself being lifted out of the truck, and lowered to the ground, where the zipper was finally unzipped all the way. Gabriel's eyes roamed around. Turnbull was stood none too close, and a slight nod was all that passed between them. Gabriel didn't react, just took in the number of men and the number of guns that were pointed at him, as he slowly got to his feet. "Water . . . I need water . . ." he spoke, motioning to his mouth in case they didn't understand English.

*   *   *

Seeing the dot on the sat-nav become stationary for the past ten minutes, JayJay studied the map closely, determining its position, and wondering where best to make his own stop. He studied the terrain. Two tributaries conjoined, as one flowed into the other from higher ground, in a mighty waterfall. The higher ground lay to the north, where a small ruined temple and village where shown on the map.

It was logical to assume that's where the base was, and JayJay was now best determining where he could set up camp to attack that base. To the East, the terrain rose more gradually, offering an overview of the village, if not the temple itself, and that, JayJay decided, was the best place to lay down fire from. He set his course accordingly, angling to with a mile of the village, before he parked his vehicle, still within the tree-line, where it wouldn't be seen or likely to catch the sun and give away a telltale reflection of light.

*   *   *

Radna came to the cave, more animated than normal, and he revealed the news of the arrivals in the camp. Two white men, one captive. One of the men was put in with the woman Julie. The other was held captive in a separate hut. From the description of the two men, and the fact that one of them had been put in with Julie, it didn't take many brain-cells to work out their identities.

"How many weapons did you manage to acquire?" Laura asked. "I have two AK-47's," she displayed.

"Three more are with my fellow priests," Radna admitted.

"Then here, take this one," Laura handed him the weapon, and quickly showed him how to use it. "Go back to your people, and when you hear gunfire, try and free those hostages. They will do most of the fighting, once armed. They are all friends of mine," she explained. "I'll create a disturbance away from the camp, and draw off most of the Khmer."

Nathaniel had no option but to stay in his cave, and simply wait, as Radna and Laura left. The priest hid his own weapon under his red robes, whilst Laura left hers slung over her shoulder, and held low and at the ready, as the two of them separated, the priest to go and rally his fellow-priests, and Laura to find a suitable place to make her diversion, in the hope that both Belle, Gabriel and Turnbull would quickly add to the mayhem, else she was going to be outnumbered rather quickly.

She headed north, to the higher ground, seeking cover in the tree-line, where she would have a good line of fire, and easily spot any pursuit.

*　　*　　*

JayJay studied the layout of the village which had sprung up around the temple ruins, sprawled out along the southern bank of the river. The training camp was set off at some distance from the main village, though the better buildings in the village had been taken over for use by the Khmer, and he had noted where Gabriel and Turnbull were currently imprisoned.

He started breaking out munitions from the truck, setting up a small mortar with which he intended creating a bit of panic down there, as and when Turnbull and Gabriel made their move, for he was sure they would eventually. A sniper rifle was to be used to pick off a few of the Khmer and their Al Qaeda trainees, going for whoever looked to be giving out the orders during the looming fire-fight. A few other guns and grenades were laid out, and he was deciding which to carry on his person, when out of the corner of his eye, he caught movement in the trees.

Staying cool, JayJay gave no outward sign that he was aware of the person stalking him. He merely continued his weapon inspection, allowing the person to get closer. He had to assume the person was armed, and an armed man at a distance was hard to fight against. Let him get closer.

The pistol was within reach, but out of the question, as it would alert the Khmer in the village below. It had to be the knife. JayJay partly turned, drawing the knife as he used his body to obscure the action, and he leaned forward as if to rearrange some of the other munitions. The stalker moved closer, more hastily, and JayJay took a handful of dirt with his free hand, throwing it backwards as he whirled around and launched himself at his partially blinded attacker.

His massive frame bowled the stalker over, but a knee up into his crotch made him gasp, deflecting the intended downward blow from the knife as the AK-47 came between them, the long blade glancing off the metal banana-clip.

A straight hand into his ribs made him cry out, and he tried to use his weight to bring the knife to bear at such close-quarters, and then he suddenly realised this was no scrawny native under him, but a rather attractive white woman, and he relaxed atop her, all offensive moves suddenly stopped, as she glared up into his face.

"Who are you?" they both asked simultaneously.

"Get offa me," Laura pushed up and JayJay rolled clear. The two of them stood up, dusting off. JayJay sheathed his knife, and Laura lowered the AK-47.

"You're not one of the Khmer, so who are you, and what are you doing here. You were setting up a kill-zone," she accused.

"Sure was, sweetheart," JayJay's face broke out into a disarming smile. "I have a friend in a bit of trouble down there, and we worked out a little scam to get him out of it. Name's Jesse James III. Pleased to meetcha, Ma'am," he grinned, eyes finding it hard to leave her braless chest which swelled from exertion under her thin khaki tee-shirt.

"Who's your friend?" Laura asked.

"Name of Turnbull, Ma'am. Nick and me go back 'aways."

"I know Turnbull. His girlfriend's down there with my daughter, and now my husband seems to be down there as well."

"Gabriel? Yeah, he's down there. I figure they'll make a move some time after dark, and when they do, I'll lay down some cover, and we can all get the hell out of here."

"Sounds like a plan. I have a few of the priests armed, and ready to help. They're waiting for my signal, and then aiming to help the hostages escape."

"The more the merrier in a fire-fight," JayJay grinned. "Hey you look hungry. I have some food and water. Want some?" he offered. Laura nodded, and put down the AK-47 as JayJay broke out some of his rations. "May as well settle down for the afternoon. We'll be fresh for when the fun starts later."

*   *   *

It was late in the afternoon when JayJay nudged Laura from a light sleep. He handed her the binoculars. "Something's happening down there. We have movement." Laura brought the binoculars to her own eyes and surveyed the village. People were milling about, ordered to and fro by the Khmer, clearing a central area of the village square.

They heard the faint thrum of rotors about a half hour later, and peered towards the horizon to make out the approaching helicopter. JayJay recognised it as a big Sikorsksy, and it had a large green cross stuck on its sides.

It made a couple of circling runs over the village, while the pilot checked out the landing area, and then slowly descended towards the cleared area, which was soon obscured by flying dust and dirt from the rotors.

After the dust settled, a ramp was lowered from the hold area of the helicopter, and figures appeared in the hatchway. Laura gasped as she zoomed in on their faces. "Luis . . ." she exclaimed, recognising Gabriel's personal physician, and some of his medical team. They were being led down the ramp in plasti-cuffs. Another figure appeared in the hatchway, crouching because of his height.

"Bird . . . ." Exclaimed JayJay. "Looks like the stakes just got a little higher, lady."

Chapter Twenty Seven

JayJay handed the binoculars back to Laura, who was obviously antsy about the situation developing in the village clearing. Gabriel was manacled, and his bearded face was still red and puffy. The irritation should have cleared normally by now, but cooped up inside that body-bag during transport, oxygen hadn't gotten to his skin. He looked physically a lot worse than he actually was, and Gabriel played on it, walking slowly and stiffly.

Turnbull was hugging Julie, staying close to him. Belle was holding back, wanting to go to her Father, who either didn't recognize her because of his puffed up eyelids, or he was deliberately not acknowledging her, to prevent their captors realizing any link between them. They had enough leverage on the current situation, without offering them more.

Radna appeared, with another of the priests. Both were now cradling Ak-47's in their arms, and appeared eager to help. The two warrior-priests looked from JayJay to Laura, occasionally paying attention to what they could see in the distance, which wasn't much without the binoculars. JayJay was checking the range on the mortar he had set up earlier. He had the shells laid out next to it on the ground, ready and waiting to be dropped down the tubes and fired into the village. He had assessed which of the buildings below were being used by the Khmer and their Al Qaeda trainees, from observation, and talking to the two priests. When the fun started, so would the panic. Few in number, they had to give the appearance of a large attacking force, to stand any chance of success, and buy enough time for Turnbull, Gabriel, Belle and Julie to either escape, or lend a hand from within.

The two priests checked the Kalashnikovs that Laura had provided them with, and they knew where the Khmer kept most of their arsenal. Hiding the weapons under their red robes, their jobs were to either secure the weapons for the villagers to use to fight back, or to prevent the Khmer getting to them, once the fighting started.

JayJay spoke to them. "Get among your people. Get them to stay away from the buildings north of the clearing. When you hear explosions, do your stuff." They nodded in understanding, folded their robes around their Kalashnikovs, and slowly headed back toward the village. JayJay was doubtful the priests would get much assistance from the frightened villagers, but if they could prevent the Khmer getting to their arsenal, it would help greatly in the fire-fight to come.

Laura studied Hongrugippon's face through the binoculars. His skin was drawn tightly across his face, and tighter still across his bleached skull. A few liver-spots mottled his face, which gave more of an indication of his age than his actual looks and manner. He looked quite mobile, though a lot of aged Asians were the same, due to practice of martial arts exercises well into their dotage. This man looked nimble and dangerous at the same time. The predator in her recognized another, one who was used to giving orders, as he did now to the Khmer, and of having them obeyed.

*   *   *

"So you're Gabriel?" Bird queried. Gabriel didn't answer. "You don't look like much," he sneered.

"Sorry to disappoint you," Gabriel answered.

"I brought you here to kill you," Bird smiled.

"I get that a lot," Gabriel simply smiled, wryly.

"Free his hands," Bird ordered, and one of the Khmer duly obliged. "My men need to be shown you're no Superman, and they need a reinforcement of my authority." Gabriel began rubbing some circulation back into his wrists. Bird pulled open his jacket, revealing a harness holding two knives against his side. He pulled one of the knives free, and threw it, so it embedded itself in the ground at Gabriel's feet.

"They tell me you're rather good with a knife." Bird sneered. "Let's see. Pick it up, and I'll try to get this over with as quickly as possible."

"Don't hurry on my account," replied Gabriel, stooping to collect the knife, hefting it in his hand to assess the weight. It was a good knife.

Bird drew his remaining knife, and addressed the watching Khmer and their Islamist trainees. "The rest of you men, watch and learn. This is just an ordinary man. One who bleeds like anyone else, as I'll shortly prove," he warned.

As Bird gave his little speech, Laura was creeping into the outskirts of the village, trying to catch the eye of Radna or one of the other priests.

Bird began to slowly approach Gabriel, who began backing away, moving in a circular movement, as he sized up his opponent. Incredibly tall and with an even more incredible reach. This was not going to be easy. Bird lunged, and Gabriel brought his knife up just in time, the blades connecting and deflecting. He tried to launch a retaliatory strike of his own, but simply could not get close, as Bird's knife danced before him. Both men were feeling each other out.

Twice more, Bird lunged, his long arm using the sharp blade like an artist would a brush, slicing at him, and catching and ripping the sleeve of Gabriel's jacket, though not yet drawing blood. The crowd were getting excited, urging on their leader as he forced Gabriel back, ever back.

Gabriel tried again, his knife ripping the lining of Bird's jacket, but he got too close, and this time Bird did draw blood, as he tried to deflect Bird's blade with his arm. The older man smiled as he saw Gabriel's sleeve darken with fresh blood, and resumed his attack. Gabriel gave ground, and Bird's knife caught his clothing twice more, as the tall figure seemed to sway back and forth, avoiding Gabriel's own attacks but still able to launch his own. The crowd began to close in around the two men. Gabriel had the jungle at his back now, as Bird forced him to give ground.

"Stay back. He's mine . . . ." Bird kept coming forward, as Gabriel backed away, trying to keep out of his reach, stumbling and almost tripping as Bird pulled and cut at the jungle foliage to keep after him. Gabriel was gasping in the jungle heat, his shirt red with blood from the superficial wounds Bird had already inflicted. As Gabriel staggered back into the undergrowth, he stumbled momentarily a couple of times, and Bird surged forward, trying to take advantage, cursing as his hand was caught by the overhanging vines. Determined, he closed Gabriel down, slicing the undergrowth to clear a path to him, following and narrowing the distance as the wounded man twisted and turned.

Out of sight of the crowd of Militiamen in the clearing, they could still be heard, urging Bird on. Laura had made contact now with Radna, and he and a few of his fellow priests were taking up positions at her direction. Above the roar of the crowd, she could still hear the sounds of threshing and combat from the undergrowth, and an occasional cry of pain from her husband.

Bird was getting increasingly more frustrated, as Gabriel now found it easier to dodge his attacks. The undergrowth was confining.

"You're right in one thing," Gabriel finally admitted in the heat. "You *are* a better knife fighter than me, and in any fair fight, you'd beat me. But your first big mistake is in thinking this is a fair fight." Bird paused in his attack, letting Gabriel's words sink in. "I fight to win. You've mistaken tactics for cowardice. I haven't been backing away from you out of fear. I'm choosing the best ground to make my stand. I lured you in here, and I'm now between you and the clearing." Bird looked around, realizing the truth in Gabriel's word. "Where we are now, the jungle and undergrowth negates your reach advantage. It's not so much a jungle as an operating table, and guess who's the patient?" For the first time, Gabriel saw fear in Bird's eyes. Gabriel lunged, his knife hand slicing down, aiming for Bird's thigh. KCHING . . . . the blades met as Bird hastily parried, but the knife in Gabriel's hand was dancing before his eyes.

Gabriel was faster in this confined environment, and Bird could not afford to lose sight of that sharp blade. Gabriel didn't use the artistic textbook strokes that Bird favored. His lunges changed direction in mid-air, sliding off to one side, and slicing instead of the normal retreat from a missed move that Bird expected. His moves were too fast for Bird to launch an attack of his own, all too conscious of the strangling undergrowth, hampering his arm movements and threatening to snare him or trip him up and thus render him helpless for the smaller man.

It was Bird who was sweating now. Little nicks began to appear on his arms, and the backs of his hands, as Gabriel whittled away. No sense trying for a kill that may leave him open for a counter, he was content to see Bird's blood flow as his own had done. The more he bled, the weaker he got. The only problem was Gabriel's own wounds. The more he moved, the more he bled himself. He wasn't quite as confident as he was leading Bird to believe. It was going to be a close thing.

As old as he was, Bird's stamina surprised Gabriel. The humidity and the blood-loss were getting to him, and he knew he had to gamble to win this fight. Putting a small distance between himself and the longer arms of Bird, his hand snapped back and forwards, the blade turning end over end, aimed for Bird's throat, but with a snarl of delight, the older man brought up his own blade KCHINNNGG . . . deflecting Gabriel's knife, and Bird lunged forward to take advantage as Gabriel staggered, dropping to one knee.

Gabriel put his hand down to support himself on the ground, forearm flexing, hand cupped to receive the knife which dropped into it, and he surged up off the ground, under the plunging arm of Bird which sought to bury his own knife in Gabriel's offered back, when Gabriel's knife ripped into his stomach.

Gabriel cried out himself as Bird's knife bit home, though not as deeply as intended, merely slicing across his back, "and your second mistake was in assuming I only had the one knife . . . ." Gabriel forced the older man's body back and off him, letting it drop to the jungle floor. Bird's hands clutched at his stomach, trying to hold in his intestines, and failing miserably. He looked up at Gabriel, eyes pleading, but Gabriel returned the stare coldly. There was no mercy in his eyes.

The undergrowth hampered their vision, as Bird's men, priests, villagers, Nick, and the two women, all tried to follow the fight. Nick debated whether to call in the fire-strike now, or wait until the contest was decided one way or the other. JayJay was waiting. He wouldn't wait forever.

Gabriel staggered out of the undergrowth. His shirt was soaked with blood, and he clutched at his chest as he took one faltering step after another, and then dropped to his knees. Laura screamed. Belle ran over to her, to try and offer some consolation. Julie gasped, holding one knuckled hand to her mouth, and Nick put a reassuring arm around her.

Gabriel stared blankly around at the grinning faces of Bird's men, and then, just as they were beginning to wonder where their erstwhile employer was, Gabriel's hand snaked out, and the knife he was hiding in his shirt, flew through the air, catching the nearest man in the throat. "Now, Nick . . . ." he cried, rolling forward to grab the dropping AK47. Nick raised the watch-communicator to his mouth.

"Hit em Jayjay! Hit the fuckers hard!" Nick cried, slamming himself into one man, forcing him against another as he also took charge of a weapon.

The scream of mortars began to fall from the skies, aimed at the small garrison of tents, and the dozen or so Al Qaeda trainees. Gabriel and Nick opened fire on those closest, the Khmer, as did Laura and the priests who had managed to arm themselves.

Seizing their opportunity, more of the warrior-priests also began attacking the Khmer overlords, and the trainees, grabbing their weapons and turning them on their oppressors. The jungle echoed to the chattering of automatic weapons, as Belle tackled Julie, trying to get the untrained civilian out of danger. Laura was now giving covering fire, as she helped Belle drag Julie into the denser jungle, keeping low.

The mortars stopped suddenly, and then the sniper fire opened up, and JayJay took great pleasure in dispatching death from a distance, moving his telescopic sight from one easy mark to the next.

It appeared to Gabriel that Turnbull was covering his mouth, and mumbling into his wrist, as discreetly as he could. The watch must be a transmitter of some sort. What was he up to? Who was he in contact with?

The firefight lasted less than five minutes. Most of Bird's men were dead, with the remaining few slinking away back into the jungle to lick their wounds. There were casualties too amongst the villagers and priests, who were now ministering to their wounded and collecting their dead.

Gabriel saw Laura, across the clearing, and started to cross it towards her. She appeared to hesitate, and then took a step back as he neared.

"Laura. It's me. There's no need to be afraid." She looked haggard, if truth be told. Nervous and frightened, as well.

"I know it's you, my love." Her broken and bloodied bottom lip trembled, as she felt her knees weakening. "Trouble is, I'm not sure if this is still me, anymore," she started to sob, and Gabriel rushed to take her in his arms.

In the aftermath of the firefight, Belle began to free Luis and his medical team, who were quick to help with the wounded. Luis came to attend to Laura, giving her a sedative. It was then that Nick's friend

JayJay strolled into the village, still loaded for bear, and alert for any stragglers. He greeted Nick and Julie, and then came over to shake Gabriel's hand.

"Thanks for the assist," Gabriel smiled.

"Ah, don't mention it. Nick and I owed these bastards, so we got a little payback. The Khmer look to have scattered, but they'll be back. Looks like the Muslim nuts are all dead. I still wouldn't hang about here too long, though. Me, Nick and Julie will be heading back in my truck up on the hill. Not enough room for everyone in your chopper anyways, and I don't want to lose the deposit on the thing," he grinned. Nick and Julie came over.

"Sorry for keeping you in the dark about things, mate. He had Julie. I didn't know about your girls. Thought I'd left them behind in Jakarta," Nick explained.

"No worries, Nick. Everything worked out for the best. I'll see you around some time, I'm sure."

"Yeah. Keep safe," he grinned, and then put his arm around Julie, to direct her off towards JayJay.

"Thank Jim for me," Gabriel added. Nick nodded.

Chapter Twenty Eight

Once Luis and his medical team finished helping the surviving villagers and priests, Luis checked on Laura and was pleased to see she had calmed down a little, and was more like her old self. The neck wound was very pronounced, and worrying, but that was something that would have to wait until they got back to Cordoba. She insisted on seeing Gabriel again, and once Luis attended to his own wounds, he came over to sit with her. "I found him. He's real. You have to see him," she insisted. "He's what you've come all this way for. His name is Nathaniel," Laura revealed, and Gabriel's eyes widened in surprise. "I'll take you to him."

Nathaniel heard the approaching footsteps, and he pressed back against the wall of his cave. He had been frightened by the noise of the explosions and the gunfire, having no idea what they were. Now people were coming for him, and he had nowhere to go.

The footsteps stopped, and he heard someone, a man, gasp. "Nathaniel?" a voice asked. Nathaniel inclined his head to the sound of the voice. "It's really you." Gabriel gave a short, nervous laugh. There was something about the voice, even though it was using modern English. Something familiar.

Then, Laura and Radna were amazed, as Gabriel began to speak in a tongue which he hadn't used in centuries. Conversation with Lucifer had always been in the modern idiom, to avoid any possibility of humans discovering they were different, but here in the cave, people already knew.

Nathaniel stiffened as he listened to a language he thought long-dead. The language of his own people, and the person speaking it was known to him.

"Gabriel? The wingless one?" he replied, in the same native tongue. Gabriel looked long and hard at his fellow angel, saddened to see the mighty wings now withered and hanging uselessly from his back. The light from the torches revealed his cataracts, causing his blindness.

"Yes, tis I. No more the last of my kind, I see. I had thought they were all gone."

"I am as good as gone myself, as you see. Blind and as good as wingless," he shrugged. *"Are we two all that is left, then?"* he asked.

"Aye. Strange bedfellows we make, eh?" Nathaniel held out a hand, and Gabriel took it, as Nathaniel warmly shook his hand.

"Your human wife said you came looking for me. Why do this? We were never close friends?"

"I had no idea who I was looking for, but I would have come anyway. We were never enemies."

"I still blame you and your foolhardiness for the loss of your and Lucifer's wings. Michael was heartbroken at having to leave you both behind."

"I blame myself, also." Laura and Radna could not follow the conversation, so Gabriel switched back to English. "Will you leave this place with me? If the Khmer return, it could be dangerous for you to remain. The priests will need to leave, and then there will be no one to care for you."

"I have no life, just an existence. Why should I care if it comes to an end?"

"Life is worth hanging on to, and I can give you back your eyes, if not your wings," Gabriel promised, after a quick examination of his eyes. Nathaniel stiffened.

"Do not mock me," he protested.

"I do not mock. Medical science has improved since you lost your sight. Doctors now can cure your affliction," Gabriel promised. "But it can't be done here, and we need to get you away from this place before the Khmer return. Do you understand what I must do?" Gabriel asked, putting a hand on his friend's shoulder. Nathaniel stood there, silently, for only a few moments, as he realised what Gabriel was asking of him. His wings were almost dead-weights on his back. To walk as Gabriel had done, amongst a world of humans, he must appear to be human.

The villagers were stunned to silence, as Gabriel and Laura led Nathaniel out into the village. They were not shocked, having tended him for all their lives, but the effect on Luis, his team, and Belle was quite different. Gasps rang out as they noticed him for the first time. The red robe of a priest wrapped around him, he was otherwise naked, but there was no hiding those wings. Limp now, and no longer fully feathered, they were still mightily impressive, and all their conjecture about Gabriel's anatomy was now answered there in the flesh.

Belle could do nothing but stare. Nathaniel was like something out of her dreams, a classic angel straight out of scriptures. Handsome, like her father, he stood a couple of inches taller, and his bearing was so regal. She noticed his eyes, and the fact that he had a hand on Gabriel's shoulder, allowing him to be guided. He was blind, but otherwise perfection. Luis and his team gathered around him, preventing Belle from getting too close, as Gabriel introduced Nathaniel to the team who would look after him. There was a lot they had to do if they were to get him back to Argentina.

"You can't do that!" Belle protested. "It's inhuman!" she pointed out, protesting fiercely. Gabriel stepped between his daughter and Luis, who was preparing his medical team to carry out a hasty amputation.

"How else can we get him out of here, Belle?" he argued. "The wings are atrophied, stunted. He can't fly with them, and likely never will again. While he has those wings, we'd never get him out of the country. Once word spreads, more people will come looking for him, particularly the Church. He's blinded, an easy target. These people won't be able to protect him, as much as I'm sure they'd like to."

Belle wanted to cry. Her Father had a strong argument, but it went against all her instincts. "Have you asked him? Have you told him?" she asked. Gabriel looked away, not wanting to see the hurt in her eyes.

"Yes," he said, simply. "He knows and he understands. I lost my own wings. Do you know how I feel about having to do this to him? We don't have time for arguments or niceties. The decision needed to be taken, and I've taken it."

"You callous, unfeeling bastard!" snapped Belle, and her hand lashed out, rocking Gabriel's head to one side as she slapped him hard. Gabriel didn't react. The imprint of her hand began to redden his cheek as he stood there, ready for whatever punishment his daughter decided to mete out.

Instead, Belle whirled on her heel, and went to tend her mother, who was now relaxing and bound into a stretcher. The drugs were beginning to kick in, and Laura was feeling drowsy. Belle could understand the logic behind her Father's decision, but deliberate mutilation of such a beautiful 'creature' if he could be called such, was abhorrent to her.

Gabriel turned again to Luis, and nodded. "Get on with it." Luis turned back to his medical team who were prepping the unconscious angel, who was lying face down on the ground. Osvaldo was using a digital camera to take photographs.

This was a once in a lifetime event, and they needed to record as much information as they could whilst carrying out the operation. The plasma supplied as part of the charter was supplemented with a couple of pints of Gabriel's own blood that Luis had brought with him from Cordoba, in case of massive blood loss, but he hoped to control that with surgical procedures and a few sutures.

Luis wielded the scalpel himself, and Gabriel forced himself to watch. It was as though he could feel the knife going into his own back, and he re-lived that dark night back in Wales, almost 2000 yrs ago, when that Druid cut his own wings from him.

Gristle and cartilage were severed by the sharp scalpel, as Osvaldo continued to use the camera, recording every cut, every muscle grouping that was revealed, as they cleaned away the blood. One wing was placed to the side, as Luis began sewing up, before turning his attention to the remaining wing.

Finally it was done, and as Luis completed his sutures, Esteban was examining the severed wings. "Take what photos you need, then burn the wings. We can't afford to leave any evidence behind," said Gabriel.

Maria and Osvaldo secured the unconscious Nathaniel on the second stretcher. Then they took him aboard the helicopter. The pilot was brought out by the villagers, once the wings had been burnt, and so was unaware of anything different about his passengers. As long as he got paid at the end of it all, he was happy.

Luis opened the false bottom in his briefcase, and took out a set of passports for Gabriel, Laura and Belle, and a blank one for his new patient. Once they got to Bangkok, one of Osvaldo's photos could be used to complete the documentation, and more money passed to enable those documents to be stamped up accordingly. Only then could they leave the country. Gabriel could charter a small jet to take them all home, back to Argentina.

Gabriel tried to check on Laura, but Belle glared at him, and wouldn't relinquish her watching guard over her. Luis reassured him. "She just needs rest for now. I'll make sure she undergoes a full transfusion and further tests once we get her back to the clinic."

Nathaniel was kept sedated for most of the trip back to Argentina. The forged papers served well, and there were no complications on the flight home. Luis phoned ahead to ready another medical team to receive them in Cordoba, and Nathaniel was moved into the private medical wing of the facility.

Laura was up and about under her steam by this time, and she stayed with Gabriel, keeping close to him, as he comforted her. Belle remained concerned for Nathaniel's wellbeing, and gave her father the cold-shoulder.

Luis allowed her to accompany Nathaniel into the private recovery room, as she ascertained the level of care Luis' staff were showing him. Then she went to see her mother, who was admitted into and adjacent room. Gabriel was with her, but left the room as Belle entered. He could see his presence was not welcome with his daughter. Best to let her get it out of her system in her own way.

"Don't be hard on him," Laura advised. "You know it was the only way we could fly Nathaniel out of the country."

"He was just so callous, so unfeeling . . . I snapped." Belle tried to explain her own feelings.

"No, he was being practical. Gabriel sometimes could do with lessons in tact, but it wasn't easy for him either. Having suffered the same amputation himself, it couldn't have been easy to suggest Nathaniel experience the same, yet as long as he looked human, the civil authorities accepted the medical papers and allowed us to medivac him back here."

"What are they going to do with you now?" Belle asked, switching her concerns to her mother. Laura shrugged.

"More transfusions, I suppose. Try and identify this parasite in my bloodstream and remove it if they can. I'm not sure they'll be able to.

She made me drink this time, Belle. I can feel changes within me. Urges I can barely control."

"This blood of Angelica's you drank, it seems to have some sort of similar affect to the 'Blood of Christ', Dad's blood, that you drank when you had me. Angelica was never given it, as far as I know. So it must come from a similar source. Vampires live longer, and have special abilities over ordinary humans, though I've yet to see anything supernatural about them. Too many similarities for coincidence."

"You'd best discuss that with your father, and Luis," Laura advised.

"I will, and with Juliana too. I'd best contact her and let her know you're okay."

"Good luck with the carrier pigeons. You know she has no phone up there. You'll have to go fetch her. I'd like to see her myself, and talk to her about things."

"I'll fly back to Buenos Aires tonight, and see her tomorrow," Belle promised.

"Okay, leave me now, and let me get some sleep. If your father is still out there, send him back in."

Chapter Twenty Nine

"How long before we know?" asked Gabriel.

"Relax, my friend. The operation went well. If his healing powers are as good as yours, we should know by tomorrow."

"Will he regain his sight?"

"Yes, undoubtedly. But the world he'll wake up to will be a lot different to the one he last remembers. How is he going to handle that? He's been very subdued since he realized we removed his wings, although he seemed resigned to it. I'm worried about his mental state."

"He'll need help, I know. Is Belle still visiting him?"

"Yes, every day. First she sees her Mother, and then she stops in to chat to Nathaniel."

"How is he reacting to that?"

"Positively. I don't know what they talk about. I haven't been eavesdropping, but he does seem to enjoy her visits. The operation went well," assured Luis, "and based on your own remarkable fortitude, we expect to be able to remove the bandages by the end of the week. I expect him to regain his full sight, but best if he wears sunglasses for a while. I understand it's been quite a while since he lost his vision."

"Yes, quite a while," agreed Gabriel. "Any complications or after-effects with the amputation of his wings?" he asked.

"Only a few complaints about how strange it felt to be able to sleep flat on his back, and some reported itching as the scar tissue pulls together. Considering the major trauma, I'm surprised he's so mobile so quickly. He's brooding a bit, though. Most amputees feel that way when they lose a limb, though he hasn't had the use of those wings in a couple of centuries from what he's told me." Gabriel nodded, remembering his own sense of loss, when the Celts took his own wings from him.

"He'll get over it. There was no other way of getting him out of there. He knew that at the time," he reminded Luis.

"Knowing it and getting used to it, are not the same thing, my friend," Luis reminded him.

"Once he has his sight back, we need to start educating him about this modern world we live in. He'll find it strange and a bit daunting."

"I'm already working on a program, mainly based around tv and films. We can't ferry him about from here to there, so we'll have to do most of it here at the Clinic. Belle's been taking an interest, splitting her time between her mother and Nathaniel, so I'm sure she'll be helpful there."

"I know. She mentioned it. Not a subject that brings us closer together, as she still blames me for amputating his wings." Luis frowned and shrugged his shoulders.

"Necessary, as you said. She'll come round, my friend." He put a consoling hand on Gabriel's shoulder as he walked down the corridor with him. "Now as for Laura, she's reacting well to the complete blood transfusion, but the virus is still in her system. I don't know if we can remove it," he warned. "Don't worry, we have a plentiful supply of your own blood in storage, so we can continue the treatment indefinitely, if necessary, while we continue our efforts to find a permanent cure. We'll just have to see how she does."

"Laura won't like being a guinea-pig, or a permanent resident here at the clinic and I can't blame her," Gabriel said.

"Vampirism is not something we deal with on a day to day basis," Luis reiterated. "We know so little about it. It's obviously more than just a blood-craving, as it's transmittable, judging by the way Angelica's bite infected her system. I'll leave you to it," Luis smiled, as they reached the door to Laura's room.

Gabriel opened the door, and Laura turned her head, smiling, as she saw it was him, and not another of the medical staff. Gabriel was glad to see the smile, and the fresher pallor on her face.

"You up for visitors?" he smiled.

"For you, always," sighed Laura, reaching out to him with both arms raised, and Gabriel closed the distance between them, sinking down onto the chair beside her bed, and allowing her to wrap her arms around him as he embraced her. It was so good to feel her in his arms once more.

"Feeling better now?" he asked. Laura nodded.

"My skin no longer itches," she confirmed. "Apart from a few bad dreams, I think I'm on the mend. I can't wait to get out of this place. I know they're all doing their best for me, but I've never been a good patient," she admitted.

"Luis says they may need to monitor you on a regular basis, and possibly continue the treatment, till they're sure of what Angelica's bite did to your system, and hopefully purge it altogether," Gabriel warned.

"Oh, shut up, and kiss me . . ." Laura complained, pulling him towards her, and he pressed his lips to hers, kissing her tenderly, and then more passionately as she responded. "Better lock the door . . . ." she moaned, in between kisses.

Gabriel smiled to himself as he left Laura's room, pleased that she was feeling more like her old self, and then he stopped in to see Nathaniel, and found Belle sat by his bed, holding his hand, and talking softly to him. At first he wasn't going to go in, but Belle looked up at the sound of the door opening, and broke the hand-contact guiltily. "Oh, Hi, Dad, I was just about to leave," she smiled, getting up from the chair.

"There's no need. I can come back," he offered, but Belle was already walking towards him.

"No problem. I've probably bored him silly already."

"Not true . . ." Nathaniel offered from his bed, turning his head in their direction, following their voices.

"Well, if you're sure?"

"Yeah, I'll call back tomorrow after I visit Mum." There was no customary hug or kiss as she brushed past him, on her way out the door, he noticed. Still pissed off at him, he guessed. As the door closed behind her, Gabriel went over to the bed, and pulled out the chair to sit down.

"Luis tells me they'll take the bandages off in a few days," he reassured him.

"Will I still recognize you?" Nathaniel wondered. "It's been a few centuries," he joked. "My eyes itch. My back itches, too. Is that what it felt like for you?"

273

"Something like that. My own operation was a bit more crude. Luis is a good physician. You're in the best of hands," he assured him. "Your English is improving."

"Belle has been helping me with that. We've talked a lot . . . your daughter with a human?"

"Yes, Laura and I were reunited with her as an adult. Laura had been told she was stillborn. It's a long story . . . ."

"How do they take the fact that they're going to die, while you live on?" he asked, somberly, remembering his own liaisons with human women.

"But they don't have to," Gabriel explained. "That's one thing the humans did for us. They found that our blood, when ingested by humans, can prolong their own lives indefinitely, as long as they can keep re-imbibing. Belle has my blood by birth, and Laura is welcome to it as often as she needs it," he explained.

"I never knew that was possible. None of us did. Where we chose to dally with the humans, it was in the knowledge that nothing lasted, and we took our leave whenever we felt the need to seek the open sky. I never stayed around long enough to know if my unions produced children," Nathaniel admitted.

"Probably a good idea," admitted Gabriel. "I have a son, also, it seems," he admitted. "I only met him briefly, and, sadly, he blames me for his mother's death."

"It must be hard to have our kind as fathers . . ." Nathaniel ruminated.

"In Angelo's case, he was an adult before he knew who his father was, same as Belle, only, fortunately, Laura is still here for her. Angelo's mother was killed when she tried to rescue Laura and Belle from White Slavers, to help me. She must have guessed who they were when she saw Belle and recognized me in her, yet she still helped me anyway, and lost her life in the process."

"My friend, I'm sorry for your loss." He reached out a hand, seeking Gabriel's. "I hope Belle looks more like her mother," he joked, to lighten the mood. Gabriel managed a wry grin.

"She's just as beautiful, but has a far worse temper," he joked. "Laura's can be bad enough, though" he added, chuckling.

"I told you to stay away from her," reminded Juliana, as she stood in the doorway of Laura's room at the Clinic. Laura looked up, and managed a smile, as she saw the old woman, leaning on her cane.

"Not as if I had a choice in the matter. She found me, not the other way around. Come on in. I could do with some company," she replied. Juliana entered, dropping her bag onto the floor next to the chair which she pulled closer to the bed, before sitting upon.

"How is your treatment coming?" she asked, concerned, as she leaned forward to take Laura's hand.

"Transfusions, biopsies. Luis is trying his best, but this isn't something you come across every day." Juliana leaned further forward, pulling down the dressing on Laura's neck to get a better look at the bite marks. She shook her head with a frown.

"You swapped blood this time, didn't you, child? This is much, much worse than before. The parasite is now in your body. You may not have been drained to death, and fully-turned, but irrevocable changes have been made to your body. You need to understand this, and learn to deal with it."

"I know. Luis told me. The transfusions relieve the symptoms, the bloodlust, but in time the parasite re-asserts itself. He can't make it go away. He's trying chemo and radio-therapy on cell tissue he's removed from my body. He still manages to smile, but more for my benefit. I can see behind his eyes. He's not as hopeful as he sounds."

Juliana reached out a hand and stroked her brow tenderly. "Listen, child . . . we spoke previously about your inherent gifts, and it is these that we must rely on, rather than modern science. I can teach you to nurture your gifts, for you will need such strengths in the trials that lay ahead of you. Only by mastering your inner self will you be able to control your urges, though even I cannot guarantee such will eventually cure your condition."

"Can your 'magic' do this, where science can't?" Laura was skeptical, even knowing of Juliana's own gifts. Years ago she wouldn't have believed that witchcraft was more than silly old women dancing naked in the fields, but Juliana oozed such power. She was far more than she seemed.

"You must come to me, spend time with me, at my home in the mountains, once they release you from this place. You need to cleanse your body of all civilization and processed foods. I will cleanse you, and

I will put you on the path to mastering your future. Whether that will be for good or evil, I cannot say. Only you can write your own destiny, but I will give you the strength, the skill, and the tools, to do so."

Laura bit her lip, as she saw the sincere love the old woman held for her, and she took the frail hand in her own. "Does Gabriel know what you plan for me?" Laura asked.

"No, but your husband is no fool. He knows more of my gifts than you do, and he knows I will do all in power to help you. He will guess, though there is no need to tell him any of the details," Juliana warned. "He arranged my flight up here to see you, so perhaps he wishes my aid in your treatment? But such secrets as I will reveal to you are not to be shared amongst others. There is a big difference between Male and Female magic. Never the twain, as they say . . . . You need to believe, girl, and you need self-belief more than anything. Don't just believe I can do these things, but believe *you* can do these things. Nothing will happen, until you put your skepticism behind you. Your bloodline shows me you share a link somewhere in your past, with those of the gift, the people who now mainly only reside in the realm of the Fey. It's a special gift, and there are too few of us left in this world. Let me teach you to use it, else this thing overcomes you."

"I'll do as you ask, Juliana. Gabriel will understand my absences."

"Good. We'll take it slow at first, just weekends, and then every other week, as you absorb my teachings, and you will need to dedicate yourself to them wholeheartedly. Now, tell me more of the effects this parasite has caused in your body."

"Apart from the craving for rare meat, for blood?" Laura turned her head away in shame. Juliana pulled her back to face her.

"If you can't face the truth, you will never face your inner demon. Now tell me," she ordered.

"My body gets hotter, my skin more sensitive. Just the sight of blood arouses me, in both a sexual and non-sexual way. In the jungle, I felt my very jaw structure rearranging itself. It ached, and felt like muscles and bone were reshaping themselves. My canines became more pronounced, and felt so sharp against the tip of my tongue. My mouth became filled with my own blood as that happened, and then, minutes later, everything re-set itself back to normal. I don't know how to explain it."

"The changes occur naturally, but only in situations of stress?"

"Yes," Laura nodded. "That's how I'd describe it."

"We know from Borgia and Angelica herself, that physical changes were not possible for them. They had no history of inherent ability before they were turned. You remain normal, and can shift from human to vampire, and back again, when the situation demands it. Laura, I fear for you. If this parasite ever runs free throughout your body, with the inherent gifts you already have within you, I fear you will become a *true* vampire of legend, with all the abilities talked of in Stoker's book. Whatever you do, you must learn to control these abilities before they control you. Do not ever consume human blood, lest you develop a taste for it."

"The thought of it terrifies me, Juliana. Sometimes, at night, Angelica taunts me in my dreams. It's as though she's inside me, staring out from behind my own eyes, and urging me to do unspeakable things."

"I am an old woman, and my life is coming to an end. It's a life that has been fraught with sadness, pain and wonder. It has also been a life full of knowledge and of power. I would like to pass on my knowledge before I die, and no, I do want to die. My time is almost done. Gabriel offered me the Blood many years ago, and I know you would do the same, but it is not for me. You can only go so far in the quest for knowledge. It is best you do not go too far. I have gone far enough, and learned things beyond my years. Some things I wish I'd never learnt, but what will be, will be. You know this," she half-accused Laura, in direct reference to Laura's rare visions of foresight. "Your daughter and I have spoken at length, about her own theories that this affliction may have been caused by the same scientist who tinkered with your father's genes. He seems to have been responsible for creating many such strange anomalies and creatures, and somehow this special blood manifests itself depending upon the DNA makeup of the person. Your own DNA is more than human, as proven by the history of magic in your own family. The enzyme in your blood has acted like a genetic trigger, and has reawakened dormant genes. Stay away from her, Laura, if Angelica does indeed still live. On peril of your soul . . . ." she warns.

Juliana sought out Gabriel on her way out of the clinic.

"Can you help her?" Gabriel asked, half pleading.

"Yes, I can help her, if she will help herself and heed my teachings. The road she must travel is dark, and there will be many fears and setbacks along the way. You know much about me, Gabriel, but only of my powers, and not of how they were obtained. They were not obtained easily. Laura will need your support as never before, and yet she needs must spend time away from you, and with me, for only I can teach her the correct paths to travel."

"I trust you, and believe in you, Juliana. Keep her safe. I'll continue to help Luis with his research, and keep donating blood so we have sufficient to keep the regular transfusions going."

"If your science cannot kill this parasite, then my magic may help to control it. That may be all we can hope for," Juliana warned.

Gabriel nodded his head. Perhaps that was all that Juliana dare hope for, but his mind kept going back to the tale Malevar had told him of his coming to their world. The spaceship which still lay buried under the Antarctic ice shelf, regenerating using the thermal energy from Mt Erebus, protected by an alien force-field, to which he alone held the key.

Aboard that ship lay Malevar's original medical facilities, and if his hunch was right, this vampirism was something else created by the alien geneticist. If so, the clues to curing it may well lie aboard that ship. Yet, how to access it? He couldn't dig down through two miles of ice by himself, even if he knew exactly where to dig.

*   *   *

"Keep your eyes closed," warned Luis, as he began unwrapping the bandages, and Nathaniel did as he was told. Luis inspected the fresh scar tissue, which was already healing at a much faster rate then he'd normally expect. Nodding to himself, he handed Nathaniel the sunglasses and helped him fit them. "Now, slowly, open your eyes. Don't be afraid to close them again if you experience any pain," he advised.

Nathaniel stiffened, staring out from behind the darkened lenses. He didn't feel much in the way of pain, but it was a shock to see anything at all. Everything was dark shapes, but they were shapes he hadn't seen in a very long time.

"Don't strain your eyes. Close them again if you feel any discomfort, and just open them again at intervals. You should soon see things clearly," Luis advised. Nathaniel nodded, and closed his eyes once more, resting his head back on the pillow. The sunglasses felt weird on his face, but he understood they were to protect his eyes against a daylight he hadn't seen in centuries.

He opened his eyes again, a few minutes later, and the shapes firmed up. Strange objects he couldn't identify were around the room, and he turned to look at Luis, seeing a small stocky man, though his features were indistinct as yet. He squinted to try and make things clearer, but felt a little pain, and so closed his eyes again.

"Don't try too hard. Your vision will come. Just rest and try again in a little while," Luis advised. Nathaniel did as he was told. He had time on his side. Sleep came easily.

"How are you feeling?" asked a friendly voice, waking him from his light sleep, and Nathaniel turned his head, opening his eyes, making out more than just shapes this time. "Belle?" He reached for the dark glasses on the bedside unit, and put them, before looking at her again. His face broadening in a smile, as he took in the details of her face. "Gabriel said you were beautiful, but I thought he was lying to me . . ." Belle blushed.

"Your eyesight is probably not fully healed," she laughed, a sweet sound to Nathaniel's ears.

"It hurts a little, if I keep them open too long, but short periods are recommended till my sight firms up. It's something I never thought I'd experience again," Nathaniel admitted.

"Close them, then. Don't exert yourself."

"But I like looking at you," Nathaniel laughed.

"Don't be silly. Close them. Please? The more rest you give them, the sooner your sight will be perfect again."

"Alright, just for you." Nathaniel lay back on the pillow, and Belle took his hand. "Gabriel told me you blamed him for me losing my wings . . ." He felt the immediate tension in her grip. "You shouldn't. He explained things to me, and I agreed to let it happen. My wings were useless, and had been for over a century. Losing them was the only way for me to leave there, and have my sight restored."

"My relationship with my Father is best left between him and me," Belle offered.

"He was right, you do have a bit of a temper," Nathaniel joked, and Belle removed her hand from his. "Just so you know, Gabriel and I were never what you might call close friends. I was a friend of Michael's, whom I believe you have heard? Whether your Father and I will become friends remains to be seen, but I am grateful for this second chance at a life that he's given me. You should be pleased for me, also."

"I am pleased, it's just . . . .when I saw you there, it was as though I'd seen a vision. I was brought up a Catholic, though that term won't mean anything to you," she apologized for confusing him, yet found it hard to find the right words. "You were like something out of a fairytale to me, and then the knives came out, and they started hacking you to pieces in front of me." Belle shuddered.

"I felt no pain, and I gladly swap my useless wings for my new eyes."

"Let's talk about something else," Belle suggested. "A lot has changed in the world since you lost your sight. Luis has come up with a program to help you learn of the new world you'll have to adjust to. He's prepared a series of films and videos."

"What's a film?" Nathaniel interrupted her.

*   *   *

Luis eventually released Laura from the clinic, with the request that she came back to Cordoba once a month for treatment and blood-transfusions. She felt like a lab-rat, and was glad to return home to the villa. It felt good to be back in familiar surroundings once more.

That first night back, after making love to Gabriel into the early hours of the morning, she lay awake beside him. The sex and intimacy had been something she craved, something normal after these last few weeks.

Laura's sleep was no longer as sound as it used to be, and bad dreams came more often. Sleep frightened her, with dreams of eyes boring into her soul, and Laura had often woke up in the clinic trembling. "Just a bad dream," she had murmured to herself, but it didn't drown out Angelica's mocking laughter in her head.

Laura sat there now, leaning back against the headboard, her knees drawn up to her chest, and her arms wrapped around them, as she gently rocked back and forth, trying to calm herself, and trying not to stare at the pulsing vein in the side of Gabriel's neck.

Preview Book 6

Frozen Roots

Achille Ratti, the de-facto head of The Sword of Solomon, the clandestine military arm of the Catholic Church, and the real power both behind and literally beneath The Vatican, studied the detailed seismology report from their man Ericsson at the Mining Camp in Antarctica. He looked up over his spectacles to his trusted confidante, Marco Falcone. "You realize the implications?" he asked, with a worried frown. Despite the miraculous Blood of Christ he had imbibed, Achille was starting to show signs of age. Times lately had been hard, and things didn't look about to get any better.

"The anomaly is spherical, and almost two miles below the ice. Spherical means not a natural formation, and the depth dates it BC. If not man-made, then something built it, and put it there. That 'something' could rock the very foundations of the Church."

"Agreed," said Achille Ratti, with a slow nod of his head. "How did Gabriel find out about this, and what is his interest?"

"I have no idea, but interested enough to fund the exploration. Ericsson says Gabriel developed the sonic drill technology himself, and offered it to the company, free of charge, providing he dictated the location of the test, and the mining crew took orders from him, until he announced the testing was over. The technology is likely to revolutionise drilling, possibly allowing the use of larger bore pipelines direct from the wellheads. The speed of this new drill is phenomenal. No wonder his company are only too happy to go along with Gabriel's request. Once they get their hands on the technology, they will be able to name their own prices in the oilfields.

Once we discovered Gabriel's negotiations with the Drilling Company," Falcone explained. "As you know there is a treaty against drilling in the Antarctic, so there must have been some serious strings pulled to get permission to test the drill there, even allowing for the pretence of scientific exploration. First it proves itself drilling through a relatively soft material like ice, and then tests continue into harder mediums, like sand and rock. The design is intriguing. Large bore to handle the removal of the powdered medium the sonic drill-head leaves in its wake, so it doesn't freeze again behind it, once the drill-head moves deeper. Once they have the patent, I'm sure they'll refine it and make smaller models, more appropriate to current drilling standards. Gabriel could have done it himself, I'm sure, but the purpose of this large drill-head is to allow him a way down there. Somehow, he knows what it is."

"What is the status of the testing?" asked Ratti.

"The anomaly was discovered yesterday, and details were sent to Gabriel over the internet. We tried tracking it, but as usual, he covers his tracks well. Ericsson sent the same information to myself, minutes later."

"We can then assume that Gabriel is en route to Antarctica, to take first hand control of the rest of the drilling. How long will he take to get there?"

"Antarctica is a hard place to get in and out of. At this time of year, there is a lot of sunspot activity, hampering radio communications. Storms make air travel haphazard, and there are only a few supply ships scheduled to sail there. The ice is closing in. Best guess, he won't be there for at least a week, unless he hires his own plane, and drops in by parachute."

Ratti frowned. "I wouldn't put it past him normally, but not in those temperatures and weather conditions. Get back onto Ericsson. I want you out there as soon as possible. Take a back seat until we have more information. Due to the difficulty in maintaining communications, I will give you clear instructions now, and allow you to use your own discretion based on what is found. If that anomaly turns out to be what we think it is, it cannot be allowed to see the light of day, under any circumstances. The Church is more important than Gabriel and his Blood of Christ. We have lived longer than mortal men because of it, and if we must die, that is as all things must," Ratti said, with a heavy heart, and added "Gabriel himself is expendable." Falcone managed to control an inward smile.